I grew up in rural West Yorkshire, right in the heart of Brontë country… and I'm still here. After graduating from Durham in 2003 I dallied with living in cities including London, but eventually came back, with my own romantic hero in tow, to my beloved Dales. I live with him in a little house with four little cats and a little rabbit, writing stories about girls with flaws and the men who love them. I go to work every day as a graphic designer for a regional magazine, but secretly dream of being a lighthouse keeper.

@MaryJayneBaker
maryjaynebaker.co.uk

The Honey Trap

MARY JAYNE BAKER

A division of HarperCollins*Publishers*
www.harpercollins.co.uk

Harper*Impulse* an imprint of
HarperCollins*Publishers*
1 London Bridge Street
London SE1 9GF

www.harpercollins.co.uk

A Paperback Original 2016

First published in Great Britain in ebook format by Harper*Impulse* 2016

A catalogue record for this book
is available from the British Library

ISBN: 9780008194598

This novel is entirely a work of fiction.
The names, characters and incidents portrayed in it are
the work of the author's imagination. Any resemblance to
actual persons, living or dead, events or localities is
entirely coincidental.

Set in Minion by Palimpsest Book Production Ltd, Falkirk, Stirlingshire

Printed and bound in Great Britain

To Mark, my very own live-in romantic hero, who deserves this dedication even though he always hogs the covers

Chapter 1

Angel Blackthorne's dream job wasn't turning out quite how she'd pictured it.

She lurked behind a Corinthian column in the ornate gilt-and-ivory lobby of the Hotel D'Azur, tugging at the barely buttock-covering Little Black Dress her boss Steve had made her wear. *Don't forget, love, tits and teeth. And then... whatever it takes.* She could smell the mint and nicotine breath lacing the gruff Yorkshire accent, gravelled with old fags, as he leaned towards her and spat out lesson one of Entrapment for Dummies.

Not for the first time that night, she wished she was wearing proper underwear. The thin, lacy strips of silken fabric covering her breasts and nether regions seemed far from up to the job of keeping everything in – which was the whole point, of course. How exactly was it she'd let Emily convince her to buy them?

The receptionist behind the white marble front desk, crisp and professional in her gas-blue two-piece and bobbed hair, was starting to eyeball Angel with suspicion. Probably wondering if I'm a 'working girl', she thought with a sour half-smile. She pulled again at the hemline of her almost-there cocktail dress and shook a mental fist at Steve, the source of all her woes.

Christ, Angel, grow a pair. Remember, you signed up for this. To the breach...

Steeling herself, she walked over to the heavy mahogany door leading to the hotel bar, gripped the brass rail and leaned her weight against it. It swung open noiselessly. Thank God for the unknown caretaker and his can of WD40!

Angel slipped through and ducked into one of the huge, high-backed armchairs immediately to her left. She noted with relief that not one of the handful of punters had looked up from their drinks.

The chair was vast enough for her to get lost in: a highly polished Chesterfield in quilted red leather that would really require a smoking jacket and fat cigar to be truly enjoyed. Not to mention a penis... The whole bar reeked of a very masculine, gentlemen's club-style opulence, all carved walnut panelling, cut-glass chandeliers and plush red damask.

Glancing around the room, Angel sought her prey.

She soon spied her man seated at the bar, watching some sort of sporting event on a wall-mounted plasma screen; the one modern touch in the place. She'd only seen one photo, but yes, she was certain that was him: notoriously private Sebastian Wilchester, film-making wunderkind.

The editor of *The Daily Investigator* had waited a long time to corner Wilchester in a public place so he could spring a honey trap. Tonight was the night – and Angel was the bait.

***

'I really don't know what you're worrying about,' Emily had said earlier that day while they shopped through their lunch break. Trust her flatmate, Miss Hump-'em-and-dump-'em, to completely miss the point. For Em, sexual hang-ups were something that only happened to other people.

Emily held up a pair of sheer red knickers and eyed them

critically. 'Honestly, Ange, only you could fret yourself to death over an all-expenses-paid night out with a sexy man in a swanky hotel. Lighten up and enjoy yourself. I mean, this is your first big assignment in six months. Isn't this what you wanted?'

'I'm not sure what I wanted, except to write,' Angel admitted. 'Bedding married strangers certainly wasn't top of my list, world-famous directors or otherwise. I thought they'd have me on WI flower show write-ups and tea-making for the foreseeable, if I'm honest. I'm only an intern, Em, even if I am a good five years older than the other foetuses on the programme. Honey trapping just doesn't seem… right, somehow.'

'Well, if he goes along with it then the sleaze has got it coming. It's a public service,' Emily said, brandishing the red knickers like a victory flag from the peak of Mount Moral High Ground. 'You'll be doing his missus a favour, Ange, trust me. No one can make a cheater cheat if he doesn't want to. And if he doesn't take the bait, then his oh-so-perfect wife's a lucky mare and we can all hate her in peace. Anyway, it's not like you've got to sleep with him, is it? I thought you were just supposed to get him down to his birthday suit and go.'

'And yet here I am in a lingerie shop, buying pants that look like a Dairylea triangle attached to a bit of string…'

'That's just to give you confidence. You can't honey trap in granny's bloomers, sweetie.'

Angel let out a little snort of a giggle. She loved her lunch breaks with Emily, bringing back memories of their days at university. This one was certainly taking the edge off the ordeal ahead. Well, almost.

With her friend's persuasion she settled on a lace-patterned black satin thong and matching push-up bra, consisting of not more than about five square centimetres of material and carrying the hefty price tag of £32.95. 'I think we're both in the wrong business,' Angel muttered to Emily, watching the shop assistant fold her tiny purchases inside layers of silvery paper before placing them carefully in a glossy black bag bearing the store logo in embossed gold. 'If we'd gone in for textiles at uni we could be multi-millionaire knicker tycoons by now.' Her friend snorted appreciatively.

Back at the office, Angel stashed her purchases discreetly under her desk and wiggled the mouse to wake up her Mac. The brushed aluminium screen flashed twenty-three new emails, all face-achingly dull corporate press releases passed on to her to filter by 'real' journalists who had better things to do. Rock and roll...

'Good lunch break?' Savannah, her fellow intern, beamed at Angel from her desk in the semi-enclosed corner of the office they both occupied. She was tucking into a princely meal of what looked like two pieces of lettuce and a cube of feta. Angel thought about the eight-inch meatball sub she'd just eaten.

'Nothing special, Sav. Just a bit of shopping and a sandwich, that's all.'

Blonde, flawless, clever, twenty-one-year-old, cloyingly sweet Savannah: film studies graduate, hotly tipped to be a future high flyer. Now here was a girl who could spring a decent honey trap. Why would Steve give Angel this assignment when he had the perfect candidate right under his nose?

'What do you know about Sebastian Wilchester, Savannah?' Angel asked. 'Have you seen many of his films?'

'God, yes, I've seen them all! He's incredible.' Savannah's reply was breathy and gushing with reverence. 'A genius, I think. I chose my dissertation topic after I saw his first film, *Unreal City*. "Sin and redemption in the British Gangster genre". Wish I could meet him.'

Don't I wish you could too...

'Oi, sugar tits!' came a rasping voice from behind her. Angel spun in her chair to see Steve at the door of his glass-fronted office, jerking a thumb over one shoulder to indicate her presence was required. 'In here for a briefing.'

'Ever the charmer,' she mumbled to herself, following him in and taking a seat at his curved IKEA desk. He sat down on the other side and swung his chair around to face her.

'Right, my little honey trap, plans for tonight.' Steve Clifton, editor of *The Daily Investigator*, didn't do small talk. Now, as ever, it was straight to business. 'Here's a pic of Wilchester. Memorise it, but don't take it with you. That could blow the whole gig.'

Angel squinted at the photo he'd handed her. It showed a tall, lean young man, good looking but apparently shy and nervous as he faced photographers on a red carpet.

She raised a quizzical eyebrow at Steve. 'This is him? I thought he was in his thirties.'

'That's at the premiere of *Unreal City* eight years ago, couple of years before he married Beaumont. Man's a bugger to get on camera, hates the press. Anyway, it should be good enough for you to identify him.'

'If you say so, boss…'

'We've booked you a suite at the Hotel D'Azur. I've emailed you the address and your reservation number. Classy place so tart yourself up a bit, Blackthorne.' Steve took in her stone-washed jeans and yellow v-neck top combo with a sneer. 'You can finish early and take your stuff over there to get changed. Don't forget to chuck a few pairs of your undies around the room, make it look lived in. We don't want him getting suspicious.'

'Nothing sexier than a total slob, eh, Steve?'

He ignored her. 'He's flying back from filming in New Zealand today. Based on what we know about his habits he should be in the hotel bar some time between 7 and 8pm. Now, I don't care how you do it or what you tell him, but whatever it takes you have to get him back to your suite.'

Angel wondered if she should be taking notes. Seduction techniques for absolute beginners.

A thought occurred to her. 'Why's he staying in a hotel anyway? He lives in Kensington, doesn't he? Why not just go home to his wife?'

Steve shrugged. 'Don't ask me, love. All we know is, he always spends the night at a hotel when he flies back from filming. Trouble in paradise, maybe.'

The editor rifled around the pile of papers on his desk, pulled one out and thrust it towards her.

'Here. Plan of the suite. When you get him back there, the most important thing to remember is there's a hidden video camera behind this two-way mirror in the bedroom's cupboard door. I'll be watching the camera feed from the computer in my home office. No mikes so I won't be eavesdropping.'

She cast a suspicious eye over the room plan in her hand. 'And this is all legal, is it?'

'Don't be daft, it's breaking every privacy law in the book. No need for you to worry though, it's my sexy little carcass on the line, not yours.' He broke into a wide, leering grin. 'Now, before you leave that room, I want a couple of compromising shots and a solid full frontal to the camera I can montage on a front page. From him, not you, although if you fancy joining the peep show I won't complain. When I've got what I need, I'll send a text. It'll just say "Done". Then you're free to make up an excuse and leave – or not, eh?' He winked at her unpleasantly.

'Do you really think I'd have sex while you're perving at me through a hidden camera?' Angel wrinkled her nose in disgust. 'Bloody hell, it's staggering the respect I get in here.'

'Don't know, don't care. You do what you like, love. It's no skin off my todger: just so long as you get me my story. Whatever it takes, remember.' He reached under his desk, pulled out a parcel wrapped up in brown paper and handed it to her. 'And while we're on the subject, you'll be wearing this. It's your size, I checked with Leo.'

Angel tore open the parcel and pulled out something flimsy, black and slinky. One eyebrow jumped up as she unfolded the dress and held it against her.

'This is a top, right?'

'It's a dress. Make sure you fill it. Remember, Princess, tits and teeth. And give him plenty of leg while you're at it: I'm told he's a leg man.'

Angel was seething now. She knew Steve was callous, misogynistic, morally bankrupt and generally a scumbag of the first order, but even by his standards this was skimming a new low.

'Christ, Steve! Dressing me, seriously? What are you now, my editor or my pimp?' She glowered across the cluttered desk at the smirking, overweight Yorkshireman, quivering with anger while she faced off against him. 'And there's one thing you don't seem to have considered here, by the way: he might not fancy me! I'm no Carole Beaumont. She's been voted sexiest woman in the world – twice. Why don't you ask Savannah? She'd be perfect. She's gorgeous, she's bright, she's ambitious, and she was just telling me what a big fan of Wilchester's work she is. She wrote her dissertation on him.'

'Yeah, yeah. She's a fan, I'm a fan, my missus is a fan: the world and his bloody dog's a fan. Of course they are, the man's brilliant.' Steve turned away from her, spinning his chair around to face the large window that looked out across the grey London cityscape. A recent fall of rain had mingled with the grease and oil of the metropolis, giving the streets a pearlescent sheen. 'You know why I need it to be you, Blackthorne? Because you're *not* a fan. Wake up, love. Sebastian Wilchester lives in a world where everyone's blonde, everyone's beautiful, everyone's a fawning sycophant or yes-man just dying to hump his leg. I picked you because you've got a nice arse and a good pair, and because you're not a part of his world. Trust me, I know people: that's why I shift papers. And my hunch tells me you're our best shot.'

It was true, Angel had never seen a Wilchester film. She knew she must be one of the only remaining people in the world who hadn't. He'd been notching up awards and critical acclaim ever since *Unreal City*, but he only made gangster movies. She hated gangster movies. Snuggling up with something vintage and classic was much more to her taste.

Still she resisted. 'Flattered as I am you put such faith in my sex appeal, boss, aren't there professionals who do this sort of thing? Private investigators? Escort girls?'

He shook his head. 'It needs to be a journalist, one I can trust. I need a report to go with the pics, and I need someone with a keen eye for detail who knows what's worth reporting.'

Even through the red mist of her anger, she felt a twinge of pride. So he did rate her journalism skills – and whatever else he was, he knew his stuff there.

'Why are you so desperate to set Wilchester up? Just out of curiosity. Is this a personal vendetta or what?'

Steve grinned, showing stained, yellowing teeth through his grizzled beard. 'I've been a newspaper man a long time, pet, and I know what the public wants,' he said with a touch of triumph, rubbing the overspilling belly under his striped shirt. 'I started in newspapers as an office boy, fifteen and straight out of a secondary modern in Bradford. Twelve years later I was deputy editor of this rag – youngest ever. I've been thirty years in the editor's chair now. I doubt anyone knows what sells a paper better than me.'

Angel wondered where he was going with this extended pat on the back. He was clearly building up to a big finish.

'You know what people love even more than a rags-to-riches success story, Blackthorne?'

'I've got a feeling you're about to tell me.'

'A riches-to-rags plummet. A failure, and a spectacular, crashing failure at that. They adore seeing someone built up only to be torn down.'

Angel curled her lip, appalled. 'Lovely picture you paint of human nature, boss.'

'Not just my opinion, love, the stark truth. And you know it. That's why we have the highest circulation of any national daily.

I sell to the darkness in people – their schadenfreude. And this scoop is going to sell me a lot of papers.'

'God, you're a piece of work, aren't you?'

'I've had my eye on Sebastian Wilchester and Carole Beaumont for a long time,' he went on, ignoring her. 'The so-called saviour of the British film industry and his beautiful A-lister wife, child-hood sweethearts, six years married with never a whiff of scandal? I mean, come on. No one's life is that perfect. And I'd bet my right bollock there isn't a man alive who can keep his trousers on when sex is offered up on a plate by any half-attractive bird.'

Seeing her shocked expression, Steve manoeuvred his bulky frame to where she was sat and put a plump, sweaty arm around her shoulders, leaning in close in a manner he probably thought was reassuring.

'Relax, love, just be a professional about it. Look, we all had to start somewhere in this business and it wasn't pretty for any of us, believe me. Enjoy yourself tonight. Have a few drinks, let your hair down. You're not doing anything wrong. If he doesn't want to betray his wife, he won't. And if he does then he deserves all he gets, and Beaumont's better off for knowing the truth while there's still time for her to chuck him out on his arse and move on.'

Angel remembered Emily's words in the lingerie shop: *no one can make a cheater cheat if he doesn't want to…*

'Do a good job on this and I'll see if I can get you some decent assignments in the next couple of weeks, a few byline pieces for your portfolio.' Steve massaged her shoulder, sensing she was weakening. 'And next time a staff job comes up, you can be sure your name will be top of the shortlist. For someone with next to no experience, that's not something to be sniffed at.'

She heaved a resigned sigh. 'Okay, Clifton, you pervy old bastard. This once, I'll do it. But this is the last time. Next time you can do your own dirty work.'

'Not got the legs for it, love. The tits, maybe,' he said with a

9

grin. 'Just remember, Blackthorne: relax, have fun and give it all you've got. You've all the makings of a great reporter. I know you won't let me down.'

But the editor's words couldn't quite calm the sickening feeling in her stomach as she left his office.

Chapter 2

Angel examined the man at the hotel bar carefully, mentally comparing him with the blurry photo of the shy young director at the premiere of his first film. Yes, it was certainly Wilchester, but eight years had made a big difference in his appearance. The man in front of her was athletic, tall and broad. His skin was tanned nut brown from foreign travel, chin flecked with designer stubble and he was soberly dressed in a navy-blue suit with a white cotton shirt open to the neck. The curling chestnut hair was just a little too long, its owner carelessly pushing back a stray tendril that was repeatedly falling into one eye.

She drew a deep breath and exhaled slowly through puckered lips, psyching herself up. This was something she hadn't prepared for. She'd expected someone good-looking, yes, but this man wasn't just handsome, he was hot: seriously hot, like a heavily Photoshopped model out of an upmarket menswear catalogue. Or that Diet Coke Break guy from the old ads. What a waste to have him behind the cameras instead of in front!

Suddenly aware of her own appearance, Angel reached up and smoothed the thick auburn hair tortured into what she hoped was a sophisticated up-do, pushing an escaping hairpin back into place behind one ear. It was pretty plain that if Sebastian

Wilchester was bored of his superstar wife, he could probably have his pick of the gorgeous starlets he worked with every day. What could the skinny little newspaper intern in the too-obvious LBD have to offer that he couldn't get anywhere else?

Well, nothing to lose except her pride…

Right, how did they do this sort of thing in the movies? 'Buy a girl a drink, cowboy?' Oh yes, very saloon-bar hooker. She couldn't remember any of what Steve had told her in the briefing, except an echo, constant and repetitive, tapping out its own rat-a-tat rhythm in her brain: whatever it takes. A reporter gets her story, whatever it takes.

She'd just have to wing it. Hopefully something would come to her as she went along.

She glanced longingly at the door. It still wasn't too late to make a bolt for it before he noticed her…

No, not an option. Steve had said there could be a staff job on the horizon for her if she got this right. After years working in dreary admin, dreaming of breaking into journalism, she couldn't afford to throw the opportunity away.

Gathering her nerve from somewhere around her ankles, she rose and tottered over to the bar on the three-inch killer heels she'd bought for the occasion, slightly swaying her hips in what she hoped was a sexy wiggle rather than a duck waddle. It felt like all eyes were on her, and she could feel her skin prickling against the taut, slinky fabric of the dress as she made her way to Wilchester.

Signalling to the liveried bartender, Angel dumped her black sequinned handbag on the bar and slid up into the empty stool next to her target.

'Double gin and slim, please. On the rocks.' That sounded pretty sophisticated, didn't it? The sort of thing a Bacall-esque femme fatale might drink. Angel cast a sly glance sideways, wondering if Wilchester had noticed.

He seemed to have abandoned watching sport on the big

plasma screen in favour of staring morosely into his Scotch. God only knew what he saw to fascinate in the amber liquid: his own reflection, perhaps? It would be hard not to stare with a face like that. She tried not to let her eyes wander over the stubbled lines of his perfect jaw, the firm-sinewed skin of his neck showing through the open collar of his shirt.

Wilchester wasn't paying any attention to her but someone at the bar was more alert to her charms, she noticed with a stab of annoyance. A ruddy-cheeked young suit with a noticeable absence of chin was swaggering over to her, a smug air of certain conquest illuminating his features. Angel cursed under her breath as he oiled up to her and leant on the bar by her elbow, reeking of self-assurance.

The barman had returned with a gin on ice and a miniature bottle of Schweppes, which he placed in front of her. 'Your gin and tonic, Madam.'

'Let me get that.' City Boy – probably a Giles or a Dom, if she had to guess – had fixed her with a one-sided smile he clearly thought was dripping with irresistible charm. 'A beautiful woman should never have to buy her own drinks.'

Angel grimaced, trying to settle her churning stomach. Seriously, that was the line he was going with?

He waved a fifty-pound note in the air in front of the barman. 'No change, mate, sorry.' Angel could practically feel her lady parts recoiling in horror.

'That's very kind of you but I, er, I'm waiting to meet my date,' she said, thinking on her feet. 'He's due here any minute.'

City Boy looked around the nearly empty bar with an air of exaggerated showmanship. 'Well, he's not here now,' he purred. 'And here's a man on £140k a year offering to buy you a drink. Come on, darling. You know which side your bread's buttered, eh?'

She curled her lip and gave the hand that had found its way to her knee a rough push. 'Look, mate, I said I'm not interested, okay? Now piss off, can you?'

'Don't come over all coy with me, darling. No one in a dress like that can say they're not interested.'

'Excuse me,' said a smooth, brushed-velvet voice at her side. Sebastian Wilchester had turned to watch the scene before him with wry amusement. 'Are you, er, Claire's friend? I think I might be your blind date. I was supposed to meet a girl here at eight.'

'Yes!' she almost barked, seizing on the lifeline Wilchester had thrown her. 'Yes, she told me to meet you here. I guess I should've asked to see a photo but, well, I'm an idiot. So lovely to finally meet you. Our friend – er, Claire – she's told me all about you. Obviously.'

City Boy was edging away now, his gaze lingering on Wilchester's six-two frame and the broad breadth of his shoulders. 'Sorry, pal, my mistake. Didn't realise the lady was meeting someone. I'll leave you to your drinks.' Angel smirked as he turned tail and sloped back to his table.

'Here, let me get your drink. Least I can do after your ordeal.' Wilchester turned to the barman. 'Put it on my account, Brad.'

Angel noticed him examining her with guarded but obvious interest while he spoke, his glittering eyes skimming over her body. She didn't know whether the sensation she was feeling in her belly was surprise or elation. He couldn't actually be attracted to her, could he, this professional connoisseur of beauty?

'It feels like I should be getting you one after that,' she said with a laugh. 'But thanks.' She topped up her gin with a small amount of tonic, glad to have something to occupy her faintly trembling hands. The ice cubes clinked against the glass as she took a sip, the liquid's zesty coolness creating a pleasant tingle over her lips and tongue. She hoped the refreshing drink would cool her down and tackle the blush rising fast to her cheeks, while the alcohol took the edge off her nerves.

'And thanks for saving me,' she said, looking up at Wilchester from over the rim of her glass. 'That guy didn't look like he was going to be put off easily.'

'Oh, there's a chancer like him in every bar, testing the gag reflex of anyone in a skirt. They usually give up after a few knock-backs.' He flashed her a smile. 'Anyway, glad I could help.'

She felt a shudder run through her, watching the smile light up his face like a fruit machine about to pay out. An attractive dimple appeared in the hollow of one cheek and his sparkling tawny eyes crinkled warmly. For some reason, Angel found herself looking down at her shoes, fighting against the ever-deepening blush.

Things were going well, though. At least she seemed to have got him talking. With a valiant effort, she forced herself to remember her brief before his attention drifted off somewhere else.

Tits and teeth. That was it, wasn't it? Looking up, she beamed at him and leant forward a little, giving him a premium view of everything her dress was failing to conceal. She saw his gaze dart over the cleft and swell of her partially exposed breasts, then quickly away again.

'Who do I owe my rescue to, then? I mean, if you don't mind me asking.'

'Sebastian. Well, just Seb usually. How about you?'

'Angel.' She grinned as he cocked one eyebrow. 'Yes, really. I know, ridiculous isn't it? My parents were just about the last of the flower children. I thought about changing it once when I was a teenager but, I don't know, Angel kind of grows on you after a while…'

Was she waffling? It felt like she was waffling. She stopped, an awkward laugh escaping from her. *Smooth, Angel, very smooth…*

His eyes scanned her face, dwelling on the tilted nose surrounded by a cluster of pinhead freckles, the large green eyes just a little too far apart, the flushed cheeks now almost bubblegum pink. His approving gaze lingered on each feature, drinking her in until she dipped her chin in embarrassment. Angel swallowed hard. Maybe Steve had made the right choice for this gig after all.

'Go on.' He seemed entertained by her discomfort.

'Um, that's all there is to it really. Not much of a story.' She managed a weak smile, twisting an escaping lock of hair around her little finger.

Her gaze flickered to the plasma screen, clutching for a topic of conversation that might get him talking before she bored him to tears with her life story. 'How's your team doing? I saw you watching the game.'

'Not really watching so much as staring aimlessly.' He laughed, taking another sip of Scotch. The glass was almost empty now. 'Just got back from a business trip, so I'm a bit spaced out. Jet lag, you know? Sorry. I'm not very good company this evening.'

Okay, strike two. Angel took another mouthful of her drink, the alcoholic tang of the gin blunted by the fast-melting ice. A pleasant fuzz had started to fill her brain and she relaxed a little into the role of seductress extraordinaire.

Leg man, was it? Right. Time to bring out the big guns.

She shifted a little on her stool to face him and crossed her legs languorously, showing off their full, silken length as she did so and just barely brushing his shin with the tip of a leopard-print stiletto. She saw him give a slight jerk as he felt her touch.

Ha! It was working! She must be better at this seduction business than she thought…

'Well, I'm enjoying your company all the same,' she heard herself say in a provocative purr, looking at him from under lowered lashes.

She leant towards him, put out her hand and rested her fingertips on his wrist with a light touch, a thrill slamming through her when she felt the throb of his quickened pulse and the warmth of flesh on flesh. At least there was no band of gold on the third finger to provoke any pangs of conscience. Was he old-fashioned, she wondered, or did he just prefer not to advertise the fact he was married?

'Listen, I really was supposed to be meeting a date here, but it looks like I've been stood up. Would you like to… I mean, do you have any plans for tonight? Here I am all dressed up with no place to go and I'd rather not be alone. Maybe we could grab coffee somewhere and, um, I could waffle on at you a bit more.'

For a split second he hesitated before shaking his head. 'Sorry, it's a bit late for me. Still on Kiwi hours. Maybe some other time, though.' Sliding his arm from under her fingers, he drained the dregs of his Scotch and set the tumbler back on the bar, fished in his jacket pocket for his wallet.

Okay, that was strike three. All out.

She couldn't understand why he was resisting. It was obvious from the way his eyes flickered with interest over her body that he liked what he saw. Even Brad the barman seemed to have noticed him checking her out. Angel could see the man smirking while he polished a shot glass, watching the pair from under veiled lids.

And yet here was Seb turning down an offer of coffee so he could catch an early night. Was the thought of his wife Carole, the porcelain-blonde screen goddess, holding him back? He must know 'coffee' was an internationally recognised euphemism for – well, any normal man would have been tearing her clothes off on one of the Hotel D'Azur's king-sized beds by now.

At her elbow she saw Seb rise and hand Brad a wad of notes to settle his account, telling the barman, to his obvious approval, that he could keep the change.

Last chance, Angel. Stall him. Cue the emergency backup plan.

Reaching for her drink, she knocked her bag to the floor with deliberate carelessness. Credit cards, lipstick, coins, hairclips and other detritus spilled out drunkenly around Seb's feet.

'Shit, I'm so sorry! What an idiot.'

'Here, let me get it.' Kneeling down, he started reclaiming her possessions from the deep-pile Persian carpet, shovelling them back into the bag's satin-lined maw haphazardly.

She could see the top of his curly head at her feet, shining burnished bronze in the mellow lamplight of the bar. Unruly locks whispered soft against her calves and she felt his breath, hot and heavy, on her ankles.

Oh God, who was seducing who here? Muscles she barely knew existed spasmed as a surging heat throbbed through her, beginning at the point where his curls unwittingly met her bare flesh.

Angel bit down hard on her lower lip to stifle a telltale gasp, surprised by her body's reaction to his touch. Squirming on her barstool, she moved her legs away from the kiss of the torturing, teasing strands.

She stared fixedly at a mirrored panel behind the bar. It shot her own flushed face, parted lips and wide, glazed eyes back to her as she struggled to regain control, to banish the too-vivid image that had risen unbidden of gazing down at Seb's tousled chestnut hair, running her fingers through those curls while he nuzzled her from ankle to thigh, flicked his tongue across the naked, yielding flesh between her legs until he reached the flimsy film of her underwear, slid his hand upwards to delve into the wetness beneath, the wetness she could feel rising now just thinking about his touch as desire shot through her nerves and hit her square between the thighs…

Jesus, where had it sprung from, this raw, unexpected need for another human being? It had been a long time now since she'd been with anyone: two years since she'd broken up with Leo. And she wasn't in the habit of having one-night stands – had never had one, in fact, even in her carefree student days. Yes, that must be it. It had been too long, and now her treacherous body was rebelling, trying to convince her she wanted to do things she knew she shouldn't.

Steve had made it clear she only needed to get Seb in a compromising position for the cameras and then it was job done as far as his story was concerned. Once the filmmaker had been papped with his trousers down she was free to make her excuses and leave before it went any further. But there was something else guiding her now – a deep, primal urgency, different from anything she'd experienced before.

Suppose she went through with it. Suppose she couldn't stop herself. Got the pictures, covered the camera and then just… let herself be with him. Could she do that? A complete stranger… a married complete stranger?

Although, of course, she'd have to get him there first.

She gave a visible jerk as Seb pressed the bag's silver clasp shut with a click and handed it up to her, dragging his gaze appreciatively along the line of her legs while he pulled himself upright.

'Thank you.' She hoped he wouldn't notice how flustered she was; the feverish cheeks, the slight breathlessness in her voice.

'No problem. Well, I guess this is goodnight then. Nice to have met you… Angel.' She felt a jolt of electricity as he tried out her name for the first time, let it linger on his tongue while his eyes, alive with golden fire in the lamplight, probed hers.

'Wait.' Okay, one last try. If this didn't work, Steve could sod his story and she'd go home and drown her humiliation in a bottle of wine. 'Look, I've got a suite upstairs and there's a pretty well-stocked mini bar in the lounge. Are you sure you wouldn't like to come up for a nightcap before bed? I mean, no worries if you're tired; there's always another time…'

She looked straight at him with an expression half pleading with him, half daring him to accompany her.

Seb was silent for what seemed like an age. Head slightly cocked, lips curving at one side, he appraised all her tiny dress revealed until she felt almost naked before him.

'Yes,' he said, giving in. 'Yes, I'd like that.'

Whatever it takes…

Chapter 3

The hotel suite was heavy with art-deco-style white bevelled panelling and opulent silver detail. The designer had obviously channelled the Roaring Twenties and the room shrieked decadence, from the grey crepe curtains to the massive Salvador Dali print on the wall. Two huge windows across one wall offered panoramic views over the lights of the city, dotted against midnight blue. A sliding panel of frosted glass led to the quilted-ivory bedroom, with its emperor-sized bed and sunken corner bath.

It probably cost more for one night's stay than Angel earned in weeks on the internship scheme. Thank God she wasn't paying!

She delved into the mini bar, hidden away inside an inlaid wood cabinet.

'Champagne okay?' she called to Seb, who was sat with one leg crossed over his knee on the plush velvet corner suite, admiring the view over the city. What the hell, the *Investigator* was picking up the bill.

He nodded assent and she dug a couple of crystal flutes out of the cabinet's lower compartment. She opened the champagne bottle with a dramatic pop that made her jump and poured them a chilled glass of golden bubbles each.

Angel handed Seb his drink and sat down a little apart from him on the sofa, the memory of the heat she'd felt in the bar still fresh in her mind. She couldn't afford to lose control again, not yet. She had to make sure Steve got those pictures.

His brow puckered slightly. It was clear the distance didn't please him, but he quickly smoothed his frown.

'So what do you do when you're not getting stood up in hotel bars, Angel?' His cheeks dimpled with the hint of a smile while he sipped the sparkling liquid, which irritated her. Nice to know he found her lack of success with men so amusing. Even if they were imaginary ones. 'Do you work?'

Did she work? What a question! Obviously she bloody worked. She had to pay the rent like all the other average joes, didn't she?

'Yes, I –' She scrambled around for a job that might sound vaguely plausible, mentally slapping herself for not thinking up a backstory in advance. 'I'm a, er, reflexologist. Staying in town for a conference,' she added helpfully.

She hoped that sounded obscure enough to be believable. Reflexology was Emily's chosen career and it had been the first thing that popped into her head.

'You don't look like a reflexologist.'

She laughed. 'Why, how are reflexologists supposed to look?'

Seb crinkled his eyes. 'I don't know, just… not like you. Not quite so…'

'Ginger?'

His voice was soft when he answered, tangling her gaze in his. 'I was going to say hot.'

Angel's stomach lurched in pleasant surprise as the words sank in. She felt a deep-pink blush creeping up from her toes, crawling along her neck and into her cheeks.

She took a deep breath, struggling to compose herself. 'Well, I'll just have to prove it to you,' she said, attempting the bright and flirty. Putting her drink down on the glass-topped coffee table, she shuffled closer and took his free hand in hers.

21

A crackling pulse of energy slammed through her body when she touched him. She caught her breath sharply and looked up at him, but his eyes were cast down and he didn't raise them to meet hers. If he'd felt anything, he wasn't letting on.

Okay, down girl. Rein it in...

His hand was large, tanned and smooth, with a sprinkling of downy hair. Angel turned it over so his palm was facing upwards and started circling gently with the tip of her thumb, just where his hand joined his wrist.

'You see, this is what we call a pressure point. When I rub just there, it's guaranteed to relieve stress and cure all known symptoms of jet lag.'

He laughed, revealing perfect straight, white teeth. God, it was an incredible laugh. Deep, bold and unrestrained.

'What I could really use for that is a shower. I've been travelling all day and this suit is starting to feel decidedly lived-in.' He closed his fingers around her hand and fixed her with a significant gaze. 'Is it okay if I use yours, Angel? Saves me having to leave you.'

She flushed, looking down at the hand now holding hers. Should she pull her fingers away? She had to find an excuse to leave the room, cool off for five minutes...

'Um, there's a pretty fancy bath in the suite. I can run it for you if you want?'

'Thanks, I'd appreciate it.'

Angel felt a surge of relief as he loosed her fingers. Standing up, she slipped through the sliding glass panel to the other room.

Okay, this certainly made things easier for her. A bath meant he'd be naked in front of the camera without her having to get too close. Too easy. All she had to do was follow him in and make sure he looked good and compromised.

Whatever that meant...

In the bedroom, she turned on two polished brass taps and watched dreamily while jets of water started to fill the corner bath. The round porcelain tub was surrounded by tiles of white marble, with small lights embedded into the stone. She flicked a switch and they illuminated the room with a candle glow.

There was a little bottle of hotel bubble bath on one side, so she threw some of that in too. The room began to cloud with fragrant, spicy ribbons of steam.

That wouldn't do: the cupboard mirror would mist over and block the camera feeding back to Steve at home. She turned the cold tap up a little and dabbled in the water with her little finger to check the temperature. Perfect.

She walked over to the cupboard now, opened it to see if the camera was doing its job. Yes, there it was, mounted at the back, an innocent-looking little black box. She gave Steve a sarcastic wave and closed the door again.

Her own reflection blinked back at her, showing her apparently now permanently pink cheeks. She noticed her hair had started to escape from its twist and, pulling out the jewelled pins holding it in place, shook it free around her shoulders. Wearing it up had given it a bouncy wave that suited her more than her usual poker-straight look.

Angel could picture Steve's look of disapproval at the other end of the camera as she kicked off the leopard-print heels and stashed them under the bed. Well, heels might be sexy, but her feet were starting to lose all feeling. She flexed the liberated toes with relief.

She knew she had to go back to the lounge and face Seb. He seemed to be relaxing now, enjoying her company with all the confidence of a man who sensed he was on a promise, but the more he relaxed, the more tense she felt. She just didn't know if she could control herself with him. If she managed to get him in a compromising position for the camera, how could she stop herself from going further? Just touching his hand had sent her shooting straight to boiling point. Two years of celibacy meant she was coiled tight as a spring, and this was easily the most magnetic man she'd ever met.

23

Angel went through to the en-suite and splashed cold water on her face in an effort to cool down. She stared at herself in the mirror, willing herself calm, cool, in control; fought the fluttering in her stomach and the bubbling in her nerves. Okay, she could do this…

Slicking on a fresh sliver of lipstick, she slid back through the glass panel to join Seb.

He'd taken off his suit jacket, which was now draped over the back of the sofa. He looked younger in just the white shirt – designer, she was guessing – and far less formal. He shot an approving glance at the loose auburn hair cascading around her shoulders as she walked towards him.

'Sorry, it's a pretty big tub. Could take about fifteen minutes to fill,' she said, plastering on a bright smile. 'More bubbly to go with your bubbles?'

Reaching out, he took her hand and drew her down next to him on the sofa. 'Actually I think I'd like to learn more about this ancient art of reflexology,' he said, his voice soft and low. 'Maybe I can discover a few of these pressure points for myself.'

She could feel her nipples puckering underneath the skimpy bra as he shifted sideways to face her and cupped both her shoulders in his powerful hands.

'For example…' He brushed her hair back over her left shoulder, running gentle fingertips across her warm cheek and down her neck. 'Here…' He pressed a delicate kiss under her ear. 'And here…' He planted another in the curve between her neck and shoulder, this time letting it linger, leaving his hot, wet lips against her skin for a moment before pulling away. She sucked in her lower lip, stifling a gasp.

Responding on instinct to the warmth surging through her body, she allowed herself to do something she'd been longing to do all evening. She reached out and combed her fingers through his unruly curls, brushing them away from the handsome face. She brought her other hand up to trace the rigid contour of his jawline with her fingertips, felt the taut skin, the coarse sandpaper stubble, the sculpted lips she was longing to feel on hers.

'We barely know each other…'

'We both want this, Angel. We're grown-ups. Does it really matter?'

In answer, she tilted her face up to his, mouth slightly open, inviting his kiss. He brought his lips down to meet hers, kissing her softly as her arms went up around his neck.

Angel felt her body spark into life as the kiss became deeper, hungrier. She parted her lips for him, giving him full access; relished the erotic embrace of his tongue with hers. He explored her mouth with expert skill, his arms reaching out to enfold her and draw her body in towards his.

She was half kneeling on the narrow sofa, her right foot on the floor and the other tucked under her thigh. Shifting a little, she hooked her right leg behind Seb's so she could move in closer to him. She could smell the musk of his aftershave, distinctive notes of woodsmoke and chocolate. Drawing back from the kiss, she moved her lips down along the sinews of his neck and under the open collar of his shirt.

She pushed her body into his with a little sigh, crushing the breasts that begged to be released from their satin prison into his chest. To her delight, a small moan escaped him when he felt the press of her hardened nipples. He slid his hands down her back to her buttocks, pulled her right up against him.

She knew what he wanted. Bringing her other leg up from the carpet, she planted one knee on each side of his athletic frame, straddling him.

Angel lowered her body to meet his, gasping when she felt the hard arousal through his clothing. Feeling him pressing into her, ready for her, the last remnant of her self-control slipped away.

Seb's fingertips were caressing her back with a delicate touch, tracing the lines of her shoulder blades before homing in on the fastening of her dress. Dragging the zip down, he slid the flimsy thing up her body and over her shoulders, helped her wiggle free and she sat astride his broad thighs in her underwear, too aroused now to feel embarrassed. He held her back from him for a moment while he scanned the creamy skin, the curves and undulations of her slim frame, and she felt his appreciation for her body stirring between her thighs.

He ran smooth, wet lips along her ears and neck. Pushing her upwards into a kneeling position until his face was level with her chest, she felt her body stiffen as his mouth found its way to the ripe swell of her breasts. He set them free, unhooking her bra and flinging it away to join her dress on the carpet.

She bit down on her bottom lip in appreciation as she felt him clamp his mouth first around one hard, pink peak, then the other, massaging gently with his tongue.

A gasp escaped her when he ran his palm down her body and began brushing a teasing thumb back and forth under the waistband of her thong with the lightest of strokes. Angel leaned forward to kiss him but he held her back, his keen gaze darting over her face to see the effect of his touch. He pressed her parted lips lightly with one fingertip, felt their moisture and the heat of her ragged breath.

His hand slid down further until it slipped between her legs. He groaned with pleasure, feeling the wetness he'd created there, how ready her body was for him. Firmly, rhythmically he moved his fingertips against her, circling and pressing with intuitive skill, smiling with satisfaction as her lashes flickered and her head fell back. She heard a low, soulful moan and realised it was coming from her.

Her brain was fogged now with a hungry need for him. She pressed herself against his hand, groaning as, insistent and unrelenting, he continued to explore her. White-hot climax simmered on the edge of every nerve ending. Oh God, she couldn't hold it back any more…

No. Too fast. It was all happening too fast.

This was no good. She had to get him to the bedroom so Steve could get his pictures. Summoning her self-control and willing it through her body with a mammoth effort, she pulled away from the feverish, exploring fingers.

'What about… your bath?' she panted. She was surprised to hear how different her voice sounded, thick and dripping with lust.

'You'll join me?'

'God, yes…'

He lifted her up and she twined her legs around his back as he carried her through the sliding glass panel into the bedroom.

The mirrored cupboard containing the hidden camera was right behind them when they entered. Aware of the great view Steve was getting of her rear, sliced by the tiny thong, Angel wriggled free of Seb's strong arms. She grabbed one of the white cotton towels that lay folded on the bed and wrapped it around her.

This wouldn't do. She was supposed to be seducing him, not the other way round, yet here she was in nothing but her knickers, breathless from his touch, while he was still fully clothed. Her backside alone certainly didn't warrant a front-page story in the *Investigator*.

'What are you doing?' His voice was hoarse and heavy.

'No more peep show for you,' she heard herself say in a teasing tone. 'Not until I get one too. Strip.'

Seb grinned at her. 'Yes ma'am.'

He unbuttoned the white shirt, now crumpled and sodden, and tossed it to one side. The tight, bronzed skin underneath was gilded with sweat. It screamed out to be touched, stroked, licked. Angel held herself back with an effort, a spasm of arousal humming through her body.

Finally he peeled off shoes and socks, unbuckled his belt and slid off trousers and boxer shorts, allowing his rock-hard erection to spring free.

'Now where's my reward, Angel?' he said in a low voice, coming towards her in the full, exquisite, quintessentially male beauty of his nakedness.

Over on the bedside cabinet, she heard a barely audible buzz from her handbag, where she'd stashed her mobile phone.

Steve. He'd got the photographs. *Thank God!*

She removed her towel and hung it carefully over the top of the cupboard's mirrored door so it was completely covered. Steve would have to get his kicks somewhere else from now on.

That was it: no more camera, no more honey trap. Just a man and a woman in a hotel room. If she wanted to make her excuses and leave, then now was the time to do it.

But clearly that wasn't going to happen.

Reaching up, she took Seb's face in both hands for a deep kiss, thirsty to taste him again.

He drew her body towards his until she felt their bare flesh meet. Then he hooked his fingers into the waistband of her thong and slid it over her hips. Wiggling, she shimmied it to the floor.

'Come on.' His breathing was husky now, almost a growl. Taking her hand, he led her to the steaming, fragrant bath, its clear water dappled with soapy bubbles. His erection sprang towards his stomach in silent tribute to the milky curve of her buttocks as she sank into the water.

She could feel the water's embracing warmth cleaving to her body, holding it tight. Seb turned off the still-running taps and lowered himself in to face her. He took her hips in his hands and eased her towards him in one smooth movement, the water buoying her up until she came to rest between his knees. She felt almost drunk, her thoughts hardly audible through the intoxicating cloud of desire.

He drew her face to him between both his hands and locked his lips into hers. The heat between them almost crackled with raw, unleashed energy while he searched her mouth. She could feel his fingers burrowing into her hair, pressing the back of her skull with an animal intensity. Oh, God, it felt good… She twined herself sinuously around his flesh, gliding her body against his; pressing, wanting.

Finally drawing back from the scorching intensity of the kiss, breathless and flushed, he guided her back into a reclining position against the side of the tub.

He seemed to be everywhere, raining down a flurry of fevered kisses on her neck and shoulders, caressing the contours of her hips and waist with his fingertips, one palm making ripples on the water as it moved along her inner thigh. But he was still in control, teasing her, never quite touching her where she longed to be touched.

His lips found their way to the inviting plumpness of her breasts, unable to resist the way they rose and fell rapidly as her breathing became a harsh pant. She could feel the buzz of his stubble while he nuzzled and sucked a hard nipple and she gave a low, longing moan, drawing an answering moan from him.

He moved below the waterline, kissing the white skin around her belly button, planting wet, lingering kisses along the bones of her hips. He looked up at her, his tawny eyes half closed and glazed with desire.

Move up, the eyes seemed to telegraph, and obediently she eased her hips higher up the curved porcelain at her back, lifting her upper body above the water.

Her breath caught in her throat as she felt his head move down between her thighs. Just like her fantasy in the bar, she looked down at his unruly mop of curls while he flicked his tongue across the soft flesh between her legs and up to where she was waiting, wet and ready for him, crying out for his touch.

She let out a shuddering groan as he lapped his tongue against her, moving its tip in a circular motion, a slow and languorous massage at first, then faster, more urgent. As he heard her pants quicken, he began broad, muffled sweeps up and down, sucking, nuzzling, dipping into her. She reached down and grabbed the hand stroking her thigh, gripped it hard until her knuckles turned white, incapable of letting go until his actions arrived at their now-inevitable conclusion. He brought his other hand up to caress one firm breast, his tongue fluttering faster as she moved her body to the rhythm he set.

'Ah! Oh… God, Seb!' Angel felt her body convulse as she surrendered, her orgasm rippling, pulsing, melting through her nerves. She bucked and cried out while the euphoria claimed her, finally sinking limp and spent back into the water.

She heaved a sigh of satisfaction, throwing back her head to savour the soft numbness of afterglow. Her vice-like grip on Seb's hand loosened and he flexed some feeling back into the fingers while he rested his head against her for a moment, breathless and triumphant.

Goosepimples stood out on her flesh, both from the now-cooled water and the still-fresh sensation of consuming ecstasy. She pulled Seb up into a kiss, tasted herself on his lips, kissed deeper in her gratitude for the pleasure he'd just given her that she longed to return.

'Over here.' Taking his hand, she rose from the water and led him over to the bed, where virginal white sheets begged to be violated.

Gently she manoeuvred Seb's broad, dripping bulk into a sitting position on the edge of the bed. She wrapped her legs around him, kissing him deeply, then guided him down on to the mattress so she was straddling the toned, taut muscles of his stomach. As she looked down at him, his dilated pupils made those overpowering eyes seem almost black. She pushed a few damp chestnut curls away from his face and leaned down to kiss his muscular neck, one hand sliding along the broad expanse of his chest and massaging a nipple tenderly.

Her eyes flickered to the cabinet by the bed, wishing she'd thought to bring some condoms so she could feel him inside her, their bodies moving together to the same rhythm. It hadn't occurred to her to come prepared. She'd never expected it to go this far.

Seb's gaze followed hers. 'You have some?'

She gave her head a regretful shake. 'There's the bar toilets. I could –'

'No. Don't go. I can't wait any more, Angel,' he panted into her ear, his breath harsh and rasping. 'Please.'

She understood. Reaching down, she took his full, swollen length in her hand. He moaned, blinking hard, as she lightly moved her hand up and down in a smooth, fluid motion, caressing the hot tip with her thumb. Moving his hand to the back of her head, he pulled her lips on to his for a kiss that startled her with its intensity, it was so raw and wildcat savage. It told her he needed this release, at least as much as she had.

She moved her mouth downward on a journey across his wet, shining torso, peppering hot and heavy kisses in her wake. She dragged a groan from his lips, tracing one nipple with the tip of her tongue and half kissing, half sucking at its hard peak. Continuing her journey down, she reached her target.

She felt him shiver as she took him into her. She could feel him, every inch of him, sliding back and forth in the snug, wet grip of her willing mouth while she moved her tongue in a circular motion around his ridge. With the flat of her nails she brushed his inner thigh, matching her speed to the buck of his hips.

The sheet tightened under her body as he knotted the cotton in a fist. It felt like his whole broad frame was ready to pop, needing her to unleash the primal energy pent up inside.

'Don't stop… ah! For Christ's sake, Angel, please don't stop now,' he pleaded, choked with delicious agony.

His moans became louder, more ragged, more vital, and his back arched as she pushed him past the point of no return. She felt his whole body convulse and he let out a groan that seemed to contain his life's essence as he fell into the oblivion of climax.

She paused a moment, then slid panting back up his body to

where he lay, breathless and satisfied, on the pillow. He tilted his head to kiss her, the lips soft, tender, the bestial intensity of before now banished.

'Oh God... that was incredible. You were incredible,' he whispered, wrapping her in powerful arms.

'Not so bad yourself.' She planted a small kiss on the end of his nose. He smiled at her in the dim light and returned her kiss sleepily.

She snuggled into him, exhausted, satiated and happier than she'd been in an age. Silencing the nagging voice of conscience, she dismissed all thoughts of Steve, work, Carole Beaumont and the honey trap, letting herself fall into dreamless sleep in Seb's reassuring embrace.

Chapter 4

Angel woke with the taste of Seb still on her lips. The bed was warm, but he wasn't there.

Had he gone into the other room? She called his name. No answer.

She rolled over on to her back and examined the carved white cornice around the ceiling as she took stock of herself. She had some idea she should feel guilty after the complete obliteration of her inhibitions last night, yet the thing had seemed so natural, somehow.

The whole experience felt dreamlike, looking back. Surreal. The second man she'd ever slept with and under such bizarre circumstances…

She'd known Leo for over a year before they'd started going out and it was months again until they'd started sleeping together. Yet last night she'd given herself to a stranger, another woman's husband, who'd made her feel her needs completely synchronised with his. It had felt almost empathic, the way he'd touched her and anticipated everything she wanted from him. She hugged herself, thinking back to his touch on her skin, a dream now in her memory. And it seemed the dream and its subject had dissolved into nothing.

She snapped back to reality. What time was it? She pushed herself over on to her side and reached for her handbag to check her mobile. 10.15, shit! Checkout was at 11.00.

Swiping across the touchscreen, she read the text from Steve that had been waiting in her inbox since last night:

Done. And nice arse by the way.

Angel felt a sickening jolt as she remembered what was coming. It was Saturday today. Steve had told her the story would break in the Monday edition.

She thought of Seb's electrifying touch, the comforting warmth of his body as he held her while she drifted into sleep, and of the pain he'd feel when he saw himself on the front page of the *Investigator* – how he'd despise her. She blinked hard, trying to hold back the tears she felt welling at the thought of the touch she'd never feel again and the man she was about to destroy.

Her gaze fell on a sheet of hotel notepaper next to her bag and she unfolded the note he'd left her:

Sorry had to shoot off, didn't want to wake you. Loved spending time with you last night. Give me a call some time. Seb x. PS Make it soon.

And then a mobile number she knew she could never dial. *Get a grip, Angel. He's married, for Christ's sake. Just another cheating scumbag who can't control himself. Now put it behind you and move on.*

It was true; she knew it was. And yet she gave in and sobbed convulsively, pushing her face into his still-warm pillow until it was soaked through with her tears.

***

34

'Hello?' Angel called out, pushing open the door of the cheap-for-London two-bed flat she shared with Emily. She'd managed to shove everything into her overnight bag and check out of the hotel with minutes to spare, closing the door on the suite she'd come to both love and hate. She'd shot off a quick report to Steve from her mobile on the train home, a few observations on Seb's mannerisms and behaviour, trying to keep it as brief and free from sordid detail as possible.

Her flatmate popped her head out of the kitchen and smirked, before pursing her lips into an expression of mock disapproval.

'Well, well, well. Look what the cat dragged in. And in the same clothes as she was wearing last night, no less. Just where do you think you've been, dirty stopout? I've a good mind to send you straight to your room.'

But her face fell as Angel burst into tears and flung herself forward into a hug.

'God, Ange, what happened? Are you okay? Did he do something to you? Did Steve –'

Angel let out a bitter snort through her sobs. 'Not them. It's – it's me. I've ruined everything.'

Emily made soft shushing sounds to her and stroked the back of her hair. Angel managed to choke back the sobs as her friend guided her to the black-leather sofa and sat down beside her, one arm around her shoulders.

'Okay, drama queen, tell me the worst. How have you ruined everything?'

Angel sniffed and blew her nose into the tissue Emily passed her from a box on the coffee table. 'God, it was the weirdest evening. I… slept with him, Em.'

'Yeah, I'd kind of got that far on my own, sweetie. Not with that sleazoid Steve watching, though, I hope?'

'No, I covered the camera after I got his text. Jesus, Em, it was unbelievable. It's never been like that before, not even before me and Leo started having all the problems.'

'That's my girl.' Emily gave the auburn head a fond pat. 'Don't you think you deserve a night of hot slutty sexifying after your gajillion years of being a born-again virgin? Why beat yourself up about it? You had a great night, you got your end away, minds were blown, the end. Put it behind you and get on with the rest of your life.'

Angel gave the pretty, hazel-eyed girl an envious glance. Ever since Emily's marriage had broken up three years ago, it seemed like she'd decided life was too short for insecurities and done just exactly what she liked.

'It's not that, Em. It's him. Seb. He was so… oh, I don't know. It's like there was this connection, or he could read my mind or something. And on Monday it'll be all over the bloody *Investigator* and he'll hate me forever. God, it's a horrible idea, him thinking I was just some call girl sent to set him up.'

'God, is that all?' Emily gave her ash-blonde curls a disapproving shake. 'You're being too sentimental, sweetie. That's what comes of swearing off men for two years. As soon as you finally let yourself have a bit of fun, it has to be bloody true love or something. Look, who cares what he thinks? Okay, so he's earth-moving in bed, hung like a stallion, buttocks like two boiled eggs in a hanky, can push your every button, whatever. That doesn't change the fact he cheated on his wife. Nice guys don't do that: trust me, I should know. Just be grateful he won't be in any position to break your heart, unlike that poor cow he's married to.'

'I guess… I mean, I know you're right, but…'

Emily took Angel's face in her hands and looked straight into her face. 'Listen, Ange. You're too good for creeps like that. And no offence, but you're not tough enough for them. Look what happened with Leo. He was a nice guy, issues aside, but you spent so many years trying to 'save' him you nearly ruined your own life. I can't see that happen again. Not to my best friend. Just chalk it up to experience and move on.'

Angel managed a watery smile. She could always trust Emily to give her better advice than she gave herself.

'What do you mean, not tough enough? Bet I could kick your arse.'

'Yeah, and don't I know it? Look, here's Groucho come to cheer you up.'

The big black cat leapt into Angel's lap with a plaintive mawk of greeting. He must be the only cat in the world who mawked instead of mewed. Angel tickled him behind one ear and he purred happily, pawing her with his claws in a way that was not doing her now very much worse-for-wear dress any favours.

'And I hereby declare this Saturday night to be girls' night, with enough wine and chocolate to drown all woes,' Emily said, brandishing her box of tissues like a snotty Statue of Liberty. 'No boys allowed except for you, Groucho, and maybe a Hemsworth brother or two if they care to beat down our door.'

'Don't you have a date with Danny the tattooed love god?'

'Oh, forget him, I'll ring up and cancel. You know the rules: sisters before misters. Tell you what, I'll even let you watch one of your soppy old films.'

'*The Apartment*?'

'Alright, alright, if the last 500 times weren't enough for you to have learnt all the words off by heart. We'll get the duvet from your room, get into our PJs and "chillax", as I believe all the cool kids are saying nowadays. You go run yourself a bath. Give me a few hours to finish what I'm working on, then I'll phone the pizza guy and we can crack open the booze.'

Thank God for Emily. Angel had no idea how she'd cope without her, but she knew it wouldn't be pretty.

***

37

Groucho's mournful wails the next morning created a throb of searing white light in Angel's brain. She clutched her temples and groaned.

'Alright, mawky, just give me a second.' She reached blearily for the packet of cat biscuits on top of the fridge and spilled a load into and around his food bowl. 'You have to be gentle with Mummy today. Nasty Aunty Emily's given her the mother of all hangovers.'

The black cat showed what he thought of this state of affairs by fixing her with an intent stare for a second before turning around and starting to wash his crotch.

'Disgusting moggy,' she muttered, tickling his neck as she pushed past him into the sitting room and plonked herself down on the sofa.

Empty wine glasses and pizza boxes littered the pine coffee table in front of her. She groaned and pushed away the stray slice of half-eaten pepperoni offending her tender morning-after nostrils. *Bleurghh*. It felt like a woolly mammoth had crawled into her mouth a couple of millennia ago and gone extinct.

Emily had popped round the corner to the newsagents to get a couple of cans of Coke and some Alka-Seltzer, tripping off brightly into the sunshine while her friend flung four-letter curses at her and her sodding alcohol tolerance.

The buzz of Angel's mobile sounded from somewhere and she flung away the detritus on the table until she found where it was hidden under an empty Maltesers packet. Emily. Probably ringing to tell her there was no Alka-Seltzer. That would be just about par for the course this weekend.

'Ange, it's in!' She sounded panicked.

'In? What do you mean, in?' Then realisation dawned. 'God, already? But the story wasn't supposed to break until tomorrow! Steve must have rushed it through last night for the Sunday edition.' She let out a heavy groan. 'Break it to me gently, Em: how bad is it?'

'Um, I think you'd better see for yourself. I'll be back in five…

my flame-haired temptress.' Angel could almost hear her friend smirking down the phone. She frowned. Flame-haired temptress? What details exactly did this exclusive include?

Emily burst breathless through the door a few minutes later and chucked her over a copy of the *Investigator*. 'Sorry, Ange, I know it's probably the last thing you want to see in your delicate state. At least your face is hidden in the photos though. Not even your best friend would know it was you, present company excepted.' She grinned wickedly. 'Looks like you had one helluva night…'

Angel's heart pumped in her throat as she scanned the front page.

Not one of Steve's best headline efforts. He'd gone with 'Unreal Titty' – a pun on the name of Wilchester's first film, *Unreal City* – emblazoned across a woman's naked back. Hers. She winced deeply. A sub-head read 'EXCLUSIVE: married director in steamy romp with mystery girl'.

You could see Seb's face, contorted with passion, over her shoulder as she straddled him on the bed. She felt a zing through her body, remembering the thrill of sitting astride him and guiding him down into the crisp white sheets, panting and wet after their bath together –

Hang on.

'Shit! Shit shit shit!'

'Oh come on, it's not as bad as all that –' Emily began.

'No, you don't get it!' Angel groaned. 'That shot – how did he get that? I hung a towel over the mirror! It must have fallen – that *perve*!'

Emily's eyes widened as she caught on.

'Jesus, you don't mean Steve watched it all!'

Angel bunched her fists into her eyes and moaned. As if anything was needed to make her humiliation more complete. Not only did she have one stonking bastard of a hangover. Not only was her bare backside splashed across the front page of a national newspaper for all to see. Not only had she, Angel

Blackthorne, spent her Friday night having oral sex with a married stranger in a hotel room. But now it turned out her letchy old boss had watched the whole thing!

'Oh God. I feel like I'm going to be sick.'

Emily patted her hair, putting on her best comforting tone. 'Look, sweetie, it might seem like you want the earth to open right now, but give it a week and this'll all be forgotten, I promise. Just tomorrow's chip paper, right? And as for Steve, he's sleazy, but he's professionally sleazy. I'm sure it's nothing he hasn't seen before, if that makes you feel any better.'

'How the hell is that supposed to make me feel better?' Angel gave another long, muffled groan, hiding her face in her hands. 'Just leave me, Em, leave me to die...'

'Oh come on. I didn't spend my hard-earned wine drowning your sorrows just so you could have a relapse next day. Look, I'll get some coffee on. That at least might help deal with the hang-over part of your symptoms.'

Fighting the surge of nausea, Angel pulled the paper towards her and began to read with kamikaze resignation:

Film-making wunderkind Sebastian Wilchester – husband of top actress and former child star Carole Beaumont, best known for her role as little Caroline in '90s sitcom *Something About Sally* – was last night caught on the other side of the cameras, romping with an unidentified redhead, possibly a vice girl, in a swanky London hotel suite.

The pair spent the evening glugging champagne and indulging in a marathon sex session in the hotel bath, while Beaumont was at home alone in the Wilchesters' Kensington mansion.

Angel felt her cheeks blazing with anger and mortification. If she'd been in any doubt Steve had stayed for the whole show, it was now utterly squashed.

A red flash in the corner promised 'MORE SAUCY PICS INSIDE! Continued on p26 and 27'.

She flicked in panic to the double-page spread and experienced a surge of relief when she saw that none of the photos showed her face or anything that could identify her. Steve may be a scumbag, but he had principles of sorts, and an absolute commitment to protecting his sources was foremost among them. Thank Christ she'd wimped out of getting that tattoo on her bum at uni, though.

Inset was a photo of Seb and his wife Carole on their wedding day, the bride glowing in a creamy silk and Seb beaming as he curled a protective arm around her. Angel felt a twinge of shame and guilt when she took in the couple's bright, happy faces.

The article continued:

The Palme D'Or-winning screenwriter and director, pioneer of the East End Noir genre, has been dubbed the saviour of the British film industry and a modern-day Orson Welles since his breakthrough film, *Unreal City*, was released to critical acclaim when he was just 22.

Neither he nor his wife of six years, former childhood sweethearts, were available to comment when contacted by our reporter. However, their lawyer has issued a statement asking for the couple's privacy to be respected at this difficult time.

Wilchester, 30, and Beaumont, 28, had just completed work on their forthcoming film, *The Milkman Cometh* – a rare foray into black comedy for the director and his wife/ leading lady.

'I didn't realise who he was when he ordered a drink at the hotel bar,' said our source, a hotel employee who witnessed the encounter between Wilchester and his flame-haired temptress. 'But I saw him meet up with this girl and they couldn't seem to keep their hands off each other. I don't know but it looked like it had been arranged in advance, and I noticed he wasn't wearing a wedding ring. He bought her a drink and they were flirting for a bit, then he went upstairs to her suite. The maid said he left looking dishevelled the next morning.'

Et tu, Brad the barman?

Angel sank down against the arm of the sofa and moaned softly. What an almighty mess she'd managed to make of her life, her love life and her career, and all in the space of one weekend! God only knew what the next day at work would bring, but a massive bollocking piece of her mind was definitely on an unstoppable collision course with Steve's face.

Chapter 5

Angel flicked on the TV as she got ready for work the next morning. She'd spent the evening ranting to Emily about Steve, professional ethics and the male sex in general, all worms of the lowest order, until her friend had begged her to stop before she either signed up for the nearest convent or took out a contract on Angel's life.

Okay, what delights did breakfast telly have in store for her today while she straightened her hair? Sex secrets of the over-nineties? How to make the perfect quiche using nothing but powdered custard? A dog that could bark the theme tune to *The Great British Bake Off*?

She switched to her favourite breakfast show. A heavily botoxed blonde presenter was delivering a piece to camera, her make-up-thick face full of one hundred per cent artificial concern.

'Theirs was the fairytale romance that helped movie fans feel true love wasn't something which only happened on the silver screen,' the presenter began in a light, trilling tone. 'Sebastian Wilchester and Carole Beaumont were childhood sweethearts from the time their parents, all four showbiz royalty, became neighbours when the children were four and six years old. Wilchester's mother was the Oscar-winning actress Abigail

Carruthers, while his father was her second husband, film-score composer Hugo Wilchester. Rick and Sally Beaumont are still well known from their hit sitcom of the 1990s, *Something About Sally*. Their daughter appeared as a regular character from the age of six, and in roles such as Little Nell in an acclaimed film version of *The Old Curiosity Shop*, but retired as a child star at the age of fourteen.'

Angel stared with car-crash fascination at the TV, her straighteners immobile in her hand, as the presenter continued.

'Wilchester and Beaumont married in a quiet ceremony while filming in Paris six years ago, two years after the success of Wilchester's breakthrough film, *Unreal City*, in which Beaumont played the lead, made them household names. But on Sunday their happily-ever-after began to disintegrate when photographs of Wilchester appeared in a tabloid newspaper, apparently showing him enjoying a sleazy romp with a vice girl in an upmarket hotel.'

Angel felt a sickening sensation in the pit of her stomach as the camera cut away to the front page of Sunday's *Investigator* and she saw her own naked body once again, the picture zooming in ever closer on Seb's lust-contorted face over her shoulder.

'The couple have so far refused to comment on the allegations,' the presenter continued, 'but we go live now to their home in Kensington as they prepare to deliver a statement.'

The camera cut to a shot of Seb, his arm around Carole's shoulders at the door of their mansion. Both looked tired and drawn. Carole's eyes were red-rimmed, her white face sort of sunken in on itself like a deflated balloon. A rolling banner at the bottom of the screen announced 'LIVE: joint statement from Sebastian Wilchester and Carole Beaumont – hotel sex-romp director and actress will not split'.

It felt strange to see someone with whom she'd shared something as intimate as lovemaking, felt to be a living, breathing force while she'd coiled herself around him, trapped in miniature within the impersonal pixels of a TV set. As if he'd somehow ceased to be a human being and become something cold and unreal, a tiny character in a drama Angel had to keep reminding herself involved her too.

'My wife and I are very much still together,' she heard Seb say in that deep, brushed-velvet voice of his. 'I am as much in love with Carole as I ever was, and I am grateful and humbled that she has found it in her heart to forgive my moment of weakness and give me another chance.'

It was Carole's turn to speak now. She seemed to have forgotten what to say, and was staring with glazed eyes and fixed smile straight ahead. Angel saw Seb give her shoulder a barely perceptible squeeze.

'I am very proud of the personal and professional relationship Seb and I have built up in the six years we've been married – or perhaps I might say in the twenty-four years we've been close friends,' Carole blurted out, gabbling her words as if reciting from a script. She gazed at her husband with a sad but loving look that really did seem genuine. Then again, she wasn't one of Britain's most celebrated actresses for nothing...

'I wouldn't be such a fool as to throw that away on my husband's single indiscretion,' Carole continued in that tinkling voice of hers, now oddly weak and emotionless as she read the words off from inside her head. 'However, this incident has shown us we need to spend more time together. We have both been working too hard on our careers; now it's time to do some work on our marriage. We would like to announce that after the launch of *The Milkman Cometh* in October, we will be taking a partial break from public life as we spend some time looking at the issues in our relationship. I would like to thank the press and public for respecting our privacy while we do so.'

Poor cow. There but for the grace of God...

Angel flicked the switch to turn off the TV. God, she could

45

wish Seb Wilchester had never come into her life, or Carole Beaumont's either, for that matter.

***

'Alright, heartbreaker?' Leo was waiting for her at the top of the stairs, a big grin on his boyish face, when she arrived at work. 'Flame-haired and tempting as ever. Boss wants to see you when you've got a minute.'

Angel groaned, furnishing him with an exasperated eyeroll. 'Don't you start. Emily's been jumping between comfort and tease mode all weekend. This flame-haired temptress thing isn't going anywhere, is it?'

'Newp. Never till the day you die. Nice pics, by the way. Just how I remember you.'

She punched him on the arm, though not without the hint of a smile.

It was always hard for good friends who became a couple who became an ex-couple to ever go back to being just good friends again. Angel was proud she and Leo had managed it spectacularly and in style, with no lingering embarrassment or jealousy. They were the same friends they had been in that first year at uni, before they got together. In fact it was Leo, the *Investigator*'s best photographer, who had recommended her for the internship in the first place.

'Morning. Do anything nice at the weekend?' Savannah said, watching Angel dump her handbag under her desk. 'As if I didn't know.'

Even she knew! Bloody hell! Had Steve sold tickets or what?
'Erm…'

'Blackthorne! My office, now!'

Urghh. Steve. Well, she had to get it over with sooner or later. At least he'd saved her from Savannah's knowing smirk.

'You've got some brass balls, Clifton!' she hissed once the door had swung shut behind her. 'What the hell did you think you were playing at, splashing those photos across your cheap little rag? You knew I tried to block that camera, and if you had any respect at all for me, any sense of human decency, you'd have turned it off yourself. Christ! I can't believe I put my arse on the line for you!'

Steve smirked. 'No pun intended, eh love? Look, don't get your thong in a twist. I didn't watch the whole show, tempting though it was. Just skimmed through the vid on Saturday and took a few stills for the story. At the end of the day, I am a family man. We had the grandkiddies in the next room. Your jiggling bum cheeks are not something I fancy them walking in on, still more explaining to their nan, thanks all the same.'

Angel felt a small twinge of relief. He was probably lying, but if she could delude herself even ever so slightly, that was better than nothing.

'And no offence, Princess, but you pays your money, you takes your choice. You didn't have to shag him senseless, I said you could go. But if a job's worth doing it's worth doing thoroughly, eh?' His mouth curved wickedly. 'You know, that's what I like about you, Blackthorne: you always see things through to the, er, bitter end.'

She winced with embarrassment. No one but her should know this much about her sex life – or, more usually, her lack of one.

'I mean, don't get me wrong, I'm thrilled,' Steve continued. 'I got a much better story out of it thanks to you. You should get the horn more often.'

'Okay, okay, so I didn't have to bloody sleep with him,' she growled back. 'But *you* didn't have to go into quite so much detail either! You were perfectly prepared to run a story based on nothing but a couple of staged photos the day before. And vice girl, Steve, seriously? What the hell was that all about?'

The editor shrugged. 'Just sounds better, doesn't it? The public loves a vice girl. Look, I kept your face out of it, didn't I? You haven't had Mummy and Daddy ringing up to ask why their little Angel's gone on the game?'

She ignored that comment. 'And what about the office? Even Savannah seems to know! I'll never hear the end of it!'

Steve waved a dismissive, liver-spotted hand. 'I wouldn't worry about it, Blackthorne. You've not been here long, have you? Something like this happens every few months in this game. It'd make you blush, the things I could tell you about the staff on this paper. Jez in accounts has got a coke habit that must be putting his dealer's kids through uni. One of our longest-serving sub-eds, sixty-four and due for retirement next year, is so addicted to high-class prozzies he's had to mortgage his flat. Even your innocent-looking little mate out there, Lord bless her, has got her dirty secret. I caught Cal, the film critic, giving her one in the stationery cupboard last week.'

'That's not the point! The point is – what, seriously, Savannah and Cal? Him with the little bum-fluff moustache?'

'The very same. Everyone's on the ladder looking to get a leg up – or a leg over,' Steve said with a leer. 'See, lass? Nothing to worry about. You're not the only one with something to be ashamed of around here. By next week no one will remember your little indiscretion, or whatever you want to call it.'

'Fine, have it your way then, you sleazy old son of a bitch. I'm dirty, you're dirty: we're all dirty, scummy little human beings. But I won't forget this, Steve. Never.' She jabbed an accusing finger at the editor's corpulent frame across the desk, her voice low and dangerous. 'You betrayed me. Those photos were… private. They weren't part of what we agreed. And you knew it.'

'Did I betray you, Princess? Or are you just taking it out on me because you feel like you've betrayed yourself?'

Trying not to consider if there was a lick of truth in his words, she drew up what dignity she could muster and turned to leave.

'Blackthorne. Wait. Before you go.'

She spun back, still seething. 'What? Have you got another

assignment for me, *boss*? Maybe head down to Battersea and kick a few puppies? Get my tits out for the Chancellor of the Exchequer in time for budget day?'

'Maybe next week. Look, I just wanted to say you did a good job on that sting. You picked it up like a pro and you really came through. I was proud of you. That was our fastest-selling edition for years. You'll make a cracking journalist one of these days, lass.'

She didn't know whether to be flattered or insulted. She didn't even know if being a journalist was something she wanted at all any more. Turning on her heel, she stormed out of Steve's office and back to her desk.

***

It was three weeks before Angel set foot in the editor's office again.

She flung open the glass-and-steel door and slammed both hands palm down on Steve's desk. Eyes and cheeks burned crimson fury as she faced off against him with an expression of thunderous defiance.

'What the *hell* was that email all about, Clifton? Are you deliberately trying to humiliate me or what? Is this punishment for something?'

To her shock, Steve actually looked surprised.

Could he really think he was doing her a favour, assigning her to report on next month's premiere of *The Milkman Cometh*? All she wanted to do was forget about Sebastian Wilchester, forget about the honey trap and get on with her life, such as it was. And now here was Steve flinging her straight into the man's path.

'Are you tugging my chain, Blackthorne? Your mate Leo had to beg me to let you take this job, with your lack of experience. Flat-out refused to work with anyone else on it. Don't you know what an opportunity it is, a lowly intern being assigned to cover a Tigerblaze premiere? If you hadn't done such a great job on that last assignment there's no way I'd send a rookie for this.'

'But Wilchester will be there!' she hissed, refusing to be mollified. 'What if he recognises me? It's both our reputations on the line, Steve, mine and yours.'

'Relax, he won't see you. These things are always packed out, and he goes out of his way to avoid the press. Hates them. Now more than ever after the stunt we pulled on him, I'd guess. You'll never even come close to him.'

Angel opened her mouth to speak, but Steve was just getting into his stride.

'And what if he does see you? He won't do anything, the story will have been out there for nearly two months by that point. Him and Beaumont are just starting to put it all behind them, he's not likely to want reminding of it. That's if he recognises you. For all we know he's Johnny Yo Yo Boxers seven nights a week. He's not going to remember one tight little arse out of hundreds, love.'

Angel felt a pain she quickly tried to smother. She wasn't allowed to be hurt by thoughts like that. She was moving on with her life. It was almost as if the whole thing never happened. It was almost as if she'd forgotten the irresistible feel of Seb against her flesh, the way his expressive eyes fired when he gave himself to her, the way he could be so tender and yet so demanding as he brought his lips down on to hers. Yes, almost.

'Fine,' she snapped, fighting the warmth surging through her gut. 'I'll do it. And I'll do a bloody good write-up as well. But I want my own byline and when Sarah goes on maternity leave next week I want my CV top of the pile for the temporary showbiz editor job.'

'It's already top of the pile, love.'

Chapter 6

The black cab slunk through the bustle of London's nightlife before pulling into the shadow of the Odeon Cinema in Leicester Square, where the world premiere of *The Milkman Cometh* was all set to take place.

On the back seat Angel skimmed her smartphone, looking again through the brief Steve had emailed her. It was the standard showbiz supplement stuff: describe what and who stars were wearing when they arrived on the premiere's red carpet, who they were with, how they looked and behaved, a brief write-up of the film itself and finally a report on the main part of the evening, the after-party. The opulence, the entertainment, and above all, the gossip. For the *Investigator*, of course, the dirtier the better.

She turned to Leo in the seat next to her, trying hard to calm the frenzied thump of heart against ribcage.

'Do I look okay, Leo? Is my hair alright?' She'd tried out a new style for tonight, sweeping the thick auburn mass into a debonair chignon and finishing with a vintage diamond and pearl teardrop pin that had belonged to her grandmother.

'Fit as a butcher's dog, Ginge,' Leo said, putting an arm around her and giving her shoulder a squeeze. 'I'm this close to ripping your clothes off.'

'Sweet boy.' She gave his hand an affectionate pat.

No slinky little dress and gravity-defying heels for her, not this time. She knew the chances of Seb seeing her were slim to none and she certainly intended to go out of her way to avoid him, but if by any chance he did catch sight of her then she wanted to be oozing pure class.

With some help from Emily, the undisputed queen of good taste when it came to matters of dress, she'd spent the best part of a week's wages on a full-length backless gown in floating silver taffeta. 'Silver will be great with your colouring. Bring out the green in your eyes,' Emily had told her. The dress had hung on her bedroom door for weeks, where she could look at it and occasionally touch it, until Groucho's evident desire to shred it up into comfy bedding for himself had forced her to put it away until the time came to wear it.

Angel seemed to be spending most of her meagre salary on clothes for assignments at the moment, and she wondered idly whether she should be putting in expense claims for them. 'Thong x 1, black satin. Push-up bra x 1, 34C . . .' Well, maybe not, although no doubt Steve would get a cheap thrill out of signing them off.

Emily wasn't wrong about the taffeta. When Angel had tried it on in the changing room, her irises had looked almost emerald set off by the silvery sheen of the material. She'd spent nearly quarter of an hour staring at herself in the mirror, turning this way and that so she could wonder at the way the light caught in the dress's glistening folds and dimples. A ruched, beaded bodice hugged the curves of her breasts and hips, extending down to her upper thighs before flowing mermaid-like into a lustrous ruffle skirt. It was stunning and she loved herself in it.

Stepping out of the taxi, Angel could taste the close air, tangy with expensive perfume, sweaty bodies and cigarette smoke. The intoxicating scent of glamour, apparently.

She understood now exactly what Steve had meant when he'd said the event would be packed out. Extending out around a fenced-off area was a deep throng of fans, reporters and photographers at least ten-deep, a sea of flash bulbs ready to blind the celebrities as they walked up the red carpet to the venue. She breathed a sigh of relief. No need to hide from Seb here, at least. This was a crowd it would be easy to get lost in.

'Brace yourself, Ginge. We're going in.' Gripping his press pass between his teeth, Leo grabbed Angel by the shoulders and started fighting his way through the crowd. She held up her skirt to keep it safe from the crush of bodies as conga-like they barged their way through. 'Excuse me, coming through, *Investigator*, coming through…'

Eventually Leo managed to manoeuvre Angel into a vantage point not far behind the mesh fencing forming the cordon. He slid himself in beside her to a spot where he could join the flash-bulb ocean. It was this winning combination of great pictures and sharp elbows that meant Leo had been Steve's photographer of choice at film premieres for over a year now.

'It'll be over faster than you think,' he shouted to Angel through the noise of the crowd. 'Better get yourself ready.'

Angel rummaged in her handbag for her notebook and waited, pen poised, for the guests to arrive. She had a pretty clear view of the carpet between the shoulders of the two photographers jostling each other in front of her. Thank God she was in heels: the inch or so they added to her usual five-six were just what she needed to guarantee her a good view, or at least the best she was going to get in this mob.

First on the carpet was a perma-tanned face Angel recognised as belonging to some reality TV rent-a-celeb, who simpered and pouted gamely for the photographers. The young woman had poured herself into a skin-tight, salmon-pink strapless dress, her surgically enhanced bowling-ball breasts bursting from the low-cut V that extended down almost to her crotch. 'Christian Dior, naturally,' she purred, twirling for the gathered press.

Angel jotted down the Z-lister's name and a description of

her outfit as per her brief from Steve, wondering if there was honestly anyone who wanted to read about this stuff.

Next came the lead actor in *The Milkman Cometh*, a big name known for his portrayal of Regency fops in period dramas. This role was his first foray into comedy and he looked suitably nervous as he faced the wolfpack, which had the power to make or break him with a word.

The thrilled-looking older lady on his arm was introduced as his mum, beaming while she posed alongside her son. 'My biggest fan,' he said. The crowd 'ahhhhed' appreciatively.

Angel scribbled away as a succession of stylish celebrities, from chefs to soap-opera stars, made their way up the carpet, those used to the limelight striding forward with unflappable confidence, others shy and diffident in the face of the blaze of cameras.

An expectant hum went through the pack and she heard Carole Beaumont's name spoken in hushed tones by the people around her. Craning her neck to get a better view over the pony-tailed photographer in front, Angel saw the film's elegant, dainty little star stepping from a chauffeur-driven limo at the other end of the carpet. A shiver slammed through her, despite the heat from the press of bodies on every side. Would Seb be with his wife? Or had he sneaked in through the back entrance? Leo said he almost always did at premieres, to avoid the gaggle of press.

Unsure whether the vibrations shooting up her spine came from fear or excitement, or perhaps a touch of both, Angel bent her strappy shoes into a tiptoe position to get a better view. She wasn't worried now about being seen. The flashes from the wilderness of cameras were as good as a smokescreen.

Her stomach did a double somersault when she saw Seb follow his wife out of the limo, his tall, athletic frame breathtaking in a classic but immaculately cut dinner jacket and black tie. The wild, curly hair Angel remembered so well running her fingers through was gelled smartly back. He gave the crowd a half-smile, but she could tell he was bored.

She hadn't realised how deeply it would affect her to see him in person again after the two months that had passed since that night at the hotel. Still on tiptoes, she almost reeled backwards into another reporter. She clutched at Leo's arm for support while she struggled to regain her footing, knocking the hand he was using to operate the flash as she did so. He shook her away with an impatient gesture.

Really, Angel, knocked off your feet? Eurghh. You are such a bloody cliché.

The glamorous couple swept hand in hand along the red carpet and Angel wondered with a wave of cynicism if their in-your-face togetherness was genuine or a stage-managed show of affection for the benefit of the gathered pack. She assumed the sharp-suited man waiting for them with arms folded at the end of the walkway was, as everything in his appearance seemed to suggest, some sort of public-relations advisor.

Seb kissed his wife on the cheek and took a step back as they neared the top of the carpet, letting Carole take centre stage. The slight scowl on his handsome face told Angel these kind of events were a duty rather than a pleasure, and only pressure from the stern PR man had convinced him not to slink in round the back as usual.

Carole more than made up for his standoffishness, however. She smiled and waved for the press, kissed adoring fans across the barrier and signed autographs until she held the crowd in the palm of her hand. She was every inch the consummate professional, the former child star who had been wowing fans almost from the cradle.

She was wearing a simple but dazzling backless dress in cream chiffon, ending in a floor-sweeping transparent train with a hemline rising in front to skim her knees. An embroidered peacock motif picked out in sparkling aquamarine beads curled down one side of the bodice. Angel felt a twinge of something – jealousy? – as she noted the shapely legs, remembering Steve's description of Seb as a 'leg man' and the way the director had seemed to approve so much of hers that night in the hotel bar. For some reason she found herself blinking back tears, recalling him scanning the curve of her crossed legs when he'd stood up to hand back her bag, and the heat that had slammed through her when she'd felt his soft curls brushing against her calves…

Carole's platinum-blonde bob was flawless as always, the fair skin was set off perfectly by delicate pencilled lashes and a slick of baby-pink lipstick, yet there was a childlike air of fragility to the diminutive actress that couldn't help but make an onlooker feel protective. Angel noticed the bruised circles indicating sleepless nights around her eyes, almost but not quite hidden by the make-up artist's skill. But Carole didn't let her tiredness show while she laughed and chatted with the assembled crowd.

'Who am I wearing?' she said in answer to a reporter. 'Why, myself, darling, of course. I make nearly all my own dresses.'

Well, of course you do. It seemed Carole Beaumont really was practically perfect in every way.

'But I do wonder why that's always the first question I'm asked,' the actress went on. 'Usually followed by a request for details of my beauty routine, while my co-star is asked about his role in the movie.'

Carole spoke lightly, with a little tinkling laugh, but her smile had a hard edge, making it clear this particular question was an irritation she'd encountered before. And it was true, her leading man had been asked just moments earlier how he'd prepared for his part in the film by the very same reporter. Angel felt her respect rise for this woman, gracious but firm, who refused to let the press reduce her to a glorified clothes-horse.

'Do you have any comment to make about your husband's recent infidelity, Ms Beaumont?' yelled a pimply young man close by Angel's elbow. 'Will you be seeking a divorce?' called someone from the other side of the carpet. But Carole Beaumont was suddenly deaf as she took Seb's arm.

She nudged him slightly and as he began to speak Angel was overcome by a sudden, vivid memory of his woodsmoke-chocolate aftershave when he drew his face in close to hers, eyes kindled with a flame that seemed to spark from his tawny irises into her green ones. She scrunched her eyes tight shut, trying hard to rid herself of the memory. The seductive embrace of his tongue with hers as he expertly explored her mouth, drawing her arched, willing body into his…

Once again she felt tears rising and blinked hard to fight them back. This pathetic habit of crying whenever she thought about Seb had got to stop.

'I'd like to thank you ladies and gentlemen of the press for turning out to the premiere of *The Milkman Cometh*,' the director said, taking care there should be no trace of emotion in his polished tones while he delivered the obviously rehearsed speech. 'This black comedy is something different for Carole and myself, but a project that has long been close to our hearts. It is also the first release to be entirely filmed at, and distributed by, our studio, Tigerblaze. Now there is nothing left for us to do but throw it on your mercy, and I hope you will not stint in either your praise or your criticism as the curtain lifts on our newest baby.'

This gave the up-and-coming reporter at Angel's elbow a new idea. He chose this moment to shout out his next question.

'Why do you think you and your wife have never had children, Mr Wilchester? Isn't a family something you want in your lives?'

Angel shrank back as Seb's gaze flickered over to the unfortunate young man beside her with a sneer of dislike. But Carole's selective deafness seemed to be catching. The question remained unanswered, hanging in the air as the couple were escorted by their PR man into the cinema.

Chapter 7

'Right, that's your lot,' Leo said, taking hold of Angel's elbow and guiding her away from the fenced-off area along with the rapidly dispersing crowd. 'Come on.'

'Where do we go now?'

'Servants' entrance, round the back. The stars all get shown into the VIP area, then we humble Newsround presspackers are allowed to go occupy the cheap seats. Have you got your pass? You'll have to show it to the security bods to get in.'

Angel reached into her handbag for the press pass. It did have a little clip to attach it, but she couldn't bear the thought of doing any damage, no matter how tiny, to her dress. Not that she'd ever admit such feminine weakness to Leo. She'd never hear the end of it.

She pulled out her phone too, scanned the screen. One new message.

Cal can't make it. Need review for Monday. Take notes and let's see what you can do with it.

Great, thanks Steve. So now she was supply film critic and supply showbiz editor. Did no one else do any work on this paper?

'Looks like I'm reviewing for the arts section as well as the summary for the showbiz supplement.' She showed Leo Steve's text. 'Cal's off sick or something. Typical. Come on, let's get round the back and try to get some decent seats.'

Leo's eyes saucered with surprise. 'Bloody hell, that's huge, Ginge! I'm impressed: from intern to film critic in well under a year. That's some jump, you know.' He gave the elbow he was holding a swift squeeze. 'Steve must think you're the dog's wotsits or something. At this rate you'll be deputy editor by this time next week. Listen, you will remember the little people who put you there, won't you, and make sure my name's in the hat for director of photography?'

She linked his arm as they joined the end of the queue snaking down towards the cinema's rear entrance. 'No worries, little person. Shame there isn't any extra money in my rapid rise to the top, though, instead of just twice the work for the same salary. I'm about one taffeta ballgown from the breadline at the moment.'

Ten minutes of very British queueing later, a beefy security guard eyeballed them as they arrived at the entrance and flashed their press passes.

'Paper, mag, blog?'

'The *Investigator*,' Leo said. 'Angel Blackthorne and Leo Courtenay.'

The guard glared at them with lowered brows. It didn't take a big stretch of the imagination for Angel to figure out why.

'That stunt you pulled was a new low, even by your rag's rock-bottom standards,' he growled. 'I don't know how you hacks have got the balls to show your faces here. Really top couple, the Wilchesters. I've worked with them for years.'

Angel examined her feet carefully, feeling the tips of her ears starting to burn. 'Look, we just work there,' she mumbled. 'The editor decides what we run…'

Oh yes, the old 'just obeying orders' defence. Always a winner. But the guard was just getting warmed up. 'A real lady, Mrs

Beaumont, and she's looked just about ready to break her heart these last few months. I mean, 'mystery girl'? Come on! One of your hired whores, more like. You know as well as I do the whole thing was a set-up. Otherwise how would you have known to plant the bloody cameras in the first place? Your white-van-men punters might have a reading age of six but even they can't be that thick.'

Behind them, the impatient queue started to rumble at the hold-up. Angel felt nauseatingly conspicuous, her cheeks blazing with shame and embarrassment.

'Listen, mate,' Leo said to the security guard, his mouth setting into a firm line. 'You'll have to take any complaint up with our editor. I'm more than happy to give you his email address. Christ, you can even have his private mobile if you want. By all means ring him, any hour of the day or night for all I care. The man's a first-class prick and you'd have my blessing. But me and this lady have got a job to do, and if your boss wants to promote his film in the country's biggest daily then you'd better tick your little box and let us in. Or you can explain to him why ours is the only paper not carrying a review, and he doesn't look like a man you'd want to cross.'

The guard's brow lowered like thunder but Leo's words did the trick. With muttered oaths and imprecations, he looked the pair up on his guest list and waved them through the barrier.

'God, Leo, how long is this thing going to haunt me? I feel awful. I deserve to feel awful,' Angel murmured when she was slumped into the uncomfortable vinyl upholstery of a cinema seat.

'Well, don't. Feel awful, I mean,' he whispered back. 'That guy was bang out of order. There's nothing wrong with exposing a cheater for being a cheater. It's not like you made Wilchester do anything he didn't want to, and in the end the only person responsible for Carole Beaumont's bleeding heart is her husband. He's the one who promised to love and snuggle her till death do they part or whatever, not you. You don't even know the woman.'

'Yeah, maybe, but…'

'Anyway, both of them were brought up in the public eye,' Leo continued, warming to his subject. 'They know how the game's played, the extra caution you have to take when you're a celebrity. You'd almost think from his willingness to give it up he wanted to get caught – or at least that he didn't care if he was.'

'That doesn't change the fact I set him up and then humiliated his wife by spending the night with him when I was never supposed to take it that far. You can't tell me you think that's okay because we both know it bloody well isn't, and if I wasn't your best mate you'd admit it in a heartbeat. Anyway, it's not a 'game' I ever want to play again, Leo, not with people's lives…'

But Leo shushed her as the lights dimmed and the curtain came up. 'We'll talk more after, okay?' He gave her shoulder a firm, reassuring squeeze. Between him and Emily, she felt like 'reassuring squeeze' was likely to be listed on an autopsy certificate under 'Angel Blackthorne: Cause of Death' any day now.

As the opening credits started scrolling across the screen, Angel fished the notebook and pen from her handbag and began scribbling away in shorthand, listing the names of the principal actors, the setting for the opening scene, some brief notes on the performances. But half an hour later the same pen hovered motionless over the page as she stared, open-mouthed, at the screen.

Steve, Savannah, everyone had been right. Wilchester *was* brilliant. Perhaps even a genius. The writing, the direction, the casting: it was all spot on.

The plot was original and yet somehow quintessentially British: a bored, ditzy 1970s housewife, Beaumont, seduces the local milkman and then convinces him to carry out a hit on her philandering businessman husband. Seb's script was the perfect combination of farce and thriller, with the audience laughing, gasping, and on one occasion, screaming on cue in all the right places. Angel couldn't tear her fascinated eyes away, watching the plot twist and turn with dizzying speed, keeping her guessing until the very end.

And Carole Beaumont! Who could have predicted the icy, regal blonde would have such perfect comic timing, delivering one sparkling line after another, or such a talent for physical comedy? She might have the looks of a Grace Kelly but her performance reminded Angel of Lucille Ball in her prime.

As the end credits rolled Angel heard a round of applause start to ripple through the press area, becoming a standing ovation as those around her rose to their feet. Angel and Leo joined them, clapping wildly with the rest.

'Does that happen a lot?' she whispered to Leo, sinking into her seat again.

Leo shook his head. 'First time I've seen it. First time it's ever been earned. He's a talented bastard, I'll say that for him. I was doubtful when he announced the next Tigerblaze film would be a comedy, but it seems like everything that pair touches turns to gold.'

Angel nodded her enthusiastic agreement. 'God, it was unbelievable. Like Ealing in its glory days, but with a dark modern edge that really gave it bite. If Carole Beaumont hasn't got a best-actress BAFTA heading her way next year I'll be amazed.'

'You were certainly paying attention.' Leo looked impressed by her insight. 'Sounds like you've got a great starting point for your review, anyway. A fresh perspective too, which I guess is a rare thing in critic circles. You've not seen any of their other work, have you? I forgot you were a Wilchester virgin –'

Leo grimaced. 'Oh God. Forget I said that, will you? I can't believe I just said that.'

'Let's just pretend I didn't hear you,' Angel said, flinching in her turn.

But it was too late: she'd seen his mouth start to curve. Before she could help herself it had affected her too and she was lolling back in her seat, giggling uncontrollably along with Leo. Other journalists squeezed past them, shooting odd-but-I've-seen-it-all looks in their direction.

Angel snorted helplessly into Leo's shoulder for a solid two minutes until the tears stung. 'Come on,' she said at last, wiping the corners of her eyes and catching her breath. 'Let's get out of here to somewhere I can sort out my mascara. I must look like a reject from an eighties pop video.' People were pouring down the aisles out of the cinema now and they were the last two left in their seats.

She gazed through the open doors of the fire exit to the freedom of the brightly lit square. 'I don't suppose we could just go home, could we?' She angled a pair of hopeful, pleading eyes up to Leo. 'I'll buy you a Domino's on the way? It's emotionally draining, this film-reviewing lark.'

'Wish we could, Ginge. A slice of stuffed-crust double cheese and I'm anyone's under normal circumstances, as you well know. But Steve'll have my goolies for garters if we don't turn in some photos and a report on this after-party. When it comes to selling papers, that's the most important part of the night. It's where all the dirt is anyway, which you must have worked out by now is all the boss cares about.'

He grabbed her arm and dragged her towards the exit. 'Look, we don't have to stay long if you've had enough. It's a great opportunity for you to get a really class piece into your portfolio. Come on, I'll call a cab to take us over to the club.'

***

The lavish Luxe nightclub announced its status as the official after-party venue for *The Milkman Cometh* with a large plasma screen mounted over the door showing clips and trailers for the film. The building's black mirror façade was illuminated with electric-blue strip lighting. Another plush red carpet, bordered by plaited ropes suspended between highly polished brass stands, guided guests up to the entrance. It looked like exactly the last place Angel would ever choose to be if her time was her own.

'Shouldn't you be crouching somewhere, taking leggy shots of celebrities as they get out of limos?' she asked Leo.

'Yeah, I actually should.' He pulled a face. 'Hey Ginge, do you think we can ever leave this gutter-press lifestyle behind us and go work somewhere really classy, like *Big Jugs Monthly*?'

'We can dream.'

Leo screwed the lens on his camera and prepared to dash off. 'Go on, you get inside. I'll meet you at the bar.'

It didn't take long for Angel to discover film premiere after-parties were everything she hated about nightclubs, with an extra coating of awful. Or rather, it took ages to discover that. She had to queue for twenty minutes to get through the security checks, watching her bag turned inside out and the assorted debris that made up the contents scrutinised by three different security officers, plus another ten minutes for them to ring head office when they discovered it was Sarah, the *Investigator*'s heavily pregnant showbiz editor, and not Angel whose name was on the guest list.

When they were finally satisfied she wasn't a terrorist with a vendetta against the British film industry and let her through, she'd spent another fifteen minutes in a cloakroom queue so she could see her favourite jacket thrown into a pile with a raffle ticket pinned precariously to the collar. By the time she made it to the black gloss bar, trying to do a bit of subtle spying into the roped-off VIP area where she knew Seb and Carole would be seated on the way past, Leo was already there with a pint of something amber and a white wine served in a miniature milk bottle. *Nice touch…*

'For the lady,' he said, nodding towards the wine. 'Probably a bit warm by now. I see you made the rookie mistake of bringing a coat.'

She threw herself on to a barstool. 'Yeah, could've warned me, couldn't you? Plus they insisted I had to be Sarah or the computer would apparently get very upset. Steve forgot to get the guest list updated.' She looked at the pint in his hand, already half gone. 'How'd you get through security so fast anyway?'

He shrugged. 'They should know me by now; I've been to a few of these things. Just had to hand my camera in at the door until the end. They don't like press photographers creeping about trying to catch out the celebrities. There'll be an official Tigerblaze camera chimp somewhere around here.'

Angel sighed and took a long swallow of wine. 'You know, I'd expected this thing to be all Ferrero Rocher pyramids and free booze, not just a glorified clubbing trip.'

She flung a worried look at the pint glass in Leo's hand then yanked her gaze away, but he'd already caught her eye.

'Just apple juice, Ginge. Still on the wagon, eighteen months and counting.'

''Em said you'd stopped going to meetings…'

He knitted his eyebrows and angled his face away from her, staring down into his drink. 'Will you girls ever stop worrying about me?' he said, swirling the liquid around the sides of his glass. 'I'm fine, honestly. I've just been busy with work stuff. Look, I'll go back just as soon as I'm on top of things again, promise.'

She put a hand on his wrist and twisted her face around to his to look into those dark brown eyes, always so mournful even when they crinkled with laughter.

'There's no cure, Leo,' she said, her voice soothing and gentle. 'Only control. Remember what you had to go through, how hard it was in those early days of cold turkey? You couldn't have done it without the meetings to support you. I think after everything we went through together trying to get you off the stuff, you can trust me on that one.'

Leo jerked his hand away and stood up, his eyes flashing with resentment. 'Yes, and you're always ready to remind me, aren't you? Still trying to 'fix' me. Well you're not my girlfriend any more, Angel. Is it really too much to be allowed to forget and move on?' Grabbing his drink, he stormed off into the crowd.

Great. Angel Blackthorne, man poison. First Seb, now her ex the recovering alcoholic, who she'd managed to take on an emotional rollercoaster from hysterical laughter to growling rage in the space of just under two hours. *You're on fire tonight, girl...*

Man poison of sorts anyway, she thought, clocking the pinstriped specimen eyeing her with interest from across the bar. Picking up guys in bars was clearly something for which she had an innate talent. If only she'd realised earlier in life, while she was still choosing her future career. She could have earned a small fortune in folded fivers as a pole dancer by now.

Angel finally pinned down the nagging sensation that the man ogling her was someone she'd seen before. Of course. It was Seb and Carole's PR guy, the one who'd waited for them on the red carpet and guided them into the cinema.

PR Guy edged smoothly over to where she was sat. 'Top up?' he asked, gesturing to the barman. She could see him skimming her body with approval. The silver taffeta had made its first conquest.

'No thanks, but there is something else you can do for me.' She forced her voice into a seductive purr, and the PR man's self-assured smile told her he had every expectation he was about to get lucky.

'And what's that?'

She dropped the simpering smile and pulled her press pass out of her bag. 'You can get me an interview with your boss.'

The man's face hardened as he took the photocard from her. 'Serves me right for going slumming in the pleb section. You do know you're supposed to wear this at all times?'

'What, and ruin my pretty dress?'

'Sorry, darling, but you're wasting your time. Wilchester never gives interviews after premieres.' He cast a cursory eye over her pass and his lip curled into a sneer. 'Particularly not with the hacks at this rag, I rather think, don't you?'

'Oh, he'll see me,' she heard herself say with a calm confidence quite unlike her normal voice. 'Just show him that, will you? I'll be waiting here for his answer.'

PR Guy gave a loud scoff. 'I told you, you're wasting your time. But if you must insist…'

'I must.'

She watched him square his shoulders and march back to the VIP area. *I hope you know what you're getting yourself into, Angel Blackthorne. I just bloody well hope you do.*

Chapter 8

Okay, top marks for speed, Angel thought as she felt someone slip onto the stool next to her a few minutes later. But when she swung round she found it was only Leo, looking sheepish.

She should have known his temper by now. A quick flare-up, a five-minute sulk and then he'd be back to his usual self, all schoolboy charm and wearing his best hangdog expression.

'I'm a twat,' he said by way of an apology.

She glared at him. He'd get no disagreement from her, not unless he could do better than that.

'I s'pose I should realise by now you're only looking out for me.' He scuffed his foot against the polished-steel crossrail of the barstool. 'But it just makes it so difficult when I know you and Em are constantly fidgeting about, watching and fretting like – well, like you're my mums or something.'

He raised his eyes to hers and searched them keenly. 'Look, Angel, I know when we were together I let you down time and again, and put you through hell besides. I know it was me and only me who ruined whatever chance we had to make it work as a couple. It means a lot that you forgave me. I can be a moody sod, but I want you to know I won't throw away what we have now. You're my best friend and this time I promise I *will* fight to keep you.'

Angel blinked, touched and surprised by the rare display of affection. 'Soppy git,' she said. He wrinkled his nose as she ruffled the rough fuzz of black hair. 'I thought you'd have realised it by now. You don't get rid of me that easily.'

He looked down at his feet, suddenly bashful. 'Alright, Ginge. You don't have to show me up in front of all the top totty in this place. I'm losing vital macho points here.'

'It is about time we both got back on that particular horse,' she said, smiling. 'The dating one, I mean. Not any other horse you might have in mind. Not that I really want to know, but how long has it been for you anyway?'

'Oh, nine months or so, give or take a few millennia. But who's counting, really? I've decided to become a tantric hippy sex celibate, actually, like Sting or one of those guys. I could live to be a hundred and thirty-five.'

'It'll certainly feel like that long anyway,' she said with a laugh. 'Come on, mate, spill. You know all about my disaster of a love life, just like every other reader of the bloody *Investigator*. Don't you have any hot prospects on the horizon?'

'Just one.' His glance drifted to the floor and Angel bit her tongue, wishing she could take back the teasing question. For some reason she was suddenly afraid to hear the answer.

Leo looked up and his gaze, full of feeling, met hers. He couldn't… not after they'd worked so hard to get to where they were now. Could he?

'It's Emily,' he confided. Angel experienced a wave of relief she couldn't even have begun to explain.

So that was it. Her two best friends…

'You must've noticed me and Em getting closer, spending more time just the two of us. But every time it gets to the point where I feel like she might care about me as more than just a friend, she pushes me away. Then the next thing I hear she's dating some bellend and we're back at Mate Zero.'

Angel felt a pang of guilt. She actually hadn't noticed, although the whole thing must have been unfolding right in front of her for months. But she'd been so tied up in her own affairs – the internship, the honey trap and its fallout – she hadn't had a thought to spare for anyone's complicated love life except her own.

'Well, you know how she's been since Peter and the way that ended.' Angel reached out to give his back a comforting rub. 'And you know what she used to be like before. Dating and sex she has no problem with, but when it comes to getting close, learning to trust someone…'

'I know, I know. But I'm hitting a brick wall here, Ginge. I really don't know where to go next.' He sighed, vengefully tearing an unfortunate beer mat straight down the middle. 'So how about you? Any irons in the fire I should know about?'

'Nah. My ex was a lot to live up to.' She grinned, perfectly comfortable with him again now the awkward moment had passed. 'To be honest, Seb was my first since, well, whenever it was you and me broke up…'

'Seriously?' His dark eyes widened in shock. 'And I thought I had it bad. You need to get yourself out there, woman. At this rate, Mad Cat Lady status beckons before you hit thirty.'

'Not sure that process hasn't already started, to be honest.'

Leo shook his head with mock solemnity. 'Poor Wilchester. I never realised he'd had such big shoes to fill that night. No wonder he looks so miserable. You know what they say: once you've had Leo, you never – er, something that rhymes with Leo which basically means I'm great in bed.'

'They don't say that.'

'Well, no, they don't say that. Not as such.'

A low 'hem' at her elbow forced Angel to look around. Seb's PR guy, looking sulky and belligerent, was trying to attract her attention. She wondered how long he'd been standing there, eavesdropping on their conversation.

'Yes?'

'Against my advice, Mr Wilchester has agreed to give an interview to the *Investigator*,' he stated formally, refusing to make eye contact while he handed back her press pass. Angel saw Leo raise a quizzical eyebrow and she gave her head a slight shake to let him know she'd explain later.

'My colleague will join us, of course?'

PR Guy eyed Leo with sneering dislike. 'That was not part of the agreement. Look, darling, you've got ten minutes with my client, not a minute more. So I suggest you grab whatever it is you need and come with me.'

What she felt like she needed if she was going anywhere with this guy was a high-powered taser and a clear shot at his groin, but nevertheless she stood up to follow as he turned back towards the club's VIP area. She made an apologetic face to Leo, snatched her bag and left him looking puzzled by the bar.

'The rules will be as follows,' PR Guy continued as she trailed after him through the dimly lit club, illuminated only by the blue LED strips embedded into the floor and bar. 'No personal questions about my client's home life, marriage, childhood, ex-partners, sexual preferences, family or future plans. No implications about my client's lifestyle, nor nuanced inferences about his private life from the answers he does choose to provide. If Mr Wilchester is made to feel uncomfortable or embarrassed by any questions put to him, the interview will be terminated immediately. If I feel the questions put to Mr Wilchester will be likely to cause him future embarrassment, the interview will be terminated immediately. If –'

'So am I interviewing him or you?' Angel interrupted, narrowing her eyes. 'If you're expecting me to write some promotional puff piece for Tigerblaze Studios you can forget it. I'm not doing your job for you, mate.'

PR Guy turned to face her, glowing with resentment. 'Let's get one thing straight. This is a film premiere. Your questions will relate to my client's work and the film you have just seen. Or this interview can and will be shut down.'

'Fine,' she snapped back. 'Suits me. It's his work that interests me, not his private life. Enthralling though I'm sure it is.'

They continued in sullen silence until they reached the VIP lounge. A plaited cord, rich electric blue like everything else in the place, barred their entrance. PR Guy unhooked it at one end and ushered her through, flashing some sort of ID at the burly bouncer stationed just inside.

The reality of what she was doing hit Angel with a solid drop-kick to the abdomen when she spotted Seb in a private booth, lounging in the corner of a round, white-leather sofa. He was drinking a mini milk bottle of champagne and chatting to the lead actor from *The Milkman Cometh* with a smile that didn't extend to his eyes. She was relieved to see Carole Beaumont wasn't with him.

Too late to back out now...

She took a few hesitant steps towards his table, but stopped dead in her tracks when he turned and caught sight of her. His eyes narrowed and the smile disappeared, his sculpted lips setting in a thin line. There it was, the very expression she'd been dreading: disdain, hard and unforgiving. She dug her heels into the thin black carpet, willed her posture into erect dignity, but he refused to withdraw his stare.

She could feel the PR man's eyes burning into her from behind too, wondering what she was waiting for now she'd finally got the coup to end all coups; an exclusive audience with publicity-shunning Sebastian Wilchester. Forcing her lips into a polite smile, she pushed herself forward and into a seat at the other side of his table.

'Thanks, George, good job with everything tonight,' Seb said to the young actor, ignoring her. 'You'd better go find your mum before she starts worrying. Catch up in a bit. Just have to do a quick press thing before I can socialise.' He jerked his head in her direction.

'You're a martyr to it, aren't you, Seb? Okay, see you in a little while then.' George nodded to Angel and the PR man as he stood up to leave.

Interview! Shit! She really hadn't thought this far ahead. Here was Seb, eyes thrusting a thousand knives in her direction, and the Tigerblaze PR manager ready to shut her down the instant she went off message, and she hadn't thought up a single question. All she wanted to do was get whatever closure she could by offering an apology, congratulate Seb on the film and go, never to darken his red carpet again. But she could hardly do that with PR Guy breathing down her neck.

'Thank you for seeing me,' she mumbled, trying not to wilt under Seb's cool, appraising gaze.

She took out her dictaphone and placed it on the table. 'You don't mind…?'

'Not at all,' he answered, with flesh-freezing good manners and just a touch of sarcasm. 'Always committed to helping the *Investigator* get its facts straight.'

The last time she'd been this close to him, his tawny eyes had been soft and heavy with post-orgasmic warmth. Now, it was obvious they could hardly stand the sight of her. Why the hell had he agreed to this? Did he just want to make her feel uncomfortable? Some sort of petty revenge?

She fumbled with the dictaphone, pressing the button to record, and pulled out her notebook.

'You're going to make notes and record as well?' the PR man asked. He glanced over her shoulder, frowning when he caught sight of the indecipherable squiggles of her shorthand. 'I'm surprised you still need to learn that, with all this technology working for you.'

'Yep. Never know when the recording might fail.' She looked up at him. 'Anyway, I wanted to learn it. Keeps what ought to be private, private.'

'It's fine, Kev. I'm sure she'll give us a fair write-up,' Seb said in a calm tone. 'She certainly looks like she has – integrity.'

There was no doubting the perfectly timed pause, the charming, chilling tone, or the killing expression hanging on his features. Cool, solid dislike oozed from every syllable.

In the dim light she squinted at the shorthand notes she'd made during the film earlier; little more than a list of actors' names. It was enough to be bluffing along with, anyway.

'Why the genre change, Mr Wilchester?' she shot out, looking down at her notepad as if the questions were right there in front of her. 'Bit of a jump, isn't it, from British Gangster – sorry, 'East End Noir' I think you call it – to black comedy?'

His face remained impassive, but she thought from the flicker in his eyes she detected a glimmer of disappointment. Not a new question then. Her 'gutsy girl reporter' routine might have carried her through in the 1930s, but it seemed to be falling a bit flat right now. So long, Lois Lane, and thanks for nothing.

'I pioneered East End Noir, Miss Blackthorne, although I wasn't the one to name it. My style of direction, and to some extent my writing, were heavily shaped by Film Noir influences. When, at the age of barely twenty, I first started experimenting in film, it was only natural they would dictate my interpretation of that most British of genres, the London gangster movie. My first film, *Unreal City*, drew on the stylistic framing I so admired in the work of John Huston, for example.' His lips curled into something like a sneer. 'But of course, I'm sure you noticed that.'

She pinkened and jutted out her chin. He was mocking her; patronising her. Did he know she hadn't seen any of his films before tonight, or was this his way of showing her that airhead little slappers on tabloid papers had no place interviewing film-makers of his calibre?

'The genre jump was, in fact, a perfectly natural one,' he continued. 'In *Milkman*, I take elements of Noir and mingle them with the traditional British farce; again, I hope, creating something that is almost a genre unto itself – dark, thrilling and funny all at once. How far I have been successful is for the public to decide, but for myself, and for the cast and crew, I must say we have been very proud of the result.'

A genre unto itself? Okay, it was true, but still... pretentious bastard.

'Your work has often been compared to that of Orson Welles.' She made an attempt to match her tone to his, hoping she was making a fair performance of reading out pre-scripted questions from the pad in front of her. And there it was again, the faint flicker that told her these questions were distinctly passé to him. Seb still looked angry, but just as mortifying to her professional pride was that he looked bored. She shuffled in her seat, swallowing hard, calculating her next move.

'Your work has often been compared to that of Orson Welles,' she repeated, meeting his gaze. 'Which, given the similarity in your backgrounds, is perhaps inevitable. But your latest venture seems to have been more heavily influenced by fifties-era Billy Wilder, with perhaps a smidge of Robert Hamer thrown in for good measure. What would you say to those who might suggest your work is not only influenced by these directors, but to a great extent derivative?'

She faced off against him, blazing defiance, feeling Kev's frown through the hairs on the back of her neck. It was a bold gambit, but it worked. Seb's mouth twitched ever so slightly, his anger tempered with a new and healthy dose of respect.

'I'm flattered, Miss Blackthorne,' he said, inclining his head towards her. 'We all want to be like our heroes, and I'm certainly no different. You have coupled my name with two of the men in this business I admire more than many others, and for that, I thank you. If my work is, as you say I'm likely to be accused of, 'derivative' – well, if it can bring even a tenth of the pleasure I've experienced while watching *Sunset Boulevard* or *Kind Hearts and Coronets* to my audiences then my time won't have been wasted.'

The men in this business. His words annoyed her, bringing

75

back the vivid memory of Carole Beaumont in *The Milkman Cometh*: that stellar performance and perfect comic timing.

'You talk of men, and those are certainly two of the greats,' she went on, all caution now gone. It was amazing how appearing nude on the front page of a national newspaper could break down your inhibitions in social situations. 'But there's a great woman in the equation here too: your wife and leading lady, Ms Beaumont.'

His face hardened and she felt Kev take a step towards her, ready to shut down the interview if he felt she was veering in any way towards an invasive personal question. She gritted her teeth and looked down again at the notepad.

'Carole Beaumont, who I think we've seen tonight is a true comic talent. Can you tell me how you came to build up this rapport you seem to have together as director and actor?'

It was a weak question and she knew it, but she was clutching at straws now, hanging on as best she could. She wished Kev would go away for just five minutes so she could extricate herself from the whole charade.

She could feel the bitterness emanating from Seb when he answered, hating her for bringing up Carole's name and reminding him of their shared betrayal.

'Carole is my wife, yes, and we have had a long – by showbusiness standards at least – and successful marriage.' He glared at her, almost daring her to object. 'But she's more than that. Carole is my oldest and closest friend. It's easy to build up a rapport, as you call it – or as I like to think of it, an empathy, an affinity – after twenty-four years in each other's company.'

She had to try hard to stop herself flinching, or bursting into tears, or laughter, in the angry beam of his gaze. She thought of her oldest friends, Leo and Emily, and the affinity she had with them. There was a difference though, she remembered, thinking of the dark circles around Carole Beaumont's eyes. She would never do anything to hurt those closest to her.

Angel felt a surge of resentment towards this man, this arrogant man, who seemed to manipulate the life and emotions of the woman he loved as casually as if she were a character in one of his films. She fixed him with a steely gaze while she framed her next question.

'Are you a fraud, Mr Wilchester? A pale imitation of the film-makers whose work you so admire?'

'That's enough!' the PR manager exploded behind her. 'I told you, if this interview got out of hand it would be shut down –'

'It's okay, Kev,' Seb said, adopting a pacifying tone much less formal and polished than the one he'd used so far. 'She's right to go hard on me. That's her job. Not everything in PR's about product placement and arse-kissing, however much your guys would like it to be. Just let me answer the question.'

He turned back to Angel and his expression seemed – but perhaps she was imagining it – ever so slightly softer than before.

'No, Miss Blackthorne. I don't think I'm a fraud.' He paused for a moment and drained the last sip of his champagne, apparently savouring the flavour while his eyes met hers across the table. 'If you're asking do I have influences, then the answer is yes, very significant ones, and I encourage them to flow into my work as much as I can. TS Eliot, the poet, said 'good writers borrow, great writers steal'. Or your readers might understand it better as that hackneyed phrase, 'nothing new under the sun'. I suppose what I'm trying to say is yes, my work borrows – and steals – and yes, it's still original, at least as long as it elicits a new emotion, creates a new sensation. All art is imitation, Miss Blackthorne. But some is, excuse me, bloody good imitation. Perhaps my work does extricate those elements it most admires in the work of others, hacks them up and monster-like assembles them again into something new. Then, to carry the metaphor to its logical conclusion, it gives them life through fresh direction and great performances by the cream of our acting talent. But without praising myself unduly, I'd say that's no bad thing.'

He leaned back with a self-satisfied half-smile. His smug expression irritated her, though she couldn't disagree with anything he'd said. She scribbled away, gibberish symbols meaning nothing, just to give her hands something to occupy them.

'But you don't have a drink, Miss Blackthorne,' Seb said in the same calm, self-assured tone.

'I don't. But there's really no need –'

He looked up at Kev. The PR man was still standing behind Angel, sullen-browed and resentful. 'Kev, any chance you could pop over to the champagne bar and get a couple of glasses? Or milk bottles or whatever?'

Kev remained the same scowling, immovable pillar of pinstripe suit and Brylcreem. 'You don't pay me to be your drinks boy, Seb.'

'No, I pay you to represent me in a good light to the public. And right now you're making me look like an inconsiderate pillock in front of this young lady. Look, go on. It'll only take five minutes.'

The PR man still held his position, looking stubborn and sulky. Seb flung him an impatient glance.

'Please, Kev. As a favour. You can get yourself one while you're there, eh?'

'Fine,' Kev growled. 'This once, then. But watch what you say while I'm gone, can you? This is the bloody *Investigator* we're talking about, don't forget.' He dragged himself away towards the VIP lounge bar, keeping his suspicious gaze on Angel to the last.

She squirmed in her chair. It was clear Seb wanted the PR man out of the way, and she wondered helplessly what was coming now.

As soon as Kev was out of earshot, the director's eyes narrowed and he leaned over the table to take hold of her wrist in his powerful fingers. The polite, polished veneer of the professional film director dropped to reveal the Seb she knew, the one she'd met that night at the hotel, and he was seething. She noticed he was now wearing a gold wedding band on his third finger. The metal felt hot and hard against her skin.

'For Christ's sake, Angel, what the hell do you think you're doing here?' he hissed. 'Don't you know you nearly ruined everything?'

'*I* nearly ruined everything?' Angel said in a furious whisper, trying to pull her wrist away from the uncomfortable grip of his fingers. 'Perhaps if you'd been so concerned about your wife and your bloody marriage that night, you would have remembered to keep it in your pants! No one made you cheat, Seb. You did that all on your own, and with very little persuasion, I might add.'

'That's not what I meant!' he almost yelled in a voice strangled with fury.

He looked around to see if anyone had heard, lowering his voice when he spoke again. 'That's not what I – listen, I had a great time with you that night. And contrary to what you or your editor might think, I don't make a habit of picking up girls in bars. Then when I saw the story I had to assume you were a private investigator, or worse, a hooker, paid to set me up. It made me sick to my stomach to think we… God! Now I find you're what, a professional reporter? Seriously, who does that to someone? What the hell is *wrong* with you?'

'Look, I'm just an intern, alright?' she muttered, looking down at her feet. 'Just a crappy intern. It wasn't like I was supposed to –'

'Supposed to what? Ruin my life? Destroy my reputation, my peace of mind, my marriage? Supposed to *what*, Angel?'

'Supposed to *sleep* with you, Seb, okay?' she blurted out in a choked voice, feeling the briny sting of tears.

His eyes widened when he saw the tears, then narrowed in anger.

'Hey. Stop it. Look, go to the toilets if you need to and get yourself sorted. This is a public place and you're making us conspicuous.' His mouth twisted in derision. 'And I presume you wouldn't want another paper to get that exclusive.'

Shooting him a look, she dragged back the salty drops with an effort. He was right. This wouldn't do, not here.

'Okay, so I was sent by my editor to honey trap you, I think that's pretty plain at this point. But I was only supposed to get you up to the hotel room, get one compromising shot and come away. The rest – well, you know the rest. I didn't know we were still being filmed. You saw me block the camera with that towel. And for what it's worth, I apologise, to you and your wife. I don't know what made me do it. I'm a sizzling mess of a human person and just like you I ballsed things up, for all three of us but especially for her. And you can bet I'll beat myself up about it every day of my life from now on. But if you want to know whether I regret the time we spent together, then I don't know how to answer you.'

Seb loosened his grip on her wrist and just stared at her. His expression was unreadable, his face unflinching. She glared back, trying and failing to make her face as emotionless as his.

'Look, I'm sorry.' Her voice cracked as he continued to stare at her in total silence. 'It doesn't fix things but it's all I've got, Seb. I'm sorry. And for what it's worth, I thought *The Milkman Cometh* was a masterpiece. Original, compelling, unbelievably tight. Wilder would have been proud to call it his.'

Out of the corner of her eye she'd seen Kev heading back towards their booth, and now he reached the table, dumping two champagnes down in front of them.

'Right, there's your drinks. Shall we get on with the interview?'

Seb stared straight into her eyes for what seemed like an age, his fingers still loosely circling her wrist.

'No need, Kev. Interview's over.'

Chapter 9

Angel staggered to the VIP lounge toilets, blinded by tears that wouldn't now be held back.

The club became a blue mist as the stinging saltwater seeped out. She lurched past the queue for the champagne bar and felt her way through the door marked Ladies, gripped the cold porcelain edge of the sink hard and gave in for a moment to convulsive sobs.

Oh God, what had made her do it? Interviewing Seb had been the single worst experience of her life. The way he'd looked at her; that hard, biting dislike…

Struggling to regain control, she looked up at herself in the mirror. The face glaring back seemed hollow, somehow catlike; the peppering of freckles standing out against ghastly white skin, a feverish spot of pink on each cheek. The green eyes were bleared and lined with red.

She splashed some cold water over her face, experienced a surge of blessed relief as it revived and healed her.

A noise came from behind and in the mirror she saw the lock of one cubicle was drawn to the red engaged position. Fantastic. So someone had heard her little meltdown.

The noise came again: a strange, strangulated gurgle. Sounded like whoever it was had knocked back one milk bottle too many...

Turning around, she thumped on the door. 'Hey. Are you okay in there? Can I call anyone for you?'

There was no mistaking the noise this time. It sounded like someone trying to speak with a tongue too thick for their mouth.

'Hey!' She banged harder. No answer, just that odd strangled sound again, something between choking and dry heaving.

This was seriously not her night.

Leaning her weight against the cubicle door with one shoulder, Angel gave it a couple of firm, hard shoves. The lock couldn't have been drawn all the way across. It snapped back with relative ease and the door swung open.

She recoiled in shock. The scene in front of her could have come straight out of a horror film. A woman was slumped in one corner, her skin so papery-pale as to be almost transparent and her lips tinged with blue. Her eyes had rolled back into her skull so only the whites were visible and the face was smeared with make-up. Blood from a nostril had dried into a trickle, staining the peacock-motif white chiffon dress that hung by one strap from her shoulder.

It was Carole Beaumont.

'Jesus Christ! What the hell have you taken?' Angel hurled herself forward and shook the lifeless figure. A stab of fear slammed through her as Carole's head lolled on her shoulders.

She moved her face to the actress's mouth and felt hot, shallow breaths against her cheek. Once again, she heard the strangulated sound gurgling from the back of Carole's throat.

She needed an ambulance. Right now. Angel turned to the mirror, which flashed her own frantic, horror-struck face back to her. Where the hell was her handbag? Did she leave it back in Seb's booth?

Then she spotted it, under the sink where she'd dropped it when she first came in. Snatching it up, she fumbled for her mobile. Oh God, what if the ambulance didn't get there in time? This woman needed medical attention right away!

Should she run outside, call for help? Someone there would be bound to know first aid. But there was also the room full of press just behind the velvet rope, all on the lookout for fresh scandal. In her mind she could already see Carole Beaumont's blood-caked face on every front page...

Seb. He'd know what to do. Surely he must have dealt with something like this before. But how could she fetch him without drawing attention to them both? And she didn't want to leave Carole alone.

With a sudden thought, she rifled through the contents of her bag. She'd given herself a mental slap at the time for being weak enough to hold on to it, but yes, there it was still, tucked into her purse behind her Visa card. The note from Seb telling her what a great time he'd had with her that night at the hotel. The one with his mobile number scrawled underneath.

Thank God she'd kept it! She tapped out the digits, hoping to heaven he'd answer. He certainly wouldn't if he knew it was her, but of course he didn't have her number.

She listened to the phone ring, once, twice... *come on, come on!* Finally she heard it click as Seb picked up, answering with a crisp 'Yes?'.

'It's Angel. Listen, you have to get to the ladies' loos behind the champagne bar right now. I'm with Carole. Jesus, Seb, hurry, can you? It's an emergency.'

Without waiting for an answer, she hung up and threw the phone back into her bag.

She shot a panicked look at Carole, wondering if she should put her in the recovery position and then what the recovery position was. She had a vague idea tongues were important and stopping unconscious people from choking on them, but that was about the sum total of her first-aid knowledge.

With an effort, she heaved Carole's small but surprisingly heavy body into a semi-upright, seated position against the smoky charcoal tiles of the back wall, then tilted her head forward so there was no chance of the tongue obstructing her windpipe. Her gurgles were becoming louder, accompanied now by hoarse, rasping breaths. Angel sat down beside her and hugged her own knees. She rocked back and forth while she waited for Seb to arrive, vibrating with cold fear.

She stuck her head around the cubicle door when Seb burst into the bathroom just seconds later, his face full of panic. 'What's happened? Where is she?'

'Here. In the cubicle. For Christ's sake, Seb, get in here!'

He almost flew across to where she was, Angel shifting to one side to make way for him, and his eyes widened in horror when he caught sight of Carole.

'Oh God, oh my God!' His voice broke with anguish as he drew the unconscious body towards him and into his arms. 'What the hell did you do this time, Car?' He cradled the blonde head, gulping out painful, swollen sobs. 'Stupid girl, my stupid girl!' he said over and over, his voice muffled, his face buried in her dishevelled hair. Angel dropped her eyes, feeling suddenly shy; an intruder into something intensely private. But there was no time for that.

'Come on, Seb! What do we do?'

He pulled himself together and turned to face her. 'Did you call an ambulance?'

'No. They'll need to know what she's taken. I called you first. I thought you'd know.'

'Okay, good.'

He pulled out his phone from the pocket of his jacket and she watched him dial 999.

'Ambulance. Quick,' he said as soon as someone answered.

With the phone still pressed to his ear, he scanned her face. 'Look. I don't trust you. But since you're already here, damage limitation tells me I've got no choice except to make use of you.'

He yanked out Carole's bag, crushed between her little doll-like body and the wall, and threw it to Angel. 'Here. See if you can find the packet. They'll ask how much she's had.'

She rifled through the little beaded handbag, her fumbling fingers eventually closing around a small plastic container. She passed it to Seb, seeing him wince when he shook it and discovered it was empty.

She looked away, trying not to listen while he talked through Carole's symptoms with the operator. 'Yes, breathing but unconscious.' He paused, shooting Angel a suspicious look and lowering his voice. 'Painkillers: codeine. Cocaine too, I think.' He hesitated again, still keeping his gaze fixed on Angel, who felt her cheeks burning. 'No. It's not the first time.'

Angel heard someone start to come in and she darted out of the cubicle. She stopped the bathroom door's progress with her foot and poked her head around it.

'Sorry, we've got a flood in here,' she said to the well-groomed brunette outside. The woman drew back in surprise when she caught sight of Angel's wild-eyed, panicked face. 'Um, best try the one over the other side.'

She closed the door and held her back against it for a moment until she could be sure the woman had definitely gone.

'How long will the ambulance be?' she asked Seb when he'd hung up the phone, her back still against the door.

'They said twenty minutes max.'

'God, that long? What if she… oh God, Seb! Is there anything else we can do for her?'

'Recovery position, stop her choking. We'll need to get her out of this cubicle first, though. There isn't space to lay her down.'

'Okay. But we have to stop anyone else coming in. If she's out here we can't hide her.' Diving back into the cubicle, Angel pulled her phone from her bag and slid her finger across the touchscreen.

Seb put a hand on her wrist. 'What are you doing?'

'Calling Leo. We need someone to guard the door.'

'What, that photographer from the bloody *Investigator*?' he hissed. 'Are you mad?'

'Look, we can trust him, okay?' She bit her lip, suddenly realising how ridiculous that sounded.

'*We* can trust him? There is no "we", Angel! I barely trust *you*, and I certainly don't trust some paparazzi bastard who'd think this was the scoop of his life! It's people like him who've put her in this state. No. I won't allow it.'

'Fine,' she snapped. 'Then the door stays open. Shall I pop outside, invite everyone in to have a look at your wife's suicide attempt?'

He flinched heavily. 'Don't use that word.'

'It's the word they'll use in the press, if this makes it out. Look, have you got a better idea?'

He glared back at her for what seemed like an age. 'Okay,' he said eventually, removing his hand from her wrist. 'Do what you have to do. But if there's anything about this in that poor excuse for a newspaper you work for…'

He let the unfinished sentence hang in the air while she pulled up Leo's number.

'Leo? Get yourself over to the VIP bit, I'll meet you by the barrier. I need a favour. Yes, it's urgent.'

She hung up. 'I'll need your pass,' she said, holding out a hand to Seb. He stared at her blankly. 'For the VIP lounge. Come on.'

Wordlessly, he unclipped it from his jacket and handed it to her.

'I'll only be a minute.' She darted out of the door and back into the club.

The blue ambiance of the lounge, with its background hum of elevator jazz, seemed indecently civilised after the drama of the bathroom. She reached up and patted her hair as she hurried towards the bouncer guarding the entrance. The sophisticated chignon was long gone now, stray tendrils falling down her neck and brushing her burning cheeks, and the silver taffeta was sodden up to her calves. God only knew what she looked like to the combed and manicured celebrities she was passing in their booths.

Leo was waiting for her on the other side of the barrier, a worried look on his handsome, boyish face.

Unhooking the rope, she yanked him through. 'He's with me,' she said to the bouncer, flashing Seb's pass. He shot them a hasty look of surprise, but he didn't stop them.

'Come on. Quick.'

'Look, what's this all about? Did something happen? You look like hell, Ginge. Is everything okay? '

'Not really. Listen, I'll have to fill you in later. Right now I need you to guard the door of the Ladies. Don't ask why.'

She saw one suggestive eyebrow raise as he took in her dishevelled appearance and realised where his mind was headed. 'No, it's not – look, there's an emergency going on in there. I can't tell you any more now. Just trust me, okay, mate?'

They reached the toilets. 'Alright, I guess you know what you're doing. You can count on me,' Leo said, pulling off a mock salute while she hurried back through the door.

'Sorry, darling, we've got water an inch deep in here. Some bugger's blocked the sink,' she heard him tell someone as the door swung shut. 'There's one at the other end if you need a whizz…'

'Angel. Here.' Seb beckoned her over.

'Any change?' she asked, joining him in the cubicle.

'Some vomiting. Hopefully that's got a bit of it out of her system. She's coming round now, I think.'

She noticed he'd taken off his dinner jacket and folded it to make a cushion for Carole's head. Without it, he looked as dishevelled as she did. His black bow tie was already hanging loose around his unbuttoned shirt collar and he was once again pushing unruly chestnut curls away from his face, the smart gelled hair of the red carpet long gone.

Between the three of them they looked like the last survivors of the Moss Bros apocalypse, Angel thought through the fog of her panic. But she couldn't help sweeping her eyes over the tousled hair, the golden skin of Seb's exposed throat.

The actress was starting to regain consciousness now. Her eyes were open but heavy and misted, pupils the size of pinheads.

'Here, help me get her out there so we can lay her down,' Seb said. 'She must've lost fluids when she threw up. It'll help if we can get her to drink something.'

They each took an arm, Angel struggling to support the weight of Carole's little frame as they guided her out of the cubicle. Between them they hauled the semi-conscious actress into a horizontal position on her side.

'My jacket. Get it.'

Obediently, Angel grabbed the folded jacket from the toilet cubicle and handed it to Seb. Lifting his wife's head, he slid it underneath her, then raised her right leg slightly so it was bent at the knee. Her dress had hitched up and on some female instinct Angel leant forward, pulled it down to cover the actress's thigh.

Carole's eyelashes started to flicker and she let out a low moan that might have been Seb's name.

'Yes, I'm here, kid,' he said softly, crouching down to run his fingers over her hair. His eyes were liquid with feeling and Angel saw a tear drop on to the blonde head. Deep in her gut she felt the wrench of some emotion she couldn't identify.

'Have you got a bottle or something in your handbag?' he demanded, turning to her. 'Any sort of container?'

'Just this,' she said sheepishly, rummaging in her bag and fishing out one of the mini milk bottles from the bar. She'd slyly pocketed it earlier; a souvenir of an evening she was now thinking she'd rather forget.

Seb stood and took it from her. 'That'll do.'

'It's… my fault,' Angel said, coming to a sudden realisation. 'This. It's my fault. Our fault. Isn't it?' She brought her eyes up to Seb's. 'The story in the paper… that's why she did this. You said it was people like Leo who'd made her this way. That means people like me.'

He gave his head an impatient shake while he took the bottle over to the sink and rinsed it out under the tap. 'No time to have that conversation.' But his expression softened a little when he saw Angel's look of wild-eyed angst. 'Look, you can't blame yourself for this. It's – well, it's a bit more complicated than that.'

'Seb… are you there?' Carole's voice was hoarse and weak, barely a whisper.

'Here, Car, I'm just here.' He turned to Angel. 'Sit with her a second,' he said in a low voice.

Dreamlike, Angel went over and crouched down by Carole's head while Seb filled the little bottle. She brushed her fingers over the untidy bob, remembering all the many times she'd seen it, lustrous and carefully styled, on television and in magazines. The actress blinked bleary eyes at her.

'I don't know you, do I? Am I at home?'

'Not just now, sweetie. You'll be home soon.' Angel tried to sound reassuring, to hide the panic she felt vice-like around every nerve.

'It hurts… God, it hurts,' Carole whispered.

Angel felt another stab of fear when she saw the actress wince in pain. She took Carole's hand in hers and stroked it with comforting fingers.

She stood up and moved out of the way as Seb came over and sat down by his wife, the bottle now filled with cold water. He slid his arm under Carole's shoulder to raise her into a semi-upright position. 'You're safe now, Car. Here, drink this. It'll help.'

He made soothing noises and stroked the blonde head, helping her drink the water down like a child. Angel flushed and turned away to face the door while she gave them a moment. When Carole had finished the water, Seb refilled the bottle and helped her drink that too.

'Angel.' She turned back to find him looking at her. 'Look, I'm going to need your help getting her outside to the ambulance. She's conscious now, and she'll be better off in the open air. But I don't want anybody out *there* –' he narrowed his eyes in the direction of the VIP lounge – 'seeing her in this state if I can help it, or a bunch of paramedics running around the place attracting attention. If this makes it into the papers, it might just tip her over the edge again.'

Angel was moved. Perhaps he was finally starting to trust her. *Then again, perhaps he just has no choice…*

Carole had managed to push herself up into a sitting position now. She was leaning against the wall for support and groaning. Looking at her glacier-white face, Angel dwelt on that word of Seb's, 'again'. She felt a jolt of compassion, wondering how many times he'd been forced to deal with this before tonight.

'Shift out of the way, then,' she commanded, signalling him to move aside. 'Let me see what I can do.'

'We'll have to take her through the lounge, it's the only way out.' Angel grabbed a paper towel and dampened it with a little water from the tap. 'But if she can walk a bit then maybe we can pass it off as drunkenness and sneak her out by that fire exit. It's only a few yards.'

Angel crouched down in front of Carole. 'Okay, sweetie, I'm just going to help you fix your make-up. Don't worry, I'll be gentle.'

She dabbed at the mingled streaks of blood and mascara with the paper towel until Carole's face was clean, then retrieved her concealer from her bag and added a smear under the eyes to hide the dark circles. She hadn't brought any blusher but a spot of ruby lipstick smudged into each cheek did the same job, taking away some of the deathly pallor, and another slick of ruby on the lips hid their bluish tinge. She combed her fingers through the blonde locks, smoothing them down as best she could.

The blood on the dress was a problem, though. Angel didn't have anything which could hide that.

She turned to Seb. 'I'll need your jacket.'

He understood at once. He snatched the rumpled dinner jacket up from the floor and draped it around Carole's white shoulders.

The buttons didn't fasten all the way up to hide the telltale trickle standing out against the creamy material, but the jacket was big enough to wrap tight around Carole's tiny frame. Angel turned up the collar to hide the blood and, detaching the pin from her now very frazzled hair, secured it from falling open. It was her nana's pin, with a lot of sentimental value. But this was an emergency.

Seb brought his face down to Carole's. 'Do you think you can walk, Car, with me and this lady to help you?' he asked in a gentle voice, far gentler than Angel would ever have imagined those deep tones could be.

Carole flashed him a weak smile, her face full of childlike trust. 'I'll try, Seb,' she said in a broken whisper. 'And – I'm sorry. I've let you all down again.'

'You know you could never do that.' He made soft shushing noises over her, planted a kiss on top of the platinum bob. 'It's not us you need to worry about letting down, kid, it's yourself. Come on, let's get you up.'

He flashed a look at Angel and she took a step forward. Crouching down, she grabbed Carole's free arm and pulled it around her shoulder. Between them they raised the actress to her feet.

Carole groaned in pain. 'Stop. It's hurting her,' Angel muttered to Seb.

'No, I'm – I'm okay,' Carole gasped. 'Thank you.' She turned guileless blue eyes on Angel.

She doesn't know who I am… Angel felt a stab of guilt through her belly.

'It's not far,' Seb said to Carole in the same tender voice. 'Just put all your weight on us.' Almost carrying her, they guided her to the door.

Leo, still on guard outside, shot the three of them a shocked look as they pushed past him. 'Back soon,' Angel mouthed and he nodded acknowledgement.

Seb forced his lips into a jovial grin when they passed George, the young actor, and his mother near the champagne bar. They stared at Carole in surprise.

'Seems like the missus has gone a bit overboard on the complimentary drinks,' he said, laughing. 'She'll be feeling it in the morning. I'll just get her into the limo, then I'll come back in and say goodnight.'

They managed to reach the fire exit without having to speak to anyone else. Keeping a tight hold of his wife, Seb leaned into the aluminium rail to push it open and they carried Carole, now a dead weight, out into the blessed respite of the cool evening air. All three sagged back against the brick wall of the club and Angel exhaled in relief.

There was a siren blaring in the distance, which she guessed belonged to the long-awaited ambulance. Not before time. Carole had lapsed into semi-consciousness, eyes half closed and mouth hanging open, and they eased her into a sitting position on the ground.

'What happened to Kev? He won't be sniffing around somewhere looking for you both, will he?'

'No, after you left he went off to get a drink at the other bar and never came back. Probably holed up somewhere by now with some unfortunate girl, luckily for us.'

Seb turned to face her, his expression impassive once more. 'Look, I can take it from here. You go back inside. Your friend will be waiting for you.'

'I'd like to stay for the ambulance…'

He shook his head. 'The more of us there are, the more likely we are to attract attention. Me and Carole, that I can explain. Just go, please, Angel. I'll look after her now.'

Her heart sank. He was trying to get rid of her, to get Carole away from her. Even after everything they'd been through tonight, he still didn't trust her. Hardly surprising, really. After all, what had happened the last time he'd put his trust in her? She stifled a bitter laugh at the thought.

She turned her weary body back towards the club. Leo would be waiting, but the fire escape locked from the outside. She'd have to go round to the front entrance and hope they wouldn't put her through twenty minutes of security checks all over again.

'Hey.' Seb caught her hand and she felt that zing of energy which seemed to shoot through her whenever they touched. How did he do that? She wondered if he felt it too. As usual, he wasn't giving anything away.

'Thanks for everything you did this evening.' He dropped the impassive expression for a moment, flashing a shaken smile in her direction. 'I won't forget it.'

She managed to return the smile. 'Thanks. That… thanks, Seb.'

'And remember what I said before. None of this was your fault. Whatever you – we – did, it would still have happened just the same way it did tonight. Trust me.'

Her head buzzing, she left him cradling Carole's head in his lap and stumbled back towards the club.

Chapter 10

It was well after midnight when Angel unlocked the door of the flat, trying to make as little noise as possible. If Emily woke up she'd have to know everything that happened at the premiere, and Angel could well spare that conversation until morning.

In the bedroom she peeled herself out of her clothes, the taffeta dress now sadly bedraggled and damp. She left it in a crumpled, shimmering heap in the corner to sort out in the morning. Too exhausted even to locate her pyjamas, she fell naked into the soft, welcoming folds of her duvet.

The window was open, letting in the oppressive heat of an early October Indian summer. A faulty car alarm wailed her a lullaby, but sleep wouldn't come. When Angel closed her eyes, all she saw was Carole Beaumont's deathlike face streaked with blood. Every time she started to drift into sleep, she jerked awake with a sudden crushing terror, her heart flapping painfully against the hollow bones in her chest.

What if Carole died in the night? What if they'd been too late to save her and the pills had already damaged her organs beyond repair? God knows how long she'd been slumped there before Angel discovered her. She thought of Seb, dragging out anguished sobs alone in a sterile hospital waiting room, and felt the prickle of sympathy drops in her own eyes.

She'd filled a shocked Leo in on the night's bizarre events as they'd made their way home. The honey trap, her ex and the man she'd set up, working together to save the woman he loved. There'd be a grim humour in the thing, if she had any energy left to appreciate it.

Obviously Leo would keep what had happened in confidence, but if anyone else had witnessed Carole's breakdown, or seen her carried into the ambulance… Seb had said if the story got out it could tip Carole over the edge. And if the *Investigator* broke it, he'd certainly blame her.

Eventually Angel gave up on sleep, threw off the duvet and wrapped her dressing gown around her. There'd be no rest tonight.

She pulled her laptop out from under the bed and switched it on. Might as well write up her notes on the premiere while the events were still fresh in her mind. It would be a distraction from worry and unpleasant thoughts anyway. Locating her dictaphone, she dug out a pair of headphones from the drawer of her bedside cabinet.

She shivered when she began to transcribe the interview she'd conducted earlier and heard Seb's deep, harsh voice again, simmering with repressed anger while he answered her fumbling questions. It reminded her too clearly of the same voice, low and gentle that night at the hotel when he'd wrapped her in powerful arms and she'd snuggled into the warmth of his body: *you were incredible…*

But those kind of thoughts weren't allowed, were they? She shook her head, as if to banish the image from her mind.

Angel switched off the dictaphone at the point where Kev had left them to get drinks. She certainly didn't want to hear her own broken, pathetic apology again, or Seb's cool dismissal. They were too firmly imprinted on her memory already.

By 6am she had the interview transcribed and the bare bones

of her film review. The other piece, the report for the showbiz supplement, could wait. After everything that had happened that night, it was hard to stay focused on which fashion designer the winner of Big Brother 2004 had been wearing.

Did she dare ring Seb to ask about his wife? She still had his number in her phone. It seemed like such an intrusion, doubly inappropriate coming from her, but she couldn't get any peace until she knew if Carole was going to make it.

In the end she decided to send a text message. Impersonal, maybe, but the idea of hearing Seb's voice, choked with a grief she had no right to hear, convinced her.

Will she be okay? Angel

That was all. Hitting 'Send', she flung her phone down on the bed.

She wondered if Seb would bother to reply, or if by now he just wanted her out of his life entirely. She wasn't a hundred per cent persuaded by his insistence Carole's suicide attempt had nothing to do with her and that front page. And who was he trying to convince anyway? Her? Or himself?

Grabbing a towel, she made her way into the bathroom. She could hear her flatmate starting to stir next door, and she wanted to get a shower before Emily commandeered the room for the next hour or five.

She let out a long, soul-juddering sigh as she turned on the shower and felt the hot water wash over her, healing and restoring her shattered body. There was a bruising pain in her right shoulder where she'd supported Carole's semi-conscious frame to the fire exit, and she stretched it uncomfortably as she rubbed shampoo through her limp, frazzled hair.

Back in the bedroom, she discovered Groucho had finally realised his burning ambition and made the neglected silver taffeta his own. He was snuggled down among the glossy folds, kneading the material and purring to himself. Angel lifted him off with an impatient cluck, shooing him out of the door while he made his objection known in a series of squawks. That Mad Cat Lady crack of Leo's earlier hadn't been too far off the mark…

She picked up the dress, rummaged around for a coat hanger and put it away in the cupboard. It wasn't looking too happy, but hopefully it could be salvaged with a good dry-clean. Although opportunities to wear it again in future were likely to be slim: she'd already decided to turn down the temporary showbiz editor position if Steve offered it to her. She'd had enough of after-parties.

Her phone was where she'd left it on the end of the bed. Picking it up, she scanned the screen. One new message.

Oh God, it was from Seb. Her stomach lurched with cold fear as she opened it.

Out of danger.

The wave of relief she felt as she let herself sink down on the bed almost consumed her. *Thank God, thank God!* She closed her eyes for a moment, let out a deep sigh and allowed her body to de-tense. She could feel the fistlike anxiety that had gripped every muscle dissolving into air.

She looked again at Seb's text. It was clear he was willing to give her only the bare minimum of information. Still worried the story would end up gracing the front page of the *Investigator*. But he'd replied. That was something.

Not for the first time that night, she wondered why it bothered her so much, the idea he didn't trust her. For some reason she couldn't fully grasp, she seemed to have this deep-seated need for his approval. Why? Just what was it about Sebastian bloody Wilchester that made her care what he thought of her anyway?

That he loved his wife was pretty much obvious. Angel remembered with a pang of compassion those liquid eyes buried in

Carole's hair, weeping while he comforted her like a child. But that he couldn't stay faithful to her, despite her fragile mental state, was just as obvious. Angel could never be anything to him, could never be part of his world, she reflected with something between relief and regret.

She knew being in his life should be the last thing she wanted. So why couldn't she stop thinking about him? What he thought of her, the remarkable quality of his work, what he was feeling and how she could make it better... her veins were poisoned with him. And it had to stop. It had to stop right now.

Clambering back under the duvet, she managed to sink into an uneasy sleep in which a disembodied pair of glittering tawny eyes followed her through each dream, eternally appraising her with a gaze of cool dislike.

***

It was nearly half-nine when Angel emerged from her room: grey-faced, hollow-eyed and yawning pitiably. Her still-damp hair frizzed an auburn halo around the top and back of her head.

Emily was in the kitchen, humming a cheesy eighties pop song to herself and doing a little bum-wiggling dance while she buttered a couple of toasted crumpets. She was dressed in a white lab coat ready for her appointment, obviously just about to bolt down some breakfast and leave.

'Bloody hell, you look dog-rough this morning, sweetie,' she said with a bright smile. 'Good time at the premiere?'

Angel gave a noncommittal grunt. At some point Emily would need to hear the whole story, but right now all she wanted to do was inhale a strong coffee and enjoy a quiet veg-out in front of the TV while she took stock of herself.

'I see Carole Beaumont had quite a night.' Emily cocked a suggestive, perfectly tweezed eyebrow. 'Shocked me, I have to say. Who would've thought Miss Perfect was as human as the rest of us?'

Angel felt a prickling horror shoot from her gut through her whole nervous system. *Shit!* Could it have hit the news already? Who could have leaked it?

'Why, what did you hear?' she demanded. 'Was there something on the news?'

'Not really. Well, not much anyway.' Emily sounded taken aback by the urgency in her tone. 'Just a bit on the entertainment programme this morning saying her hubby had to take her home early from the after-party because she was leathered out of her skull.'

'Photos? Video?'

'No, just one line in the weekly gossip round-up. That actor, George Seward, tweeted about it apparently. Why, Ange, what's it to you?'

Angel felt a surge of relief. 'Oh, nothing. Well, something, but no time to go into it now. You go to your appointment. I'll fill you in later.'

'Right, okay.' Emily shot her a worried look. 'Nothing wrong, is there? You don't want me to cancel?'

Angel summoned a tired smile. 'No, it's not important, Em, honestly. Nothing that can't wait. Definitely nothing you should be cancelling work stuff for.'

'Well, if you're sure…' Emily was still hesitating.

'Look, I'm fine, I really am. Go, go!' Angel laughed as matador-like she tried to shoo her friend out of the door with a tea towel. 'Get a jiggle on or you'll be late. And I'm not paying your share of the rent when the Reflexology Illuminati or whoever have blacklisted you.'

'Right. Talk later then.' With one last concerned look over her shoulder, Emily left the kitchen, a half-eaten crumpet hanging nearly forgotten from one hand. Angel heard the door slam as she left the flat.

She had enough time before Emily got back to finish her film review of *The Milkman Cometh*, under the tentative title of 'Carry On Hitchcock'. Writing it was sort of fun and Angel felt her spirits lift a little while she tapped away at the laptop, watching her half-formed ideas take shape into what she sincerely hoped was a well-thought-out critique. As soon as it was finished she whizzed it off to Steve. The showbiz supplement piece he could wait till morning for.

It was evening before she had chance to talk to Emily about what had happened at the premiere. Sunday was Angel's night to cook, and she and Mr Dolmio had whipped up her famous, or possibly infamous, Spaghetti Pomodoro. They ate it from their laps on the sofa with the TV humming in the background, Groucho watching their plates with a proprietorial eye from the floor, staking his claim to any leftovers.

Emily listened in shock while Angel told the story of the previous night's events.

'Jesus, it was terrifying, Em. I really thought she was going to die. She kept making this horrible gurgly noise, and you should've seen her face. Like a stunt double from *The Exorcist*.'

'Shit, Ange! Sounds like you kept your head, though. Bet I would've just sat there dribbling if I'd been faced with something like that.'

'I'm not sure I did really – keep my head, I mean. When I first found her I nearly peed myself. It was just… luck, more than anything. God, I'm so glad she's going to be okay.' She shook her head sadly. 'Poor cow.'

'And what did that bastard have to say for himself?' Emily asked, her lips thinning in anger. After Angel had told her about his behaviour during the interview and Carole's suicide attempt, Seb was well out of Emily's good graces. Not that he'd ever really been in them. Cheating husbands were always a sore point with her.

'Not much. He seemed pretty traumatised when he first saw

her but he managed to hold it together. To be honest I don't think it was the first time he'd had to deal with something like that.' She twisted a strand of hair around one finger, remembering. 'Have to say, Em, it was sort of sweet. The way he looked after her.'

'Pfft! Yeah, when he's not sneaking around behind her back getting laid in hotel suites. No offence. I hope he *was* traumatised, given it was probably all his fault. Serve him bloody well right.'

Angel knew her friend's brutal response had nothing to do with Seb and Carole and everything to do with Emily and her ex-husband, Peter. They'd lived the stereotype when it came to cheating spouses: Emily had come home early one day after a cancelled appointment and found Pete in bed with his assistant. It's one thing to find your husband cheating, she'd observed with a grim laugh long after, but he could at least have taken the time to be original. That had been her last long-term relationship.

'Leo was great last night, anyway.' Angel watched her friend's face while she spoke. 'Didn't bat an eyelid when I asked him to keep guard. You'd think he had mates asking for his help with suicidal actresses every day. He really came through for me.'

Emily looked down at her hands with a warm smile. 'Yeah. He's a good boy.'

Angel wondered if she should bring up what Leo had told her at the premiere about his feelings for Emily. She didn't want to risk scaring her commitment-shy friend off. And it really wasn't any of her business.

Then again, they should know by now she was a nosy, interfering cow.

'Em…'

'What?'

'Do you ever think I did the wrong thing, ending it with Leo?'

'Absolutely not.' Emily gave her bouncy curls a firm shake. 'You spent too much of your life trying to help him through his

101

issues, Ange. I love Leo, you know I do. But you two just weren't right for each other. You're too… mumsy.'

Angel drew herself up in indignation. 'Huh! Thanks a lot, Em.'

'Oh, you know what I'm on about. I'm not talking support tights and frumpy M&S cardigans. It's just when it comes to lost causes, you've got a salvation complex. You're too prone to trying to look after people. And someone like Leo is always going to let you. Come on, sweetie, you know I'm right.'

Angel felt Groucho weaving around her legs as if to prove Emily's point. He'd been a stray when Angel had found him outside the flat; just a mangy ball of fur and bones with two big green eyes staring out. She'd had to beg her friend to let her adopt him and nurse him back to health in spite of the no pets clause in their letting agreement.

'Good relationships don't work that way,' Emily went on. 'There has to be that give and take. You and Leo are great together as mates, but much as I hate to say it, as a couple you were probably doomed from the off. Even if he could've stayed sober.' She gave her friend's shoulders a squeeze. 'Sorry, Ange, but it's true.'

Was it true, though? Did she have a salvation complex? Okay, there was certainly a time when worrying about Leo, trying to 'cure' him, had taken over Angel's whole life. She couldn't picture that happening to independent-minded Emily.

She found herself wondering about Seb's relationship with Carole, if he'd also been through the sleepless nights and angst-ridden days that came when you shared your life with an addict. It had been a lonely time, she remembered too well; all those nights lying awake crying when Leo failed to make it home again, then the bitter recriminations, the slurred excuses.

Was Seb lonely too? Was that why he'd seemed so hungry for her body against his that night at the hotel, as if it had been an eternity since he'd been touched by anyone?

She kicked herself for this weakness. Trying to find excuses why Seb Wilchester would cheat on his wife would do Angel's mental state no favours. Her subconscious was just telling her what it knew she wanted to hear, as usual. If Seb wasn't a 'proper' adulterer then she could continue to let the idea of him haunt her.

Rousing herself, she turned back to Emily. 'So you think Leo's a lost cause?'

'For you? Yes.'

Angel took her friend's hand and gave it a squeeze. 'And what about you?'

Emily shook her head, looking down at her feet. She didn't seem surprised, though. This wasn't a new idea to her then...

'It'd be too weird. You know – my mate's ex.'

'Oh come on, Em, that's just an excuse. You know I'd be thrilled to see you together. You'd be perfect for each other. Someone like you is just what he needs. You almost said it yourself a minute ago. And I know he could make you happy now he's... well, better.'

Drawing her hand away, Emily stood up. She took Angel's empty plate from her lap and turned towards the kitchen. 'Hey, want some ice cream? There's some in the freezer, toffee fudge.'

'You're changing the subject.'

'Goddamn right I am. To ice cream, always a happy-making topic of conversation.' Her usually bright expression darkened a little. 'Take the hint, Ange, eh?'

Angel took the hint. The subject was closed – for now.

Chapter 11

'Sorry, sorry, sorry. Piccadilly Line's mental this morning,' Angel said to Savannah, sinking breathless in front of her desk nearly an hour late for work.

Her alarm had failed, there was chaos on the Tube, the lift was out of order and she'd had to bound up the two flights of stairs to her floor... were all excuses she knew wouldn't hold any weight with Steve. And as for 'I was knackered because I spent Saturday night hoisting suicidal actresses around toilet cubicles' – well, that one could just stay right in the box where it belonged.

'Did he notice I wasn't in for nine?' she asked, jerking her head over her shoulder towards the editor's door.

Savannah looked a little pale and drawn and Angel wondered in passing if everything was okay.

'Yeah, sorry. I tried to cover for you but he's been out twice to ask if you're in yet. Wants to see you in his office soon as,' the young intern answered. 'And I'd tread lightly if I were you. There's a rumour going round he's trying to get off the fags again.'

'Oh Christ.' Angel had never seen it herself, but Steve's intermittent attempts to quit smoking were the stuff of *Investigator* legend. Coffee mugs were said to have collided fatally with walls as the cravings gnawed frayed nerves – even, on one occasion back in the day, a typewriter. Angel looked over to his office and saw him pacing the carpet, wolf-like, through the glass.

'Wish me luck,' she said, pulling a face. Savannah held up crossed fingers and flashed her a weak smile.

She gave the door to Steve's office a gentle shove and walked in without knocking. No need to set his nerves on edge any more than they already were. The editor was still pacing, chewing on a thumbnail. A row of dirty mugs on the edge of his cluttered desk seemed to indicate one bad habit had replaced another.

'You wanted to see me, boss?'

'Yeah, about a week ago,' he barked. 'Where the hell have you been?'

She opened her mouth to frame an excuse, but Steve raised a hand to silence her. 'Never mind, just remembered I don't give a flying toss. Don't let it happen again, that's your last warning. And you can stay late tonight to make up for it too. That piss-poor excuse for an article you emailed me for the showbiz supplement needs a bloody good tidy-up before it goes to the subs. It's littered with typos.'

She shuffled her feet, not daring to tell him she'd dashed it off in a hurry on the train into work that morning.

'Well then, how was it on Saturday?' he demanded.

'The premiere?'

'No, the bloody Lithuanian State Caber-tossing Championships. Of course the sodding premiere, you silly bint!'

The insults were coming out earlier than usual. He really was in a foul mood.

'It was… fine, Steve. You've got my piece. Not much to tell other than what's in there.'

'I heard there was an ambulance out the back of Luxe about 11.00.' He searched her face, but she kept her expression fixed.

'Sorry, didn't hear anything about that.' How did he always know these things? 'I was with Leo at the bar most of the night.'

'Yeah, that's what he said.' Steve's gaze continued to hold her.

'And I suppose you didn't hear anything about Carole Beaumont getting taken home by your boyfriend in a rather, er, "tired and emotional" state at around the same time, did you?'

She felt her cheeks heat when he mentioned Seb and scuffed one shoe against the carpet. After spending much of the weekend in heels, she'd given her feet a break today and worn her trainers. She could sense Steve drinking in this new informal look with disapproval.

'I told you, I was with Leo…'

'…at the bar. Yeah, you said. Bloody hell, love, you're about as useful to me as a ribbed-for-her-pleasure johnny machine in the Vatican today, aren't you? Do you think I pay you and Courtenay to get rat-arsed on the paper's time?'

He stormed across to his desk and Angel wondered if one of the mugs was about to be on a collision course with her head. But he just rummaged through a pile of papers and fished out printouts of her showbiz report and film review.

'Here,' he said, thrusting the showbiz report into her hand. 'And a bigger pile of wank I've never read. I've scribbled a few notes on it for you. See if you can't smarten it up a bit, since unfortunately it's the best I've got. I want it sorted by the end of the day, and I don't care how late you have to be here to do it either.'

She nodded, dropping her eyes to the carpet. She felt like a teenager being told off about sub-par GCSE coursework.

'And you can forget the temporary showbiz editor job, Blackthorne. Sarah's off to pop the sprog some time after next week, and I'll be interviewing for it from tomorrow. You've made it abundantly clear you don't have what it takes to fill those ugly maternity flatties of hers.'

Even though she'd already decided she didn't want the job, Angel felt close to tears under the onslaught of criticism. It wasn't like he went in for touchy-feely people management at the best of times, but it was obvious a Steve who was off his Benson &

Hedges was a Steve who really didn't bother with the whole 'compliment sandwich' thing.

He looked down at her other piece, the film review, which included her interview with Seb.

'Now this,' he said, waving it at her in a fist. 'This is bloody brilliant.'

Angel reeled in shock at the sudden change in tone. So apparently Steve was less of a 'compliment sandwich' and more of a 'beating you round the head with a massive compliment baguette' sort of employer.

'Well-informed and thought out, not too brown-nosed or bitchy, insightful and fresh assessments of character, plot and influence, and my favourite bit, an exclusive interview with the director.' She saw Steve's mouth twitch into a half-smile through his greying beard while he lingered over his favourite word, 'exclusive'. 'It takes a lot to impress me after all these years in the business, Blackthorne, but I have to admit you've managed it. With some of Courtenay's photos, I'm going to get a double-page feature out of this.'

Maybe it was the lack of nicotine, but he seemed almost giddy as he ran his eyes over the review once more. Angel was speechless.

'There's a film critic opening with your name on it if you want it, Princess. You've shown yourself more than capable. Double that internship pittance you're on now, starting soon as you like.'

Her eyes widened in shock. The man didn't do things by halves!

'But… what about Cal?' she managed.

'Gone.' Steve waved a dismissive hand. 'It's a tough business, this. You don't pull your weight, you're out. Gave him his marching orders first thing this morning when I found out he blew that *Milkman* job off for a mucky weekend with his blonde bit outside.'

'Savannah?' No wonder she'd looked so pale. 'And is she –'

'No, she's not going anywhere. She wasn't the one who was supposed to be on the clock, just him. Gave her a bollocking you could hear in Aberdeen about her stationery-cupboard antics, though. She won't forget that in a hurry.' He grinned to himself, relishing the memory.

'But I'm not qualified to be film critic,' she muttered, still trying to get her head around what was being offered. 'I mean, I'm an English graduate, Steve. What's that got to do with films?'

He shrugged. 'You've got wit and insight in spades, Blackthorne, and you're a great writer. That's all that matters to me. That pretentious bastard Cal came down the film studies route and he never wrote anything up to this standard.'

'That's… well, thanks, boss.'

She grimaced in disgust as Steve pulled out a well-chewed lump of nicotine gum, still attached to his mouth by a thin cobweb of saliva, and sent it to join the hairy wodge already stuck to the underside of his desk before popping another little square tablet through stained teeth.

'Well?' he demanded. 'Do you want this sodding job or don't you? I should warn you, Blackthorne, if you're after something glamorous or easy you might as well say no now. You'll have to review hundreds of films a year, in all genres, including those bloody awful British rom-coms that use the word "gosh" every five minutes. Most of them will be utter toss. And I mean that most sincerely.'

'I don't know, boss, I'll have to think about it. Okay, thought about it. I'll take it.' Angel beamed at him. 'Of course I'll bloody take it! And… thanks, Steve. I do appreciate you giving me the opportunity. I won't let you down.'

'Alright, don't get all hormonal on me, pet. It's yours because you've earned it, I'm not doing you any favours. Anyway, since you want it you can start next week.'

She smiled at him and turned to leave, but he hadn't finished with her yet.

'Oi. Blackthorne. Before you go, just tell me this: how did you get that interview with Wilchester? He hardly ever gives interviews, he hates the press, he hates *us* with a blazing passion, and I'd guess you'd be just about public enemy number one in the Wilchester/Beaumont household. Come on, enlighten me, or I won't be able to sleep tonight.'

Angel twirled a tendril of hair around one finger. The honest answer was she had no idea why Seb had agreed to an interview that night, unless it was to tell her exactly what he thought of her, and she certainly didn't want to be thrashing out ideas about it with Steve. The editor already seemed suspicious about her dealings with Seb and Carole, for some reason.

'Can't reveal my sources, boss,' she said, adopting what she hoped was a light-hearted tone. 'You know that.'

'Don't be daft. I know who your source was. What I want to know is how you got him to talk to you. This isn't the flaming magic circle, love.'

'I… it was the Tigerblaze PR guy. Kev. He came to chat me up at the bar, offered to buy me a drink. I sort of flirted my way back to Wilchester in the VIP area. Then once I was there I, um, think it threw him off balance a bit. He could hardly admit he knew me, so he had no choice but to go along with it when I started waving a dictaphone at him.'

'So you got an interview with Wilchester by dry-humping charmless Kev, the human suit?' Steve looked impressed. 'Good way in, that, lass. This femme-fatale business seems to be right up your street.' He hesitated a beat. 'But, er, you weren't in the lounge when Beaumont got carried out, you said?'

Just what was it he knew?

'No. That must've happened later.'

He shrugged. 'Pity. Could've been a front-pager if we had the details. Well, good job anyway. Go sort that showbiz piece out, if you can do anything with it, and we'll schedule an induction for your new role later this week.' He gave a hoarse chuckle as she opened the door to leave. 'Our competitors'll think I've gone soft in my old age, handing jobs out like sweets to young tarts with no experience. Still, I think you'll do alright. Well done, Blackthorne. Welcome to the team.'

Angel spent the rest of the morning in a daze, working through the notes Steve had made on her showbiz piece and tidying up a few of the typos. The writing was still pretty poor but at least the spelling was immaculate. Once she'd beefed it up with a few pieces of trivia about the celebs at the premiere lifted from Wikipedia, it might be almost passable.

She'd decided not to say anything to Savannah about her new role just yet. The intern still looked pale, and it occurred to Angel she might be upset about Cal's sacking. It didn't seem like a particularly good moment to break the news she'd be jumping straight into the ex-film critic's job.

She whizzed off a couple of emails though, one to Emily and one to her mum and dad, letting them know about her promotion. Her parents would just be going to bed over in Melbourne, where they'd retired a few years ago, so they wouldn't see it until tomorrow, but Emily replied almost immediately with enthusiastic congratulations and an animation of a hula-dancing otter in a grass skirt. Angel smiled and closed it quickly before anyone noticed.

As soon as lunchtime hit she darted off to the staff canteen, where she'd arranged to meet Leo, desperate to share her news. She brought him up to date while they waited in the queue to order.

'Wow, that's massive, Ginge!' Her friend drew her into a bear-like hug, squashing the shrink-wrapped tuna-melt panini she was holding between them. 'I knew Steve was lining you up for big things. It usually takes years to get into a job like that. Right little editor's pet, aren't you? Bloody brilliant!'

'I know, right? I still can't believe it. I'm dangerously close to actually going "squeee".' She grinned at him as he released her from the hug and tried to plump her panini back into shape. 'Oh, and don't make any plans for tonight, will you? I'm taking you and Em out for a meal to celebrate. On me.'

'Hey, you know this means you probably outrank me now?'

Leo said. 'I hope there won't be any abuse of power going on around the office.'

'Depends how you feel about coming to work in a PVC French-maid's outfit.'

'What do you think I'm wearing under this?' Leo gestured to his smart black jeans and grey polo neck. Angel giggled and gave him a friendly whack with her panini.

'And thanks for not letting Steve get any information out of you about Saturday. I guess that's the last thing Carole Beaumont needs right now,' she said in a low voice, quickly glancing around to make sure no one in the queue was paying attention to them.

'No problem, Ginge. Not that Wilchester really deserves to have us covering for him, selfish bastard. But I'm glad Beaumont's going to be okay.' Leo frowned as though something had just occurred to him. 'You know, Cal had to show his face at a few events when he was film critic. I sometimes went with him to be the camera monkey. Not premieres too often – there's usually an advance critics' screening, unless they're editing right up to the last minute. But awards ceremonies, film festivals and stuff. Are you going to be okay if you run into Wilchester or Beaumont at one of them?'

She hadn't thought of that. Her heart gave a treacherous leap at the idea of seeing Seb again, but she slapped it back down.

'I guess I have to be. Anyway, I can't avoid them forever in this industry, and I'm not turning down an opportunity like this for Seb Wilchester or anyone else. I think after the whole thing with Carole, he must hate me marginally less than before. Hopefully we'll be able to keep things professional.'

Professional. It had a cold, leaden sound that hurt her tongue.

***

Angel was two weeks into her new role when she got back from lunch to find Steve standing by her desk, examining a huge vase of pink and white flowers wrapped up in cellophane.

'Er, thanks boss, you shouldn't have,' she said, drinking in the mysterious bouquet.

'Don't look at me, Blackthorne. I'm more from the 'drink up, love, you've pulled' school of wooing. Got a secret admirer, have you?'

Angel frowned. She didn't know anyone who'd send her flowers, except maybe her parents, but they'd already given her a shopping voucher as a 'congrats on the new job' present. And this looked like a far more expensive bouquet than they could justify buying on their pensions. She buried her face in the medley of lilies and roses and gave an appreciative sniff.

Scanning the flowers for a card, she soon spotted one tucked into the petals of a half-blown white rose. A short message was handwritten in a rounded, feminine style. 'Thanks for everything. C x'. That was all.

Underneath the flowers she could just see what looked like the glint of jewels. Looking closer, she found it was coming from her nana's diamond-and-pearl teardrop hairpin, the one she'd used to fasten Seb's dinner jacket the night of the premiere…

Carole.

'There was one delivered for you and another for Courtenay,' Steve said, watching her closely. 'Anything you want to tell me, love?'

Angel shook her head. 'I'm as stumped as you are, Steve. No name on the card.'

The editor stared at her, once again giving the impression he knew more about the whole business than he was letting on.

'Heard today Carole Beaumont's checked into a health spa,' he said, as if he wanted to change the subject. 'Which is the standard celebrity euphemism for rehab. You know anything about it?'

'Me? No, why would I?'

He shrugged. 'Just making conversation. Well? Do you?'

She met his gaze steadily. He couldn't *make* her talk.

'Nope. Not a thing.'

It was strange though, Carole Beaumont sending her flowers at work, she reflected as Steve stomped back to his office in a sulk. Seb must have told his wife she and Leo worked for the *Investigator*, but he couldn't have told her about the honey trap, surely. Carole would hardly send flowers to the woman who'd tried to ruin her marriage. And sending flowers to their work, under the watchful eye of dozens of tabloid reporters always on the lookout for a good celebrity scandal story, wasn't exactly a clever move either.

It was the first she'd heard of Carole since Seb's text two weeks ago, letting her know his wife was out of danger. She, Leo and Emily had staged a ritual deletion of his number from her phone when they'd gone out to celebrate the night she'd been promoted, removing any temptation to drunk-dial him in the future.

Still, much as she wanted to put Seb, Carole and their world behind her, Angel was relieved to know the actress was out of hospital and getting help for her problems. And here were her flowers and the returned pin. It was a kind thought.

'Oooh, what beautiful flowers! Are they yours?' Savannah asked as she came back from her lunch break. 'I didn't know it was your birthday.'

'Actually it's not,' Angel said with a smile. 'My birthday, that is. These just showed up today, no name on the card. Wish I knew who'd sent them.' The lies were falling thick and fast today...

'Ooooh!' said Savannah again. 'You lucky thing, that's so romantic! I wish I had a secret admirer.'

She looked a little depressed, and Angel guessed she was thinking of Cal again. She wanted to ask if they were still together and how the girl was bearing up since his sacking, but then she'd have to admit Steve had told her all about it. She didn't want to humiliate Savannah any more than the editor already had that day he'd bawled her out in his office.

'I'm sure you could have as many as you wanted. You know you're drop-dead gorgeous, Sav.'

Savannah flashed her a grateful smile. 'You're sweet. Thanks, Angel.'

'Blackthorne. Here.' Their conversation was cut short by Steve's barked instruction from behind her.

'Oh God, now what's he want?' She made a face at Savannah, stood up and headed towards the increasingly familiar glass door leading into the editor's office.

'What is it this time?' she demanded. 'I told you, boss, I don't know who the flowers are from —'

'Never mind that,' Steve snapped, tossing back the dregs of another coffee and pulling up an email on his computer screen. 'What I want to know, *Princess*, is why I've just had this land in my inbox from your old mate Kevin Hancock at Tigerblaze Studios, asking for you personally to write a profile piece on Sebastian Wilchester — at his particular request.'

Chapter 12

'*What?*'

Angel sank down into a chair, limp with shock.

Seriously? Seb was making contact now, like this, with his wife only just out of hospital? Jesus Christ! Emily was so right about that man. He was trouble.

Steve began reading aloud from the screen. '"Mr Wilchester is willing to offer a one-time-only opportunity for a journalist and photographer to shadow him for an afternoon. The journalist will write a profile piece as part of the ongoing promotion surrounding the release of *The Milkman Cometh*. My client is willing to grant this profile exclusively to the *Investigator* on the condition your new film critic" – and get this, Blackthorne – "who he feels has some *depth of insight* when it comes to his work, writes the piece." Well, pet?'

Yep, that certainly sounded like Kev's clipped, sulky tone. And from the mention of a photographer, it sounded like they wanted Leo there too.

But why? Everyone knew Seb Wilchester hardly ever gave interviews, and actually requesting someone write a profile piece on him was unheard of. That was even worse than a standard interview: he'd be expected to discuss his private life too. Something he never did, even on those rare occasions he did speak to press.

Angel had a flash of inspiration. Could he see this as some sort of reward for helping Carole? That would make sense. Paying off a debt or something.

Why go through Steve instead of coming to her directly, though? Contacting the editor, ever alert for fresh scandal, was always a risky business. She still didn't know how the sleazy old bastard had found out that little nugget he'd let slip earlier about Carole being in rehab.

Perhaps Seb was worried she'd refuse if he asked her himself. Whereas Steve Clifton would rather hack off his baccy-yellowed fingers than miss out on this opportunity to scoop all his competitors.

'Wilchester must have seen something he liked in my review, I guess.' Angel shrugged, trying her best to look disinterested. 'Makes sense though, doesn't it? Whatever happened between me and him, he'll want his film to do well. And as you're so proud of pointing out, boss, we do have the highest circulation of any national daily.'

Steve glared at her through narrowed eyes. 'Look, love, contrary to appearances, I'm not so green as I'm cabbage-looking. I've got enough sixth sense left in my old journalist's balls to spot when someone's trying to hide something from me. Come on, Blackthorne, don't be a pillock all your life. I know that ambulance was there for Carole Beaumont the night of the premiere. I know you were involved in the business somehow, and maybe Courtenay too, or he's covering for you. So you might as well just pack it in and come clean, eh?'

How could he *know* all that? Angel tried to keep her features from twitching while she faced off against him, her spine stiffening as she drew herself up.

'I told you, *boss*, I don't know anything about it.' She tried to sound calm and self-assured. 'I interviewed Wilchester and I went back to Leo at the bar, okay? I don't know how many times you need to hear me say it before you'll believe me. And what exactly has Carole Beaumont got to do with me anyway that I should be doing her any favours? I don't know her, and I guess I'd be just about the last person she'd want to get friendly with after what we put her through.'

'Who said anything about favours?' Steve's eyes glinted in triumph.

Angel mentally kicked herself as she realised she'd given more away than she'd intended. Steve was too good at this Bad Cop, Knobhead Cop routine.

'Well if you're so bloody cock-sure the ambulance was there for Beaumont, why are you grilling me about it?' she snapped, a sudden determination to call his bluff sweeping through her. 'You've got your story right there, haven't you?'

Steve scoffed, continuing to hold her in an interrogative, blood-shot gaze. 'Oh, yeah, that'll fly. A story based on what, my half-hunch and some extremely circumstantial evidence? Come on, love.'

'Well it's never stopped you before,' Angel countered nastily. 'Aren't shoddy reporting and not-quite-libel kind of the *Investigator*'s thing? Why break the habit of a lifetime, eh Steve? And I'm not talking about the fags, by the way.' She eyed his shaking manila hands with distaste. His commitment to cold turkey was still going strong.

'Even we have to have some standards, Princess.' He allowed himself to break into his usual mocking grin and popped another tablet of nicotine gum into his mouth. He always seemed to enjoy it when she insulted him. 'Beaumont's lawyer would be up our backsides like a dog on heat if we went down the publish-and-be-damned route. Now, if you'd seen something you might be willing to share with your old boss, on the other hand…'

She shook her head, meeting his eyes with steely determination as her mouth set into a thin line. 'Sorry, Clifton. Afraid I can't help you.'

'Have it your way then, *pet*.' Real anger edged into his voice this time and his grin settled back into a scowl. 'I suppose I can't make you tell me what happened that night. But I won't lie: I'm bloody disappointed in you. This blind spot you've got for Sebastian sodding Wilchester… well, let me make it quite clear to you. I don't care how damp your knickers are for that bastard. When it comes to him, his missus and the *Investigator*, it seems to me it's time for you to work out exactly where your loyalties lie.'

Angel could feel her cheeks burning, but she refused to be the first to break eye contact.

'I'm going to ring that prick Kev and tell him we agree to run the piece,' Steve went on, turning away from her and looking out to the pearl-grey dome of St Paul's. 'Although of course, he already knows that. I shouldn't need to tell you this is the opportunity of a lifetime. I expect you to put this paper first, and I expect you to get me the dirt. Do *not* let me down on this, Blackthorne. I'm counting on you.'

***

'Get your teeth in, Ange!' Emily called out, barging through the door of the flat that evening. 'I've brought company.'

Angel was lying face down on the sofa in her hippo pyjamas getting ready to watch a DVD, Groucho curled comfortably into the small of her back like a hairy black cushion. She gave a muffled grunt in lieu of a hello as Emily made her way into the sitting room, followed closely by Leo.

'Jesus, who died?' Emily asked, plumping herself down on Angel's legs. 'What's with the lying down in a darkened room, Ange?'

Grumbling under her breath, Angel yanked her legs out from under her friend and sat up, dislodging Groucho, who yowled an indignant complaint.

'Poor old feller. Stuck in a house full of girls.' Leo picked the chubby cat up and chucked him under his chin. 'Don't worry, mate, Uncle Leo's here now for a bit of manly bonding.' Groucho stared, wide-eyed and puzzled, as Leo put him back down on the carpet and aimed some playful shadow boxing at his fluffy ears, making a 'Psht! Psht! Psht!' sound between his teeth.

'Leave him alone, Leo.' Angel grabbed the remote and turned off the DVD player. 'He's one of the girls now, aren't you, Grouch?' The cat turned his backside towards her and started washing a paw in disgust at this assault on his machismo.

'So what are you up to, then, Ginge?' Leo asked, leaving Groucho to his bath. 'Wallowing in self-pity?'

'Actually I was about to have a film night until you two showed up.' She gestured to the pile of shrink-wrapped DVDs on the pine coffee table. 'Had a bit of a splurge with that voucher Mum and Dad sent me.'

'Oooh, what've you got?' Emily picked up the open case on the table and her mouth wrinkled as she looked at the title on the cover. It was *Unreal City.*

She threw it back down in disgust. 'Oh, for Christ's sake, Ange. What is it with you and that cheating prick? It's been months, you should be well over him by now. These are all his as well, I take it?' She examined the pile of DVDs still in their packaging and tossed her ash-blonde curls in indignation when she confirmed they were, as suspected, Seb Wilchester's entire back catalogue.

Angel sighed, sensing a battle ahead. 'Hey, it's research, alright? Look, I don't know why, but Seb's PR guy contacted Steve today and asked for someone from the *Investigator* to shadow him for a profile piece. Or, not someone. Me. He asked for me specifically. And I don't want to make a tit of myself like I did in that last interview by being totally ignorant of his work.'

Emily was staring at her, eyes narrowed in disbelief. Angel held her hands up in front of her face in protest. 'Look, Em, it's strictly professional, I promise. I mean, I'm film critic now. This sort of thing's bound to happen sometimes.'

'It's true, I'm going too,' Leo chipped in, coming over to join in. 'Steve sent me a brief for it today. The old sod can't believe his luck, getting a coup like this. We're supposed to be off to Tigerblaze tomorrow afternoon.'

Emily scowled her disapproval. 'I don't know why you both don't tell Steve to shove it,' she said, her voice savage. 'That Wilchester bastard seems to spread misery and destruction wherever he goes.'

She turned to Angel, her eyes filled with worry. 'And why do you think he asked for you anyway, Ange? Reckon he's still got a boner for you or what?'

Angel shrugged. 'No idea, if I'm honest. You'd think I'd be the last person he'd ever want to see again. All I can think of is he's trying to somehow pay me and Leo back for helping Carole the night of the premiere. Cancel it out or whatever.'

Leo responded with a slow, thoughtful nod. 'Yeah, you might be on to something there, Ginge. Wilchester doesn't look like a man who could bear to owe anything to anyone. Have to say, though, I don't like it. I was half tempted to do what Em said and tell Steve to forget it when I got his email today, except I wanted to be there for you to do the whole moral-support thing.'

'Yes, well, that's something.' Emily was looking through the pile of DVDs, but she tore her gaze away to flash him an approving glance. 'At least you'll be there to keep an eye on the bastard, Leo. And her.' She tossed a thumb towards Angel in a way that made it quite clear she thought her friend was not to be trusted.

'Yeah.' Leo fixed Angel with keen eyes. 'I mean, God knows I was never going to win any boyfriend-of-the-year prizes when me and you were together, Ginge. Even, you know, before… everything.' He flashed a sideways glance at Emily, but she was still busying herself with the DVDs. 'But the way that dickhead treats his wife, the way he treated you…'

Angel looked down at her fleecy slippers. 'I don't know, Leo. He didn't treat me any worse than I deserved, setting him up like that. I'd be bloody angry too if it had been me. And if you'd seen him with Carole – the way he looked after her, how devastated he was at what she'd done to herself – I think you might give the guy a break.'

But Leo's expression was hard. 'Sorry, Ginge. A cheat's a cheat. No matter what state my head was in, I could never have done that to you. Not to anyone I claimed to love. Be warned and steer clear, eh?'

Emily nodded her approval and reached out to give Leo's arm a friendly squeeze. 'Listen to the man, Ange. Sound advice, that. The kind I could've used a few years ago.' Leo turned to smile at her, but she didn't meet his eyes.

Angel couldn't stop a note of irritation creeping into her voice. 'Look, you guys, I'll be fine, okay? I'm big enough and ugly enough to look after myself, thanks all the same.' She picked up the DVD remote. 'Anyway, are we going to watch this film or not? I've still got a profile piece to research by tomorrow.'

Leo looked over at Emily. 'Actually, we were planning on having a game of Wii Tennis.'

'Yeah.' Emily nodded. 'I haven't seen Danny in three weeks. Got to blow off steam somehow, Ange.' Angel noticed the crumpled look of pain that flashed across Leo's face, but he quickly smoothed it away.

She took the hint. Leo wanted a bit of alone time with Emily. He wasn't giving up just yet. 'Alright, no worries. I can watch on my laptop upstairs if you want the big telly.'

'Well, I guess we could watch the film first. It's pretty early,' Emily said, apparently failing to pick up on Leo's signals. 'That okay with you, mate?'

'Yeah, course. Always up for a film night with my girls.' If he was disappointed, he was doing a good job hiding it. 'I'll want popcorn at half time, mind. Budge up then, Ginge.'

Angel smiled as the two of them piled on to the sofa either side of her. Sometimes when all three of them were together it felt like they were back at uni, young and full of the future, and the last five years – Emily's unhappy marriage, Leo's struggle to get sober, her relationship and career woes – had never happened.

***

Angel reflected on her first encounter with East End Noir while she lay in bed that night.

Once again she couldn't help being overawed by Wilchester's skill as a director and screenwriter, in spite of her prejudice against the gangster genre. And yet *Unreal City* had been a completely different experience than *The Milkman Cometh*. There was none of the polish of the seasoned filmmaker evident in his latest production. The film was buoyed along by sheer energy and enthusiasm, with occasional flashes of genius, such as could only belong to someone young and untrained, yet fired by an unleashed and innate creative power.

It had been shot on a low budget around the city, entirely in black and white. A twenty-year-old Carole Beaumont – oozing a naive vulnerability, with her blonde hair in a platinum sheet extending below her shoulders – had once again played the lead to perfection. The woman defined versatility.

Angel wondered what exactly she'd expected when she'd thought of British Gangster as a genre. Probably characters with names like Sid the Spiv, chewing on gold-plated toothpicks while they ordered the removal of people's earlobes in dark Soho alleys. But *Unreal City* hadn't been anything like that. It had been… beautiful somehow, with a haunting, otherworldly quality. At its heart, it was a love story. Angel, Emily and even Leo had all been in tears by the time the credits rolled, although Groucho, as the man of the house, had, of course, remained impervious.

There had been a political element to the film she hadn't

expected as well, touching lightly but with a repressed, bubbling anger on the homelessness and poverty too evident in the streets of her home city. It had given her a glimpse of a different Seb to the one she thought she knew: a man who was principled, passionate and idealistic, who wanted his work to make a difference not just artistically but in the hearts and minds of the people who saw it. Angel wondered if the Sebastian Wilchester of today, eight years older than the Wilchester who had made *Unreal City*, still felt that way. Then as she drifted into sleep she reminded herself with a twinge of guilt, for just about the hundredth time, that Seb's thoughts and emotions were no concern of hers.

Chapter 13

Lying crooked on his elbow next to her, Seb nuzzled her neck and earlobe, his breath a harsh, feverish pant on her tingling flesh. 'My God, you're beautiful,' he breathed softly into her ear. 'You do know I've been waiting for this, Angel?'

She dragged in her breath, brought her arms up around his back and ran her cupped palms and fingertips along the muscular contours of his shoulder blades. 'You think I haven't?'

Suddenly he thrust one hand between her legs, a gasp catching in his throat as he felt the wetness he'd made there. She let out an aching groan when his two fingers slipped inside her and searched her expertly, and she pushed down on his shoulders to bring his lips to hers. She kissed him with an untamed hunger, moving her hands up his back and burying her fingers in his wild chestnut hair.

Eventually drawing away, Angel's green eyes met his tawny ones, heavy-lidded and full of feeling. 'Now, Seb. Please,' she begged.

His sparkling eyes darted across her face, a teasing half-smile appearing on his sculpted lips as the exploring fingers moved faster, more urgent, and his thumb spiralled and pressed against her. Oh God, where had he learned how to do that? She groaned again and arched the small of her back, tilted her hips towards him in silent pleading.

'Now, Angel? Are you sure?'

'Yes, oh God, yes, please…'

His smile disappeared and his fingers stilled suddenly. 'It's no good,' he whispered, his breath ragged, his voice thick with lust. 'I want you too much to play games.'

With one fluid movement, he removed his hand and pulled her over on top of him, raised himself up into a sitting position so he could feel the whole of her body pressed against his. She moaned into his ear, wrapped her legs around his back and felt him, all of him, as he slid into her and her body absorbed his in a tight, clenching fist.

Seb gave an answering groan, pressed his fingertips into her buttocks while he pushed himself further inside her. 'Oh, Jesus, Angel, oh my God, you feel so good…'

Her breath became a frenzied pant as she felt him buck beneath her and rocked her hips in time to his rhythm, slow at first then faster, faster, as if they were being guided by an external force. She slid her hands up his sinewy, sweat-beaded arms and along the rigid lines of his face to his untidy hair, dug her fingers deep into the damp chestnut curls while she moved herself against him, crushed his handsome face against her breasts.

Over and over she moaned his name, so delicious on her tongue, as he filled her with sweet, rippling ecstasy. 'Sebastian… oh, God, Sebastian…'

Seb gripped a pillow in one large fist, his eyelids flickering and his wet lips parted, gasping as they moved instinctively together. 'Oh Christ, what are you doing to me?' His voice was harsh, wild; needing her. 'It feels so, ah… just please don't stop, don't ever stop. Angel, oh, my Angel…'

She awoke with a jerk, breathless and shuddering, as Groucho bounced onto her stomach with a plaintive mawk to demand his breakfast.

Angel pushed him off her with a frustrated groan, rolled onto her side while she got her breath back. She'd writhed the sheets into an uncomfortable lump, and she attempted to smooth them out beneath her while she willed her heart rate down.

Not content with replaying the time they'd spent together at the hotel every few days while she slept, her subconscious was now inventing new Seb dreams to torture her with. Just what did she have to do to exorcise that man? At work, at home, awake or asleep, he couldn't let her be. And the worst thing was she couldn't convince herself she wanted him to.

Perhaps the profile piece was just what she needed to finally get some closure and stop him haunting her.

Then again, perhaps it was just the opposite…

Well, sleep was shot now, she realised that. Steve had given her the morning off to prepare for her afternoon shadowing Seb, though, so she still had a few hours until it was time to get up. And she needed something to take her mind off Dream Seb and his magic touch. It was a bit early for a cold shower.

She pulled out her laptop and popped one of her new DVDs into the tray. This one was called *Winter Dawn*, a sort of prequel to *Unreal City*, made some years later when Seb and Carole had both become big names in their own right.

She made a few notes on the film while she watched. Again, it was a tour de force: a big-budget blockbuster showing the same polish and tightly pruned script she'd admired so much in *The Milkman Cometh*. Still, in the end she couldn't help preferring the energetic rollercoaster of *Unreal City*. There was something raw in that breakthrough film missing from this later work. It didn't improve the film, if she thought about it objectively. Perhaps, she thought, angry with herself, she liked it because it told her more about the man.

When the film had finished she started it again, this time flipping on the director's commentary. She was curious to know what Seb had to say about his own work. Somehow he managed to give little away, though, commenting on everything from the

126

set design to the actors' talent but never on his own input into the creative process.

Angel felt the familiar jolt in her stomach when she heard his deep tones, already too fresh in her mind from her dream, but she managed to settle herself relatively quickly. She knew she had to be in control when she saw him again that afternoon for the profile, and it was as well to get some practice in now.

By the time the film had finished, she could hear Emily beginning to stir next door. She jumped out of bed and went out into the hall, gave a few short, sharp raps on her friend's door before poking her head around it.

'Wer…? S'not time to get up, s'it?'

Angel flashed her flatmate a bright smile and twitched the corner of the duvet. 'Yep. Today it is. I need some help getting ready. Your expert fashion sense is required, if you don't mind, Em.' She had no idea what to wear for the profile. She knew she had to be dripping professionalism, but everything in her wardrobe seemed to scream either smart casual (with a definite emphasis on the casual) or frumpy middle-aged divorcee.

Back in her room, Emily rifled through the wardrobe, shaking her head. 'None of this'll do. Haven't you got any sort of skirt suit? What did you wear for your last job interview?'

'I just wore a blouse and black trousers for the internship interview. Will that do?'

'Maybe, if I lend you a jacket. I'll fetch one and you can see how it looks.'

Fifteen minutes later, Angel grimaced as she looked at herself in the mirror. Emily had scooped the auburn hair back into a severe bun, which made her look even paler than usual somehow and about ten years older. She couldn't help feeling her friend's disapproval of Seb was causing her to overcompensate.

'Eurghh. I look like a librarian at a funeral.'

'Good,' Emily said, not without the hint of a smirk. 'Then he'll see you're not standing for any of his nonsense, won't he? Nobody interferes with librarians. Especially not at funerals.'

Angel yanked out the bobble and pin holding her bun in place, shook her hair around her shoulders and unfastened the top button of her smart white blouse. She undid the jacket Emily had loaned her so it hung open. Better. Formal, but not quite so severe.

Emily shrugged. 'Fine, then, if you don't want my help…'

'Come on, Em, you know I do. I didn't mean to hurt your pride as London's top fashionista. But looking professional isn't the same as looking like Morticia Addams's ginger sister. You don't need to protect me from Seb's advances by making him think I want to suck on his neck.' Em raised a highly suggestive eyebrow. 'God, like a vampire, I meant! You know, vampires: pale, undead, serious iron deficiency? Look, when it comes to me and Seb Wilchester, there will be no sucking on necks, faces or anything else, okay? You have my word as a lady.'

'Oh right, as a *lady*,' Emily scoffed. 'Well that's worth approximately sod all.' She gave a theatrical sigh. 'Still, I suppose I have to let you kids grow up some time. Breaks my old heart, mind. Just remember to stick close to Leo, won't you, Ange? Don't let that bastard Wilchester get you anywhere alone, where he can start whispering sweet wotsits into your ear. I'm not saying I don't trust you to control yourself, but…'

'…you don't trust me to control myself?'

'Right. Oh, and make sure you wear heels, eh? Heels are empowering, they'll make you feel more confident. And they're also handy for a swift kick to the plums if he comes on too strong.'

'They're bloody painful on my poor old toes, is what they are. But alright, just for you I'll wear the small ones: the ones I can actually just about manage to hobble about in.'

Angel darted out to answer the door when she heard Leo knock. She'd asked him to call on her so they could share a taxi over to Tigerblaze. Time to get the ordeal over with and put Seb Wilchester out of her mind forever.

Now where have I heard that before...

***

It was just after midday when Angel and Leo's cab pulled up to the huge metal gates of Tigerblaze Studios.

She'd never visited a film studio before, unless a school trip around the *Coronation Street* set at Granada Studios when she was eight counted, and she looked around her with great curiosity as she got out of the cab. The sprawling lot looked like a cross between an army barracks, an airport and a travelling carnival, with metal huts, trailers and portakabins of various sizes dotted haphazardly around the focal point: a large Edwardian manor house, converted into offices for the Tigerblaze staff. The place seemed enormous, although Angel knew from her research that even including the backlots it didn't cover more than about fifteen acres. Squinting into the sunlight, she tried to make out where the rows of corrugated metal huts ended.

A petite, fair-haired girl with a pixie cut was waiting to greet them. Angel guessed she was probably about her own age, mid-twenties, although her air of bashfulness as she scuffed her shoes against the tarmac made her seem much younger. Kev was standing next to her, looking even sulkier than he had the night of the premiere, if that were possible. Any notion Angel might have entertained that the profile was his idea, part of his promotional efforts for *The Milkman Cometh*, was put firmly to rest as she took in the familiar scowl.

'Mr Courtenay? Miss Blackthorne?' said the pixie-cut girl, smiling at Angel and Leo. They nodded, and she handed them each a clip-on ID. 'I'm Suzanne Haynes, Seb's – I mean, Mr Wilchester's – personal assistant. I'll be here to answer your questions, show you around and so on until Mr Wilchester is ready to see you. And I think you've already met Mr Hancock, our head of PR.' She gestured to Kev, who remained the same immovable suit on legs. 'He has also kindly agreed to be on hand throughout the afternoon for as long as you're on the lot with us.' Yeah, to keep an eye on us, Angel thought sourly, giving the PR man a frosty nod of recognition.

Kev offered a haughty nod back, eyeing the pair with his customary expression of dislike. The man was such an evident misanthrope, Angel wondered whether anyone had explained to him that the P in PR stood for 'public' when he'd picked it out as a career. She wasn't sure he'd bothered to look up the 'relations' part of the job description either, for that matter.

'Mr Wilchester will mainly be going through storyboards for his latest script this afternoon, and reviewing some of the promotional posters for *The Milkman Cometh* DVD release.' Suzanne gabbled a little through what was obviously a carefully rehearsed welcome speech. She sounded like an air hostess on her first flight, trying to remember that the emergency exits were here, here and here.

'He's happy for you to observe him while he goes about his work,' she continued, 'but he would ask you to kindly reserve any questions you may have until afterwards so he can work without distraction. I've scheduled in a Q&A session and photoshoot for the end of the day.'

That didn't sound too scary. It certainly didn't sound as if she would be left alone with Seb at any point, or as though there'd be much opportunity for idle conversation. Perhaps she could get through this with minimal embarrassment after all.

'So, um, welcome to Tigerblaze, I guess,' Suzanne said, beaming at them with relief as she reached the end of her little talk. 'If you'd like to follow me, I'll give you the guided tour.'

Angel got out her notebook so she could make a few notes and prepared to follow.

'Oh. Will you be okay to walk or shall I ring the office and ask them to send a car for us?' Suzanne was eyeing Angel's heeled shoes with concern. 'I know it doesn't look far from here, but it's probably about a half-mile to HQ.'

Damn Emily and her bloody 'empowering' heels…

'Oh, no need to worry about me, I'm used to walking in these,' Angel lied, smiling. 'That distance is no problem at all.'

'Here, take my arm,' Leo whispered, crooking an elbow towards her. 'I can bear some of the weight. It's not like there's much of you.'

'Thanks, Leo.' She shot him a grateful smile.

Tucking her notebook under one arm, she hooked her other through his and leaned her weight against him with a sigh of relief. Suzanne flashed them a knowing look and Angel felt her cheeks blaze as she realised what the PA was thinking. Cringe. Still, it didn't matter, they wouldn't be here long.

Kev swiped an electronic keycard against the little black box by the huge gates and they swung open to let the party through.

'Seb and Carole were chuffed to bits with your *Milkman* review,' Suzanne said conversationally to Angel while they walked together, Angel leaning on Leo's arm and the PA keeping pace at her other elbow. She seemed to be relaxing a little, and Angel detected the very slight lilt of an Irish accent under the practised RP English. She also noticed Suzanne seemed to have stopped reminding herself not to slip into first-name terms with her employers.

'What was that line you wrote about Carole in it?' Suzanne was glowing with something like pride as she remembered. 'I think it was "Her performance as Edna Pewter in *The Milkman Cometh* proves Carole Beaumont is one of the greatest post-war actresses this country has yet produced". Her face just lit up when I read it out to her in the hos-'

She bit her lip, lowering her eyes to the floor. Kev, walking ahead, turned to scowl at her, sending the clear message she needed to watch her mouth.

'Miss Haynes, why don't you start the tour?' His voice was low and dangerous. 'I'm sure our guests –' he sneered as he pronounced the word – 'would like to know a little bit more about the history of the place.'

'Yes, sorry, Kev – er, Mr Hancock,' Suzanne mumbled to her own feet. Angel shot the PR man a nasty look for embarrassing the shy girl, which he returned with at least equal venom.

'Er, yes, so this is the Tigerblaze lot,' Suzanne began, mustering a weak smile and waving a hand around her. 'Still very much a work in progress, as you can see. Se– Mr Wilchester and Ms Beaumont purchased it two years ago after they decided they wanted to set up a studio of their own, so they could have more creative control over their work. Before that, um…'

Suzanne stopped, confused. Kev fixed her with an unpleasant glare while she fumbled for another sentence.

'I presume it hasn't always been a film studio, has it?' Angel prompted. 'The house looks pretty old.'

'That's right, it used to be a country club.' Suzanne remembered her spiel with relief and flashed a grateful smile at Angel. 'Around the turn of the century the house was built as a private club for parties of fashionable young men during the shooting season. This was all woodland then. It wasn't until the 1930s that the house and grounds were bought by a wealthy American director who'd settled here. He levelled the trees and turned it into a studio, Hollow Crown Pictures.'

'Were there any important films made here?' Leo asked, looking interested. 'Anything we might know?'

Suzanne laughed, relaxing a little. 'Well, Hollow Crown's time was pretty short-lived. But it does have the dubious honour of being the set for Britain's biggest ever musical flop, *The Lamplight Pirouette*, in 1938. And there were a couple of Hammer Horrors shot here too. The war put an end to its brief heyday, though. It closed in 1940 and was used by the War Office as a munitions store until peace was declared, then it fell into disrepair. It cost Seb and Carole a fortune to bring it back from the ashes as

Tigerblaze, but it was worth it. Critics are saying *The Milkman Cometh* is their best film yet. That's all thanks to having this place.'

Suzanne was settling into full-on tour mode now. She gestured towards a huge khaki-green building in curved corrugated metal that looked a bit like an aircraft hangar. 'This is the Zimmerman Stage,' she told them. 'Named after the director who originally bought this place and turned it into Hollow Crown. It's the biggest one we have, where we did most of the non-location filming on *Milkman*. And over there –' she pointed to an almost identical but slightly smaller building ahead of them in the distance – 'is the Wilchester Stage. That's being let out at the moment for filming on a new television drama.'

'Seriously, he named the stage after himself?' Leo whispered to Angel. 'Can someone say 'ego trip'?'

But Suzanne overheard and her face fell as she turned towards them.

'Oh no, you mustn't think that,' she said, sounding upset. 'It was Carole who named the stage, not Seb. She said he should have something as a monument to all his hard work. Seb hated the idea – well, he always does hate anything like that – but she usually gets her own way with him in the end.'

'I bet she does,' Leo muttered. Angel dropped his arm, frowning at him. She'd made him promise to behave himself in the taxi on the way over, and here he was going off on one before they'd even got to Seb.

Kev had overheard their conversation too and his brows tightened. 'Okay, Miss Haynes, that's enough,' he muttered to Suzanne. 'Just remember what Seb told you and stick to the bloody script, can you?'

She blushed again under his warning and gazed at her feet. 'Sorry.'

Leo looked guilty. 'Don't apologise, please. You were doing great: it's a fascinating place. It's me who should apologise. I was rude. I'm sorry. Please do go on, Miss Haynes.'

'Yes, please,' Angel echoed. 'Is that another stage over there?' She pointed to a third hangar-type covered area up ahead; large but nowhere near as big as the other two.

Suzanne's face lit up as she followed Angel's finger. 'Oh, that's Carole – er, Ms Beaumont and Mr Wilchester's – pet project.' She beamed at them. 'I love telling that story.'

Angel's curiosity was piqued. 'Story? What story?'

'Well, it turned out when they bought the studio, included in the sale was a load of old equipment belonging to Hollow Crown – cameras, sound gear, projection equipment and all sorts, all from the thirties and early forties. Some of it was broken beyond repair, but Seb was able to have a lot of items fixed back up into working order. Have you heard of ReelKids?'

Leo shook his head, but Angel suddenly remembered something she'd read in a magazine that had sparked her interest. 'Yes. I think I have. I didn't know it was based here, though. It's a charity that teaches kids traditional filmmaking techniques, isn't it?'

Suzanne smiled at her, pleased she'd heard of it. 'Yes, sort of. It gives kids from disadvantaged backgrounds the chance to use a range of equipment, from the 1930s through to the present day. Groups can come and take part in day workshops here, all run by professional filmmakers, and learn how to make and screen a film of their own.

'But the charity's not just based here,' she continued. 'It's Seb and Carole's baby. They started it up with all the old equipment they got with the studio, plus some more modern stuff they donated, and they help run the workshops whenever they have a break in their schedules too.'

Angel's eyebrows lifted in surprise. There'd been nothing in what she'd read about any link between Tigerblaze and ReelKids.

'Really? I never knew that.'

The PA smiled. 'No, Seb likes to play it down. Doesn't want people to think he's just doing it to promote Tigerblaze. The focus has to be on the kids and their work, he says.'

'That's very… noble of him,' Leo said doubtfully.

'So do you want to go in and look around?' Suzanne asked with a bright smile. 'We can't go take a look at the bigger stages this afternoon, they're both in use. But there's a schools workshop going on at ReelKids and I don't think they'd mind us dropping in. Is that okay, Kev?'

The PR man gave a slight nod. They had reached the ReelKids building now, and Angel and Leo followed Suzanne through a corrugated porch leading into a long covered stage area.

'Shit, sorry!' Angel muttered as she stumbled over her increasingly sore feet, bumping against a tall man in a dark-blue suit standing just inside the doorway. A handsome man with curling chestnut hair and shining tawny eyes, and aftershave that reminded her of slowly melting chocolate.

She reeled backwards in shock as she realised she'd just walked straight into Sebastian Wilchester.

Chapter 14

The notepad under Angel's arm fell to the floor and she staggered sideways into Leo, who caught her and pushed her back upright with an impatient noise. Loose sheets of paper spilled out all over the grey concrete floor. She felt the blood rush to her face while she bent to pick them up, and tried not to meet Seb's eyes.

'Oh God, I'm so sorry! Here, let me…' Seb knelt down to help her, then drew back in surprise when he realised who it was he'd knocked for six.

'Angel.'

'Seb. Er, hi.' She nodded to him, trying not to let her confusion show. There was something about the way that man said her name that just seemed to do things to her…

To her surprise, a smile lurked at the corner of his lips.

'Sorry. Deja vu,' he mumbled, collecting up handfuls of paper. She laughed, remembering him retrieving the contents of her handbag in the hotel bar the night of the honey trap, then stopped suddenly in confusion.

Okay, it couldn't just be her. This was definitely weird…

They quickly collected a sheaf of papers each and stood up together, bashful and flustered. It was obvious she'd caught him off-guard and his defences were down. For once he seemed just as ill at ease as she was.

She let out another awkward laugh, feeling a blush prickling up her neck while she held out her hand for the papers he'd collected. Their fingertips brushed as he handed over his pile and she jerked her hand away quickly, trying to stop herself fumbling the papers to the floor again. She shoved them back inside the cover of her spiral-bound notebook and tucked it away in the canvas record bag she was carrying across her shoulder.

Seb quickly seemed to have recovered his cool. He was watching her quite calmly now, his eyes flashing and the little smile still playing about his lips. Self-conscious under his gaze, Angel pushed a stray strand of hair away from her heated cheeks.

Suddenly, she remembered the others in their group: Suzanne and Leo to either side of her and Kev bringing up the rear, all waiting for the director to acknowledge them.

'Oh, er, you know Leo Courtenay, my photographer, I think?' she said, gesturing to Leo as she struggled to conjure the calm professionalism of Film Critic Angel up through her shoes from somewhere deep inside the concrete floor. Her friend gave Seb a cool nod.

'Wilchester.'

'Mr Courtenay.'

The atmosphere was distinctly frosty, and Angel sensed no amount of underprivileged kids' charities could buy Seb's way into Leo's good graces.

'Hi, Seb!' Suzanne was beaming at her boss. 'I hope you don't mind me bringing them here. Only, they seemed really interested in ReelKids. Sorry, did I do it wrong? You know what I'm like, I just started jabbering on…'

She pinkened when she saw Seb frown momentarily, but as quickly as his brow puckered it was smooth and he made an effort to give her a cheery grin. 'You know anything you do is alright with me, Suze,' he said in an affectionate, teasing tone.

Now here was a different Seb again. She'd seen him as a husband, a lover, a director. Was she seeing him now as a friend? This certainly seemed like more than the bog-standard relationship between employee and employer.

With Kev he just exchanged a cool nod. *No change there, then…*

Angel peered over Seb's shoulder to see what was behind him. She could hear a buzz of young voices, but a screen of upright pallets hid the speakers from view. A small rectangular hole of a doorway with a strip of black fabric hung in front indicated the way into the main stage area.

'The kids are just through there, working on their film,' Seb said, seeing where her eyes were directed. 'Don't suppose you'd like to come in and watch for a little while? I don't think they'll mind, if you're quiet. I was just taking a break for five minutes before they killed me with enthusiasm.'

'Erm… yes, why not? If that's where you're going.' She winced, realising how that must have sounded. 'I mean, we can get some material for the profile. Are you running the workshop?'

'Not all of it. I had some time this morning so I said I'd drop in to give a bit of direction. Ended up staying longer than I'd intended. Come on, let's go through.'

She followed him through the curtained opening. Inside the large, high-raftered building, a crowd of teenagers and ReelKids volunteers were busying themselves around lighting rigs, cameras and sound equipment while their teacher sat sipping a coffee, evidently grateful for a time out.

A respectful hush fell on the room when Seb entered, all eyes turning an awestruck gaze on him. Angel actually saw the calm, cool director blush under the stare of the group of young people, none of them more than about sixteen.

'Hi, guys,' he said. 'I'm back. Er, these are some of my staff.' He gestured towards Suzanne and Kev. 'And this lady and gentleman are here from the *Investigator*. They've come especially to see what you're working on. I told them to prepare to be impressed.'

That was a pretty radical interpretation of their brief, but Angel wasn't going to object. The kids shot doubtful looks at her and Leo. She managed a press-lipped smile and gave them a nervous half-wave. Then, almost as soon as their interest had been sparked, it was gone. They turned back to their equipment and the volume of chatter increased as they carried on with their work.

The four of them sidled into a corner while Kev peeled off from the group to sit, scowling and silent, next to the coffee-drinking teacher.

'Bloody hell.' Leo gave his brow a comical wipe. 'If I'd known there'd be feral teenagers running around the place I would've brought some Haribo and tear gas, just in case we needed to cause a diversion and make a run for it.'

Seb laughed, dimpling one cheek. 'Oh, they're okay. Bit scary en masse, maybe. But you should see what they can produce when they work at it. Amazing stuff.'

Leo fixed him with a cold gaze. 'Zat so?'

Angel frowned at her friend but he ignored her, continuing to glare with cool dislike at Seb.

'Well, the set's certainly impressive,' she said, turning to Seb with an apologetic smile. In front of all the cameras and sound equipment was what appeared to be a perfect replica of a 1940s kitchen, complete even down to the old wireless playing 'As Time Goes By.' Dooley Wilson. She loved that song. 'Incredible detail. Did the kids build it?'

'Yes, partly.' Suzanne joined in the conversation now, beaming with pride while she looked over at the kitchen. 'Each workshop we've had here has added something to it – a prop, a painted backboard, an ornament – so the detail now is amazing. Every group that comes in creates and films a different story, all based around the same set. We're going to release a DVD of the best ones at some point, call it *Tales of the Kitchen*, or something better we haven't thought up yet.'

Seb smiled at Angel and Leo. 'You see, Suze knows far more

about this than me.' He put an arm round the PA's shoulders and gave her a squeeze. 'We always say she's ReelKids' biggest fangirl.'

Out of the corner of her eye Angel could see Leo's scowl, the look of disdain. She understood what he was thinking. Leo seemed to see Seb as some sort of sexual predator extraordinaire, with a woman on each arm and a spare for Sunday best.

She could tell, though, there was nothing more to Seb's relationship with Suzanne than straightforward friendship. She knew, somehow, by the brotherly way he touched her.

'Right, I'd better go schmooze that tweedy teacher, see if I can get permission to take some photos of the kids while they work.' Giving Angel's arm a quick squeeze, Leo grabbed the bag containing his camera equipment and headed over to the bench where Kev and the teacher were seated.

'I should get back to the kids in a minute,' Seb said. 'I have to be back in the office soon for those storyboards. Miss Blackthorne, if Suzanne doesn't mind, could I have a quick word with you in private?'

Suzanne nodded her consent. It was obvious whatever Seb wanted to do, now or in the future, was fine by her. Angel frowned though. What could he have to say to her he didn't want the others to hear? Did he have something to tell her about Carole?

'Um, okay.' She could see Emily's disapproving face rising up before her, scowling at her weakness in agreeing to be alone with him, but she really couldn't think of a good enough excuse to refuse.

She turned to follow Seb through the black curtain leading to the backstage area. Leo shot a worried look in her direction and she flashed him what she hoped was a reassuring smile over her shoulder.

'Your boyfriend seems a bit overprotective,' Seb said as soon as they were alone together.

'Oh, he's not my – he's my ex.' She bit her tongue. Why would she tell him that? 'I mean, um, we're just friends.'

'Oh. Right.'

Seb had said he wanted to talk to her, but now they were alone he just stood there, scanning her face. It felt like he was looking for something there. She wondered what it was. Something he'd lost…

She felt her skin prickle under his gaze and reached up to smooth her hair, running downcast eyes over the cracks and undulations in the grey concrete floor.

'You ever play poker, Angel?' he asked her suddenly.

'What? No, never. Why?'

'Don't. You'll be ruined inside a week.'

He reached out to stop the progress of the hand patting her auburn hair, took it inside his own. She drew in a sharp breath, feeling the familiar crackle of energy shooting from his fingers through her body as flesh met flesh, the lurch of muscles deep in her belly.

Seb dropped her hand like he'd been burnt. So he did feel it too…

His eyebrows gathered and he shook his head as if trying to free himself of something, diverting his eyes away from her face.

'You said you wanted to say something in private,' she prompted, desperate to get away from there, back to the safety of a crowd.

'Yes. I did say that.'

He relapsed into conflicted silence. What was it he'd brought her out here for, if he was just going to stand there frowning and not saying a word?

Angel tried again. 'How's Carole doing?' She flinched to hear herself say his wife's name, remembering everything that had passed between the three of them. 'I wanted to ask you to thank her for the beautiful flowers she sent me and Leo.'

Seb brightened a little. 'Did she send you flowers?'

'Yes. Didn't you know? She sent them to the office.'

'What, to the paper? That was foolish.' His brow tightened again. 'Still, it was like her to think of doing it.'

'And is she…?'

'Yes, she'll be okay, I think. She's getting stronger by the day, and she's with people who know how to help her. It's the best place she could be right now.'

'I'm glad, Seb, I really am. God, that night… I couldn't sleep till I got your text.' She winced at the memory, the cold grip of fear around her innards while she'd wondered if Carole would make it through. 'I hope she can go home soon. You must miss her.'

'I do.' His face darkened and he fell into silence again.

Angel began to get impatient. If he had nothing to say to her, why didn't he let her go?

'Okay, well if that's all, I'd better get back to Leo.'

Seb seemed to rouse himself from whatever black thoughts were causing him to direct a threatening scowl at the floor. 'Wait. Don't go back yet. I'm not done.'

He reached towards her and she thought for a second he was going to take her hand again, but he pulled back as if he'd suddenly remembered himself. Instead, he reached up to run distracted fingers through the chestnut curls, pushing them away from his forehead in a way that made Angel lower her eyes from his face.

'I suppose I just wanted to thank you properly for everything you did at the premiere. Leo too. It means a lot to me. And to Carole.' His eyes delved into hers, shining with gratitude and something else she couldn't quite identify.

Angel blinked, touched and a little embarrassed. 'It's only what anyone would have done,' she mumbled.

'It isn't at all, and you know it. You stayed in control where others would have panicked. And it's certainly not what any normal redtop reporter would have done.' He sneered as he considered that hated breed, the tabloid journalist. 'I half expected

142

to see it on the front page of the *Investigator* the next day. You could've had quite a scoop, Angel.'

'You know I'd never do that.' She bit her lip. Ridiculous thing to say. Of course he didn't know that. Hadn't she set him up and sold him out for a story once already?

'And this is our reward, is it?' she said, shifting the focus of the conversation. 'The profile piece instead of the scandal story?'

He smiled. 'Maybe a little of that. And –' the words seemed to tumble out of him in a rush before he was able to stop them – 'and I guess… I wanted to see you again.'

'See me again?' She frowned in confusion. 'Why would you… I mean, see me as what, Seb? A reporter? A friend?' Her face darkened. 'Something else?'

'I don't… know!' The last of his calm seemed to disappear in an instant. He bunched fists into his eyes in anguish and frustration, turned away from her while he struggled with the sudden outburst of emotion.

His voice cracked when he spoke again. 'Nothing. Anything. I don't know, okay? I wanted to see you, that's all. It doesn't matter, Angel.' He turned and strode away from her towards the exit, as if he was going to leave the building, then changed his mind and came back again.

It seemed as though there was some sort of battle raging inside him he didn't know how to win, and it was devouring him from the inside out. Angel felt as if she wanted to reach out, put a comforting arm around him, but she remembered touching wasn't allowed. Too dangerous. What should she do? She felt powerless to do anything for him. She stood in silence for a minute, digging her fingernails into her palms while she waited for him to regain his composure.

'Seb.' When she spoke again, her voice was gentle and soothing. 'Calm down. What's up? Can I do anything?'

He was breathing deeply, holding his gaze away from hers, twisting the gold wedding band around his finger.

'Sorry. I'm sorry, Angel. I'm… well, it's been a tough few weeks. Didn't mean to frighten you.'

She could hardly drag the words from her mouth, but she knew she had to bring it up. It was there, palpable, hanging in the air between them, and she'd have no peace until she'd dealt with it.

The honey trap.

'Look. That night… at the hotel. I need to know if it's okay, Seb.' Her cheeks were blazing scarlet but she forced herself to look at him, her green irises full of feeling, begging forgiveness. 'And if not, I need to know how to make it right.'

Seb's face blackened into a scowl. 'I had it coming. I could have kicked myself for being so stupid when the story came out. That expensive suite should have been a dead giveaway the whole thing was a setup. And I should know better than to trust strangers who strike up conversations in bars, no matter how –' He broke off, sucking in his lower lip in a way that made Angel avert her eyes.

'I'd like to forget it, Angel, I really would. But…'

'…but you still don't trust me.' She felt a mortifying prickle in the corner of her eyes, the familiar salty drops rising. She blinked hard, pushing them back.

'Any reason I should?'

'Only one I can think of.' She turned away from him to head back through the doorway.

'Angel. Wait.' He grabbed her elbow and spun her around to face him. 'I shouldn't have said that. It was uncalled for. I'm sorry.'

'No.' She dragged out a heavy sigh. 'No… it was fair. I'd feel the same, I suppose. I lied to you and I humiliated you, Seb. You don't get over something like that in a heartbeat… Mind you, you weren't exactly up-front with me either.' She cast a bitter glance at the wedding ring now encircling his third finger. 'Weren't really shouting about the fact you were married, were you?'

'Well, you never asked,' he said, his mouth curving slightly at one corner.

She fixed him with a stony glare. 'It's not funny, Seb.'

'I'm not smiling because it's funny. I'm smiling because it isn't.'

'That doesn't even make sense. Come on. I don't have time for riddles.'

'It makes sense if you're me.'

This was going nowhere. He was calmer now but his behaviour was odd, and she had no time for his nonsense talk.

'I don't understand you. Let me go back in to the others now. Please. You can't have anything else to say to me.'

He sighed. 'Yes, you're right. They'll be wondering where we are. Come on then, I guess we're done here.'

Seb turned and marched past her back towards the door, quickly reassuming his usual mask of stern, professional composure, and Angel followed him behind.

'Wait.' She grabbed his arm and pulled him back as he was about to walk through the curtained gap in the pallets. 'I forgot, I have to tell you something. Something important.'

His eyes widened with concern when he caught her worried expression. 'What is it? Is everything okay?'

'I'm not sure. Look, it's Steve.' She lowered her voice to a whisper. 'He knows about Carole.'

Seb's eyebrows lowered. 'You didn't.'

She shot him an irritated glance. 'No, not me. Not Leo either. He just knows, okay? I don't know how: journalist's hunch or something. He heard about the ambulance, and somehow he knows I was involved. And then there were the flowers. I denied it but he *knows*, Seb. He told me he didn't have enough evidence to run a story, but… just… the two of you watch your backs, okay?'

She gave his arm a comforting squeeze then dropped it quickly as they headed back through the curtain together and immediately separated.

Chapter 15

Making a beeline to where Leo was setting up his camera equipment in the corner, Angel wondered why she'd warned Seb about Steve. To protect Carole? Was that it? Well, it was as good an excuse as any to be going on with. She realised she was reaching up to pat her hair again and brought her hand back down to her side. Seb was right. She'd never make a poker player.

'It's okay, sorted it,' Leo said, not looking up from adjusting his tripod. 'We can take as many photos of the kids as we want, so long as they're only used for ReelKids promotional purposes. That includes our piece. Kev sorted it, actually, got me all the paperwork I need.' He nodded over to the bench, where the coffee-drinking teacher in the tweed twinset was talking animatedly. The PR man was looking rather windswept in the path of her constant flow of chatter. 'That teacher seems quite taken with him. No accounting for taste, I suppose. Anyway, what did that James Bond wannabe want?' he asked, jerking his head towards Seb, who had joined Suzanne and a group of students in the mock-up kitchen. 'I've got instructions from Em to report back to her if he tries it on with you.'

'You two really need to stop bloody worrying about me. And be *nice*, will you?' Angel hissed, jabbing him in the ribs with her elbow. 'Or be polite, at least. We've still got the rest of the afternoon to get through, and if Wilchester chucks us out on our arses then you can be the one to explain why to Steve. Can you imagine what he'd say if we went back with nothing?'

Leo put on a letchy smirk. 'Eeee, 'appen tha's buggered it right oop, sugar boobies,' he rasped in imitation of Steve's Yorkshire accent. 'Show us yer bum and I'll forget all about it.' Angel giggled and punched him on the arm.

'So?' Leo said, dropping the Steve impression. 'What did Wilchester want, then? Didn't touch you up or anything, did he?'

'Look, I can take care of myself, okay?' Angel said, folding her arms across her chest. 'He didn't try anything on, I promise. Just thanked me for helping Carole then stood around looking gormless for five minutes. I don't know, he seemed a bit distracted actually.'

'Why, what's up with him?'

Angel shrugged. 'Dunno. Worried about his wife, maybe. Anyway, after today we'll be done with them both and we can all get on with our lives.'

Leo looked doubtful. He held up crossed fingers. 'Here's hoping…'

'Right,' Angel said, taking her notepad and pen out of her shoulder bag. 'I guess I'll go talk to some of these kids, see what they're working on.' She looked nervously over at the groups of teens, who were buzzing away in excitement while they planned their film project. 'Er, on second thoughts, maybe I'll start with the teacher, check she's okay with it.'

Angel headed over to the bench where the middle-aged lady in tweed was still talking away at a silent Kev.

'Um, sorry to interrupt. Angel Blackthorne, from the *Investigator*. I wondered if you and I could have a chat, Mrs…?'

'Oh, hullo, dear. It's Simons. Miss.' The teacher shot a sly sideways glance at Kev.

'Hi.' Angel shook the manicured hand held out to her and

took a seat at the teacher's side, absorbed into a Miss Simons-shaped haze of lavender scent.

'So the kids seem to be having fun. Is this part of a media studies course or something?' Angel asked, looking over at them. They'd separated out into four groups of five or six each. One was working on storyboards in a corner, with another painting scenery backdrops and a couple more learning how to use some of the cameras and sound gear. The kids with Seb and Suzanne in the kitchen seemed to be the designated 'actor' group and were running through the script. A number of volunteers milled about, helping the young people with anything they didn't understand and showing them how the specialised equipment worked.

'No, it's extracurricular. It does tie in with their schoolwork, though,' Miss Simons answered. 'I must say, it's an incredible opportunity for them to be able to come somewhere like this. Such amazing facilities, and then someone like Sebastian Wilchester, *the* Sebastian Wilchester, giving them a crash course in filmmaking too.'

'What is it they're actually working on?' Angel tried hard not to be distracted by the way the teacher constantly pushed one squeaky shoe into the floor, making a repetitive 'eee-ee' sound with the rubber sole. 'Is it a script they've written themselves?'

'Yes, they've been working on it in my classes for the last four lessons.' She laughed. 'Don't ask me what it's about though, I've been sworn to absolute secrecy.'

'Sounds intriguing.'

'I'm sure it'll be something special.' Miss Simons glowed with pride. 'They're a creative bunch. I do hope you can stay for the screening, Miss Blackthorne. They'd love it if you mentioned it in your newspaper. Kids with their backgrounds don't get much positive press, and, well, it would be something for parents or carers to put on the fridge.'

'Er…' Angel looked over at Kev, who was scowling at her as usual. She summoned a non-committal smile for Miss Simons.

'That's probably a decision for Mr Wilchester. We'll see what we can do.'

'You can ask him now, look,' the teacher said, nodding over to the kitchen set. Angel turned and saw Seb striding towards where they were sitting.

He avoided making eye contact with her as he arrived at the bench, instead addressing himself to Kev.

'Kev, can you pop up to HQ for me and pick up those storyboards and the *Milkman* posters? I may as well go through them here. I'd like to stay until the group finish their film, if our guests from the press don't mind. Normally Carole would take over, but...' He hesitated, giving the teacher a wary glance. '...but she's not available,' he finished.

Miss Simons looked disappointed. It was clear she was happy enough with a Sebastian Wilchester if that was all she was going to get, but she could dine out for weeks on a big star like Carole Beaumont.

Kev's brow lowered. 'Since when does fetching and carrying for you come under the heading of PR, Seb? Get Suzanne to do it, she's your assistant.'

'She's working with some kids over there, I don't want to interrupt her.' Seb looked over his shoulder to where Suzanne was now chatting enthusiastically with the storyboarding group. He turned back to Kev with a frosty look. 'Whereas you've done nothing but sit on your arse for the past hour.'

Kev stood up, face fixed into its usual sulk. 'Fine.' He lowered his voice. 'But you need to get rid of that girl, Seb. As if it's not enough she's bad at her job, now she's not even making any attempt to do it.'

Seb's expression hardened. 'She's not going anywhere. Just go get those things, will you?'

Kev stood up to go, turning a suspicious look on Angel. It clearly worried him, leaving her and Leo with unrestricted access to Seb, even if only for quarter of an hour.

'I don't believe I've congratulated you on your promotion yet, Miss Blackthorne,' he said with an exaggerated, sneering politeness. 'I've been hearing all about you from my other media contacts. From intern to film critic in, what, just under eight months at the *Investigator*? Your editor must think very highly of your, er, *skills*. Whatever they may be,' he mumbled in a nasty voice, turning on his heel and stalking off towards the door.

Had to get a parting shot in, didn't he? So that was what people were saying. That she must be sleeping with Steve. *But of course…*

'Sorry about him,' Seb said, turning to her at last.

'Oh, don't worry. I should be used to him by now. He certainly takes his job seriously when it comes to watching your back.'

'Yeah. A bit too seriously. I think he'd stand over me while I slept if I let him, fighting off hostile journalists with a sharpened implement as they tried to sneak in my bedroom window.'

Miss Simons was smiling with a glazed, puzzled politeness while this conversation washed straight over her head. Now, she saw her moment to chime in.

'Oh, Mr Wilchester, thank you so much for all you're doing with the children,' she gushed. 'It's such a wonderful opportunity for them.'

Seb winced under her fulsome praise. 'It's me who should thank them. They're a privilege to work with. So many creative ideas. You must be very proud of them, Miss Simons.'

'Thank you, I am. Very much so. Oh, er, I'm a little embarrassed, but would you…?' Miss Simons bent down and fumbled in her laptop case under the bench, fished out a DVD copy of *Unreal City* and a marker pen and held them towards him with an expectant expression on her round, heavy-jowled face. 'It's not for me, you understand, but it would mean the world to my, er, niece. She's such a huge fan of your work.'

Seb looked blankly at the DVD cover. 'Oh, right, yes. Of course.' He scrawled his signature across the front and handed it back to her. 'I hope your niece likes it.'

Miss Simons beamed. 'Oh, wonderful, thank you so much! I was hoping to get Miss Beaumont to sign too, but, well, if she can't come… I hope she's alright?'

'She's fine,' Seb lied calmly. 'Just a bit tired after all the work on *The Milkman Cometh* publicity recently. I told her to take some time off, get some rest. Can't have my star getting burnt out.'

'Oh. Well, you know best, of course. Please tell her we're all massive fans of hers at the school. The rest of the staff couldn't believe it when I said I was coming here.'

'Glad to. Erm, I actually came to ask if I could poach Miss Blackthorne from you.' He turned to Angel with an embarrassed smile. 'I thought you might like to come and see one of the groups at work – if Miss Simons here has no objection.'

'Oh, none at all, I assure you,' the teacher said, preening at being asked her consent. 'And I do hope you won't mind if she and her colleague stay for the screening later, Mr Wilchester. I'm sure the children would love them to see it – and maybe write about it in the paper.' She turned an ingratiating smile on Angel.

'Would you like to?' Seb asked her in a quiet voice. 'I'm more than happy to arrange it.'

'I… er, maybe. I'll need to talk to Leo. Thank you.'

She stood up and walked with him back towards the group in the kitchen.

'That DVD will be on Ebay tomorrow,' he said with a grin. 'Hope she gets a good price for it, anyway. Shame Carole wasn't here, she'd have got at least triple with a Beaumont signature on there.'

'Seb,' Angel said in a low voice. 'This is all really interesting, the workshop and everything. But you do know I was sent to write a profile on you, not a promo piece for ReelKids? If I don't turn something in fitting that description, Steve's going to hang me out to dry.'

Seb's brow darkened. 'Oh, bugger Steve.' But his scowl disappeared as he turned to her. 'Sorry. I know it's your job. And I know it was me who asked you here. Listen, how about we grab a coffee after this and talk? I'll answer any questions you like, I promise. And then if you want to stay for the screening, that's up to you.'

We? Coffee? Talk? That sounded worrying. Worryingly date-like. And she didn't want to get caught alone with him again, not after his bizarre behaviour backstage.

'Leo too?'

'Oh yes, the photographer who doesn't like me.' He flung a look over at Leo in the corner. 'Well, I don't see any reason we can't do pictures at the same time. Suze said she'd scheduled in a Q&A, might as well bring it forward.'

Okay, that wasn't so bad. At least they wouldn't be in a tête-à-tête situation. And he didn't seem to be pushing to get her on her own again, she reflected with a mixture of relief and disappointment.

Angel plastered on a fixed smile for the group of teens running through their lines in the kitchen as she and Seb approached, trying to look confident and self-assured. The trick was not to let them smell your fear, she told herself, while they stared at her in all the narrow-eyed, suspicious curiosity of youth.

'This is Miss Blackthorne from the *Investigator*,' Seb told them. 'She's come to see what you're working on and make a few notes. Is that okay with you lot?'

A girl of about sixteen, her black hair piled on top of her head in a grungy sort of way, glared at her. 'My dad says the *Investigator*'s full of bollocks,' she said in an accusing tone, turning to Seb. 'He says they make stuff up all the time and they're always stirring up shit. And he says they've got blood on their hands because they supported that thing that time or whatever.'

Seb opened his mouth to reply, but Angel held up her hand to let her answer.

Okay, I can do this…

'What's your name?' she asked the girl.

'Kyra,' the teen answered with a sulky shrug.

'Why are you telling us what your dad thinks, Kyra? You can think too, can't you?'

'Well, yeah, I guess…'

'Then don't believe something just because you've seen it in the paper or on the telly, or because your dad or your teacher or someone else tells you it's true. Use the thing swimming about between your ears and find things out for yourself. That's what it's there for.'

Kyra grinned. 'Yeah, well, my dad's full of shit an' all. Tell you what, you're alright, you are, Miss.'

'Thanks.' Angel smiled back at her.

'I like the *Investigator*,' said a swaggering boy in the group, treating his peers to an arrogant smirk. 'Coz there's always tits on page three, yeah?'

'You *badly* need the Internet, mate,' Angel said. The group laughed and elbowed the lad playfully.

'Well, you seem to have tamed the savage beasts,' Seb muttered under his breath, smiling at her. 'Good job.'

'Thanks. You think they spotted I don't know what I'm going on about?'

'No, you're doing fine. Just never let them see the whites of your eyes.'

But the swaggering lad wasn't done yet. 'I seen *him* in the *Investigator*,' he told the group, pointing at Seb. 'Cheating on his missus, that famous actress, wassername… Beaumont.'

'Yeah, me too.' Another boy nodded, sniggering. 'Shagging some ginner slapper in the bath. Nice one, mate.' He gave Seb an exaggerated double thumbs-up.

Angel felt her cheeks burn deep scarlet and turned away, pretending to examine the vintage radio on the kitchen counter. She flashed a sideways glance at Seb from under lowered lashes as she wondered how he'd respond. To her surprise she found his eyes were seeking hers, crinkling slightly at the corners.

God… he can't possibly think this is funny?

'Thanks,' Seb said to the lad, his tanned cheeks pinkening just a little. 'Glad to hear you find my sex life so fascinating. Maybe one day you'll have one of your own to entertain you instead, eh?'

The lad scowled, flushing with anger, but the rest of the group laughed. 'Ooooh, Jordan, slapdown!' giggled Kyra, nudging him in the ribs. 'You so had that coming.'

'I get girls,' Jordan mumbled, sulking at the attack on his manliness. He raised defiant eyes to meet Seb's. 'Loads.'

Seb slapped the boy on the shoulder. 'Alright, son, never mind. Just having a laugh. Come on, let's get on with the script run-through, shall we?'

Angel scribbled down notes while Seb worked with the group. She couldn't help but be impressed by the way he guided them, advising them on their delivery and positions, suggesting amendments to their script's dialogue and plot but always allowing himself to be overruled if his suggestions weren't accepted by the kids. His brow knitted with concentration, and it was clear he took his role as director just as seriously here as he would on the set of any of his big-budget films. He seemed to know just how to talk to the group to get the best out of them, adopting a tone that was both informal and respectful.

This was all he wanted to do, Angel realised, watching the energy and passion flowing from him and the kids' eyes firing as they caught it too. She could tell this was where he wanted to be, and the glitzy world of premieres and celebrity was just something to be tolerated so he could continue doing what he loved: making films and teaching others to love making films.

'Okay,' Seb said after they'd been through the script twice, pushing a stray curl away from his face. 'Let's take a break. Good job, guys. There's squash and sandwiches over by Miss Simons if you want to help yourselves.'

Full of animated chatter about their script, the kids made their way over to a snack table in the corner, Seb leading the way.

Chapter 16

Angel followed, finding herself walking next to Kyra, the girl she'd spoken with earlier.

'He's good, ain't he?' Kyra pointed to Seb over by the snack table.

Her brown eyes were still glowing with enthusiasm from the script run-through. She'd been cast in the main part. Her first read-through had been a little wooden but she'd blossomed under Seb's direction, eventually bringing the lines to life with a passionate delivery all her own.

Angel nodded, looking down at her too-tight black heels. 'Yeah. He is.'

'I'm totally going to be an actress when I finish school.' Kyra preened a little while she confided this burning ambition. 'Mr Wilchester says I could be, for definite. He says not to give up, just keep practising at it. My mum reckons I should get a job down Asda like my sister and start bringing money in, but she can sod that. I'm not getting stuck in that shithole the rest of my life like everyone else round our way.'

Angel was moved by the girl's determination. 'You should listen to him, Kyra, he knows his stuff. I mean, ignore all that 'follow your dreams and you can do anything' bollocks some adults are always doling out, obviously. Not everyone who dreams of being an actor can actually be one. But you've definitely got a talent, I can see it. Don't give up on that.' She gave the teenager a warm smile.

Kyra grinned back at her, pleased and proud. 'Thanks, Miss. I knew you was alright.' She looked over at Seb and lowered her voice. 'Oi, don't look now but I reckon that Mr Wilchester's checking you out. Better keep your eye on him. He's married, you know.'

Angel glanced over at Seb, standing near the sandwich table, and discovered Kyra was right: he was watching her. He smiled as he caught her eye, one of those rare, full, double-dimpled smiles she hardly ever saw him use. She felt the blood rush into her cheeks, but he didn't withdraw his gaze.

'Don't I know it,' she muttered to herself. She turned back to Kyra, but the girl had wandered off. Angel grabbed a polystyrene cup of sludge-like coffee for herself and wandered over to where Suzanne was squatting, looking over the storyboards the kids had produced.

'Pretty good, don't you think?' she said to Angel, who crouched down beside her.

'Yeah. He really seems to know how to bring out the best in them.' She glanced over at Seb again, who'd been joined by Kev with the posters and storyboards.

'How long have you been working for him, Suzanne?' Angel asked. 'I mean, sorry, Miss Haynes.'

'Oh, no, Suzanne, please. That's much better.' The PA gave her a friendly smile. 'And, not long. I mean, I've known Seb and Carole a few years, but I only started working as his assistant about four months ago. I was just a runner before that. I met them on set.'

Angel lifted her eyebrows, surprised. 'Really? That's a pretty big promotion.'

The PA dropped her eyes, fumbling with the storyboards. 'I

guess. But that's just like Seb, wanting to give someone an opportunity like that. He's a really nice guy.' She laughed. 'Shame I'm so rubbish at it.'

'Oh, you'll get the hang of it. Trust me, from someone else in the 'new job' boat. And for what it's worth, I think you're doing great.' Angel threw her a smile.

Seb and Kev were heading over to join them now, carrying the pile of paperwork the PR man had fetched from Tigerblaze HQ.

'Suze, change of plan,' Seb said, crouching down beside his PA. 'We're going to go through the posters here and save the storyboards until tomorrow. I'd rather have a look at them tonight at home and make a few notes. It'll give me something to occupy me, anyway. It's so quiet there at the moment.' He nodded towards the papers under Kev's arm. 'Let's take a look at the posters, shall we?'

Seb rose. Kev was standing beside him, his long, thin face fixed into the trademark resentful scowl. 'I don't know why we need to involve her, Seb,' he muttered, gesturing to Suzanne. 'She's only a bloody runner. What does she know about publicity?'

'Hey, I'm right here, you know,' Suzanne said, giving him a dirty look. 'And I'm not deaf, Kev.'

'I want her to take a look.' Seb's voice was firm as he spread the posters out on the floor in front of them. 'I trust Suze to give me an honest opinion.'

He turned to Angel. 'I'd like to know what you think too, Miss Blackthorne, if you're happy to give your feedback.' He flashed her another warm smile, which took her by surprise. The day seemed to be full of them. 'I thought very highly of your *Milkman* review. It shows you have a natural talent for seeing what others don't.' Almost the same words Steve had used when he'd promoted her. She flushed under the compliment, trying her best to ignore Kev's humph of disapproval.

'These are the designs we're considering for billboards and bus shelters when the DVD's released next month,' Seb told her. 'I want something a bit different from the ones we used to promote the cinematic release.'

There were five posters, all in different styles. Angel's gaze darted over them, brows knitted with concentration. Seb's eager eyes were fixed on her face while she examined each one.

'Well? What do you think?'

Suzanne drew one towards her. It showed Carole's character in the film, Edna, rising up over the skyline of a suburban neighbourhood. 'This is my favourite.'

Angel shook her head. 'A bit simplistic for my taste,' she said. 'Sorry, Suzanne. It is a great shot of Carole, but it doesn't say enough about the film itself.'

She drew out a minimalist design, a simple pen-and-ink drawing showing a gunshot wound bleeding milk. 'I love this one, but...'

'But?' Seb said, watching her carefully.

'It's very powerful. Iconic, even.' She shook her head. 'But I don't think it'll sell your film. People want something more... obvious. I mean, save it for merchandising, by all means. But I'd have to say... this one.'

She picked up another poster and handed it to Seb. It was an ensemble shot of the main characters: black and white, deliberately over-exposed photograph cut-outs arranged on a textured blue background. Carole, centre front, was trapped inside a giant milk bottle, banging against the glass.

'I just think it shows that sort of cloistered suburban madness Carole brought out so well in the film,' Angel said, glancing up at Seb. 'And the genre is nice and obvious too. People know they'll be getting something funny, but something dark.'

Seb nodded, impressed. 'Yes, I think you're right. Good choice.' His eyes flickered over her face before he turned to the PR man, and she couldn't help wondering if this had been some sort of test. 'What do you think, Kev?'

He gave a grumpy shrug. 'Well, if my opinion matters again all of a sudden, I'd probably have to agree. Not the strongest design, but the one that'll sell it for us.'

'Good enough for me, then. Sign it off with Publicity. We'll get it to print before the end of the day.'

Kev nodded. He left the three of them together and pulled out his mobile to make the call.

Seb turned to Suzanne, who was collecting up the rejected poster designs under her arm. 'Miss Blackthorne was asking if we could move the Q&A forward a bit. Is that okay by you, Suze? I want to make sure they get a decent profile piece for their editor.'

'I'm starting to wonder who this guy is and what he's done with the real Seb,' Suzanne said to Angel with a laugh. 'I don't know when this brave new world where Sebastian Wilchester cooperates with journalists came into existence. But yes, shouldn't be a problem. We can do it now while the kids are having a break, if you and your photographer are ready.'

'Thanks, Suzanne. I'll fetch Leo.'

Angel headed over to Leo and his camera in the corner. The teacher, Miss Simons, had joined him and he was showing her some of the digital photos he'd got of the groups working on their film.

'Oh, those are fabulous, Mr Courtenay,' she heard the teacher gush. 'You will be sure to let the school have a copy for our autumn newsletter, won't you?'

'Course. More than happy. Just be sure to credit the paper or I'll get a bollocking from my boss.'

'Leo,' Angel said, nodding a hello to the teacher as she approached. 'We've decided to shuffle things around a bit. Are you okay to come and get some photos of Seb now?' She saw Miss Simons raise one eyebrow at her familiarity in drifting into first-name terms with the director and kicked herself for the slip-up.

'Fine by me, Ginge. Where shall we do it?'

'Up to you, I guess. Better see what Suzanne thinks.'

'Right.' Leo headed over to where Suzanne was in deep conversation with Seb, leaving Angel alone with Miss Simons and her tweed twinset.

The teacher beamed at her. 'What a talented young man he is, that Mr Courtenay. You must be very proud of him.'

'Me?' Angel frowned. 'Ah! Right, I see. No, er, we're just good friends.'

'Oh, I do apologise. I thought... but never mind.' She let out a little girlish giggle. 'I do have a habit of putting my foot in it, don't I?'

Angel smiled distantly. Miss Simons was starting to remind her of the stock ditzy teacher character in a *Girl's Own* boarding-school story. It was only one small step from girlish giggles to midnight feasts. And then the woman would have to be stopped.

'We're going to do them up at Tigerblaze HQ,' Leo said when he rejoined them, commanding Angel's attention away from the ever-smiling Miss Simons. Finding herself in a conversation she had no part in, the teacher wandered off in the direction of the coffee-making facilities, much to Angel's relief.

'The old house will make a great backdrop for the photos.' Leo started to dismantle his equipment while he spoke. 'I can get a few outside and a few of Wilchester in his office, then you can do your Q&A. You did remember to write some questions this time, didn't you?'

Angel furnished him with a theatrical eyeroll. '*Please*, Mr Courtenay. I am a professional.' She flicked an imaginary speck of dust from the cuff of her borrowed jacket with comic hauteur, making Leo laugh.

'Alright, star reporter Lois Lane. Didn't mean to wound one's fragile ego. Help me pack this stuff up and we'll hobble on over.'

She helped him unscrew the tripod legs and put his equipment away in the camera bag. Seb, Kev and Suzanne were already waiting by the black curtain for them.

Her feet were killing her now, and she wished she could take off the evil shoes and feel the cool concrete against her poor aching heels. It was still another quarter of a mile to the main Tigerblaze building. She let out a quiet groan as she followed her party out through the metal porch.

Leo heard and held out his arm to her. 'Hey. Want to put your weight on me again?'

She threw him a grateful smile, but shook her head. 'I'm fine, Leo, it's okay,' she lied. Somehow, she didn't want to be arm in arm with him while Seb was just there ahead of her. Enough people had assumed they were a couple that afternoon to make her feel self-conscious about appearing too cosy with him.

Angel and Leo fell a few yards behind the others as they walked across the tarmac to the big Edwardian mansion, her sore feet forcing her to slow her pace. She saw Seb fall back too, deliberately letting Kev and Suzanne go on ahead. He fell into step with Leo on her right and gave him a pleasant smile.

'You looked busy this afternoon. I hope you were able to get some decent snaps of the groups.'

Angel could tell he was making a conscious effort to win Leo over and felt a ribbon of excitement unfurl in her as she wondered if it could be for her benefit.

Leo gave a belligerent shrug, not meeting Seb's eyes. 'Yeah, not bad. That teacher seemed to like them anyway.'

'Doesn't surprise me. I've seen your photos. They're bloody impressive, seriously.'

Leo shrugged again, grunting.

Seb stopped walking and turned to confront him, exasperation written all over his features. 'Look, mate. Do you and I have a problem here?'

Leo glared at him with dislike. 'That's something you might want to ask your wife, *mate*,' he snarled, the resentment that had been bubbling up all afternoon finally bursting free. 'If you can remember you've got one for five minutes.'

162

'So that's it, is it?' Seb held Leo's gaze, refusing to break eye contact.

Eurghh. Angel felt like she was drowning in an excess of testosterone. Any minute now she could see this ending in headlocks and nude wrestling. Or maybe that was just the two years of near-celibacy talking...

'Leo.' She grabbed her friend's arm, tried to force him to look round. He attempted to shake her away, but she curled her fingers around his wrist and gripped hard until he had to face her.

'What?' he hissed. 'Let me deal with this, Angel, okay?'

'For Christ's sake, Leo, can you cut out this macho bullshit?' she said in a fierce whisper, watching Seb trying hard to calm his furious features over Leo's shoulder. 'You're supposed to be a professional on a job, not a bloody five-year-old arguing about your dad being bigger than his dad or whatever.' She glared at him. 'And since when was Carole Beaumont your problem anyway, oh great protector of the womenfolk? When was I? Come on, Leo. You're better than this. Please.'

Leo's brow lifted a little, picking up the note of quiet pleading in her voice. He exhaled slowly, willing himself calm, as she continued to glare at him. 'Alright, Ginge, fine. For you then,' he said in a whisper.

He turned back to Seb, summoning a cool, polite smile from somewhere with an effort. 'I'm sorry, Wilchester, that was out of order. As my friend here has kindly just reminded me, I'm a dick. Your relationship with your wife or – or with anyone else is none of my business.'

'Bloody right it's not,' Seb muttered. But he managed to raise an answering smile, one that extended to his lips if not his eyes, as he caught Angel's pleading look over Leo's shoulder. 'But... apology accepted, I suppose, in the interests of peace and harmony. Let's just get on with this, shall we?'

Angel felt like a schoolteacher settling a playground fight. She wondered if she should force them to spit-shake on it as well.

'Is everything okay?' Suzanne called in a concerned voice from up ahead, noticing they'd stopped walking.

'Yeah, fine.' Seb attempted a careless tone. 'I'm right behind you, Suze.'

'Hey. Courtenay,' he said, furnishing Leo with a half-smile far more sincere than the full one he'd summoned with great effort seconds earlier. 'I really do like your photos.' Leaving them, he strode off ahead to join Suzanne.

Angel glared at Leo. 'Didn't you see that? He was trying to be nice.'

'I noticed,' Leo said, his eyebrows gathering. 'The problem with that guy is he's "nice" to all the wrong people.'

'Oi. Unfair.'

'Why the hell are you always sticking up for him? You've got as much reason to hate him as anybody.' Shooting a quick look at the group ahead to make sure they weren't paying attention, Leo cupped a hand around her shoulder and drew her around to face him, lowering his voice. 'Maybe it isn't any of my business, but I am your friend, Ginge, and sorry, but you won't shut me up. The man cheats on his wife, practically pushes her into a breakdown, it seems to me, then acts like *you're* the bad guy because he couldn't keep his pants on. And then he summons you here like God's bloody gift and drags you off into quiet corners so he can, what, get you to become his regular bit on the side or something?' He jerked his hand away from her shoulder, turned away in disgust and resumed his walk. 'I might've been a pretty shit boyfriend to you, all told, but I never treated you or anyone I cared about like they existed purely for my convenience. Jesus Christ, Angel, grow some self-respect, why don't you? Do me and yourself a favour and tell that cheating prick where to go.'

Angel felt the tears rise and turned her face to the ground while she composed herself. Leo was harsh. Leo was… Leo was… Leo was right, wasn't he? She didn't know why she was defending

Seb, except... no, there was no reason she could explain. Not right now.

It was a cheap dig, though, about her self-respect. She hadn't exactly thrown herself into Seb's arms, had she? Not recently anyway, she thought, grimacing. And he hadn't made any advances, not really, not if she thought about it. He'd been sort of nice to her all afternoon, which she hadn't really expected given their history to date. Then he'd acted pretty strangely when they'd been alone backstage together. True, he'd said he'd wanted to see her again... but that was hardly some prime seduction technique. He'd barely even been able to touch her.

It was just this... whatever it was, crackling between them all the time, making things all weird. Leo had picked up on it, and she was starting to think Suzanne had noticed something too. The PA certainly seemed to shoot worried glances in their direction whenever she spotted the two of them together.

Angel felt an apologetic hand squeeze her arm, and turned to see Leo wearing the familiar baby sheepdog expression he always had five minutes after they'd rowed.

'Sorry, Ginge. Did it again, didn't I?'

'Well, you weren't wrong this time, much as I hate to admit it. He hasn't tried it on, I promise. But... I have been thinking about him. I know I shouldn't. When I remember Carole's face that night... but I just can't help it, Leo.' She turned damp eyes up to him, wishing she could stop for a hug without the others noticing. Suddenly she really felt she could use one. 'It's like you with Em, I guess.'

'Yeah.' He cast a morose glance down at his shoes. 'I know what you mean. Sometimes someone just gets inside your head like that, no matter how bad you know it is for you.' He looked back up at her, his eyes fierce. 'But you owe it to yourself to fight it, Angel. It's bastards like that who'll break your heart, and I'm the first person entitled to tell you that you deserve better. Do it for me and Em, eh?'

She gave a tiny, sad little nod. 'I'll try, Leo. I will.'

He attempted a bright smile. 'Come on, kiddo. Let's get this over with and hole up in a pub to eat peanuts and cry on each other's shoulders. There's an apple juice behind the bar of a Wetherspoons somewhere with my name on it.'

'Best suggestion you've made all day, mate,' she said, flashing a smile back to him. 'Come on then, let's get this thing over with so we can get out of here.'

She forced her poor feet into a faster pace to catch up with the others, who were waiting for them outside the large white-washed manor looming up ahead.

Chapter 17

'Okay, Wilchester – er, *Mr* Wilchester. You here, please.' Leo was in businesslike mode, previous animosity put to one side as he directed Seb to where he wanted him for the photoshoot. The imposing, classically styled white front of the Tigerblaze head-quarters made the perfect backdrop.

He really was very good, Angel reflected, watching her friend put Seb into poses like a human Action Man. He never skipped a beat as he deftly moved the director from one position to the next, then the next and the next, in a whirlwind of lenses and flashbulbs.

Seb looked over at her with a comical grimace, his eyes a little glazed while he submitted to being pushed here and there by Leo. She couldn't help laughing as she shot an answering smile back to him.

She knew Seb hadn't been idly flattering Leo when he'd told him his work was impressive. He'd been studying philosophy when he, Emily and Angel had met in halls during freshers' week at King's College, but photography had quickly become his real love. It was his passion all through their uni years, never going anywhere without a camera, and some of his pictures had won prizes in national competitions while he was still a student. He'd even been invited to take part in a couple of exhibitions. But that was before the drinking had really taken hold, and his camera had become just another way to earn a living.

Once Leo had finished with him, Seb made his way over to Angel, looking a little shell-shocked. Leo remained in the building's covered porch area, leaning on a Doric column and scrolling through the images on his camera's LCD screen with an expression of intense concentration. Suzanne was next to him, giving appreciative 'oohs' and 'aahs' when he let her see the best shots. Even Kev seemed reluctantly impressed, scanning the pics over Suzanne's shoulder.

'I guess it's pretty obvious I'm not used to this,' Seb said to Angel. 'Much more Carole's area than mine. It's interesting to be directed for a change, though, see how it feels.' He ran his fingers through his curls in that way he had which made Angel's nerves quiver. God, she wished he'd stop doing that... 'Your friend certainly knows his stuff, I'll give him that.'

'Look, Seb, I'm really sorry about before,' she said with an apologetic smile. 'Leo was totally out of order, having a go at you like that. And – thanks, for not rising to it. He just worries about me, you know?'

His expression hardened. 'Yeah, so I see. Takes very good care of you, doesn't he?' He flashed Leo a resentful look. 'How long is it since you broke up?'

Angel looked blank.

'Sorry,' he muttered, his face furrowing into a frown as he turned away from her. 'That was personal. None of my business, I know.'

'Two years.' Why was she telling him that? 'It's been two years. That was the last time I was... with anyone.'

She felt the blood rush to her cheeks. It felt like life was all blushing, crying and heaving bosoms these days. She was a walking Jane Austen novel, wasn't she? How very depressing.

'That's a long time.' Seb didn't look round as he spoke. Instead he stared away into the distance, over to the silhouetted Zimmerman stage, where filming for *The Milkman Cometh* had taken place. 'A long time to be alone, anyway.' His voice was dreamlike, almost as if he'd forgotten she was there. Angel threw a puzzled frown in his direction.

'Seb…'

He jerked as if he'd been shot. 'Sorry. I'm a bit distracted today.' He seemed to be deliberately avoiding meeting her eyes. 'Shall we go in and get on with the Q&A? You must want to get out of here by now.'

She gave a confused nod, wondering about his strange behaviour. One minute he was all friendly smiles, the next scowling with emotions he didn't seem to be able to handle. Was it Carole? The fallout from the newspaper story? Stress from the film publicity? What?

Not for the first time, she wished she knew what was going on behind those perfect features of his. And then she wondered why she cared. And then she remembered caring wasn't allowed: hadn't she promised Leo not half an hour ago she was going to try to put Seb out of her mind?

Well, perhaps her own conflicted emotions were just as much of a mystery to her as his. She shook her head, impatient with herself.

Inside the building, Suzanne pointed to various rooms as they walked along a third-floor passage to Seb's office. 'This is where the distribution arm of Tigerblaze is based. Publicity department's in there. And this is PR: Kev's domain, of course.'

Angel looked over at Kev: the human suit, as she remembered Steve calling him once. Or The Incredible Sulk might be a more fitting nickname. She'd almost forgotten he was with them. He'd barely spoken a word since they'd left the ReelKids stage.

'And this is my desk.' Suzanne pointed it out to them with all the enthusiasm of a child showing her parents around her new school for the first time. 'Seb's office is just through this door here. Carole's got one too, next door, but, um… she's not in, obviously.'

The PA ushered them into an office, smaller than Angel had expected, and decorated in a period style to match the age of the building. A mahogany desk bearing two computer monitors was placed in one corner, overlooking a large window with a view across the studio lot towards the military-green Zimmerman stage. There was an ornate open fireplace in the centre of the room and a very faint smell of cigar smoke hanging in the air.

'Oh, don't mind that,' Seb said with a smile, watching her take a whiff. 'Just our resident ghost.'

She lifted a sceptical eyebrow. 'Ghost, seriously? Whose is it supposed to be, an actor who committed suicide after a contract dispute?'

She saw Seb wince and bit the inside of her cheek, realising what she'd said. He was thinking of Carole. God, what the hell was wrong with her? Serious foot-in-mouth syndrome…

He turned his face away as he smoothed his expression and spoke to Suzanne. She was facing away from them, gazing out of the window over the lot. 'Suze, could you sort us out some hot drinks? Just get one of those big Thermos things in and we'll help ourselves.'

Once the PA had left he turned back to Angel, managing a smile. 'Actually I think it's supposed to be the ghost of a young dandy killed in a shooting accident in the days before this became a studio. But the more mundane explanation, I'm afraid, is it's the accumulated smell of decades of upper-class sorts using this as a smoking room drifting down from my chimney. We only ever get it when the wind blows. I actually find it quite comforting.' He took a seat at his desk and gestured to her and Leo to pull up one of the high-backed executive swivel chairs on the other side. 'That's why I chose this office, even though it's a bit on the small side for meetings. There's something about that musty old smell.' He looked absently into the fireplace. 'Reminds me of Christmas.'

'I like it too,' Angel said, smiling. 'Makes me think of my dad. He quit years ago, but when I was a little kid and he used to hug me his clothes always smelled of it.'

She gave a little awkward laugh. 'Sorry. I'm doing that thing again. That waffling thing.'

'I like it when you do that thing.' He smiled at her, another of those rare, tummy-melting double-dimplers.

She coloured and looked away, then felt Leo plant a light kick on her ankle under the desk. A warning. 'Don't fall for it,' the kick seemed to say.

Her friend cleared his throat at her shoulder. 'Er, I believe we're here to do a profile, Wilchester. If you want to tell us ghost stories we can come back for Halloween.'

Seb chose to ignore him. Instead he turned to Kev, lurking behind his boss like an ever-present shadow and fixing Angel with an even deeper scowl than usual while she busied her hands with her notebook.

'Kev, I don't want you here for this.'

Angel almost pitied the sullen PR man when a hurt look flashed over his face. 'You can't seriously expect me to leave you here with *them*, Seb? Come on, don't be a fool.'

Seb shot an exasperated look at him. 'Look, I've made up my mind, okay? You're not my personal bodyguard. Believe it or not, Kevin, I can actually manage to look after myself.'

'Of course you can.' Kev's chilled tone bit with sarcasm. 'I think me, you and every reader of the damn *Investigator* are aware of that, aren't we?'

The director's face remained immovable. 'Just go, Kev, will you?' he snapped. 'Go and play with your bloody Meccano set or whatever it is you do in your downtime.' But his face softened a little when he noticed Kev's hurt expression. 'Look, I can't have you hovering over me, it just makes me nervous. And there isn't enough room in here for five of us. I'll be fine, I promise. Suzanne will be here to mind me. Please. Go.'

'Fine. You're the boss. But I'm taking no responsibility for whatever they get out of you.' Kev turned to stomp towards the door, like a sulky child who's first out at musical chairs. Suzanne, heading back through with the tea and coffee-making stuff, shot a surprised look at him as he thundered past her.

'Sorry about that,' Seb said to Angel and Leo. 'I'm sure he's got a mother somewhere who loves him.'

'Not so sure, myself,' Leo muttered to Angel. 'I'll go get us some drinks.' He stood up and headed over to the side table, where Suzanne was laying out the mugs and Thermos.

'Well, shall we make a start?' Seb asked her. Angel nodded and rummaged in her bag for her dictaphone. She saw a smile curve one corner of his mouth when she placed it on the desk in front of her.

'What?' she asked, smiling too.

'I'm just remembering the last time you interviewed me. You called me a fraud, I recall.'

She felt another deep blush burning on her face. They certainly seemed to come thick and fast whenever she was in his company.

'Oh God, Seb, let's not talk about that. Worst night of my life.'

His expression darkened. 'Yeah. I've had better myself.'

Angel fumbled with the dictaphone, waiting for the awkward moment to pass. It seemed to her there was only one real ghost in the room here, and that was a phantom Carole Beaumont.

They fell silent when Suzanne and Leo came back to join them. Leo handed Angel a mug of tea. 'Here. White, one sweetener, right?'

'Yeah. Thanks, Leo.' She took it from him, nursing it between her hands. She couldn't help noticing Seb watching the two of them, his expression inscrutable.

Angel took a long swallow of the refreshing brew and put the mug down on the desk so she could rustle through her notes. *Get me the dirt. Don't let me down…* she could hear Steve's voice at the back of her mind while she looked over her questions.

172

People expected something more personal from a profile piece than a bog-standard interview. Work, family, relationships – it had to offer the whole package. And everyone knew Sebastian Wilchester never answered personal questions. He seemed happy to cooperate with her, for some reason only he knew – but how far did she dare go?

'Look, if there's anything that makes you uncomfortable, feel free to tell me where to go,' she told Seb, seeking his gaze. 'I don't want you to answer anything that –'

'It's fine, Angel,' he interrupted. 'I owe you a decent piece after –'

He stopped suddenly, glancing over at Suzanne, who'd pulled up the one remaining chair and sat a little apart from them by the large window. The PA was gazing across the lot, one hand wrapped around her upper arm. She looked tired, Angel noticed, and a little sad too. Angel wondered how much she knew about that night at the premiere.

'– after you gave up your afternoon,' Seb finished weakly.

Leo just sat swirling his coffee absently next to her, not paying much attention to what was going on. He'd started to rub his cheek, a habit that always worried her. When they'd been together, and later when he'd been struggling through cold turkey in the early days of AA, it had always been a sign he was trying to fight off a craving. She wished she could press his arm without the others noticing, remind him she was there.

'Ask me whatever you like, don't go easy on me. There's no Kev here this time to jump down your throat.' Seb was smiling at her again, and she found herself unconsciously twisting a strand of hair around her finger. What was it he'd said about poker earlier? 'I promise I'll do my best to answer any questions.' His gaze darted across her face. 'I trust you, Angel.'

Angel felt her heart jump and her muscles clench alarmingly as he said those words, 'I trust you.' She hadn't realised how much she'd needed to hear them.

'Um,' she said, trying to gather her thoughts. 'That's – thanks.'

She'd done her research this time, and she knew where the difficult areas lay. His composer father's early death, his mother the actress's drug overdose twelve years ago, Carole's – well, anything to do with Carole, it seemed.

'Erm, this isn't a question, really, but ReelKids – do you mind me mentioning it in my piece? Suzanne said you liked to keep your involvement quiet.'

He shrugged. 'I like to play it down if I can. You saw what that teacher, Miss Simons, was like. It does tend to distract from the main purpose of the charity. Then again, the fact that Carole and I are founders and directors is a matter of public record so it's not exactly secret. I'm sure I can leave it to your discretion.'

Flustered, Angel skimmed through her notes, wondering where to begin.

It wasn't a question on her list, but he'd sparked her curiosity with something he'd said earlier. Well, she guessed it was as good a starting point as any.

'You said earlier cigar smoke reminded you of Christmas.'

'That's right.'

'Your father used to smoke them?'

'No, not exactly.' He smiled. 'My nanny.'

'Your… you had a nanny?'

'My childhood wasn't exactly what you'd call ordinary, Angel, as the son of what the press like to call "showbiz royalty".'

'How do you mean?'

'Well, alright, here's an example: do you remember what you got for your sixth birthday?'

'Me?' She frowned. 'God, I don't remember that far… no, wait, I do!' She almost yipped when a memory came surging back. 'It was this, well, it was like a spy kit. My parents made it up for me because they knew I loved making secret codes, solving mysteries and things.' She coloured slightly. 'Silly, I know.'

His eyes crinkled, amused by her sudden excitement. 'Not silly at all. Your parents obviously put a lot of thought into a gift you'd like.' He paused to take a sip of the coffee Suzanne had placed in front of him. 'I got a tiger.'

'You got a… sorry, can you say that again?'

'A real tiger. For my sixth birthday. My mother bought him for me as a pet.'

She shook her head in disbelief. 'Bloody hell, Seb. Was he… safe?'

'Well, Blaze was a wild animal at heart, so probably not. But he was very tame, like a big lazy cat. We had some good times together.'

'Blaze…' Something clicked. 'Like Tigerblaze.'

'That's right.' A smile illuminated his handsome face. 'In memory of an old friend.'

'And your nanny. Is she still around?'

'Moira. Yes, she's retired now, living in Somerset. An incredible woman. She brought me up, really. Closest thing I had to a mother.' His brow darkened again with some unpleasant memory.

Angel looked down at her notes, but there was nothing there to help her. Tigers, nannies… none of this had turned up in her research. She was on her own. 'Um… so what about Abigail Carruthers? I mean, your actual mother. Was she away a lot? Filming commitments, perhaps?' she asked.

He winced with some powerful emotion. 'Seb,' she heard Suzanne say from the window in a low voice. 'Are you sure you're okay to talk about this?'

'I'm sorry,' Angel said. 'I didn't mean to stir up… anything. If you'd rather not…'

'No,' Seb said with an effort, rubbing his temples with his fingertips. 'I promised I'd answer. I should be able to talk about this with you.'

Odd thing to say. With her? Why with her?

'My mother was… detached, shall we say.' He continued to press his head between his fingers, not meeting her eyes. 'The day I got Blaze, she gave me a big hug, wished me a happy birthday and then took a bucketload of Valium and went to bed for three days. That was her all over: a big gesture, then she'd disappear. I got used to it. And Moira was always there, steady as a rock, to keep me sane.'

Angel's pen hovered motionless over her pad while she listened, fascinated.

'From the age of about five, she demanded I stopped calling her "Mother", as she'd taught me to do until then, and insisted I call her by her name, Abigail,' he continued, his tone bleak. 'She thought it made her sound old, you see. She was obsessed with ageing. The loss of her beauty. Her career.'

'Seb…' Suzanne voiced a soft warning, but he ignored her.

'By the time she died it didn't really matter what I called her. She hardly seemed like my mother at all by then.' His voice dropped as with an effort he forced himself to meet Angel's eyes. 'At the end… at the end she was a monster, Angel, emotionally and physically. Scarred by cosmetic surgery, drugs and bitter memories. I know she loved me, in her way, but it wasn't enough to – to fix her.' He made a choking noise that might have been a stifled sob, looked down at the desk while he tried to recover his composure.

Angel's eyes were wide with shock. Even Leo was paying attention now, staring at Seb in disbelief.

'And… your father?' she heard herself say, almost in a whisper.

He gave a grim snort of laughter. 'It was life and fame that made my mother a monster. My father, he was different.' His mouth set in a hard line. 'That bastard was born one.'

His eyes were fierce, locked hard into Angel's. He spoke quickly, as if, once begun, he felt compelled to get his story out. 'My parents were married for about eight years, until my father's death at forty-two. Nearly every night for eight years, Hugo Wilchester would go to bed drunk and cursing his life.' His features were twitching with emotion when he delivered the next sentence. 'And every night before he went to bed… every night he'd take this antique cane he kept above the wardrobe in their room, hand-carved bamboo – funny how you remember the little details. And he'd thrash my mother until she screamed. On rare occasions, me too, but always Abigail, always. I don't think he could sleep until he'd heard those screams. Like some sick, hellish lullaby. And the more she screamed, the harder he beat her, cursing her for the loss of her looks, the string of lovers he accused her of having – any bastard thing he could think of.'

Suzanne had approached him from behind and laid a gentle hand on his shoulder. 'That's enough, Seb. Time to take a break.'

But he pushed her away with an impatient motion, unable to stop until the full story had tumbled out of him.

'One day when I was about seven years old, Moira had put me to bed. She usually stayed with me until I was asleep and read to me, but that evening she couldn't stay, or I'd woken up again after she went to bed. I forget which it was. I woke to Abigail's screams. Nothing new. So I sobbed and I put the pillow over my ears like I always did, but I could still hear my mother screaming, swearing to Hugo he'd kill her this time if he didn't stop, and him telling her he hoped he did. That's when I knew it was time to grow up.'

He stopped, rested his head on his hands and blinked back tears. Angel met Suzanne's eyes helplessly, but it seemed Seb wouldn't, or couldn't, stop.

'So I sneaked down to the phone and I called the police,' he said, his voice cracking. 'I told them my father was trying to kill my mother. I begged them to come and help her. When they came –' he gasped out a broken sob '– when they came I heard the officer ask Abigail what she'd done wrong. To provoke him. Because she must have done *something*. Ha! Then they went away. Left her there with him to scream him to sleep.'

His eyes were soaking wet and blazing with anger as they met hers. 'The happiest day of my childhood was the day that bastard finally succeeded in drinking himself to death.'

'Jesus *Christ*, Seb,' Angel whispered, appalled. 'I – I had no idea. Oh God, I never would have... I didn't know. I honestly didn't know.'

'No. Why would you? At Home with the Wilchesters wasn't exactly a *Hello* magazine centre spread.'

'Interview's over, I think,' Suzanne said in a quiet voice, patting Seb's shoulder. He reached up brokenly and grasped her hand for support.

'Mr Wilchester.' Leo broke his silence. He was looking at Seb with sympathy in his eyes. 'If you can overlook the fact I've been the most insufferable prick to you all day, I'd be proud if you would agree to shake my hand. You've reminded me of – something. I'd like to thank you for the lesson.'

Seb managed a weak smile as he took the hand Leo offered. 'Thanks, Courtenay – Leo.'

'I don't think we'll stay for the kids' screening,' Leo said, looking over at Angel, who was fiddling with her dictaphone as she tried to wrestle her emotions back under control. 'Not after... well, I think it's best we leave now.'

Suzanne nodded. 'Miss Simons will be disappointed, but... we understand.'

'Come on, Ginge,' he said, standing. 'Time to go.' He held out his hand to help her to her feet and she grabbed it in a half-daze.

'Angel.' Seb looked up at her as she rose to leave. 'Before you go.'

'Yes, Seb?' Her voice sounded strange to her when she answered: hoarse and cracked.

'I just wanted to say – I don't regret it if you don't.' He shot her a look full of meaning. 'I know I should, but – well, I don't. I thought you should know.'

Suzanne looked across at her, puzzled. Probably wondering if he meant the interview, Angel thought: wishing she'd done Kev's job better and stopped him spilling so much personal information to the press.

But Angel knew better. She remembered her words to him the last time they'd ended an interview. *'If you want to know whether I regret the time we spent together, then I don't know how to answer you.'*

The honey trap.

Chapter 18

'Hey! Wait up a sec!'

Angel and Leo turned to see Suzanne, racing after them as they walked across the tarmac away from the Tigerblaze office building.

They stopped to let her catch up.

'Sorry. He just – wanted me to give you – these,' she panted, holding out four red cards. 'He forgot before. I think he was a bit – distracted, after the interview and everything.'

Leo took them from her and read what was printed on them, then raised a questioning eyebrow.

'Tickets to Hollywood Dreams? What's that?'

'It's a fundraising gala for ReelKids next month. Seb thought you might like to go, since you're not able to stay for the screening. There's a ticket each and two for plus ones, if you've got anyone you'd like to bring.'

'Oh. That's a nice thought. Thank him for us, will you?'

Suzanne turned to Angel with a worried look. 'Are you going to print all that, what he told you in there? About his dad and everything?'

'I… don't know, Suzanne. I'll have to turn something in to my editor, obviously. But I will try to keep out anything that could cause him or Carole pain. You can have my promise on it.'

The PA shot her a smile of trust and gratitude. 'Thank you. I don't know why he told you all that, I honestly don't. I've never heard him open up like that to press before – not to anyone, really. He's been working too hard, I think. The stress has started to get to him. And he misses Carole.'

Angel gave an absent nod. She looked up the building to what she thought must be Seb's office window. 'Yes. That must be it.'

'Anyway, thanks for coming. It's been a funny day, hasn't it? But it's been lovely meeting you both.' She beamed at them, and Angel could tell she really meant it. Suzanne seemed to be someone whose heart was firmly on her sleeve at all times.

'Well that was definitely in the top five strangest afternoons I've ever spent,' Leo said as they headed towards the exit. 'Poor Wilchester. I never realised… God, I've been such a prick.'

'I won't argue with that,' Angel said, nodding. 'But you did alright in the end. Apologising to him and everything.'

'Yeah.' Leo scowled at the floor. 'I didn't just mean that.' He turned to her. 'Look, Ginge, do you mind if I cry off the pub tonight? I think there's a meeting I need to be in.'

'Really, Leo?' She grabbed his arm and gave it an affectionate hug. 'I can honestly say I've never been happier to be stood up. What's brought this on?'

'Would've thought it was obvious,' he mumbled. 'I mean, I know I'm not Hugo Wilchester, but we've got one thing in common. I made life miserable for the people I loved for years before I sobered up. The number of nights you must've spent crying because of me. I don't want to be what Wilchester was talking about – a monster, whose death would be the happiest moment of my own son's life.' His eyes flamed with determination. 'I never want to get back on that stuff, Angel – never.'

'You could never do what that bastard did, Leo,' she said fervently. 'You don't have it in you. But I'm glad you're going back. I really am.' She squeezed his arm again, genuinely happy for the first time in ages.

181

'So are you going to this, then?' Leo asked, changing the subject as he handed her the tickets to the ReelKids fundraiser.

'Yeah, I guess. Probably stag, though. Doubt I can get a date that isn't furnished from Em's little black book, and we both know how that's likely to look.' She grimaced, thinking of Emily's usual taste in men.

Leo shot her a suspicious glance. 'You're not going just so you can see him again, are you?'

'What, Seb? I hadn't really thought about it.' The lie burned her tongue, and quite possibly her pants. She wondered who she was trying to kid – Leo or herself. 'Anyway, I thought all was forgiven and you were best mates now. You shook hands. That's boy for hugging, isn't it?'

Leo shrugged. 'I'm willing to admit I may have been too hard on him. He's had a rough time of it, poor bugger. I thought he was just some spoilt little rich boy with the usual massive sense of entitlement, but no kid should have to go through what he did. Have to say, he seems pretty well adjusted, all things considered.' He stopped walking and turned to look at her. 'But what I said before still stands, Angel. He's bad for you. He's got a wife and you're not her. And he's probably got some serious issues under that chiselled face of his, after what his old man put him through. Don't forget what you promised me. Stay well away.'

It was true, Seb's revelations hadn't really changed anything. But she wondered why he'd shared so much, in front of Leo too. And he'd said he trusted her. And that he didn't regret their night together…

With her head spinning and feet throbbing, she hobbled away from the Tigerblaze lot.

***

As she went through her notes in the flat later that night, Angel struggled to work out what she should write about for her profile

182

piece. She had a headline she wasn't particularly happy with, 'The Reluctant Celebrity' – sounded like a 1970s Mills & Boon, but it was the best she could do for now. But when she tried to make an outline out of her scribbled shorthand her head reeled.

Seb had said he trusted her – what did he mean? Did he expect her to quit her job, not turn in the piece? Or did he want her to publish everything he'd told her about his family – some sort of catharsis – like balm on a troubled soul?

She started making a list of everything she wanted to include. As Seb had said, his role as director of ReelKids was a matter of public record. Still, she knew he liked to play it down when he could. The fact he was one of the industry professionals who ran workshops for the charity, on the other hand... she added it to the list. Yes, that was good. She'd watched him closely while he'd worked with the kids and there was lots of detail she could include. It would give people an insight into how he worked, and his interests outside his own filmmaking. Steve would like that.

Then she looked again at the notes she'd made during the Q&A. Okay, so there was the pet tiger. That was fine, and a nice little anecdote about how the studio got its name. She jotted it down. Oh, and the office ghost, that could go in. She smiled when she remembered the cigar-smoke smell of his office, inhaling deeply as if the scent still hung in the air.

What else? The nanny, Moira, he was so close to, and her cigar on Christmas Day. Yes, that could go in too.

She hesitated for a moment, then jotted down 'mother's obsession with fading youth'.

She didn't know how Seb would feel about that, but she had to give Steve something. Abigail Carruthers was a big star in her own right, so that little nugget would be a draw for readers.

But it wasn't enough. 'Get me the dirt,' Steve had said. An actress's obsession with her looks was hardly that – it was bordering on the bleeding obvious. She needed something else.

She hesitated even longer before adding 'Hugo Wilchester –

alcoholic' to the list, wincing when she remembered Seb's damp eyes while he'd shared his memories of his monstrous father.

That was all. The abuse, the bamboo cane, the phone call to the police – that could stay out. Steve would never know it, and nor would the reading public.

'Hiya. Genius burning?' Emily asked as she came in.

'Not exactly. It's hard to work out what I should put in and what I should leave out.'

Emily shrugged. 'Put it all in. He knew it was an interview when he told you, didn't he? And it was him who asked you there. Seems like he wants it publishing.'

Angel had filled her friend in on the day's events earlier in the evening. Unlike Leo, though, the tale of Seb Wilchester's tortured past didn't seem to inspire any more kindly feelings in Emily.

'If his dad was such a dick to his mum, you'd think he'd think twice about screwing up his own wife's life,' she'd commented darkly, showing no mercy to a chicken she was stuffing for their dinner that evening.

'So you don't feel even a little bit sorry for him?' Angel had asked.

'Maybe. But it's not an excuse.'

'Poor bastard, though. No one should go through that.'

In reply, Emily had given a fake cough that sounded very like 'salvation complex'. 'Not everyone's a mangy cat you can nurse back to health, Ange,' she'd said, nodding over at Groucho asleep on a chair.

Maybe Em had been right. She was doing it again, everything that had doomed her relationship with Leo.

'Oh, I know what I wanted to ask you!' Angel suddenly remembered the fundraiser tickets in her record bag. 'Are you doing anything on the 22nd, Em? Wondered if you wanted to come to this Hollywood Dreams thing with me. Fancy dress, all for a good cause. Come on, it'll be a laugh.'

'Are you asking me out, Ange?'

'Ha! Yeah, you know you'd love a piece of me. Well, come on, how about it? Girly night out?'

Emily coloured slightly, something Angel couldn't remember seeing her do in years. 'Actually, I, er, I've got a date that night.'

'Danny?'

'No.' Her friend seemed to be examining her feet with great care. 'Actually, Ange, it's… it's Leo. He rang me earlier to ask if I'd go with him. As his date – not just mates, you know? And I said I would.' Emily looked up, seeking Angel's eyes. 'Sorry. I should've told you before. You don't mind, do you? It won't be weird or anything?'

'Wow, Em, that's – that's brilliant news!' Angel stood up and flung her arms around her friend in genuine pleasure. 'I can honestly say I couldn't be happier to let you have my sloppy seconds. What was it made you change your mind in the end?'

Emily returned her friend's hug. 'You might think I'm a stubborn old mare, but I do listen to you, you know. I've been thinking about what you said that night – that we'd go well together. And you're right. I've been pushing him away, afraid of I don't know what. Liking him too much, I guess, and of ruining our friendship if it all went tits-up. But if there's a shot at happiness, why not grab for it? Life's too short, carpe diem, and other meaningless clichéd bollocks of that kind.'

'That's so great, sweetie. I don't want to speak too soon and jinx everything but I'm sure it's the right thing, giving it a go. Did he tell you he was going to his AA meeting tonight?'

'Yes. I said I'd go out with him on the condition he started going back to them regularly. Was pretty thrilled when he told me he was already on his way.'

Angel drew out a happy sigh. Her own life was as complicated as ever, but at least for Emily and Leo things seemed to be heading in the right direction.

***

It was a few days later when Steve threw a copy of the *Investigator*'s showbiz supplement down on her desk, open at her profile with Seb.

'Good piece, that, Blackthorne,' he growled, leaning over her and resting a rough hand on her shoulder. She could smell the familiar scent of nicotine and mint on his breath. Another attempt to quit the fags seemed to have bitten the dust. Probably explained his relative good mood.

'I don't know how you got all that out of him about his mam and dad. Never known Wilchester talk about his childhood in an interview before. Your, er, charms seem to have quite an effect on him, Princess. And yes, that was a euphemism for your tits, by the way.'

'Thanks, Steve, glad you approve. Of the piece and my tits.' She scanned the article with an anxious eye, trying to remember exactly what she'd written.

There it was in unalterable black and white: ReelKids, pet tigers, nannies, alcoholism, but nothing about the domestic abuse he and his mother had lived through. She wondered if Seb had read it yet, how it looked through his eyes. He'd told her he trusted her. Would he be angry when he saw what had been printed? Had she said too much?

'You know, I've been editor here long enough to remember the day we covered Wilchester Senior's death,' Steve told her, drawing up a chair. Now the cravings were gone he was evidently in the mood to be chatty. 'I remember Carruthers, all stretched skin and collagen, and your boyfriend, pale little bugger of seven or eight, standing out in front of their big house appealing for privacy at a difficult time – the usual spiel. Blamed it on an undiagnosed heart defect. No one mentioned the booze. Don't know how they managed to keep it quiet all those years.'

'Is that right?' Angel wasn't really listening. She'd been distracted by one of Leo's photos, an arty black-and-white shot of Seb in front of the Tigerblaze building's Doric porch pillars.

The director was looking moodily into the distance with that determined expression on his face, the same one she'd seen while they'd worked together to help Carole the night of the premiere. His curls were swept back by the wind and he looked more like an underwear model than ever. Angel felt her stomach clench as she took in the open-necked shirt showing his exposed throat, the glittering eyes, the compressed line of his lips. It was so hard to look at them without imagining them pressed against hers…

'Blackthorne. Did you hear me?'

'Hmmm?' She turned to Steve. 'Sorry, did you say something?'

'Hellfire, love, you're not with it today, are you? I said I want your review of that screener DVD we got sent yesterday by 2pm. You know, the horror with the clown thing on the cover? Get a shift on, eh?'

She shuddered. Eurghh. Clowns. She hated clowns. Steve hadn't been kidding when he'd told her this job wasn't all glamour. About ninety per cent of the films she was invited to review were one-star B-movies.

'Yep. On it, boss.'

'Make sure you are. And well done, lass.' He gave her shoulder another satisfied pat and wandered back towards his office. She could see resentful eyes turned towards her from other desks. She'd have to be deaf not to have noticed the bitchy comments around the office. The rumours mentioned by Kev that afternoon at Tigerblaze were spreading like melted gossip butter.

Savannah's eyes were red and swollen when she arrived at her desk, twenty minutes late for work. 'Morning. Sorry I'm late,' the intern muttered. She fumbled the mouse to wake up her computer.

'No problem.' Angel shot her a look of concern. 'Hey, everything okay, Sav? You look knackered.'

'Yeah, I guess.' She hesitated. 'Okay, no, that's a lie. Cal broke up with me last night.'

'*What?*'

Savannah turned to Angel with a watery smile. 'Oh, no need to pretend you're surprised. I know everyone in the office knew about us. I'm not thick, you know, Ange. Just blonde.'

'That wasn't I-didn't-know surprise. It was what-an-idiot surprise. Oh God, Sav! I'm so sorry.' Angel reached out and patted the girl's hand. 'Let me get you a cuppa. Not much help, I know, but tea and sympathy are the best I can offer right now.'

As she stood in the kitchen, watching the yellow wisps of fragrant jasmine and ginger infusing into Savannah's favourite herbal tea, she remembered what was sitting in her desk drawer.

'Hey, I know what might make you feel better. Are you doing anything on the 22nd?' she asked as she put the steaming mug down on Savannah's desk. 'I've got a spare ticket for this Hollywood Dreams thing. It's a fundraising event for that charity, ReelKids. Movie-themed fancy dress.'

She fished it from her drawer and held it out to Savannah with a smile. 'Yours if you want it.'

Savannah grabbed at the ticket as if it had been issued by Willy Wonka. 'Oh my God, Ange, where did you get this?' Her still-damp eyes were wide with surprise and excitement.

Angel responded with a puzzled frown. 'Wilchester's PA gave it to me when I went to Tigerblaze for that profile piece. Why? I didn't realise it was a big deal.'

'Are you kidding? These things are like gold dust! The ReelKids fundraisers aren't exactly sausage rolls in a pub function room, you know. They're really glitzy. Packed with big names.'

'Oh.' Suddenly the whole thing seemed much less appealing.

Savannah threw her arms around Angel, something she'd never done before. 'Thanks so much, this is brilliant! We'll have a great time!'

Okay, no backing out now, then…

'Angel…' Savannah had fixed her with a quizzical look. 'Can I ask you something personal?'

Something personal. That never heralded anything good. Angel gave what she hoped was a careless laugh. 'Why do I get the impression you're going to ask me anyway?'

'It's just… Sebastian Wilchester. He's supposedly got this perfect marriage, and yet he spent the night with you at that hotel. And no offence, but you don't exactly seem like the femme-fatale type. And then you'd think he'd hate you for publishing the story, but instead he gives you an exclusive interview. The man who hardly ever gives interviews. And then he invites you to his studio to do a profile piece, tells you things about his family he's never shared with the press before. Gives you tickets to a big charity fundraiser.'

Angel's mouth had set into a compressed line. 'Is this leading to a question, Savannah?'

'I guess I was just curious to know… are you and Wilchester, you know, involved?'

'Involved?' Angel coloured. 'No, Sav. We're not involved, what-ever that means. Just two professionals occasionally forced to work together. The honey trap thing… well, I don't know why he forgave me for that, if he did. But he's got films to promote, I've got films to review. That's just the way it is.'

'But he'd like you to be, wouldn't he? Involved, I mean?' Savannah smiled a coy little smile. 'He must like you. I bet he does.'

'I'd be lying if I said I didn't wonder sometimes,' she confided with a sigh, meeting Savannah's eyes. 'But the truth is, everything I've seen of Seb Wilchester, everything I know about him, screams out that he loves his wife. And if he likes me, it can't be as anything more than… something I'd never be willing to become. That's the bottom line.'

'Oh.' Savannah reached out and covered Angel's hand with hers, eyeing the photo of Seb, in sexy black and white, in the still-open showbiz supplement on her friend's desk. 'That's sort of sad, isn't it? I wish I was as strong as you, Angel. I don't think I could help myself. I mean, he's so talented and handsome and everything…'

'I'm no stronger than you or anyone else really, Sav. I just know what I owe to myself. I won't be someone's bit on the side, no matter how… well. Let's not get into that.'

She jumped when she heard her phone buzz. Picking it up from her desk, she opened the new message. It was only two words:

Thank you.

'Sorry,' she said absently to Savannah, dismissing the text. 'Just Leo.' Another lie. They seemed to fall from her easily these days. She didn't recognise the number, although the last three digits looked familiar. But she knew there was only one person it could be from.

Seb.

She understood now. The profile piece hadn't been a reward for helping Carole, or a way to pay off a debt for keeping back the story about her suicide attempt.

It had been a test. And he wanted to tell her she'd passed.

Chapter 19

Savannah was almost vibrating with excitement as she and Angel shared a cab to the ReelKids fundraiser a few weeks later. She ran her hands down her costume anxiously.

'I don't know why I wore this,' she said to Angel. 'I bet there'll be loads of Marilyns.'

'Probably. But there won't be any who fit the part as well as you, Sav, trust me.'

Savannah made the perfect Marilyn. She had the hourglass curves, the pout, the perfect skin and she'd had her blonde hair cut and styled especially for the occasion. The fact she was willing to sacrifice her shoulder-length locks proved how much she'd invested in this event. With the new short style, she could almost have passed for Carole Beaumont's younger sister.

Her costume was a pretty original one, too. Angel would be willing to bet every other Marilyn there would be *Seven Year Itch* Marilyn, she of the billowing white dress and the grate, whereas Savannah was *Some Like It Hot* Marilyn, in a figure-hugging black silk dress with beaded fringe skirt, white faux-fur wrap and long pearls that screamed flapper chic.

'Who did you say you were supposed to be again?' Savannah asked, looking Angel up and down. She was dressed in a modest black trouser suit and bow tie, figure-hugging but not at all revealing. A plastic revolver was tucked into the waistband of her trousers. That had been the only part of her costume she'd bought for the occasion. Everything else was an Emily loan, apart from the tie, which had been furnished by Leo. She'd maxed out her clothing budget for the year recently, so this was fashion on the cheap.

Savannah examined her with a puzzled frown. 'Oh, I know! Chaplin, isn't it?'

She giggled as Angel looked down at her costume with a hurt expression. 'Oh come on, Ange, I'm only teasing. I know who you are. You're James Bond, right? But like a lady Bond. It's very you; really original. And you look great, promise. Classy.'

'Thanks,' Angel said, grinning. It wasn't often Savannah made jokes. Tonight seemed to be doing a good job so far of putting Cal out of her mind.

She'd offered seats in their cab to her other two friends, but Leo had told her he and Emily wanted to make their own way there. 'No offence, Ginge, but if we go with you then that's just another mates' night out. We do those all the time. This has to be different. It's our first date and I want it to be exactly that: a date. Just us two, you know?'

'Happy to be abandoned, lover boy,' she'd replied. 'I just hope you'll find time to have a few drinks with me before you start getting off with each other in a corner.'

Angel spotted the red carpet as their cab slunk up to the hotel where the event was being held. God, she hated the sight of them. They reminded her of that night, that awful night, when Carole Beaumont's life had hovered on a knife edge.

She felt a moment's guilt, seeing the guests answering questions from reporters, before she remembered she wasn't here for work. Sarah's replacement, the new temporary showbiz editor, would be around somewhere with a dictaphone and a simper getting the quotes in for Steve.

The evening began with a champagne reception in a bar area hung all around with red velvet curtains, two giant Oscar statuettes flanking the entrance. A row of Walk of Fame stars led the way to the bar, where complimentary glasses of champagne, each with half a strawberry submerged at the bottom of the flute, waited for them.

Looking around the throng of people, dressed as everyone from Indiana Jones to Nosferatu, Angel spied Emily and Leo near the bar, chatting animatedly. That had to be a good sign. She waved to them.

Emily beckoned her and Savannah over. She grabbed a couple of champagnes off the bar for them and handed them over

'Nice jacket,' she said, running her eyes down the ensemble she'd lent Angel for the evening. 'Could swear it looks familiar.'

'Meh. Looks better on me.'

'Bloody cheek!' Emily elbowed her friend in the ribs.

'Alright, Ginge?' Leo said, sipping from a champagne flute of orange juice. 'Dicky bow suits you. Stan Laurel, is it?'

'Don't you start.'

'Hiya, Norma Jean. Looking good.' Leo nodded at Savannah, his *Investigator* colleague, who beamed back at him. 'Oh, this is Emily, my – er, our friend.'

'Nice to meet you.' Savannah and Emily exchanged nods.

'So who are you, then?' Angel asked Leo. He was wearing a plain charcoal suit, white shirt and tie.

'All in the props, Ginge,' he replied, pulling out a black umbrella from under the bar and slinging it over his shoulder.

Angel gave a puzzled frown. 'Mary Poppins on her way to a business meeting?'

'Funny girl. I think it's pretty clear to those of us who know our films that I'm *Singin' in the Rain* Gene Kelly. But I wouldn't expect you to realise that.'

'You mean that film I made you watch when we were going out?'

'Yep.'

'That you hated?'

'Yep.'

'And fell asleep during?'

'The very same.'

'Shoddy, mate, very shoddy.'

She turned to Emily.

'Don't know why you agreed to go out with the lazy sod, Em. At least you made the effort, though.'

Emily was wearing a low-cut black halter top, black shorts, stockings and suspenders, showing off her curves and shapely legs to perfection. A bobbed wig and bowler hat finished her Sally Bowles costume. It was certainly having the desired effect. Leo couldn't keep his eyes off her.

'I mean, if you can't use a fancy-dress party as an excuse to get all dolled up as a cabaret-singing 1930s prostitute, when can you? That's what I always say,' Angel said with a grin.

'Oh, is it fancy dress?' Emily asked in mock surprise. 'This is just my usual Friday night clubbing gear.'

Angel giggled. 'To be honest, I'd expected you to be another Marilyn.'

'Nah, too easy.' Emily downed the dregs of her champagne and crushed the half strawberry between her teeth. 'For me, I mean,' she said to Savannah, who looked a little downcast at this slight on her costume choice. 'The hair, you know? I'm all blonde and curly under this wig. To be honest, it was either Marilyn, Shirley Temple or Harpo Marx, and I didn't think any of them were good enough to impress my date.'

'Thanks, Em.' Leo shot her a fond smile. 'And, by the way, please don't do that thing with the strawberry again,' he said, lowering his voice and bringing his mouth close to her ear. 'Not sure I can stand that and the suspenders.'

She giggled. 'Turning you on, lover?'

'Always.'

Angel cleared her throat loudly. 'Ahem, guys. Other people here. Enough with the sex-strawberry talk.'

Leo grinned. 'Sorry, Ginge. What were we talking about? Oh yeah. Costumes. Have to say, if there's a prize, none of us can compete with that guy over there.'

He pointed out a figure at the other end of the bar. Angel followed his gaze and laughed. A man in just his underwear, covered in gold body paint, had come as an Oscar. He was sipping his champagne calmly, as if this was just another night out to him.

'Oh my God! That's George Seward!' Savannah grabbed Angel's arm in excitement. 'You know, that actor from all those period dramas. Oh, I love him!'

Angel squinted at the gold man and realised Savannah was right. It was the young actor she'd met briefly the night of the film premiere, who'd played the lead in *The Milkman Cometh*. She wondered if his mum was hanging around somewhere too. Possibly dressed as a Golden Globe.

Savannah was scanning the room, seeing if she could spot any more celebrities. 'Oh, there's that soap-opera actor, the one who was arrested for drink-driving last month! And him from that new fantasy series on Sky. Oh!' She gripped Angel's arm tighter with a quick intake of breath. 'Oh my God! Isn't that Nicolas Cage?' she whispered, pointing to a man in a sharp suit drinking champagne in the corner.

Angel laughed. 'Okay, calm down, film groupie. That's just Kev, the Tigerblaze PR guy.'

'Oh. He's very handsome, though,' Savannah breathed, apparently not too disappointed, as she examined Kev more carefully. He caught her eye and smiled. It seemed he could remove his perma-scowl fast enough when a pretty girl was in the equation. He even managed to exchange a cool nod with Angel and Leo. The champagne must be going to his head.

Angel shook her head at her friend in disbelief. Cal had been no looker, but Kev? Seriously?

'Honestly, Sav, no offence, but your taste in men is appalling.'

But even while she teased Savannah, she could feel her heart rate speeding up. If Kev was here, that meant Seb must be somewhere about. She wondered where he was, if he would come and speak to her.

She cast a cursory glance around the room. It was thronged with people, but she felt pretty certain Seb wasn't one of them. She felt she'd know, somehow, if he was close by.

The master of ceremonies, a convincing Clark Gable lookalike in a cravat and white waistcoat, hemmed loudly into a microphone at one end of the room.

'Ladies and gentlemen, if you'd like to make your way into the adjoining ballroom and find your places, dinner will shortly be served.'

By the entrance to the ballroom, Angel scanned the list of guests to find their names. There they were, seated all four together on a table to themselves near the back: 'Mr Leo Courtenay and Guest, Miss Angel Blackthorne and Guest'. She scanned the list for Seb's name, but the crowd began to jostle her into the ballroom before she could find it.

He would be there, wouldn't he? She felt a sudden jolt in her stomach as she realised the tickets might have been nothing more than a way to thank her for the interest she'd shown in ReelKids. Perhaps Kev wasn't there with Seb. Perhaps he was there instead of him, representing Tigerblaze.

It all made sense now. Why would Seb be at a social event when his wife was still in rehab? *Silly girl, Angel. Assuming he'd arranged the tickets so he could see you again.*

Savannah gripped her arm again while they made their way to their table, letting out an appreciative 'Ooooh!' as she drank in the impressive decor. Plush red and black velvet was everywhere, with dripping teardrop-beaded chandeliers extending from the ceiling to brush the tops of the round tables laid out for groups of six. Black curtains set with stardust fairy lights adorned the walls. At the front of the room was a stage area, currently occupied by a huge replica of the Hollywood sign.

As Angel took her seat and downed the last sip of her second glass of champagne, she could feel a headache starting, nasty little pinpricks behind her eyeballs. Bleurghh, fizzy booze. Evil stuff: it always went straight to her head. She poured herself another glass from the chilled bottle on the table.

Emily and Leo were whispering together while they took their seats opposite her. Not wanting to intrude on their date, Angel turned to Savannah.

'Enjoying it so far, Sav?'

'God, yes, it's amazing!' Savannah's eyes were huge as she looked around the room, drinking in the luxurious decor, the many celebrities she recognised. 'Thanks so much for bringing me, Ange. You're a good friend.'

Angel smiled at her. There was a time when she'd wondered if she and the young intern would ever become friends, with their very different personalities, but she was discovering she'd become rather attached to Savannah.

'Hey, isn't that –' Savannah clapped a hand to her mouth. 'Oh my God, it is!' said the muffled voice. 'Sebastian Wilchester, I can't believe it! Oh, you lucky thing, Ange. He's gorgeous…'

Angel's heart bounced into her throat as she turned to follow Savannah's gaze. Yes, there was Seb, sitting between Kev and the gold-painted George Seward two tables away. He looked thoroughly bored but incredibly sexy, Angel thought, taking in his costume.

She wondered which Hollywood legend he was supposed to be. This might be the first time she'd seen him in something other than a suit of some kind, she reflected, then blushed when she remembered that wasn't quite true. She had seen him in a lot less, just once…

He was wearing jeans and a tight white t-shirt with very short sleeves, his hair gelled and ruffled into a deliberately tousled style.

Angel tried not to let Savannah notice her eyes lingering over the bronzed, distractingly muscular arms on full display, glad at least her other two, usually uber-protective friends were too wrapped up in each other to notice her pinkening cheeks. God, she remembered those arms, solid yet so, so gentle as they'd held her astride him that night in the hotel suite, held her slightly back while he took in her naked body and moaned his appreciation...

Savannah was fanning herself as if she'd just won a beauty contest, passed Go and collected £200. 'Do you think he'll come over?' she whispered to Angel. 'You know, when he sees you? I bet he will.'

'Oh no, I doubt it...' Angel began, but Seb was already giving the lie to her flustered denial. He threw a warm smile her way when he noticed her looking over at him and stood up as if to head to their table.

Kev plucked his elbow, rose too and whispered something in his boss's ear. Seb's face tightened into a frown, but he nodded to the PR man and sank back into his seat. Angel tried to fight back the surge of disappointment as he directed his eyes away from hers, scowling down at the table.

At that moment the lights dimmed and the curtain went up on the stage ahead of her, taking her mind off Seb for the time being.

'Ladies and gentlemen, while we serve your first course, it's time to start the bidding on the ReelKids charity auction. All the lots here tonight have been donated by philanthropically minded businesses and individuals for the benefit of ReelKids, to help it continue the work it does with young people for many years to come – so please give generously!'

The lots were unbelievably indulgent and way, way out of Angel's price range. Even the cheapest, a day at Silverstone racetrack in the company of a famous comedian, went for well over £20,000.

'Jesus, who has this kind of money? You could put a deposit

on a flat for that!' Angel muttered to Emily, making a start on the dessert placed in front of her by one of the silent, sharp-suited waiters who'd glided up to their table. She tried to put a hand over her glass before he topped her up as well, but it was too late.

Oh well, rude not to really… she chased down a spoonful of sticky-toffee pudding with another mouthful of bubbles.

'Hmmm?' Emily turned away from Leo, who'd been whispering something in her ear. 'Sorry, Ange, did you want me? Hey, stop it, you!' she hissed, giggling as Leo started playfully nibbling her earlobe.

Angel pursed her lips. 'Yeesh. Get a room, you two. Honestly, young people today.'

Leo looked up from Emily's neck. 'Actually, we were just talking about that…'

'Yeah.' Emily cast a shy look over at Leo. 'We, er, were thinking we might skip coffee and cake, head back to the flat. If that's okay with you, I mean, Ange. You and Savannah can look after each other, can't you? Leo and me, we've been talking and I think we've got some catching up to do.'

Angel's face spread into a smirk. 'Ha! You're telling me you have. Go on then, off you go, you two. Have fun. And stay safe, won't you?'

Emily grinned back at her as she and Leo stood up to go, holding hands tightly. 'Thanks, Mum. We will.'

'And put some earmuffs on Groucho, will you?' Angel called after them. 'Otherwise you can pay for any therapy he'll need from whatever he happens to see or hear.'

'What was that all about?' Savannah asked. 'They seemed in a bit of a hurry.'

'Er, yeah… first date.'

'Oh.' Savannah shot her a knowing smile. 'I see, is it like that? Well, good for them.'

'Yeah,' Angel said, watching with a dreamy expression as the

199

MC announced the last lot, a milk-crate prop from *The Milkman Cometh* signed by Seb and the two leads, Carole and George. Bidding was already at £10,000. 'They've waited a long time to be together. I'm glad it worked out for them in the end; they're perfect for each other. Lucky sods.'

She was happy for Leo and Emily, of course. Happier than she'd been about anything in a long time. Happy she'd played a small part in helping it happen. But she felt sad as well, and envious, and sort of lonely.

She pinched the bridge of her nose, her worsening headache thumping her between the eyes and pushed away the half-full glass of champagne – her fourth. Or was it fifth? Her brain was starting to cloud with the noise, the crowd, the alcohol.

The meal and the auction were over now and she wished she could go home, rest her aching head on her cool, soft pillow and let herself sleep. But Emily and Leo were at the flat. She wanted to give them a few hours' alone time at least. She groaned to herself, thinking about two more hours of what apparently with some people passed for fun. A live band, some sort of Queen tribute act, had started playing now, and a few people were making their way to a dancefloor area in front of the stage.

'Hey, I'm going to the bar. You want anything?' Savannah asked with a bright smile. She'd had just as much to drink as Angel, but apparently her tiny frame hid the constitution of an ox.

'Not for me, thanks. Or, actually, a Coke or something would be nice. Something to dilute this stuff.' She waggled the half-empty champagne flute at Savannah.

Her friend smirked as she headed off. 'You old folk just can't hack it, can you?'

'Hey! I'm only five years older than you!' Angel called after her, watching Savannah wiggle her shapely backside over to the bar. 'Cheeky young whippersnapper,' she muttered, smiling to herself.

She leaned her arm on the table and rested her forehead on

200

her palm. She could feel her eyes closing. Sweet, sweet sleep… if only she could let herself give in. The pounding music kept time with the throb of her temples as she drifted into a half doze, waiting for Savannah to come back with her Coke.

Angel jerked awake when she felt a hand come to rest on her shoulder.

'Savannah?' she said, dazed. 'You've been ages, what happened?'

No. Not Savannah. That silhouette, the broad, powerful shoulders…

She looked up to see Seb Wilchester regarding her with a look of deep concern.

Chapter 20

'Seb. You're here.' Angel blinked hard, trying to focus.

'Are you okay?' His voice was gentle and she was aware of his hand still resting on her shoulder. She should probably brush it off. That's what Emily and Leo would say. But they were back at the flat, probably listening to Barry White and doing the no-pants dance by now. She shot a dazed grin up at Seb, stifling a little giggle.

'How much champagne have you had, Angel?' he asked. 'Can I get someone for you? Leo?'

She shook her head from side to side, whipping her hair about her shoulders in an effort to sober up a bit. It wasn't like she'd had enough to be fall-down drunk – well, okay, not quite. But the headache that felt like it was nutting her between the eyes was making the room's dancing disco lights into a solid, buzzy blur.

'I'm okay, Seb, really. Just a few glasses. Got a splitting headache, that's all.'

She blinked again, bringing him into soft focus. She could see one powerful arm in front of her while he leaned on the table, still staring with that worried expression into her face. His tight t-shirt really did leave nothing to the imagination.

'You're really bringing the gun show tonight,' she said, running her eyes along the sleek ripple of his muscles. Okay, so it seemed she'd definitely had enough wine to send her inhibitions on an all-expenses-paid holiday to Nowheresville. If she didn't know herself better, she'd think she was almost flirting.

'Who are you supposed to be, anyway? *Rebel Without a Cause* James Dean or *Streetcar Named Desire* Marlon Brando?'

Seb let his face loosen into a grin. 'Brando, of course. That's the first rule of fancy dress in the Wilchester book. If you can be Brando, always be Brando.'

'Couldn't agree more.'

'Bit slutty though? Cheapening myself by showing too much arm?' He gave the muscles a comical flex, making her giggle.

'View looks good from here.'

Seb laughed, deepening those gorgeous dimples. Angel remembered the last time she'd seen him, his face stained with tears while he'd struggled to tell her the story of his childhood. She was glad she could make him laugh.

'And now I have to guess who you are, don't I?' he said. 'I'm thinking someone who goes by the name Bond, James Bond? Unless you're one of the penguin waiters from *Mary Poppins* and that bulge under your jacket means you're just pleased to see me.'

Angel giggled again. She pulled out the plastic gun from the waistband of her trousers and placed it on the table. The throbbing had subsided a bit now and she was starting to feel more like herself. She put one hand on his arm, smiling up at him. 'I like you when you're funny.'

Seb cast a look of surprise down at her fingertips on his skin. Wincing, she jerked her hand away, embarrassed by what she'd just heard herself say. Okay, so it turned out her inhibitions hadn't quite gone…

'Hey, are you sure you're okay?' The note of concern had crept back into his voice. 'You seem a bit out of it, Angel. Where are your friends?'

'Well, Emily took Leo home over an hour ago. Hopefully by now they're at least at third base.'

'Leo?' Seb looked confused. 'I thought he came with you.'

'With me?' she said, looking at him with surprise. 'Seb, I told you. We're not together like that, not any more. Just friends.'

'Oh. I thought... well, you guys seemed so close that day at the studio. Sorry. I had no right to assume.'

'No. You didn't.' She pushed the bridge of her nose into her fingers again and screwed up her eyes to shut out the juddering haze of disco lighting, trying to relieve the thump-thump pounding in her brain. It was getting worse, and this conversation wasn't helping. It was all... confusing. And she had to remember Carole. Carole was his wife. Carole was ill and getting help. *Mustn't forget... mustn't let myself forget.*

'Hey, have you seen my friend Savannah anywhere, the blonde girl?' she asked. 'She went to the bar a little while ago to get me a Coke. I could really use something cool and non-alcoholic right now.'

To her surprise, she saw the corner of Seb's mouth twitch into a smirk.

'That girl dressed as Marilyn Monroe you were sat with?'

'Yes. Why, Seb? What's funny?'

'I, er, think she might have got a bit distracted.' He nodded in the direction of the bar. Angel looked over to see Savannah in her Marilyn costume, kissing passionately in the corner with a tall man in a pinstripe suit. His hands rubbed down her back as she pressed herself against him in a get-a-roomy sort of way that should really be reserved for teenagers hanging out at bus shelters.

Angel clapped one hand over her mouth. 'Oh my God! Not – Kev!'

'Afraid so,' Seb said, laughing. 'Disgraceful, isn't it? Apparently the man's just irresistible.'

'More like arrestable.' She pulled a face. 'Ouch. That girl really knows how to pick them.'

'Well, let me get you that Coke instead,' he said. 'Don't want to disturb the young lovers, do we? Then we'll see about sorting you out a taxi home.'

Angel struggled to free herself of the drowsy, headachey, half-drunk feeling in her brain while she waited for Seb to come back with her drink. What should she do? She didn't want to go back to the flat, not yet. Emily and Leo had barely had the place to themselves for an hour. But her head was killing her, Savannah had abandoned her and she wasn't sure she could face another few hours of 'Don't Stop Me Now' being sung by an out-of-tune Glaswegian in a harlequin jumpsuit who dreamed of being Freddie Mercury.

'Here you go.' Seb was back with her drink. Apparently being a world-famous film director and underpants-model hot meant getting served at bars was a very streamlined process.

'Thanks.' She took the ice-chilled liquid from him and held the glass against her hot forehead. It felt good; reviving. She rolled it across her brow, felt it cooling her and relieving the painful pulses behind her eyes.

'Drink that up and I'll sort you out a cab,' he said, drawing up a chair next to her and watching as she gulped down the Coke. 'You look like you've had enough partying for one night.'

'What a lightweight. Half a bottle of champagne and I'm practically under the table.'

'Half a bottle?' He cocked a sceptical eyebrow.

'Okay, two-thirds of a bottle.'

She looked over at him. 'But I can't go home yet, Seb. Leo and Emily… well, it's their first date. I want to give them some alone time. I'll stay a bit longer, I think. Another hour will be okay. And if Savannah's ready to leave by then we can share a taxi. It'll cost her a fortune to get back across London on her own.'

She pushed the cool glass against one temple and let her eyes fall shut, blocking out the dancing neon. If she could only stop that relentless throbbing…

'Don't be daft, you can't stay here. You look like your head's about to burst.'

Seb looked around, as if to check no one was watching them. 'Angel.'

She opened one bleary eye when she heard the soft voice he only seemed to use to say her name. Those glittering eyes, flickering over her face. This wasn't another dream, was it? This was a real thing happening right now. She had to react, be alert. She shook her head again, trying to shift the fog. Hopefully the caffeine in the Coke she'd just finished wouldn't take too long to kick in.

'Let me take you somewhere.'

She blinked hard, tried to wake up. 'Take me somewhere?'

'Yes. A place I know. I don't really want to go home yet either. The house seems so empty right now, without… with just me. No reason we can't get out of here together, is there?'

'But… just me and you?' She hesitated. 'I don't know, Seb.'

'Why, Angel?' he said. 'Just what is it you're afraid of? I hope you know I'd never… try anything. Or is it that you can only spend time with me when you're chasing a story?'

'That's unfair.'

'Is it?' He angled his face away from her, sucking in his lip in that way he had which always caused her to look away.

'Hey.' She put a hand on his arm. The pain in her head was searing now. She could barely form her thoughts and she longed to get out into the cool night air, feel the breeze against her burning cheeks.

'You told me last time I saw you that you trusted me, Seb. Though God knows I'd done bugger all to earn it. Well, I think I can return the compliment. I mean, I know you wouldn't… look, if you think it's okay then we'll go. I'd like to. And you're right, I do need to get out of here.'

It seemed strange he couldn't see what she thought must be obvious: that it wasn't him she didn't trust. It was herself.

**

Out in the open air, Angel sagged against the wall. She loosened her bow tie so it was hanging open and unfastened her top two buttons.

Seb was on the phone, sorting them out a taxi. She knew she probably shouldn't be doing this, but through the thick mist in her brain the voice of reason was having a tough time making any sort of case.

She hadn't been able to bring herself to interrupt Savannah and Kev. In the end, she'd sent a text to let her friend know she was taking off. Sav would be okay. Angel could settle her half of the taxi fare at work on Monday to make it up to her.

That was assuming she didn't go home with Kev. Was the Suitbot 2000 even programmed for sex? Angel shuddered at the unwelcome visual.

'It's on its way,' Seb said, hanging up his mobile and coming back towards her.

'I thought you'd have a driver or something, to ferry you to these places.' She hugged her arms, shivering. The tight, sparse November air was helping her headache, but Emily's light jacket wasn't doing much to keep out the chill.

'I have, but I sent him home. I'm sure he'd rather be with his wife and kids than waiting for me in the cold half the night.'

Was that all there was to it? Or would the chauffeur report back to Carole if he wound up driving Seb around with another woman?

'Here.' He took off his coat and draped it over her shoulders. 'That jacket you've got on looks as thin as paper.'

'Thanks,' she said, pulling the jacket he'd given her tight around her body. Her gaze flickered over his bare arms and thin t-shirt. 'Won't you be cold, though?'

'I'll be fine. I don't really feel it.'

Liar…

She ran her hands along the battered leather biker jacket he'd

207

wrapped around her. 'Part of your Brando costume, I'm guessing? Or are you a closet Hell's Angel?'

'Both,' he said with a laugh.

He moved closer to her, leant one arm against the wall where she was resting so he could look directly into her face. 'I like you when you're funny,' he said softly, echoing her words to him earlier. She dropped her eyes.

Blinking hard, she tried again to clear her head. At least the throbbing between her temples had started to subside.

'How are you feeling now?' he asked. The black cab he'd called for them was just pulling up by the side of the hotel. 'You look exhausted. Are you sure you wouldn't just like to go home? I'm sure your friends won't mind, if you're not feeling well.'

This was it, her last chance to back out. She could go home, crawl into her bed, rest the eyeballs that felt like they'd swollen to twice their usual size and bury her head in a soft, welcoming, fluffy pillow. She was so tired now, Emily and Leo could spend the night whooping sex noises through the walls and she probably wouldn't hear a thing.

But then Seb would think she didn't trust him. That she only wanted to be with him when there was a story on offer. Somehow she couldn't bear the thought of it. And he'd have to go back to his big house alone, to think about Carole and Hugo and Abigail, another sleepless night, probably…

'I'm fine,' she said, summoning what she hoped was a bright smile. 'My head's much better. And I'm not ready to go home, Seb, not just yet. Come on, let's get out of here.'

Angel fell into a semi-doze as the cab slunk through the London streets. She was in the back and Seb was up front with the driver, giving occasional directions. Through a drowsy haze, she wondered where they were heading. A lot of the pubs and bars would be shutting now, and he was hardly likely to take her to a noisy nightclub. A hotel? No, surely not: not after last time.

I know a place. That's what he'd said. He couldn't be taking her to his house in Kensington, could he?

'This is it. Anywhere round here,' Seb said to the cabbie as they pulled up into what looked like a row of old terraces in some dark backwater of the city. Just a few empty shops, houses whose occupants were long in bed and some big, decaying old buildings.

Angel squinted through the car window. Why would he bring her to this place? There wasn't much nightlife here unless you enjoyed getting mugged, by the look of it.

'Don't worry,' he said, smiling at her expression while he held the door open for her to get out. 'I've not brought you to spend the night in a crack den or anything.'

He fumbled in his pocket, pulled out a small key and led her towards one of the rotting buildings, its dirty white-tiled façade tinted orange in the streetlight glow. There was a large arched porch over a red door. Seb unlocked it and she followed him along a corridor with exposed brick walls, feeling like someone in a dream. Everything seemed too big, overexposed and a ringing sound like an old GPO telephone was assaulting her brain via her ears.

He ushered her through another door and flicked a switch by the side to illuminate the room they'd just entered.

'Jesus, Seb!'

She was in a high-ceilinged, teal auditorium. Five rows of velvet-upholstered seats were laid out in front of a cinema screen, with an old-style projector window set into the top of the tall wall. There was even a pit at the front for an organ. The back half of the room and a balcony area above were still in a state of near-decay, but the front looked just as it must have done before the war.

'Is it… yours?' she asked.

'Yes. The Hippodrome. Built in 1926, just in time to bring *The Jazz Singer* to London audiences. I bought it last year when it was in danger of demolition. Thought it would be something ReelKids could use in future, if I could get it in a decent enough state. But for now it's just a bit of a den, really. I come here to screen rushes sometimes, and when I want to get out of the house.'

'Bloody hell, Seb,' Angel muttered, looking around the old cinema. 'You know, other men have garden sheds...'

'You like it, don't you? I knew you would.'

'How did you know I would?' she asked, smiling.

'I don't know. Maybe because I do.'

He turned away from her, tanned cheeks flushing when he realised what he'd said.

'Hey. Come see this.' He nodded towards a door above the balcony, to the right of the projector window.

'What is it?' she asked, following him up an old, recently restored staircase to the second level.

'The projection room,' he said, eyes shining with boyish enthusiasm. 'Can't wait to see your face.'

He showed her into a small tiled room where a large 1940s two-reel projector peeped through the window, ready to show the latest John Wayne or Judy Garland blockbuster. Against the back wall were shelves upon shelves of old film reels in aluminium cases, each labelled with the name of a different movie – from the 1920s through to the '80s.

'Oh my God!' She touched a reel gently with one finger. 'Oh my God, Seb! These are old... some aren't even in print any more.' Drawing her hand back, she lowered her voice to a reverent whisper. 'They must be worth a fortune. Are they really all yours?'

'They are now. Some I've collected myself, and some that belonged to Abigail. She was a collector too, before... well, you know, before.'

'This is amazing,' she muttered, scanning the rows of silver cases. She smiled as she thought of something. 'Reminds me of that bit in *Beauty and the Beast*.'

'What, Cocteau?' Seb looked impressed.

Angel gave an embarrassed laugh. 'Er, no. Disney.'

'The cartoon? With the dog-bear thing?'

'Beast.'

'Beast. Right.' One corner of his mouth twitched into a half-smile. 'And that's me, is it?'

She looked at the bare board floor, trying not to laugh. 'I can't help thinking of it. It's just there's this library, with all the books Belle could ever imagine. It's incredible. The beast shows it to her and she's sort of...'

'...blown away. I know, Angel. I love that bit.'

She let out a dizzy giggle. 'Really, Mr Director? A kids' film? Surely not.'

'A classic. A masterpiece of its genre.' He grinned. 'And one of the finest talking teapots this side of an LSD trip.'

He came over to her, ran his fingertips over a row of reels. 'Now come on, Miss Blackthorne. What's it to be? Take your pick.'

'You don't *watch* them, do you?' She looked up at him in horror, making him smile.

'Not the originals. I had them all digitised. Here.' He gestured upwards and she noticed a modern ceiling-mounted LCD projector with a small hard drive attached. 'The old reel projector's just here for atmosphere, really.'

'Oh. Right. So... you want to watch a film?'

'Since you don't want to go home. It's the only entertainment I can offer you, I'm afraid. I admit it's no Queen tribute band.'

The only entertainment allowed anyway, Angel thought through the woozy numbness in her brain. Her headache was gone but she still felt pretty out of it from the champagne.

She ran her fingers along the titles printed on the spines of the film cases, resting on one that struck her. *Some Like It Hot*. It reminded her of Savannah in her slinky black Marilyn dress.

'Good choice,' Seb said, casting an approving glance at the

211

case. 'I knew you were a Wilder fan.' He squinted one eye, puzzled. 'How did I know that? Did you tell me?'

'It was at the after-party for *Milkman*,' she said, pleased he'd remembered, embarrassed she had to refer to it. 'I mentioned Wilder… in the interview. You know. That night.'

'So you did. Told me I was a derivative hack, didn't you?' he said with a grin. 'Any other filmmaker and I might have been offended. But Wilder? Fair comment. Everyone's a hack compared to Wilder.'

'Oh God, don't remind me what I said then. That's not what I think at all. Well, you know that now, you read my review. I don't know what I was trying to prove, really. Once I was sitting there with you glaring at me like something you'd wiped off your shoe, I wondered why I'd tried so hard to get you to see me.' She flushed as she met his gaze. 'I… hadn't even prepared any questions.'

'Really?' She'd expected him to be offended, but he sounded impressed. 'You did that whole interview just off the top of your head?'

'Pretty much. God, Seb, I was so rude to you! I suppose I wanted to show you I wasn't just another bimbo.'

'You certainly did that.' His voice was suddenly deeper, more intense, in a way that made Angel feel afraid and excited in equal measure. She fixed her eyes on the ground, hoping he'd move the conversation on.

He took the hint. 'Or how about this one?' She looked up to see which case he was pointing at.

'*The Apartment*? Oh, I love that film!' she breathed in what, to her disgusted ears, sounded like an almost Savannah-esque gush. 'It's the one I always watch when I need cheering up. My mum and me, that used to be our favourite.'

'Really? I always think it's quite sad, for a comedy.'

'That's why I like it,' she said. 'Feeling sad can be soothing sometimes, don't you think? And at least there's a happily-ever-after. Well, sort of.

'"Shut up and deal." True. There is that.' He pulled his keen gaze away from her face and turned to the ceiling-mounted projector. 'So how about it, then? Haven't seen it recently, have you? I can queue it up if you like.'

Angel blinked, remembering the last time she'd watched it to cheer herself up just a few months ago. It was with Emily at the flat, the night after the she'd been with Seb at the hotel. The night she'd sobbed, upset at the thought of never seeing him again. The night before the story broke and everything in her life changed.

'No, not for ages. I'd love to watch it with you.'

***

Angel groaned as she flailed her arm to one side, reaching for her mobile phone to check the time. It hit something warm and solid where her bedside table should be. She tried to blink her gummed eyes open, wondering if Groucho was sleeping on her mobile again and why someone had shaved him.

'Angel.' Dream voice. She'd heard this one before. 'Angel, Angel.' Why was it always saying her name? Could it never just let her sleep? *God damn you, dream voice, you haunty weird bastard.*

'Angel.' The dream voice was more urgent now and she could feel something heavy on her shoulder. She forced her eyes open, wiggling to shake herself free, and felt the weight drop away from her. A hand. A man's hand.

Seb. He was leaning over her, looking all gentle and sexy. He did that a lot in her dreams, to be fair, but not usually dressed as Marlon Brando. Although she was sure her subconscious would be working that one in for the future.

Of course. The cinema. They'd been watching *The Apartment*... then what?

She wriggled in discomfort, realising she was jammed into an odd shape in the velvet upholstery of a cinema seat. A warm plaid blanket covered her.

'How long was I out of it?' she asked, her voice thick with sleep. She struggled to bring the room into focus. 'What time is it?'

'After two. You slept through the whole film. Brought you a blanket from the back room.' Seb's voice was pleasant and warm. It made her want to snuggle back into sleep, safe knowing he was with her.

With an effort she pushed herself upright. 'Oh God. I'm so sorry. You must have been bored to death.'

He smiled at her, one of those soft little smiles he seemed to save just for her. God, those smiles, the way they made his cheeks dimple and his tawny eyes crinkle at the corners, illuminating his features like Christmas lights…

'It's fine, Angel, I was enjoying the film. Anyway, I didn't want to wake you up when you looked so tired. Let me sort out a cab to take you home, okay?'

'I… thanks. That'd be great.'

She struggled to banish the drowsy feeling. 'Seb. Let me say this thing before I sober up completely.' Her head was spinning, but she was determined to get this out. 'Look, I had a nice time tonight. And I wanted to say… I'm sorry. Not for the honey trap thing, I apologised for that already and you can take it or leave it.' She scowled, then broke suddenly into a woozy grin. 'And I guess you've decided to take it, since you're all here with me and everything. I meant, you know, I'm sorry about your dad and all that stuff you told me. No little kid should have to go through what you did, and no adult should have to live with the memory of it. Especially not you, Seb, because you… are nice. And that's what I have to say. You are nice. So… that's that, I guess.'

Seb was staring at her, one eyebrow quirking up in amusement as she let herself waffle on.

'God, I'm a ridiculous mess.' She gave a dreary laugh. 'I don't know what brought that on. It is so definitely the champagne talking. Ignore me, please. Everyone does.'

He reached over and rested his hand very gently on her shoulder. 'I could never ignore you, Angel.'

But before she could even look up to meet his eyes, he'd pulled his hand away and was rising from his seat. He was already swiping at his phone for a taxi to take her back to the flat.

***

They waited at the front of the building for the cab to arrive, Angel leaning back against the wall, dizzy and exhausted, Seb quiet after her odd little speech.

'Here,' she said, taking off the old leather jacket he'd lent her. 'You'll want this back.'

'You keep it. It might be cold in the taxi. I've got plenty of jackets.'

She smiled at him and wrapped the jacket back round her. 'Thanks, Seb.'

'Hey,' he said as the cab pulled in and she unpeeled herself from the wall. 'I had a great time tonight, Angel.'

'Me too. Thanks for bringing me. Sorry if I was… weird. Or, you know, asleep.'

'Give me the quiet life any time.'

Angel threw him a weak smile, her head already beginning its familiar throb. Thank God there was a packet of paracetamol back at the flat. Opening the car door, she started to climb into the back of the taxi.

'Angel. Wait.'

She stopped, turning back to him.

'What?'

'Would you… can I see you here again?' He caught the expression on her face. 'I mean, not anything… just friends, you know?'

'Just a sec,' she said to the driver. She closed the car door and leant back against it.

215

'I don't know, Seb. Do you think it's a good idea? We've got… history, you and me.'

'I like spending time with you, Angel. More than anyone I've met in a long time. The truth is, I don't let many people into my life. It's hard to, when you live like me. There are maybe three people I'd say I was really close to: that I'd call friends. If I could make it four, I'd like that other one to be you.'

She felt her skin prickle at the sincerity in his voice. He really wanted this. He was really prepared to put the honey trap and everything else behind them and let her in.

'Seb…'

'Yes, I admit the way we met was… unusual, to say the least.' He cut her off before she could reply. 'But it's done now. And if you were up for it, I'd like to try and get to a point where me and you could maybe have what you've got with your friend Leo. I guess you two had a history too, but you worked past it because you obviously care about each other. I know this is different. But I'll give it a shot if you will.' He fixed her in an intense gaze. 'All I know, Angel, is I'd like you in my life.'

'I don't know, Seb,' she said again, trying with a mammoth effort to stay strong, resist the gentle pleading in those soft eyes. 'Leo and me, when we were working at rebuilding our friendship, we only had ourselves to worry about. You've got Carole.'

His face darkened when she said his wife's name. 'I don't need my wife's permission to have friends, Angel.'

'Unless they're ex-lovers. Then I'd say maybe you do.' She climbed back into the taxi. 'Goodnight, Seb.'

'So is that a no?'

She couldn't help smiling at his persistence. 'Let's say I'll think about it.' She slammed the door closed behind her and the cab pulled off into the early hours of Saturday morning.

Chapter 21

Angel's Saturday started with two paracetamol and a long lie-in. It was after 11.00 when she finally forced her eyes open with a heavy groan and pushed herself up on to one elbow. She was still far from feeling human, but at least the throbbing in her temples had finally subsided.

That was it. She had to stop doing this to herself. First thing tomorrow, join a gym, buy some healthy food, chuck any booze in the flat down the sink.

Yeah. That's going to happen.

She flinched when she remembered the events of the night before. 'I think you are nice' – seriously? Ouch. That had to be a new low in man-repelling, even for her.

Seb hadn't seemed too repelled though, she thought, hugging herself. He'd asked to see her again, hadn't he? Told her he wanted to be friends.

But watching films with a married man in his private cinema was distinctly date-like, no matter how little hanky panky was actually going on. And spending time with Seb platonically when they could barely touch without the crackle of that weird magnetic sexual-tension thing – how realistic was that, really? Eventually it would be torture. No, it seemed like the whole thing would be doomed to fail, came the morose thought as she skimmed absently through her Facebook feed on her phone. It could only end in heartbreak: either for her, Seb or Carole Beaumont. Or more likely, all three.

But spending time with him last night – no pressure, no story to get, nothing physical – had been so… nice. And sort of sweet, somehow. She'd had fun, she couldn't deny it. He liked the things she liked. He made her laugh. She liked talking to him, being with him, feeling him close by. When she was with him, it felt like… like she was where she should be.

And they had one other thing in common. Seb had said there were only three people he was really close to. Well, who did she have in her life? Just her two best friends, a soppy old cat and her parents, far away on the other side of the world. Her existence was pretty isolated, when she came to think about it. And now Emily and Leo had each other, she was feeling more alone than ever.

Could she and Seb be friends, just friends? After all, things hadn't always been the way they were now with Leo. It had been pretty awkward just after they'd broken up and were trying to get their friendship back on track. Things had been weird for a long time – months. It had been hard work, but they'd powered through because they cared too much about each other to just let it go.

Could she do that with Seb? Could they push through everything making things awkward – the strange chemistry between them, the fallout from the honey trap, Carole, his unusual childhood, that exotic show business world he occupied and she didn't? Could they ever have something like what she had with Leo and Emily?

Emily. She was dreading telling her she'd given in to temptation and spent the night with Seb alone, after all her friend's warnings about giving him the brush-off. She could already see the scowl of disapproval on her flatmate's pretty, round face.

Then again, she could really use some good advice and a hug right now.

With another groan she swung her legs out of bed. Dragging a dressing gown around herself, she pushed her frazzled hair through a bobble and made her way to the sitting room to seek out Emily.

Angel smirked when she noticed a pair of men's shiny black brogues by the front door. So Leo had stayed all night, then. Well, good. Advice from two friends had to beat advice from just the one prejudiced one she happened to live with.

She scrunched her eyes closed as she flung open the door to the sitting room, feeling her way in blindly.

'Is it safe? Can I open them yet?'

She heard Emily giggle. 'It's okay, Ange, we're decent.'

'That's up for debate,' Angel said, opening her eyes.

Emily and Leo were sat on the sofa in bathrobes, draped over each other. Emily glowed with contentment as she flicked through a magazine, Leo reading it over her shoulder. The picture of happy coupleness.

Go on, rub it in...

'Morning, Ginge.' Leo looked up from the mag to give her a bright smile. 'Good night last night?'

'I think I should be asking you that, mate,' she said with a laugh. 'Except it seems like the answer's pretty obvious. You certainly look pleased with yourself today anyway.'

'Hey, I'm entitled. I won't deny the earth moved for our friend Em here.' He smirked at Emily, running fond fingers through her curls. 'If I'm not mistaken, twice.'

Emily hit him with the magazine. 'Oi, stop it, you. Have you no shame?'

'Nope.' He moved one arm around her and gave her shoulders an affectionate squeeze. 'Only pride, because you're gorgeous and I'm a sex god.'

'Well, I can't argue with that.' She giggled and leant into him for a kiss.

'Alright, alright, love's young dream,' Angel said, wrinkling her

219

nose. 'Since unfortunately we're fresh out of sick bags, I'll go make drinks. And when I come back I expect all snogging to be completed and some friendly advice to be forthcoming.'

'Friendly advice?' Emily pulled her lips away from where they'd travelled to Leo's earlobe and flung a suspicious look at Angel. 'Why? What did you do, Ange? What did *he* do?'

'Nothing awful. I promise.' She tried to look reassuring. 'Look, I'll tell you in a minute. I really need coffee before I can face getting into it.'

'Girl-talk for five minutes, okay?' Emily said to Leo, giving him a quick peck on the cheek and standing up to follow Angel into the kitchen.

She closed the door behind her and folded her arms, pursing her lips at Angel like a school caretaker who'd discovered her having a crafty cig behind the music block.

'Well?'

Angel shook her head. 'Oh no you don't, Em. Not this time. You first.'

'What do you mean, me first?'

'*Twice*, Miss Graziana?' Angel's mouth spread into a wide smirk and she waggled her eyebrows suggestively. 'Some night, eh?'

Emily blushed. 'Actually it was three times,' she mumbled. 'But don't tell Leo. There'd be no living with him.'

Angel grabbed Emily's hand and drew her friend into a tight hug. 'Well, you deserve it,' she said sincerely. 'You've waited long enough to see what was right in front of you. And a nicer guy you couldn't hope to find. Keep hold of him, eh? I want to see you guys wrinkly and grey together, cuddling on Brighton pier when I'm all alone in the old folks' home crying into my boiled cabbage.'

'Trust me, I won't let him go without a fight.' Emily returned her squeeze. 'I've kidded myself for too long. Ever since Pete, and how that ended. To be honest –' She hesitated. 'No, I don't think I can bring myself to say it.'

'Can't say what? Go on. I'm your friend, I can take it.'

'Truth is, I think I might be – oh God, it'll sound so soppy when I say it out loud.' Emily groaned and pinched her nose, smiling at her own embarrassment. 'I think I'm falling in love with him, Ange.'

Her face relaxed into an expression of relief as she managed to tell Angel what was on her mind. The words tumbled out of her now in a rush.

'Phew, that felt good. Finally getting it out. Been falling for him for ages, probably, only like the pig-headed cow I am, I wouldn't see it. Fooling around with Danny, trying not to think about what I was really feeling. Shutting you down that night when you tried to give me some perfectly good advice. And now, after last night, it's all come rushing over me like a huge – rushy thing.' She bowed her head. 'I've been a proper pillock. Wasting all this time when I could've been happy. When we both could.'

Angel gripped her friend by the shoulders in pleasure and surprise. 'Oh my God, Em, that's amazing! Arghh! I can't believe it, my best friends! I'm so happy for you both.'

Emily laughed as Angel pulled her into another hug. 'Alright, calm down, sweetie. I don't think you need to be writing out the wedding invitations just yet.'

Angel drew back and nodded over to the door. 'Have you told Leo?'

'No. Not yet.' Emily began examining the pattern on the lino, uncharacteristically shy all of a sudden. 'Don't want to scare him off. I mean, first date one night, true love the next morning? There isn't a bloke in the world who wouldn't be lacing up his Reeboks at that revelation.'

'Are you kidding? Leo? He wouldn't do that, you're mates. And he's wanted this for ages, you know. Wanted *you* for ages.'

'Really?' Emily's face brightened. 'I mean, I did know he fancied me, but you know how he does that jokey flirty thing –'

'More than fancied you.' Angel's face was serious now as she

221

looked her friend straight in the eye. 'He's been eating his heart out over you for an age. He told me so that night at the film premiere, and it sounded like it'd been going on since well before that, only I was too thick to see it. He's spoony for you, Em. Totally head over heels.'

'Really?' Emily said again. Her face glowed with surprise and happiness as she glanced in the direction of the sitting room.

'Go on.' Angel shoved her towards the door. 'I'm sure I can busy myself with the kettle for quarter of an hour before I goose-berry back in. Go tell him. You'll make his decade.'

'But what about your thing?' Emily asked vaguely, eyeing the door handle with obvious longing. 'You needed my advice on something.'

'I'll tell you both in about fifteen, twenty minutes and we can do the tissues and issues thing all together. Until then, go be with Leo. I've got some complicated hot drinks to make and I may be some time.'

She opened the kitchen door and pushed a hesitant Emily through.

Grabbing her phone from the marble worktop, Angel fired up a music app and tuned into some classic rock. Queen seemed appropriate, after the insult to their talent that had been the tribute act at the fundraiser last night. She turned the volume up high enough that it was impossible to hear anything being said next door, boiled up the kettle and thoughtfully stirred the three steaming mugs while she waited.

Leo's tea was well brewed by the time she carried it through on a tray; a real builder's concoction, and getting on for lukewarm as well. Her and Emily's coffees weren't much better. Brown sludge the temperature of bathwater. *Ick.*

'Here you go.' She dished out drinks to the jumble of limbs she'd already christened the Lemily. Her friends' eyes were wet and the pair of them were pulled in so close to each other it was hard to see where one body ended and the other began.

222

'You guys okay? I can go to my room, if you want to be alone.' She picked up her coffee and stood hesitantly by the table.

'Oh no you don't. Sit down.' Emily extricated her face from the crook of Leo's shoulder and fixed Angel with an icy stare. 'There's an elephant in this room and in all the rooms wherein you sit, Angel Blackthorne, and I'm not talking about that fat, moth-eaten old cat. Sebastian bloody Wilchester. Tell. Now.'

'Straight to the point, as always,' Angel muttered, throwing herself down on the other sofa next to the sleeping Groucho and staring down into her mug as she swilled the uninviting liquid around the sides.

'Hey. It was you who wanted to talk. So come on, what happened?' Emily asked. 'That girl Savannah was with you, wasn't she?'

'Yes.' Angel looked up from her coffee with a half-smile. 'At first. She, er, got a bit side-tracked on her way to the bar not long after you left.' She sought out Leo's eyes. 'You remember that PR guy from Tigerblaze? Pinstripe suit, face like a slapped arse?'

'What, Kevin?' Leo's eyes widened as he caught her drift. 'No way! Savannah and Kev? Christ almighty! I mean, Cal was no looker but he was nice enough when you got to know him. But Kev! The man must've had a charisma bypass at birth. And he's practically old enough to be her dad as well.'

Angel shrugged. 'I really don't know what's wrong with that girl. Supermodel looks, absolutely no taste.' She smirked at Leo. 'Reckons Kev looks like Nicolas Cage.'

'Ha! Which bit of Nicolas Cage, though? That's the real question.'

'So come on then,' Emily said, impatient to hear the rest of the story. 'Never mind Savannah. What happened with Wilchester? God, Ange, I knew I should never have let you out of my sight.' She planted a kiss on Leo's neck. 'Your fault for being irresistible, sexy thing,' she muttered into his ear.

'Nothing,' Angel said. 'That's just it. Nothing happened, Em.'

'What do you mean, nothing happened? What, so he just ignored you all night?'

'No.' Angel stroked the dozing cat next to her in a vague sort of way. 'He came over to talk to me. Asked if I wanted him to sort me out a taxi. I was a bit, er, the worse for wear by that time. Stonking headache, and maybe just the teensiest bit tipsy.'

'What, you? Surely not.'

'I know, hard to believe, right?' Angel grinned at her. 'Anyway, I didn't want to come back too early and gatecrash all your hot sexifying. So he asked if I wanted to get out of there somewhere with him.'

'Somewhere? Where somewhere?' Emily's mouth wrinkled in displeasure. 'Honestly, Ange, you should've just come back. Don't be alone with that bastard for our benefit.'

'Hey, let's not be hasty,' Leo muttered, cuddling Emily closer to him and nuzzling her ear.

'What, and interrupt your twelve orgasms in a row or whatever it was?' Angel said with a laugh. 'No thanks. And it's fine, honestly. I'm not completely helpless, you know. Unlikely as it may seem, at the ripe old age of twenty-six I can look after myself.'

'Actually I think it was more like fifteen orgasms. Possibly a few more.' Leo turned to Emily. 'And Angel's right, Em. She's a big girl. We need to back off and let her make her own mistakes.'

'You've changed your tune. It wasn't too long ago you were warning me to stay the hell away from Seb Wilchester at all costs,' Angel said, smiling. She cocked a sarcastic eyebrow. 'Hmmm. I wonder what can possibly have brought on the change of heart.'

'Funny how getting your end away can give you a whole new perspective,' Leo said with a smirk. Emily nudged him in the ribs. 'Ow. Anyway, Wilchester's alright. Seems a nice enough bloke, the issues with his missus aside. I don't think he'd try and push you into anything you weren't comfortable with.'

'As if he could. And when did you decide this, anyway?'

'I guess I've been warming to him since we were at Tigerblaze. Saw him in a whole new light that day. Poor sod.'

'Okay, so he asked you to go with him. Then what?' Emily said to Angel, radiating impatience. 'I'm guessing you went, since you didn't roll in until ridiculous o'clock this morning. Where'd he take you? His house?'

'No. It was… well, okay, don't laugh, but he's got his own cinema.'

Emily gave a loud snort. 'You what? His own *cinema*? Bloody hell, Ange!' She shook her head in disbelief, one side of her mouth curling upwards. 'What is it with you, anyway? You can't just go out with normal blokes, the kind who think they're going it some if they take you out in their Skoda for a white-wine spritzer and a bag of chips.'

'Pffft, what? Chips *and* wine?' Leo put one finger under Emily's chin and tipped her face up to look at him. 'If I'd realised you were such an expensive date, Em, I might've thought twice about asking you to be my girlfriend.' He gave a loud fake cough that sounded very like 'high maintenance'.

Angel smiled to herself, noticing Emily flush happily when she heard Leo use the word 'girlfriend'.

'Yeah, well, this cinema's not exactly the bloody IMAX or anything,' she went on, picking up their conversation. 'It's this little old 1920s place, half rotten, hidden away in some inner-city dive. Seb said it was in danger of demolition so he bought it to do up.'

'Well? What happened when you got there?' Leo's eyes held a wicked twinkle. 'Did he offer to show you his popcorn trick?'

'His popcorn – no, don't tell me.' She held up her hand as Leo opened his mouth to explain. 'Knowing you, I think I'll be happier in my ignorance.'

'Ignore him,' Emily said, giving Leo a playful punch on the arm. 'Just get on with it, will you? The suspense is quite figuratively killing me.'

225

Angel shrugged. 'Not much to tell, really. We watched a film, I slept pretty much through the whole thing, he called me a cab and I came back here.'

'That's it? He didn't try it on?'

'Nope. Perfect gentleman. Just covered me in a blanket when I fell asleep and then told me to keep his jacket so I wouldn't be cold on the way home.'

Emily scowled. 'The old coat routine, eh?' But Angel could tell she was softening.

'Well then? What's your problem?' Leo said with a shrug. Angel noticed his fingertips brushing Emily's hip while they talked and she felt a pang of loneliness, wishing she had someone with touching rights to her body. Not just someone. One person in particular. The one person she couldn't have. She sighed heavily and wondered when she'd become the walking one-woman soap opera.

'It was just… well, at the end of the night, when I was getting into the taxi. He asked if he could see me again. Just as friends, you know? He said… said he wanted it to be like us. Me and you, Leo. Work through the weirdness and come out the other side as shiny happy mates.'

'And are you going to?' Emily asked, her face filled with worry.

'Honestly? I don't know. I don't know what to do. I like hanging out with him, but… well, there's Carole. I can't imagine she'd be too thrilled about it, platonic or not. And then there's… the other thing.'

'Other thing? What other thing?'

The lust thing, she wanted to say. The sexual tension that fizzled in the air between them whenever they got close, that stopped her feeling she could trust herself around him. You'd think actually having had sex would alleviate it a bit, but if anything it seemed to be getting worse.

Somehow, though, she felt strange talking about it in front of the two of them, wrapped around each other as they bathed in the afterglow of newly declared love.

'Just, you know, our history and everything. The kiss-and-tell in the paper, all that stuff.' She limped along her sentence to the finish line. 'Well? What do you two reckon?'

'I don't know, Ginge,' Leo said. 'Do you really trust him not to try it on?'

'Yes.' She heaved another deep sigh, drew a floppy, purring ball of Groucho-shaped fur over on to her knee and cuddled him. The sight of the Lemily was making her feel even more isolated than usual. 'Yes, I trust him. He's never done anything that would… well, let's just say it's not him I'm worried about.'

'Oh. I see.' Leo frowned. 'Well, it's your choice, Angel. You're an adult. And he seems like a nice enough guy overall. But if something's going to bring you more pain than pleasure, you need to think about whether you'll be able to mop up the mess later. I'd hate to see you get hurt.'

'What do you think, Em?'

'Hmm?' Emily was busy tracing the line of the sinews in Leo's neck with the tip of one finger. 'Oh. Yeah, Leo's right, Ange. No one can make that decision for you. But if you want my considered advice, then it's to run as hard and as fast as you can in the other direction. Look at the state of that poor cow Beaumont and be warned, okay?'

'Yeah. I guess.' Angel cast a morose look down into her now stone-cold coffee, but there were no answers for her in the brown scum that had formed over the top. 'Okay, well, I'll leave you lovebirds alone. If anyone needs me I'll be upstairs, shopping for cat accessories and researching nice retirement villages where I can go to die alone.'

Leo made exaggerated side-eyes at Emily. 'She's not going to let us enjoy this, is she?' Extricating himself from the mass of intertwined body parts, he stood up. 'Come on, Em. You know what to do.'

Angel's friends came over to her, each grabbing an elbow and manoeuvring her off the sofa.

'Ow. Get off, you two. What're you doing?'

'Taking you to the pub for lunch, drama queen,' Emily said in a firm voice. 'See if a basket of chips can stop you whingeing. Come on, go get dressed.'

Chapter 22

Angel was sitting sipping a coffee and watching *Murder She Wrote* one Saturday morning, Emily's feet on her lap and Groucho on top of them, when she jerked as she heard her phone buzz from the coffee table. She'd been jumping at every call and text since the night of the ReelKids fundraiser, wondering every time if it would be Seb. But so far, not a word. And she still hadn't decided what answer to give when he did eventually get in touch.

Or if he did. It had been over a fortnight now. Maybe he'd changed his mind.

'Jeez, Ange,' Emily said next to her, jumping in her turn and dislodging Groucho. He gave the pair of them a filthy look, then stalked off into the kitchen. 'You have to stop doing that. You're turning me into a nervous wreck.'

'Well, who is it?' she asked, watching Angel reach over for the phone and swipe to open the message. 'Wilchester?'

'No.' Angel tried not to sound disappointed. 'It's your boyfriend.'

Emily giggled. 'Still not got used to hearing him called that. Well, what's he want?'

'Wants to know if we fancy the pub later. What do you reckon? Sounds good to me. I've got a sudden irresistible craving for a Guinness and a bag of roasted peanuts.'

Emily groaned. 'What, get out of my PJs and leave the flat? I dunno, Ange. Sounds like a lot of effort. But yeah, go on then. Tell Mr Sexypants we're in.'

'Yeah, might just call him Leo, actually.' She shook her head, smiling. 'You two really need to work on your pet names.'

Angel jerked again as the phone buzzed in her hand while she typed her reply to Leo. A message popped up.

Film night tonight?

Her heart jumped. Seb. Finally. And, as usual, the man's texting defined terseness.

'Shit!' Emily said, propping herself up so she could read it over Angel's shoulder. 'It's him, isn't it?' She glanced up at her friend. 'Well, Ange, looks like it's making-your-mind-up time, in the words of the immortal Bucks Fizz. What are you going to do?'

Angel made a snap decision. 'I'm going.'

Her friend put one hand on Angel's shoulder and twisted to face her, radiating concern. 'You sure about this, sweetie? Really sure?'

'No. But I'm still going to do it. You weren't there that night, Em. He said some things… about wanting me in his life. And, well, I've been thinking about it, and I feel the same. I like spending time with him, so why not spend time with him? Nothing wrong with that, is there? I mean, imagine if I'd let Leo slip out of my life just because it was too awkward or whatever. This could be the same thing, couldn't it? I don't want to let someone who could mean something to me go and then regret it for the rest of my life. It's just a case of… powering through. You know, all the weirdness.'

'Seb isn't Leo, Angel,' Emily said, frowning. 'You were mates well before you were a couple. The groundwork was already done. And Seb's married, don't forget.'

'Yeah. And as long as we both remember that, we'll be okay.'

'Right.' Her expression darkened. 'If you think you can. Shall I text Leo then, tell him pub's off?'

'No, don't do that. I'll ask Seb if we can make it an early one and meet you after. Not seen you guys to hang out with for ages.' She gave Emily a suggestive grin. 'Heard you quite a bit, though…'

Emily smirked. 'Well, it's your birthday next week, isn't it? Maybe we'll both chip in to get you some earplugs.' She gave her curls a haughty toss. 'Mind you, I think you should be grateful. There're premium websites out there that'll charge you a fortune for the kind of action you're getting gratis.'

'Oh? And how do you know, missy?'

'You know, just my many years as an adult film star. I'll have to send some in to the *Investigator* for you to review. You'll love me in *Randy Reflexologists 4*.'

Angel giggled and hit her with a cushion.

***

She got off the Tube just before 6pm for her not-date with Seb, dressed in bootcut jeans and a long-sleeved emerald-green top that matched her eyes. Nothing too dressy. He'd wanted to send a car for her, but she'd insisted on making her own way there. Chauffeur-driven limos didn't seem very her, somehow.

Seb was waiting on the platform to meet her, kitted out for the early December chill in black jeans and a chunky cream jumper. His gorgeous face broke into a warm smile when she stepped off the train and came towards him.

'Hi,' she muttered, suddenly shy. Seeing him face to face again brought back the memory of her ridiculous 'You are nice' speech last time they'd been together, when her brain had been groggy with sleep and too much champagne. She felt her cheeks start to burn, wondering if he was remembering too.

'Hi.'

Okay, so already things were weird. If she was meeting Emily or Leo, there'd be a hug of greeting now, probably a kiss on the cheek. With Seb, she seemed to have developed a tacit understanding that touching wasn't allowed. Even a handshake would be treading dangerous ground.

She stared at the floor bashfully, waiting for him to break the silence.

'Glad you could come, Angel.' He scanned her casual outfit with approval. 'You look nice.'

'Er, thanks. You know, you didn't need to meet me,' she mumbled, looking up at him. God, those dimples, when he smiled like that... why did he always have to smile like that? 'You already texted me the address. I could've found my own way there.'

Longest message she'd ever had from him.

He shrugged. 'Didn't want you walking around this neighbourhood in the dark on your own. The Saturday drunks will be out and about by now.'

'So I need a big strong man to protect me, do I?' she said with a laugh, starting to feel at ease as the awkwardness wore off and she relaxed into his company again.

'Something like that. Although my kung fu skills are a bit on the rusty side. Come on.'

For a minute she thought he was going to take her hand, but he stopped before his fingers met hers, instead tapping her elbow and pointing to the exit.

'Mind the gap,' intoned an automated robot voice from the wall-mounted tannoy. Angel looked at the distance between her and Seb while they walked out together and sighed.

***

'What's this?' she asked as Seb opened the door of the Hippodrome's auditorium and ushered her in. 'Did you do all this?'

'Yes. Like it?'

She looked around at the fresh teal paint, walked over to the seating area and ran her hand along one of the handsome, comfortable-looking black-leather chairs he'd had fitted. A sudden thought struck her.

'Not for my benefit, I hope?'

He smiled. 'Call that the catalyst. I've been meaning to get the place tarted up a bit for ages. Knowing I might be having company gave me some much-needed motivation.'

Angel shook her head, smiling at something in what he'd said that had struck her. 'Can I ask you something, Seb?'

'Of course. Anything.'

'It's… well, it's sort of personal. I don't want to say anything that might bring back bad memories for you.'

'I said anything,' he said in that special soft voice he only seemed to use for her, coming over to where she was standing and arresting her eyes with his. She tried to fight against her blush reflex but it was too late. She could already feel her cheeks starting to burn.

'Just, well, you had this unusual childhood,' she said. 'Tigers, film stars, a swimming pool filled with asses' milk and a team of diamond-studded unicorns to pull your carriage…'

'Ha! Come on, Angel, it wasn't that bad.'

'Okay, rhinestone-studded unicorns, then. But then you use phrases like "tarted up a bit". When you're not being all professional and film director-y you talk like, I don't know…'

'…like a normal person?' he finished for her, smiling. 'I can see that's what you're fumbling for.'

'Well, yes, I guess. If you want to put it like that. You seem pretty down to earth for someone who's had the sort of life you have, that's all I mean.' She gave an awkward laugh. 'There's a compliment in there somewhere if you want to grope around for it.'

Seb shrugged. 'I suppose you can thank Moira for that.'

'Your nanny?'

'My mum, really. She loved me like a son anyway, and vice

233

versa. She was a tough old biddy, though. A no-nonsense, plain-speaking woman from the wilds of Lancashire. If it hadn't been for her and Carole – my real family – I suppose I'd have been just as screwed-up and spoilt as the kids Abigail used to bring round to try and make me be friends with.'

She'd been examining his face while he spoke, watching the different emotions playing out on his features. She ran her eyes appreciatively over the hard cut of his jaw and cheekbones, the buzz of stubble she remembered too well, though it was so many months ago now, tingling across her bare flesh. She jerked, catching herself, as he said Carole's name. No more of that, she remembered. They were powering through, weren't they? Yep, powering through. That's what they were doing.

'How is Carole?' she asked with a guilty pang. She was so used to seeing him frown whenever she mentioned his wife's name, it was a surprise to see him break into a smile for a change.

'Home,' he said simply. 'They let her come back yesterday. You wouldn't recognise her from that night you saw her, Angel. Her cheeks are pink, actually pink, and she's even gained some weight. I've never seen her looking so healthy and happy.'

Angel smiled, a little sadly. Really did love her, didn't he?

'I'm glad, Seb. I'm glad you've got her home safe again. Really.'

'Yeah.' He dropped his eyes from hers. 'Me too.'

'Don't you need to be with her, though? She's not alone, is she?'

'No, she's with Suzanne.'

'Suzanne? Your PA?'

'Yes. They're friends. I told them I'd clear out for a bit so they could have a girls' night. Probably just what she needs right now, after months of being shut in with a load of strangers.'

'Oh.' It struck Angel as odd he wouldn't want to spend her first few nights out of rehab with his wife. But she supposed Seb knew Carole and what she needed best.

'So what are we watching, then?' she asked, changing the

subject. 'I picked last, so it must be your turn this time, yes?'

He nodded. 'Sounds fair. Actually, I've got something picked out I think you'll like. Just a sec.'

He jogged up the stairs to the projection room, and she could hear him firing up the equipment. Pretty soon the sound of tinny piano music filled the auditorium. The screen begin to flicker and a card bearing the words 'The General, starring Buster Keaton' in old-fashioned American-West lettering appeared.

Seb came back to join her and she raised one eyebrow at him. 'A silent?'

'Yep. Have you seen it?'

She shook her head. 'The only silent films I've seen are a couple of Chaplins and a Laurel and Hardy short I watched with my mum. I like my classics, but usually I'm strictly a post-talkie girl.'

'If you only see one, it should be this one,' Seb said, passion firing in his eyes as he looked up at the screen. 'Keaton was a genius. Way ahead of his time.' He gestured to one of the new soft leather chairs and she sat down, Seb settling into a seat beside her.

'It was a flop when it was made, you know,' he told her with enthusiasm. 'Broke the bank at the studio and nearly ruined Keaton's career into the bargain. But I'd say it's easily one of the best films of the silent era. You'll see what I mean.'

He turned to her, his eyes flickering as they reflected the silvery image of an old steam train from the screen above their heads. 'Anyway, there's another reason for the choice of a silent,' he said. 'I thought we might try this new thing all the kids are into these days, called having a conversation.'

Angel smiled. 'We have conversations.'

'We do. And yet somehow, I still feel like I know almost nothing about you.'

She saw him smile in the dim light. 'You've interviewed me twice, Angel, which is more than any other journalist in the known world. I've told you things about myself I've never shared with anybody before. That means you could now claim status as the country's leading expert in Sebastian Wilchester. Whereas all I know about you is that your favourite film's *The Apartment* and you look great in nothing but a towel.'

'Don't, Seb, please!' She twiddled a lock of hair around her little finger, avoiding his eyes. 'Aren't you embarrassed to mention that night? I can hardly bring myself to think about it. I thought I'd die at ReelKids when that boy Jordan started teasing you about it.'

'I should be embarrassed, shouldn't I?' he said. 'But to be honest, once the anger had subsided it seemed sort of… funny, in a darkly comic sort of way. I mean, not the night itself. Just the absurdity of the whole situation. Plus, it'd happened, and I just had to learn to accept it.' He brought his face down to hers, trying to catch her gaze, but she kept her eyes fixed on the screen above. 'Don't you feel like that?'

She thought back to herself and Leo, rolling in their seats that night at the *Milkman* premiere in uncontrollable laughter at the ridiculousness of the whole thing. 'Yeah, I can see your point. But please, Seb, don't talk about it any more. God, I don't know what made me agree to do it! Those aren't memories I want to deal with right now, not here. Not with you. Sorry. It just doesn't seem appropriate, that's all.'

'Okay.' His voice was gentle. 'Not if it makes you uncomfortable. I'm sorry.'

She shook her head. 'No, it's my fault. I'm just… not ready yet. Maybe one day we can laugh about it together, but not right now. It's too soon. Let's just be glad –' She wanted to finish 'it brought you into my life', but that sounded too much like something a lover would say. 'Let's just be glad it got us to where we are now.' *Wherever the hell that is…*

He smiled at her, holding eye contact without speaking until she had to withdraw her gaze.

'So come on then, Seb, what do you want to know?' An abrupt

change of subject seemed to be in order. 'Interview me.'

'Okay. But I warn you, Miss Blackthorne: I won't be going easy on you.'

'Good. I like it rough. I mean…' She blushed, laughing. 'Oh God, just ask me things, before this gets any more awkward.'

'Right, well, we can start with your accent and where in this sceptred isle of ours it's from. It doesn't seem to belong anywhere I can place it.'

'It doesn't, really,' she admitted. 'Nowhere fixed, anyway. It's a bit of a nondescript sort of hybrid. My parents are from Chester originally, but I was a Forces brat, you see.'

Her eyes watched his arm as he stretched it across the back of her chair.

'Sorry,' he said, following her gaze and dropping the arm to his side. 'Wasn't thinking.'

They lapsed into awkward silence for a moment, watching the action on the screen.

'So your dad was in the army?' Seb asked, rousing himself.

'Medical officer. We got moved around a lot when I was a kid. Germany, Cyprus, South Africa… Wales. You know, all the exotic locations,' she said, smiling. 'Dad wasn't always around, so it was just me and Mum a lot of the time.'

'And where are they now, your parents?'

'Melbourne. Retired there three years ago. They were in their early forties when they had me, so they're pushing seventy now. Thought they'd like to spend their autumn years in the warm.'

'Brothers? Sisters?'

She shook her head. 'Just me,' she said with a sad little shrug. 'By the time I was born, they'd left it a bit late to try for any more.'

He looked at her intently, his eyes soft and sympathetic. 'Sounds like a lonely life for a little girl.'

'Yeah, I guess. Getting moved from place to place, school to school. It was hard to make friends my own age and keep them.

Maybe that's why I'm so close to Emily and Leo now. I always had Mum, though.'

'And was it her who introduced you to classic films?'

Angel nodded. 'She loves that era. Calls it the golden age of cinema. My grandparents died when I was tiny but Mum used to tell me about the films they'd taken her to see when she was little in the fifties, and before she was born when they'd go to the pictures for a double feature then spend the night in each other's arms at a dance hall. It sounded so glamorous and exciting and romantic. I loved the idea of it.'

She grinned, remembering a conversation she'd had with her mum earlier that year. 'Mum's been nagging me to see *your* films for yonks,' she confessed. 'Told me you were a modern-day Hitchcock. But I always resisted.'

'What!' Seb drew himself up in mock indignation. 'Are you seriously saying you've not seen my films?' He put on a fake French accent, flourishing a hand affectedly. 'But they are, how you say, masterpieces!'

Angel giggled. 'I've seen them all now. But no, when we first met I hadn't seen a single one. Not even *Unreal City*. Sorry.'

'Why not? Not to sound too arrogant, but they're really rather good.'

'Typical British understatement there. They're bloody brilliant, as you know perfectly well. But your modesty is appreciated.' She gave a shrug. 'I suppose it was a genre thing really. I'm not a fan of gangster films. I thought it'd be all kneecapping and hanging people upside down in meat warehouses.'

'Meat warehouses?' Seb pretended to look thoughtful. 'Maybe I should be writing these solid-gold script suggestions down.'

'Sorry. Copyright Angel Blackthorne. But they may be available to you for a small fee,' she said with a laugh. 'I don't know, Seb. I always thought that East End Noir thing was a bit of pretentious made-up bollocks. But you were right. Your films are genre-defining.'

'Don't look at me,' he said, shrugging. 'I didn't coin the term, as I told you once before. Actually, I think it was your predecessor who gave my work the name East End Noir. Moustache guy. His writing always was a bit up itself for the *Investigator*.'

She looked up at the screen and laughed as she watched Keaton bundle his girlfriend head-first into a large mail sack, wearing his trademark deadpan expression. 'I take it you didn't know Cal well enough to bring him here for private film screenings then?'

'Funnily enough.'

They lapsed into silence for a little while, the train chase scene they were watching claiming their undivided attention.

'So,' Seb said, turning back towards her. 'Now you're basically my biggest fan, yes? I charge for autographs, you know.'

'Sorry, that would still have to be my mum. You'd better watch out if you ever meet her, Seb. She may well have to be restrained from throwing her knickers at you.' She stopped suddenly. Had that sounded a bit like an invitation to meet the parents? *Remember, Angel. Not a date...*

Seb was looking at her with a little smile playing at the corner of his mouth. 'Know what?'

'What?'

'You're sneaky. You've been doing journalism on me, haven't you?'

'Um, have I?'

'You asked me to interview you, and yet we've spent the last quarter of an hour talking about my films. See what I mean? Sneaky.'

'Ha! I suppose we have. Well, go on, then. It's your turn to change the subject this time.'

'Okay, well, since it's come up: why journalism? I can see you're committed to it, and you certainly seem to be the rising star all of a sudden.' In the silver glow of the cinema screen, she saw him grin. 'Assuming the rumours about you sleeping with your editor aren't true.'

239

'You heard those, did you?'

'Yeah. Kev told me.'

She shook her head in annoyance. 'For a man who hardly speaks, he's a bloody leading expert in shooting his mouth off when he shouldn't.'

'Well? Are you going to answer the question or do I need to strap you to a chair and shine a lamp in your face first?'

'Who told you I was kinky?'

'A boy always knows.'

Angel giggled. 'Well, I suppose it started when I was a kid, the journalism thing. Do you remember when you asked me what I got for my sixth birthday?'

'I do. Your parents made you a spy kit.'

'Yeah.' She smiled at him, touched he hadn't forgotten. 'It was a shoebox with all sorts of bits and pieces in it. A code wheel, a miniature tape recorder, magnifying glass...' Her eyes shone when she remembered the excitement of opening the box and exploring the sawdust filling for hidden treasures. 'We were living in family quarters at a barracks in Cyprus then and Dad was with us. I think I drove him and Mum crazy the next few weeks, trying to record secret conversations and explore our rooms for clues.'

'No wonder you wanted to be Bond at the fundraiser.'

'No, that was just stinginess. I didn't want to buy a costume.'

'Ha! Well? What's the journalism connection then?'

'One Christmas I got this storybook, *Rebecca the Reporter*. There was this little girl, Becky, and she'd go around with her hair in a bun and a pencil tucked behind her ear, cracking crime syndicates and getting interviews with celebrities. Then she'd write it up for the school paper and win twenty points for her House.' Angel gave a sheepish laugh. 'It was silly, but I wanted to be just like her. Even started getting Mum to put my hair up in a bun. So my spy obsession sort of evolved, and I'd be running around with my tape recorder trying to interview people and writing it up into these little articles I'd put into my own home-made newspaper. *The Blackthorne Bugle*, I called it.'

Seb was staring at her in silence and she felt her skin prickle with embarrassment. 'Like I said. It's silly.'

To her surprise, he reached over and brushed a strand of hair away from her face, drawing the back of one fingernail gently along her hot cheek and down the arch of her neck while he did so.

'You're a rare thing, Angel.' His voice was deep and gentle, washing over her like warm treacle. 'I don't know when I've met anyone quite like you.'

She looked down at the floor, her face burning. No. This wasn't the way it was supposed to go.

'Seb…'

'Oh God, sorry. I shouldn't have done that,' he mumbled. When she looked up, his eyes were scrunched tight closed and his fingers buried in the long curls. He looked like he had that day backstage at ReelKids, fighting a battle he couldn't win.

She gave her head a sad shake. 'I should go.'

'Wait. Don't, please.' He looked up at her with pleading in his eyes. 'I'll be good, I promise. It won't happen again.' He sat on his hands with such a penitent, schoolboyish air that Angel couldn't help but laugh.

'Okay, how about we both go then? I'm meeting my friends at the pub.' She watched his features for his reaction. 'Come with me.'

'Your friends?' He frowned. 'Won't they mind? Leo's not exactly my biggest fan.'

'He's warmed to you, apparently, since that day at Tigerblaze. His words, not mine. And… I'd like you to meet them properly. You'll like them. Well, probably. Sometimes.'

'If you're sure they'll be okay with it.' He shot her a grateful smile. 'Thanks, Angel.'

'What about the film?'

'Almost over. Oh, wait! This is the best bit.'

Angel looked up at the screen and watched, fascinated, as the huge steam train The General fell through a railway bridge and into a river before being dashed to pieces on the rocks below.

'Bloody *hell*, Seb!' She lifted her eyebrows. 'That looked expensive.'

'It was. You remember I told you this film nearly bankrupted the studio? No special effects in those days. Keaton literally destroyed a whole train,' he said. 'The man was rock and roll long before there was any such thing. Okay, come on, let's go.'

Angel grabbed her coat and followed him to the door, hoping the spectacular wreck of The General wasn't any kind of metaphor for the future of their not-quite friendship.

Chapter 23

The Cap and Motley had somehow managed to survive the general gentrification of Angel and Emily's bit of Greater London. The drinks still cost a bomb, but otherwise it was your traditional British pub: dark-wood tables, a selection of real ales on the bar, a pool table and an eclectic jukebox. Possibly the owners meant it all with hipster irony, but still, it was theirs.

Seb looked nervous as they walked up to the oak-panelled door together. 'Are you sure your friends won't mind me coming?'

'I told you, they'll be fine.'

He looked down at his jeans and chunky sweater. 'I'm not really dressed for it.'

'You look great, Seb. Anyway, it's a pub, not a film premiere. Come here.'

She reached up and tucked in a flap of polo shirt collar poking out from the top of his jumper. 'That's better.'

'Thanks, Mum,' he said with a smile.

She winced. 'Don't call me that. Sounds odd, coming from you.' She pushed open the door and he followed her through. 'Come on, let's go find them. They're always in the same corner.'

'You come here a lot?' he asked as they made their way through the throng.

'Yeah, when we've got a free Saturday. It's great. You can get any Meat Loaf song on the jukebox free, and there's pie-and-pea suppers for a fiver after eight.'

'Er, yeah, sounds fab…'

She looked up at him, smiling. 'Welcome to my world, Seb. I'm guessing you don't go to pubs much, do you?'

'Not really.'

She lowered her voice so they wouldn't be heard over the noise of the crowd. 'People recognise you?'

'No, not often,' he answered, speaking close to her ear. 'Film directors are a bit of a mystery to the general public, I think. People know the names, not the faces. Maybe someone like Spielberg, but even he'd probably have to be wearing his "I made *ET* – ask me how" t-shirt. Happens a bit more now, though, since… well, you know.'

She felt her cheeks heat, remembering the now legendary *Investigator* front page: her naked body and Seb's lust-lashed face over her shoulder.

'Carole, on the other hand…' he continued. 'There's a reason we don't go out together much. She's the star, and she's been on people's TVs and in the papers since she was tiny. People know her face almost as well as they know their own. It's not so much a case of recognised as mobbed.'

'Poor Carole. That sounds pretty horrific.'

'Yeah.' Seb scowled down at the polished floorboards.

'So how come you don't go to pubs, then, if you're Mr Incognito?' she asked, swiftly changing the subject.

He gave a morose shrug. 'No one to go with, I suppose. Except sometimes Moira when I visit.'

'Well, you have now.'

'Thanks, Ange.' He sounded touched and she noticed him using the shortened form of her name at once: the name her friends used for her. He'd never called her that before and somehow it seemed significant. She turned away to hide a sudden surge of emotion.

'You could always ask Kev,' she said once she'd recovered. 'I bet he's a laugh a minute after a few pints.'

'Ha! That guy couldn't be a laugh a minute without a full-on personality transplant.'

'My friend Savannah reckons he's the strong, silent type. An alpha male,' Angel said with a grin, remembering a conversation she'd had with her colleague the Monday after the ReelKids fund-raiser. Sav's blooming relationship with the sulky PR man was still going strong.

Seb snorted. 'More like an alpha hole,' he muttered. 'Still, he's good at his job. Most of the time.'

'I bet he doesn't know you're here with me. He'd be apoplectic.' She had a sudden thought. 'Hey, it won't cause trouble for you, will it? I mean, if you're recognised?'

'We are in the same industry, you know, Angel. You're the *Investigator*'s film critic. It's not completely unbelievable we might socialise. Plus Leo's here as well. I'm sure we could fudge it as a work thing if anyone started asking questions.'

'Yeah, I suppose we could. Didn't think of that.' She laughed. 'Actually, it'll look worse for me, won't it? Letting you schmooze good reviews out of me.'

'I do like a good schmooze. Whatever a schmooze is.'

Angel waved to Emily and Leo in their corner, draped over each other as was now the norm, and led Seb over to them.

Emily shot her a quizzical look when she noticed Seb standing just behind her friend, waiting to be introduced, but she quickly fixed her face into a polite smile. Angel beamed at her, pleased to see she was making an effort to be nice.

Disentangling himself from his girlfriend, Leo stood up and shook the director's hand, meeting his eyes with a manly frank-ness. 'Seb. Nice to see you again.'

'You too, mate. Hope you don't mind the gatecrash.' He looked over at Angel. 'Your friend seemed to think you wouldn't.'

'Did she now?' Leo gave her a one-sided smile. 'Well, then she must be right. Pull up a pew, guys.'

'Ahem,' Emily said loudly. 'Anyone going to introduce me?'

'Oh, sorry,' Angel said. 'Em, this is Seb, as you've probably worked out by now. Seb, my flatmate, Emily.'

'Nice to meet you,' he said, offering a polite handshake. Angel felt a pang as she watched them link fingers with careless abandon. Why couldn't she do that? Em made it look so easy…

Seb turned back to Angel. 'Okay, I'm going to brave the bar. What can I get you?'

'Guinness, please.'

'Really?'

'Yes, why?'

He shook his head, smiling. 'Nothing. Just never seen you drink a pint before, that's all.'

'I know. How unladylike of me. You must be appalled.'

'Oh, I am. Disgusted to the core.'

She flinched when she noticed Leo and Emily staring at them, taking in this display of what even she had to admit was some pretty blatant flirting.

'What about you two?' Seb asked politely.

'White wine for me, please,' Emily said, flinging a glance at Angel. 'Some of us ladies know how to behave, you know.'

Angel snorted her derision. 'Don't forget to stick your little finger out while you drink it, Lady bloody Penelope.'

'How about you, Leo? Top up?' Seb asked.

'Just an apple juice, please, mate.'

'Sure I can't get you anything stronger?'

Leo's brow knitted slightly, but he quickly smoothed his expression. 'No, I'm good with this stuff, thanks. Dosing up on Vitamin C.'

Angel looked up at Seb. 'I'll meet you over there in a minute and help with the drinks,' she said. She watched him walk away until he was out of earshot.

'And how goes it with the non-fuck buddies?' Emily asked as soon as she was sure Seb couldn't hear her. 'Good fake date?'

Angel shrugged. 'Yeah, I guess. Bit… weird.'

'Anything happen?' Leo asked, glancing over to Seb at the bar, where, as usual, his good looks meant he seemed to be having no trouble getting served right away. The pretty Australian barmaid was fluttering her lashes and simpering while she poured the drinks. Angel wondered if her own face ever looked like that when she was with him. God, she hoped not.

'Not really. Just this one odd thing where he said… said he'd never met anyone like me.' She gave an awkward laugh, her stomach somersaulting with pleasure and pain at the memory of his words and how his fingers had brushed her skin when he'd stroked her hair ever so gently away from her face. 'That's when I dragged him off to the pub. It's safer here.'

'He said that?' Emily cast a suspicious look over at him. 'Keep your eye on him, Ange.'

'Please. He can barely even touch me,' she said with a note of sadness in her voice.

'Then what was all that flirting about?' Leo asked. He threw his hands up in front of his face effeminately, putting on a high-pitched voice. '"Ooooh, Seb, get me a Guinness and I'll show you my lady parts."'

'Er, yeah, pretty sure that's not what I said…'

'Well, it was something like that. Since when do friends without the benefits speak to each other that way?'

'Ha! Is that Leo Courtenay I hear, talking out of his backside as per usual? The only man who can flirt in his bloody sleep? Please, mate. I hear worse from you every day.'

'She's got a point, Leo,' Emily said. 'I probably would've realised you liked me a lot sooner if you weren't such an almighty flirt.'

Leo shrugged, putting both hands behind his head and leaning

247

back against the high-backed mahogany bench he and Emily were occupying. 'Hey, if you've got a gift, use it, I say. Mine happens to be pleasuring the ladyfolk.'

'Well, clearly,' Angel said with a laugh, watching Emily run her fingers affectionately over Leo's short black hair. 'Look, I'm going to help Seb with the drinks. Don't go anywhere, you two.'

The barmaid was just handing over the Guinness when Angel approached Seb at the bar. She found him squinting into it with a puzzled expression on his handsome face.

'What's that supposed to be, do you think? An aubergine?' he asked, nodding to the device in the foam.

'I think it's meant to be a shamrock,' she said, laughing. 'Here, let me take that.'

'Did I say something wrong before?' he said in a low voice. 'Your friend Leo looked a bit pissed off.'

'Oh. Yeah, that. No, it wasn't anything you did. He doesn't drink, that's all. Not any more.'

'I see.' Seb shot a glance over at Leo. 'Oh! Right. I *see*.'

To her surprise, she felt a quick, gentle pressure on her free hand. Seb was looking down at her, his tawny eyes soft and full. She nearly dropped her Guinness, caught unawares by the sudden, unexpected warmth of his touch.

'That explains a lot. I'm sorry, Angel. I didn't realise.'

'It's… thanks. I'd rather not talk about it here, though.'

'Okay.' He squeezed her hand again, a quick, soft, reassuring press, and just as quickly pulled his fingers away. 'Just want you to know I understand. I know what it's like. Living with addiction.'

She shot him a feeling look. 'Your dad?'

He shook his head, his mouth tightening with anger. 'Not *him*. My only worry there was that he couldn't drink the stuff fast enough to get him out of our lives forever. Bastard.'

'Oh. Carole.'

He gave an almost imperceptible nod. Angel returned the quick pressure on his hand.

'Come on, Seb. Let's get back to the table. We can talk about this another time.'

'Another time?'

'Yes, I think so, don't you?' She cast a warm look up at him and he smiled back, his eyes full of feeling.

'So, Seb,' Emily said when they'd handed round the drinks and sat back down, fixing him in an appraising gaze. 'How's your wife?'

Angel shot her friend a warning look, shaking her head ever so slightly. She wished she was a bit closer so she could manage a well-aimed kick under the table.

'Er, fine, thanks,' Seb said, frowning at the abrupt question. 'She's at home, having a girls' night with her friend Suzanne.' He summoned a friendly smile from somewhere. 'What exactly happens at those things, anyway? Perhaps you ladies can enlighten the two of us.'

Emily shrugged. 'Oh, you know. Truth or dare. Giggling about boys. Plaiting each other's hair. The occasional topless pillow fight.'

'Now *that* I'd like to see,' Leo muttered, leaning in to nuzzle her neck.

'Um, guys,' Angel said, nodding towards Seb. 'Company. Public. Other people. You remember that little talk we had?'

Leo grinned. 'What, you think a man's girlfriend can drop the phrase "topless pillow fight" into the conversation and he'll just sit there? I'm not made of stone, Ginge.'

'He always call you that?' Seb asked, turning to Angel.

'Yeah. Rude bastard.' She flung Leo an affectionate smile over the foamy top of her Guinness. 'Pretty much since the day we met, I think.'

Leo shook his head. 'Nah. Your hair was blue the day we all moved into halls, remember? That was before you fully embraced your inner gingerness.'

'So it was.' She reddened at the memory. 'My punk phase.'

Seb lifted his eyebrows in amusement. 'You had a punk phase?'

'Just a little one.'

'You should've seen her, mate,' Emily chimed in, giggling. 'All tartan and safety pins, this thick blue hair piled up on her head. She looked like a smurf on the run from a Bay City Rollers gig.'

'Ha! I can't quite picture it, somehow.'

'Good.' Angel scowled, her cheeks flaming. 'Now I just need to go home and burn all the evidence.'

'Too late,' Leo said, passing his smartphone to Seb, who let out a ripple of laughter as he looked at the photo of an eighteen-year-old Angel on the screen.

Angel glared at her two friends. 'God, I hate you guys.' Emily smirked at her, blowing a theatrical kiss across the table.

'It's not so bad,' Seb said, passing back the phone and trying to stop his mouth curving upwards. 'The nose stud suits you, Ange.'

'Can somebody please, please change the subject before I start hacking off body parts?'

'Okay, okay,' Leo said, waving a dismissive hand. 'Let's talk about something else then, and come back to embarrassing you later. Are we still on for your birthday thing next week?'

'Course. We do it every year, don't we?'

Seb turned to face her. 'I didn't know you had a birthday coming up. When is it?'

'Wednesday. We've had a bit of a tradition since uni. Takeaway and a film in our PJs. Seems as good a way as any to mark the depressing hurtle towards thirty.'

'Oh, it's not so bad once you get there,' Seb said with a smile. 'Anyway, how are you fixed for the Thursday?'

'Er, dunno, why?'

'I wondered if maybe you'd like to have a post-birthday drink with me.'

'Oh.' She blushed, suddenly very aware of her friends' eyes burning into her, waiting for her answer.

'I mean, all three of you, of course,' he said, reading the embarrassment painted on her cheeks.

Leo shook his head. 'You'll have to count us out, I'm afraid.' He made a face at Angel across the table. 'Em's got us tickets to see *Les Misérables*.'

'Ouch. Rather you than me, mate,' she said with sympathy. 'It's about twelve hours long, isn't it?'

Emily hit Leo with a beer mat. 'You'll enjoy it when you see it,' she hissed. 'Honestly, it's supposed to be a great show. Five-star reviews and all that.'

He gave a comical sigh. 'I knew there had to be a catch to all that sex we've been having. This boyfriending lark isn't all it's cracked up to be.'

Emily planted a fond kiss on his cheek. 'Look me in the eye and say that, lover.'

'You know I can't,' Leo said in a soft voice, pulling her towards him for a proper kiss.

Angel rolled her eyes and turned to Seb.

'Sorry about them,' she said, jerking a thumb across the table to the snogging couple. 'Young love and all that. Nauseating, isn't it?'

'Looks like fun from where I'm sitting.'

'Perve,' she muttered, grinning at him.

'Well, how about Thursday then, Angel? Meet you in the usual place?'

So the cinema was the usual place now, was it? Okay then…

'Yeah,' she said, smiling. 'Yeah, why the hell not?'

***

'Well?' Angel asked Emily as the three friends opened the door of the flat three rounds and four games of pool later and collapsed exhausted onto the sofa. 'Now what do you think?'

'Of your married boyfriend?'

She frowned. 'He's not my boyfriend.'

'Whatever.' Emily twined herself around Leo, snuggling into him. 'I don't know, Ange. I mean, he seems like a nice guy, putting aside whatever this thing is with him and Beaumont. Good laugh and all that. And kind of, I don't know, humble I suppose, for someone with his background. But… he likes you.'

'Well, yeah, I hope so.'

'No, I mean, he *likes* you. Not just as friends, and not just because he'd pretty clearly be up for getting you in the sack again. He boyfriend likes you. As in, Angel and Seb sitting in a tree, etc, likes you. It's obvious. The way you're the only person in the room to him, and his face lights up when we talk about you. He reeks of it, sweetie.'

'It's true, Ginge,' Leo chipped in, twirling Emily's curls around his fingers. 'I guess I noticed it that day at ReelKids, too. Something more than just awkwardness because of that honey trap thing, or sexual tension or whatever. I mean, the way he looks at you. He likes you. You do know that, don't you?'

'I… don't know. Suppose I do.' She pushed her index fingers into her temples and pinched her eyes closed. 'Still. He can barely even bring himself to touch me. Not so much as a handshake. He's not exactly trying to jump my bones, is he?'

'Look, I know what you want us to say,' Emily said, frowning. 'It's not an affair because you're just friends, right? But there's more to cheating than sex, Ange: trust me, as someone who's seen it from the other side. Feelings come into it too. And in the end, it's those that hurt most.'

'I guess…'

'I don't know if the two of you can ever just be mates,' Emily continued, shaking her head. 'Not really. Because you'll always want to be more than that, won't you? Not like when you guys were working things out.' She tossed her curls in Leo's direction. 'That stage of your relationship was already over.'

'Yeah. I think by that point we both knew there was no going back, didn't we?' Leo shot Angel a pressed-lip smile of camaraderie that she did her best to return. 'It was tough at the time, but… made things easier, in a way.'

'The problem with you and Seb, sweetie, is you're neither one thing nor the other,' Emily said. 'And the more time you spend together, the worse it'll get. It'll eat away at you and make you miserable until you either give in to it, let yourself become just The Other Woman, or get your heart broken. Simple as that. I'm sorry, but it's the truth.'

The hard words brought the tears stinging into Angel's eyes. She blinked hard, struggling to fight them back.

'Hey.' Emily's voice softened when she registered the emotion flickering across her friend's features. She untangled herself from Leo and came over to where Angel was sitting, lowered herself down beside her and put an arm around her shoulders.

'Can you give us a minute, Leo?' Emily asked. 'Go stick the kettle on or something? I think we need some girl time here.'

'Of course,' he said, his face radiating concern. 'Take as long as you need, ladies.'

'Sorry, Ange, that sounded harsh,' Emily said once Leo had moved into the kitchen.

Angel buried her face into the crook of Emily's shoulder and let the tears flow freely. 'It's not that,' she whispered through sobs. 'It's me, Em.' She looked up into Emily's soft hazel eyes. 'Because I like him like that too.'

Emily smiled and stroked her hair. 'Please. Tell me something that isn't right in front of my face. I could've told you that the day you got back from that stupid hotel. We both know he's been the only thing on your mind for months.'

Angel gave a muffled, tear-choked laugh. 'That obvious, is it?'

'And then some, sweetie.'

'God, it was so weird tonight, Em. One minute it could seem like we were just mates, mucking about and teasing just like the three of us always do. Really enjoying spending time together, getting to know each other better. Then he'd look at me and I'd feel something jump inside me, and I'd know it was… more than that. I guess there's a difference between a night out with a friend and a date with no touching.'

Emily gave her head a sympathetic pat. 'Yeah, I know. Me and Leo were trapped in the same holding pattern for months before I agreed to go out with him. Nights out just the two of us, kidding myself we were mates and nothing more… Well? What do you think you'll do, Ange?'

Angel was silent, but she knew what the answer had to be. She had to end whatever this thing was, before her feelings for Seb tore her slowly apart.

Chapter 24

Angel ran her hands over her red pencil skirt, brushing it free of some stray Groucho hairs clinging to it, as a taxi dropped her off in front of the Hippodrome for her birthday un-date with Seb.

Its now-familiar white tiles looked lustrous after a recent clean. His handiwork, presumably. He seemed to be going all out to make the place inviting for her, she reflected with biting sadness, remembering this would be her last visit.

Somehow it hadn't seemed right to go through with their non-breakup over the phone. And yet she eyed the cinema's red door with trepidation, trying to crush the stabbing, gut-wrenching pain in her chest.

It felt like she was about to sever a limb. Every time she thought back to that night in the pub, when she'd promised Seb in not so many words she'd always be there for him, she felt guilty tears rise in her eyes.

He opened the front door when he heard her cab pull away, a warm, dimpled smile spreading over his handsome features while he welcomed her. God, he wasn't going to make this easy for her, was he? Already she could feel tears rising and struggled to push them back.

He was wearing jeans with an open-necked cotton shirt, a look that always suited him, and as usual her eyes were drawn to the magnetic bronzed skin at his throat. With an effort, she willed herself not to imagine how it would feel to run her fingers along those taut sinews. Her lips…

'Come on in, birthday girl. Haven't eaten, have you?'

'Er, no. Why?'

'Come see.' She followed him along the brick corridor to the auditorium, gasping when he opened the door to show her inside.

'Seb! You did all this? Why?'

'Well, you only turn twenty-seven once,' he said, looking at her with glowing eyes. 'Hope you like it, Angel.'

At the front of the room, in the hollow of what would once have been the organ pit, he'd spread a red-and-white gingham blanket. On it a picnic was laid out: five or six plates of rustic breads, little sandwiches and delicate pastries, plus a bottle of wine chilling in an ice bucket and a cupcake with an unlit birthday candle on it. A couple of bigger candles and a string of glowing fairy lights bathed the room in a soft, creamy glow.

'This is… amazing. I can't believe you did this for me, Seb.' She looked up at him, her eyes liquid. 'Thank you.'

'You haven't seen the best bit yet. Over here. I had it brought over from home.'

He guided her to the corner of the room, where he'd placed what looked like a small, highly varnished walnut cabinet. She ran her fingers along it, discovering when she lifted the lid it was an old-style record player set into its own free-standing case.

'There's some records in there. I brought the ones I thought you'd like.' Seb pointed to the cabinet's double doors. Angel opened them and looked at the stack of vinyls inside. She took out a few and read the titles. Crosby, Sinatra, Holliday…

'I remembered what you said about your grandparents going out dancing and how you fell in love with the idea,' he said, his voice soft. 'I thought you might like to listen to some of these.

They're all from that era. And there's something about vinyl that just beats anything digital hands down for the old stuff, isn't there? I think it's the crackle.'

'You shouldn't have gone to all this effort,' she mumbled.

Seb turned fervent tawny eyes on her, holding her gaze until she felt the too-familiar blush creeping up from her shoes. 'You're worth it, Angel.' He crouched down to rifle through the stack of LPs and pulled out a Nat King Cole record. 'How about this one?'

She nodded, feeling half dazed, and he put it on. Nat's silken, dreamy tones filled the candlelit room. Angel closed her eyes to listen for a moment, struggling again with rising tears. God, why was he making it so hard for her to do what she knew she had to?

She followed him over to the chequered picnic blanket and lowered herself down opposite him, feeling as if she was in a dreamscape version of her own life, hazy and unreal, everything slightly wobbly and out of proportion. She could sense her resolve weakening with every second she spent in Seb's company. One thing was perfectly clear to her, though. Touching or no touching, this was, without any shadow of a doubt, a date.

'Crusts trimmed off and everything. Very Oscar Wilde.' She tried to sound like her usual self as she picked up a cucumber sandwich.

'Well, what do you want first?' he asked, pouring them both a glass of wine. 'Food, cake or present?'

'Oh, no, Seb! You didn't get me a present?'

'Well, it's no spy kit I'm afraid. But I think you'll like it. Back in a minute.'

Jumping up, he bounded up the stairs two at a time to the projection room and came back carrying a longish, rectangular box, all wrapped up in light-blue paper with little yellow cartoon frogs wearing party hats on it. She smiled at the childish pattern on the wrapping as he handed it to her and tore it off with great curiosity.

'Er, thanks,' she said with a puzzled frown when she'd lifted the lid off the cardboard box, casting her eyes over the old-fashioned tennis racquet inside. It was varnished wood with a rubber-tipped handle, nestled carefully into reams of gold tissue paper. 'You shouldn't have. Are we taking up mixed doubles or something?'

'Look on the handle.'

Angel lifted the racquet out of its box, brought the wooden handle up to her eyes and squinted at it in the candlelight. She could just make out a signature there. It looked like...

She clapped one hand to her mouth, almost dropping the racquet when she realised what she was holding. 'Oh my God, Seb! Oh my God! It isn't!' she said in a muffled voice, her eyes filling with tears as she experienced at least three different emotions at once.

'Yep. It's the one Jack Lemmon uses as a spaghetti strainer in *The Apartment*. The real one. Signed by Wilder himself.'

'Seb! Oh God... I can't believe I've really got it in my hand,' she whispered, holding the precious object like the most delicate butterfly-wing crystal. 'It must be priceless.' She looked up at him. 'I really can't accept it from you, you know.'

'You can and you will, or I'll be highly offended. Please, Angel. I want you to have it.'

'But... where did you even get this?' she asked, awestruck, placing the prop gently back inside its cardboard box.

He shrugged. 'It was Abigail's. She was a big collector of that type of thing. But I think you'll appreciate it more than she ever did. Once she had something, she used to just shut it up in a room and never look at it again. Just something to brag about to dinner guests, I think. Not that there were many of those, in later years.'

He coloured, fiddling with his wine glass on the blanket. 'I, er, met him once, you know,' he said with a sheepish expression on his face. 'Wilder.'

Angel's pupils looked about the size of the vinyls she'd been

258

examining earlier. 'No. Way. Are you seriously telling me you met *Billy Wilder*, Seb? And you never thought to mention it until now?'

'Well. Sounds a bit name-droppy, doesn't it? The illustrious director and his celebrity pals.' He threw her an embarrassed smile. 'It was Abigail who took me to see him, when I was about five or so. She'd brought me over to the States with her while she was working on a film. Just came into my room in the middle of the night and threw some of my clothes into a bag, then we were off. Never said a word to Moira, or to my father, of course.' He looked down sadly at the chequered blanket. 'Strangest trip of my life. All I remember about it was spending a lot of time on my own in this huge hotel bed while she was out at parties, missing Moira and wishing she was there with me. Then one afternoon my mother took me to see this little bald old man with a German accent who smelt of brandy and pinched my cheeks, in a big white house that looked like an art gallery. And it was him. Wilder. I didn't understand who that was then. Wish I had. I'd have liked to have shaken him by the hand, if I'd been a bit older.'

Angel shook her head in disbelief. 'You've had some life, Seb.'

'Yeah.' He let out a bitter snort. 'It's been a bastard.'

It was a haunting image: the pale, lonely little boy, lying in a strange bed all by himself, wanting his mother. Responding to a sudden impulse, Angel flung herself forward, wrapped her arms round him and hugged him tight. She held him against her for a few seconds then broke away, hot and confused.

'Whew! What brought that on?' Seb looked a little windswept from her sudden embrace as he pushed his curls out of his eyes.

'Sorry,' she mumbled. 'Don't know what came over me.'

'You should let it come over you more often,' he said gently, his eyes sparkling. She looked down in confusion and grabbed another sandwich to give herself something to do with her hands.

Seb picked up the birthday cupcake with the little candle in it, pulled a pack of matches out of his pocket and lit it. He waggled it at her, making the little flame dance. 'Go on then. Make a wish.'

'I don't know if wishes still work the day after your birthday. But okay.' She scrunched her eyes tight and blew out the candle.

'Well? What did you wish?'

Angel shook her head with a rueful smile. 'Sorry. You know the golden rule.'

'If you tell me, it won't come true?'

'That's the one.' *But I bet you could take a fair guess…*

She cocked her head to one side when a new song came on the record player. 'Oh! I love this one.'

Seb smiled a soft little smile into her green eyes, twinkling with candlelight and appreciation while she listened to Nat singing 'Unforgettable'.

'Stand up, Ange.'

'Why?'

'Come on. Humour me.'

'Er, okay.' She lifted herself off the blanket and followed him out of the organ pit to the empty space between it and the row of chairs, wondering what unpredictable thing he was going to do now.

Seb turned to face her. 'May I have this dance, Miss Blackthorne?' he asked as he bent forward into a solemn bow.

Angel couldn't help laughing at him looking up at her with merry eyes. She dropped a passably gracious attempt at a curtsey in return and held out her right hand to him. 'Well… I believe I have a space on my card, Mr Wilchester.'

She stifled a gasp when he took hold of the hand she was offering and wove his fingers through hers. He curled his left arm around her waist, keeping her back from him at a little distance. All of a sudden he was touching her, holding her. She knew she should pull away, give him the kind but firm little speech she'd prepared after her conversation with Emily, but… she closed her eyes, absorbing the song, letting the moment wash over her.

260

Unforgettable, that's what you are. Unforgettable, though near or far...

She sighed as he began swaying her gently to the hypnotic ebb and swell of the music she loved. 'I didn't know you could dance,' she murmured, feeling suddenly shy. She could feel his thumb tip stroking softly along the curve of her hip, and she tried to slow the feverish pounding that had sprung up in her chest at their sudden contact.

'I can't,' he whispered. 'Don't let it get around, but I'm making this up as I go along.'

Angel opened her eyes and raised them to his, smiling. 'I won't tell if you don't.'

Abandoning all resistance now, she let Seb draw her into him and wrap her in strong arms, rocking her body dreamily in time to the softly crackling record. She knew she should stop it before things went any further, but all power to remove herself from those arms was gone. She rested her cheek against his chest and felt him bury his face in her hair, breathing deeply. He made a little noise when he caught her scent and pressed her tighter against him, as if scared she might slip away.

She drew out a long, blissful sigh, allowed herself to get lost in the moment, in that beautiful old tune and the comforting warmth of Seb's arms while they held her. She felt him press his lips to the top of her head, letting them linger there as the dance went on, but she had no strength to pull away. She inhaled deeply against him, relishing the smell of his woodsmoke-chocolate aftershave as it owned her senses.

Angel laughed as he twirled her like they did in the old-time films, then swung her back along his arm's length and into a tight embrace.

...like a song of love that clings to me, how the thought of you does things to me, never before...

She could feel his warm, deep breaths against her ear. He brought his hand up to her face, drew light, caressing fingertips

261

along her cheekbone, then moved them up into her hair. She shivered when he brushed the auburn strands back behind her shoulder, stroked along them tenderly, curled one strand around his finger. Her cheek, resting against his as they danced, was damp now from his tears.

'I love you,' she heard him murmur into her ear in a barely audible whisper. 'God, Angel, I love you so much.'

What did he just say? She jerked out of the dream, wriggled free from his embrace and jumped back as though she'd been stung.

'What the *hell*, Seb?' She backed away from him in shock.

'Oh God. I know, I know. I'm sorry.'

'Then say you take it back. Tell me it was just the music talking,' she challenged him.

'I… can't.' He brought full, anguished eyes up to meet hers. 'I can't. I don't want to.'

Coming close, he reached out for her but she pushed him away with both hands, eyes blazing fury. 'Jesus *Christ*, Seb! How long has Carole been out of rehab and you're already trying to find a new way to screw her up! Do me a favour and stay the hell away from me, can you?'

'Look, I was weak. I'm sorry. I said I was sorry. Can't we start again, Angel? Friends? Please.'

She gave a loud snort. 'Friends?' Her voice had risen almost to a shout as she faced off against him. 'I swear, I don't know at this point if we're supposed to be friends, lovers or a bloody film club. This is not *normal*, Seb. Friends don't have candlelit picnics and slow-dance to old records and tell each other –' she swallowed hard, fighting back tears – 'tell each other… they're in love. We are not *friends*. We can never *be* friends. I don't know what in the hell we are, but whatever it is it's pretty screwed up.'

He slumped down into one of the cinema seats and buried his fingers in his long curls. She looked away, willing herself not to break, to allow herself to pity him.

262

'This isn't going to work.' Her voice was soft now, soft and sad. 'But I think you know that, don't you?'

Exhausted, she sank down into a chair next to him and let her tears flow. 'Oh God. Why did you have to say it, you stupid bastard? Why?'

'I don't know,' he muttered in a broken, hollow voice. 'Maybe because I can't stop thinking about you. Because you're not like anyone I've ever met. Because you make me laugh. Because I can hardly even touch you without feeling that I – that I never want to let you go. Because – because I *love* you, Angel.' He choked back another muffled sob. 'Should've known I'd ruin everything.'

'Okay, well while you're feeling sorry for yourself, here's a question I never asked you in any interview,' she snapped, her anger rising again when he repeated the words. She grabbed his wrists, tore his hands away from his face and forced him to look at her. 'But I'd be bloody fascinated to know the answer. Do you love your wife, Seb?'

'I…'

'Go on, tell me you don't.' Her eyes flashed furiously. 'I double-dare you.'

'I… can't.' He wrenched his gaze away from hers and glared down at the gold wedding ring on his left hand. 'I can never say that.'

'Then this conversation's over. And so are we.' She stood up and dragged herself away from him towards the exit.

'Angel. Don't leave it like this.' Following her, he grabbed her hand to draw her back and she felt again that familiar pull, the need to be close to him, slamming through her treacherous veins and into every part of her body from the point where his skin met hers. God, if she could just let it take her. Let herself be happy, complete, as she had been in his arms moments ago…

No. She could fight it. It couldn't own her… could never own her.

Steeling herself, she clamped her fingers around his and met his eyes with a steady gaze.

'I'll stay and talk if you can tell me you don't feel that.'

'Oh God…' He looked down for a moment, sucking in his lip. 'Okay, fine, if that's what you need to hear. I don't. I don't feel anything.' He kept his face fixed, but she could see his eye flickering slightly at the corner, the little shudder that ran through his broad frame and along her arm.

'So you don't want to hold me?'

'No, I… no.'

She gave a grim snort. 'Don't lie to me, Seb. We're too far on for that. It's insulting.' She dropped his hand with an effort and spun back around to the exit.

'Ange. Just wait a second.' She looked over her shoulder at the note of quiet resignation that had crept into his voice. His features were twitching with emotion now and his tear-filled eyes flickered, reflecting the flame of the candles. 'If you really want to go, I won't try to change your mind. But your gift. Take that, at least.'

She shook her head. 'You know I can't accept that from you.'

'Please. I picked it out for you.'

'It's too valuable, Seb. It wouldn't be right. And… I don't want it.'

'But I want you to have it.' His voice was pleading as he retrieved the tennis racquet in its cardboard box from the organ pit and thrust it towards her. 'Here. Keep it. For me, Ange.'

'I… okay. If it means that much to you.' She was too drained to argue any more. Tucking the box under her arm, she walked away from him.

Standing in the doorframe, she turned back to look into the room.

'Seb.' He had sunk back into his chair and was staring up at the cinema screen, his face expressionless now, his eyes glazed and empty.

'What is it, Angel?'

Her voice sank almost to a whisper. 'I love you too.'

Before he had time to respond, she flung open the door and strode out of the auditorium, and out of his life.

Chapter 25

The first thing Angel did when she got back to the flat was to take the leather jacket Seb had given her the night of the ReelKids fundraiser out of her wardrobe. It still smelt of his aftershave and she held it against her face, inhaling deeply while she let it muffle her broken sobs. Then she wrapped it around the cardboard box containing the signed tennis racquet and shoved them both under the bed, out of her sight.

By the time Leo and Emily arrived back from their night out, she was huddled on the sofa under her duvet, cuddling an oblivious, purring Groucho and drinking wine straight from the bottle in the dark.

She sat, immovable, while Leo switched on the light and waved a hand in front of her spaced-out, tear-swollen eyes. 'I think she's broken,' he muttered to Emily as they packed in on either side of her.

'I'll just take this,' Emily said gently, prising the wine bottle out of Angel's clutches and putting it down on the coffee table. She drew her friend towards her, guiding Angel's head down on to her shoulder. 'Want to talk about it, kiddo?'

Angel gave a grim, slightly hysterical laugh, still staring straight ahead and stroking the cat absently like a stoned Blofeld. 'I can give you the executive summary if you like. The sweetest guy I've ever met made me a candlelit picnic, gave me an incredibly thoughtful birthday present that's probably worth more than this flat, slow-danced with me to Nat King Cole and told me he loved me. I screamed at him and left him forever. Now I literally have no tears left inside my actual body. And I'd appreciate it if you could give me back my wine so I can carry on getting steaming drunk, thanks, Em.'

'Je*sus*, Angel,' Leo said in a shocked voice. 'He told you he loved you? Bloody hell! Anything else?'

'Yeah. I told him I loved him too. Oh, and there were cucumber sandwiches. No crusts.'

Angel reached across Emily for her phone, vibrating on the arm of the sofa. She snorted as she dismissed the incoming call.

'Seb?' Emily asked.

'Yep. He's been trying to ring me all night.'

Emily stroked her hair, making all the right noises for sympathy and reassurance. 'Well done for staying strong, sweetie. Look, I know it doesn't seem like it now but it is for the best. I promise. I mean, realistically, how could this ever have a happy ending? Even if he left his wife and you two were together, you'd always be thinking about how you met. Wondering if you could really trust him. Once a cheat, always a cheat.'

'He wouldn't leave her,' Angel said vaguely. 'He loves her. He told me.'

Emily frowned. 'I thought he said he loved you?'

'He did. While we were dancing. It was… beautiful.' She gave another odd, high-pitched little laugh. 'Bastard.'

The phone buzzed again. Leo reached over the two women for it and swiped the screen. 'Look, she doesn't want to talk to you, mate,' he snapped into the microphone. Hanging up immediately, he flung it down on the table.

'I can tell you that self-medicating with this stuff won't do your bleeding heart any good, anyway,' he said to Angel, picking up her half-empty bottle of wine and eyeing it with distaste. 'Is this all you've had?'

Angel sniffed and snuggled her numb face into Emily's shoulder. 'There's an empty one in the kitchen.'

'Christ almighty, Ginge! Okay, I get that you need to wallow right now, but let's not go mad. It's a school night, you know. Work in the morning. You know you'll regret it.'

'Alright, Mr Sensitive,' Emily said, frowning at him. 'Why don't you go and get her a coffee, if you want to help? Bugger off so I can do the "good cop" routine for a bit. And put this wine in the fridge too, can you? She's already had enough for a blinding hangover tomorrow.'

***

Leo burst into her room the next morning without knocking. 'Wakey wakey, campers!'

'Ouch! No need for it, mate.' Angel groaned, rubbing her temples at the unwelcome boom of his voice. 'Why are you here again, anyway?' she grumbled, her voice muffled as she lay face down on her pillow. 'Your flatmates must've forgotten what you look like by now. I think you need to check yourself into one of those sex-addiction clinics.'

'Never mind that.' He jerked open the curtains to let the runny winter morning through the panes and yanked the duvet off her. She groaned in hangover-induced pain, the dawn light stinging into her salt-sore irises. 'Time for work. Come on, Ginge.'

'Hey! I could've been naked under here,' she complained groggily, feeling the duvet slip away.

Leo shrugged. 'Nothing I haven't seen before. Come on, up you get.'

She groaned again. 'I'm not going in today. Tell the boss I'm ill.'

'With what, Sad Bastarditis? Get a shift on, woman: heigh ho, heigh ho. We're late. There's no Tube today, don't forget.'

She pushed herself up on to one elbow with an effort and blinked at him through bleary eyes. 'I mean it, Leo. I'm pulling a sickie. Break-up's a perfectly valid reason for missing a day of work.'

'If you think Steve's going to be convinced by heartbreak and hangover as an excuse for skiving, even from his pet journo, then you're more deluded than I thought you were. He'll be forced to give you a lecture about working fourteen-hour days down t'pit from the age of five with a ferret down his trousers, or whatever it is his people do up there.'

She reached for her mobile, buzzing on the bedside table. Leo gave it a wary look.

'Wilchester again?'

'No. Just my morning alarm.'

'You think he's given up?'

She gave a gloomy shrug. 'Dunno. I'll find out today, I suppose. He will eventually, if I keep ignoring him.'

Leo sat down on the bed next to her prostrate form and patted the frizzy auburn mass of her hair. 'Come on, Ginge,' he said, gentling his voice. 'I know yesterday was tough on you. But you'll only be moping around this place feeling sorry for yourself otherwise. Work'll be good for you. Take your mind off it.'

'I can't feel my eyes, Leo,' she mumbled, rubbing where she remembered they used to be. 'Or my brain.'

He grabbed the limp arm that hung over the side of the bed and pulled her up into a sitting position. 'Go on, bathroom's free. Get in before Em sets up camp in there for the next few hours. A shower'll help you feel better.'

Leo was a liar. A shower didn't make her feel better, at least not for any significant period of time. As they bussed into work, their usual route cut off by yet another Tube strike, she could feel the thin, cold fingers of white sunlight prodding her right between the eyes.

269

The bus was crammed and she was forced to pack in next to some Sniffy McNoTissue and his pestilential germs. Even the sight of the Christmas decorations adding some colour to the dirty streets couldn't lift her spirits. And she noticed the posters for the DVD release of *The Milkman Cometh* seemed to have started appearing on billboards and phone boxes around the city. She blinked back tears, remembering the day she'd spent at Tigerblaze helping Seb pick out a design. He was everywhere. How could she forget about him when he was everywhere?

Everything seemed empty now, a ghoulish imitation of her world. She'd spent months trying to free herself from the idea and the reality of Seb Wilchester. Now that he was actually out of her life with something like finality, she felt as if the one thing that had been buoying her up for the last four months, since that night at the hotel, had been wiped out in an instant. Not just Seb but hope, excitement. And, she realised now, something that had been growing the more she'd learnt about him: love. But she couldn't think about that any more, it hurt her face. That or the wine did, anyway.

There was a life lesson for the twenty-first century, she thought dryly. Love was a bitch and it hurt your face. If this film-critic thing ever fell through, she could probably get freelance work selling gems like that to *Cosmo*.

By the time they reached work, they were more than half an hour late. 'Morning,' she said in a tired voice to Savannah.

The intern examined her with concern. 'Are you okay, Ange? You look awful. Too much celebrating for your birthday, was it?'

'Er, yeah, something like that.'

She fished in her pocket when she felt her phone begin to buzz, giving a bitter snort as she dismissed another call from Seb.

'Who was that?'

'Oh, no one. Sales call.'

Angel wasn't sure how she managed to drag herself through the morning, but somehow she did it. She had some shorthand notes to transcribe for a screener DVD she'd watched the day before, so she started with those. A nice, easy job. Then she wrote them up into what had to be the world's worst-written review and sent it with reckless abandon off to Steve.

She couldn't work out if she was hungover or still drunk from the quantity of wine she'd necked the night before, but she felt oddly detached, as if she was having an out-of-body experience or something. Anyway, she certainly couldn't face lunch. She spent the break at her desk, resting her temples on her fingers with her eyes closed.

'Oh, I forgot!' Savannah said, coming back from her break. 'Here, this is for you.' She rummaged in her desk drawer and handed a rectangular gift-wrapped object to Angel, beaming as usual. 'For your birthday. Sorry it's late.'

'Thanks, Sav,' Angel said, surprised and touched by the thought. 'You didn't have to do that.'

'I hope you like it. Just released, so I knew you wouldn't have it. The newly remastered special edition,' Savannah said, beaming as she watched Angel peel off the paper. 'I asked Leo, and he said it was your favourite.'

To Savannah's surprise, her friend took one look at the copy of *The Apartment* and burst into a flood of tears.

'Hey,' Savannah said, distressed at the sudden outburst. 'What's up, Ange? Is it the wrong thing?' She came over to her friend's desk and put her arms around her neck in a comforting hug. 'I didn't mean to make you cry. I'm sorry.'

'It's – nothing.' Angel struggled to choke back the tears. 'Just – reminded me of something, that's all.' She summoned a watery smile. 'Boy trouble, you know? It's perfect, Sav, really it is. Leo was right, it is my favourite film.'

Was that even true any more? She wondered if she could ever watch it again without thinking about Seb. Another thing which up until then had brought joy into her life. He'd taken that away with him too.

Savannah shushed her softly, rubbing a hand around her back. Angel tried hard to push back the stinging drops. Her eyes were still dry and puffy from last night's bout of crying, and she rubbed the angry red skin with a wince of pain.

Her phone buzzed again. It was a text message this time:

Need to talk to you.

It was probably best she'd broken up with Seb, she thought sourly. His text message etiquette was really appalling. Still, at least he didn't 'lol'. Small mercies. She swiped the screen to delete his message and put her phone back on the desk.

'Blackthorne.'

Steve was calling her from the door of his office in that way he had, eyeing her with a look of deep concern. She knew he couldn't have avoided seeing her crying and Savannah comforting her. Mentally, she cursed whoever had designed that bloody glass-fronted office of his.

'Coming, boss,' she said wearily. Savannah flashed her a sympathy eyeroll as she went to join Steve.

'Keeping you up?' the editor asked as she took a seat at his desk and yawned heavily.

'Muh.'

He ignored the zombified reply and picked up a printout from his desk. 'Right. Firstly, love, this review is absolute shite. Take it away and try again,' he growled, handing back the piece she'd emailed that morning. It was scrawled all over with his notes in angry red biro.

She nodded her tired, aching head, stifling a groan. 'And?'

'And, you came in half an hour late this morning looking like death cooled down, spent your dinner break groaning at your desk and you haven't eaten all day. I'm not stupid, pet, despite all appearances to the contrary. I know a pissing hangover when I see one.' He glared at her. 'Well?'

'Sorry, Steve,' she mumbled. 'Won't happen again.'

'See it doesn't.'

'Anything else?' she said quietly. She had absolutely no energy to do battle with Steve. Not today. Just agree and get the hell out of there. Get through the day. That was the best thing.

'Yeah. Stop crying over that bastard Wilchester and pull yourself together. You're no bloody good to anyone in this state.'

She almost reeled in shock, if it was possible to reel while still sitting down.

'How do you know that?' she whispered. 'How can you possibly know that?'

He shrugged. 'Right though, aren't I? Come on, Princess. What sort of journalist would I be if I couldn't see what's right there in front of my face? You've had him on your mind for months.'

So apparently there were at least two people in the world who knew what she was feeling better than she did: Emily and Steve. Maybe she should just hand over the keys to Operation Lost Cause, codename Angel Blackthorne, and let them drive.

Christ. She knew she was hungover when she could mix that many metaphors in one sentence.

'Go on, get your stuff and go home,' he said. 'Take the rest of the afternoon out of your holiday allowance. You can give that crap review to blondie outside to finish, it'll be good experience for her. Don't want my star critic making herself ill.'

'Really, you're sending me home? Bloody hell, did you get visited by the Ghost of Christmas Past last night or something?'

'Let's say I'm going soft in my declining years. Now go on, bugger off before I change my mind. Get yourself home for some Alka-Seltzer and sleep. And make sure you're in all the earlier on Monday.'

'Er, okay… thanks, boss.'

'What's happening?' Savannah asked when Angel arrived back to her desk and started collecting her things.

'Steve wants me to go home. Take the rest of the afternoon as

273

holiday and get some rest. And he says to give you this, see what you can do with it.' She handed over the biro-scrawled review.

'What?' Savannah looked over at Steve's office, frowning. 'That's not like him. I mean, I know you're his favourite, but…' She smirked at Angel. 'You know, Kev told me…'

'Yeah, yeah. I'm shagging the boss, right?' Angel managed a watery grin. 'And what do you think, Sav? Am I that hard up?'

Savannah looked over at Steve scratching his backside by the window of his office and curled her lip. 'Good point.'

'You're still seeing him, then? Kev?'

'Yes.' Savannah dropped her eyes, fiddling with a pen lid on her desk. 'I don't want to jinx it, but it's actually going really well. I'm seeing him again tonight. He's taking me to that new restaurant in Islington, the expensive one.'

'All the restaurants in Islington are expensive, Sav,' Angel said. She couldn't help wondering where this blind spot came from, the one that seemed to cause Savannah to imagine Kev as the strong, silent type rather than just the miserable git he so clearly was. Still, she seemed happy. That was the main thing.

The office phone on Angel's desk started to ring, making her jump. It was pretty rare she got calls at work. Everything was done by email, usually. Probably some ambulance-chaser wanting to ask if she'd ever had an accident in the workplace.

'*Investigator*?'

'Angel. Don't hang up.' The voice at the other end was deep and warm, like the hints of chocolate in the aftershave he always wore. And it sounded tired.

'How did you get this number?' she hissed, looking around to see if anyone was listening. Savannah was staring at her with wide eyes.

'It's a newspaper office, Ange. They've got a website.'

'Look, I can't talk to you here. I'm at work. There are people around.' She lowered her voice. 'Reporter people who can hear every word I say. And I told you last night…'

274

'I just want one minute. Please, Angel. I'm not going to say anything to upset you.'

'Well?'

'What are you doing tonight?'

'What! Why is that any of your business?'

'No, it's not… Look, can you come to my place? I mean, to the house. I can text you the address.'

'I thought I told you to stay the hell away from me!' she whispered furiously.

'Wait! Don't hang up.' His voice became urgent as he sensed her about to put down the receiver. 'It's not like that. Carole will be there.'

'What?' Surprise crept into her voice.

'We want to talk to you. The two of us. It won't take long. Then you can go and I'll never bother you again, I promise.'

'I can go now and you'll never bother me again. Not once the restraining order comes through.' She tried to keep up an angry tone, but she had to admit she was intrigued. What could Carole Beaumont possibly have to say to her?

'Come on, don't be like that. Are you going to? I'm not planning on stalking you, Angel. I just want five minutes, that's all. It's important.' He paused. 'This is probably a good time to make it clear I'm not trying to rope you into a threesome, right?'

She tried to stop herself, but she couldn't help it. She burst into a laugh.

'You absurd bastard.'

She could practically hear him grinning down the phone. 'Then you'll come?'

She frowned, hesitating. 'Well… okay. But five minutes. And for once, I'll let you send your bloody car for me. It'll cost a fortune to get to Kensington during a Tube strike.'

'Who was that?' Savannah asked, watching her hang up the phone.

Angel looked her friend straight in the eye. She felt giddy and her head was almost inside out, but she kept a straight face. 'That was Sebastian Wilchester, Savannah, the Palme D'Or-winning film director, who wants to know if I'll go to his house tonight to have a threeway with him and his wife.'

Savannah smiled uncertainly. 'You're joking.'

Shaking her poor sore head and laughing, Angel grabbed her bag and left the office.

***

The black-liveried chauffeur was silent and professional, hidden from Angel by a tinted-glass screen while she sat in luxury in the back of Seb's limo. She leaned back and stretched out her legs comfortably. So this was how the other half lived, was it? It certainly beat the sardine-tin hell of the Tube.

She felt marginally more human after squeezing in a few hours' sleep that afternoon. The odd detached feeling had started to dissolve and the world was no longer spinning alarmingly. If she could only get rid of the throbbing behind her eyeballs. Even paracetamol didn't seem to be helping. Nor did nagging anxiety about her upcoming encounter with the wife of the man who, despite everything, she couldn't help being in love with.

The driver got out to open two huge iron gates with a security pass and she gasped as the car crunched up a gravel track to Seb and Carole's house.

It was easy to forget, when she was spending time with him, the sort of life Seb lived and how different it was from her own. Easy to forget they were anything more than just a man and a woman. Seeing his house brought the difference between them home to her with a solid sucker punch between the eyes.

She'd seen it before, of course, in photos and on TV. But never in real life. It was a huge mansion made of some golden stone, sandstone probably, nestled into its own carefully mani-cured grounds. Ivy curled around the two rows of seven or eight mullioned windows, flashing formidably at her in the winter sun.

How could this be a home for just two people? It looked like a Victorian orphanage.

Seb was waiting for her at the door when she got out of the car, which quickly disappeared around the back of the house. He was looking gorgeous as usual, the wind whipping his chestnut curls around his face in zigzags, but grey-skinned and tired. The bags under his eyes told her he hadn't passed the night any more happily than she had.

'Come on,' he said, taking her elbow to guide her into the house. She jerked her arm away from his touch.

'Where's this all going, Seb?' she said in a low voice, following him along a lengthy passage towards a large oak door. 'What is it you want to talk to me about? We said everything we had to say last night.'

'It's Carole who wants to talk to you, not me,' he said, his gaze still focused straight ahead. 'Through here.'

He opened the door to a large sitting room that looked more like a library: plush, dark and woody, smelling of oranges and cedarwood. A huge, twinkling Christmas tree in the corner lent an inappropriate festive air to the occasion.

Angel's stomach knotted when she caught sight of Carole Beaumont, in black leggings and a long, flowing pink top, waiting for her. She noticed with surprise that Suzanne, Seb's PA, was there too.

What, was he starting a harem or something?

'Hi, Angel,' Carole said, blushing.

'Hi,' Angel said with an answering blush.

Well, this isn't awkward...

Carole laughed suddenly. 'Oh, this is silly,' she said, taking Angel's hand and pulling her into a hug. She planted a kiss on each cheek and Angel's eyes widened in surprise. 'I shouldn't greet someone who helped save my life so coolly, should I?'

Angel stood, confused and blank, staring at Carole. Okay, what the hell was going on here?

'Oh, I think you know Suzanne?' Carole said, taking the girl's hand and bringing her forward. Carole locked her baby-blue eyes into Angel's green ones. 'My girlfriend.'

Chapter 26

Suzanne coloured to the roots of her pixie cut and flashed Angel a shy smile. 'Hi again.'

Angel actually staggered backwards. She could feel Seb behind her, putting strong hands on her hips to support her, and she leaned against him in shock.

'I'm sorry, your…?'

'My girlfriend.' Carole looked up at Seb. 'She knows what that means, doesn't she?' she said in a stage whisper. 'We don't need to have the birds-and-the-bees talk?'

'Yeah, Car, she knows how it works. Trust me.'

'I'll go stick the kettle on or something, sweets,' Suzanne said, giving Carole a peck on the cheek and turning to leave the room. 'You three need to talk, I think.'

Angel shook her head in bewilderment. She let Seb guide her over to a large, heavily cushioned leather armchair, sank down into it and fixed her vacant stare straight ahead.

'I'm sorry, I'm confused. What the hell is going on?'

Seb sat down on the sofa opposite her and started twisting his wedding band around his finger. 'It's simple really, Ange. Well, no, it's complicated, but what it boils down to is that those guys are a couple. Me and Carole – well, we're family. But we're not together. Not like that.'

'Not –' Angel stared at him in shock and disbelief. 'You mean you… you can't mean you… you… *bastard!*' she hissed. 'All these months we've been – for Christ's sake, Seb!' She pushed her temples into her hands, trying to get her head around this new information. 'Why didn't you tell me before?'

'Hey.' Carole Beaumont moved behind her chair and put a warning hand on Angel's shoulder. 'Calm down a bit, darling. It wasn't him, it was me.'

She walked across to Seb and took a seat next to him.

'Don't get me wrong, I was grateful for what you did for me. You know, at the premiere,' she went on. 'Or I was, once I started to get my head straight again. But – well, what you do for a living, you know? I'm sorry, but I've had some pretty bad experiences with that myself. And then after what you did to Seb…'

'The honey trap.' Angel rubbed the bridge of her nose. 'I'm so sorry, Carole. God, you must have hated me.'

The actress shrugged her perfect shoulders. 'I wasn't always your biggest fan,' she admitted. 'Seb told me everything that happened that night at the hotel.'

'Everything?'

'Well, maybe not quite everything. There are some things I don't need to hear.' Seb wrinkled his nose as she ruffled his curls in a sisterly manner. 'But he told me enough.'

'So? What changed?'

She laughed, that little, tinkling laugh Angel recalled from every time she'd seen the tiny actress interviewed on TV. 'It was pretty hard to stay mad at you after the premiere. I don't really remember it, but… Seb told me you probably saved my life that night.' Her blue eyes sparkled with sincerity and gratitude. 'Thanks for that, darling.'

'And what about you?' Angel glared over at Seb.

'I guess I always planned to tell you at some point, Ange. But it was for Carole to decide when the time was right. I couldn't make that decision for her.'

There was more, though. She could see it in his eyes. 'You still didn't trust me,' she said, dropping her eyes to the hands folded awkwardly in her lap. 'Did you?'

'No,' he confessed. 'Not a hundred per cent. Not right away. You can understand that, can't you, after what happened? I needed to be sure. I couldn't take any chances with Carole and Suze's happiness: two of the people dearest to me.' Carole looked up at him with a fond smile and linked her arm through his.

'When he came back here last night I couldn't stand it any more,' she said to Angel. 'Having his miserable old face on my conscience. Gave him carte blanche to tell you everything.' She locked Angel in an earnest gaze. 'He loves you, you know.'

Angel turned crimson as Seb frowned at Carole.

'So?' he said, turning to Angel.

'So, what?'

'Me and you. What do you think?'

'I don't know, Seb.' She felt dazed. Needed time to process everything that had been said. 'I don't know.'

Before she knew what was happening he was standing up and walking towards her, his eyes full and heavy-lidded. When he reached her chair, he grabbed her hand and pulled her to her feet. Tilting her chin to bring her face up to his, he brought his thin, sculpted lips, those lips she'd fantasised about for so long, on to hers. His thumbs came to rest on her cheeks, his fingers under her hair...

Angel felt the room fizz away while he kissed her: not the hungry, devouring kisses he'd rained down on her that night at the hotel, those hot kisses that had seemed to draw her sensuality sweetly, painfully up by the roots and leave it pooling and frothing at his feet. This kiss screamed to something in her soul.

She felt his tongue part her lips, insistent but gentle, and gave in to the crushing, engulfing warmth as she opened her mouth and

281

let herself kiss him back. The hot breath from his nostrils burned against her cheek, one arm travelling around her back and tender fingertips caressing the nape of her neck. And she was lost in him.

She brought her hands up to grasp his shirt collar, pulled his solid mass closer to her, deepened the kiss until it owned every sense. Her head was swamped, double-reeling like a fairground waltzer... and then he was gone, drawing back from her, and her glazed eyes flickered open again.

'How about now, Angel?' he whispered, those expressive tawny eyes searching her face.

'Huh.' Her mouth seemed to have lost the ability to form speech. As if all the words had been kissed right out of her.

He smiled. 'That's what I like to hear.'

As he moved out of her line of sight and she sank back, breathless, into her seat, Angel noticed Suzanne had come back into the room and taken Seb's place on the sofa. She was hand in hand with Carole and the pair of them were grinning at her.

'Come on, my fellow gooseberry,' Carole said, turning to Suzanne. 'All this snogging is getting a bit voyeuristic for my taste. Let's get out of here. These two need some space, I think. If you're very good I'll let you take me back to yours for dinner and have your way with me.'

Suzanne blushed. 'Sorry about her,' she said to Angel, shooting Carole an affectionate sideways glance. 'She seems to think I can't resist her.'

'You can't resist me, Suzie.'

'Well, okay, fair point. Come on then, sweets.'

'Look after him, won't you?' Carole said to Angel. She reached up to ruffle Seb's unruly hair again as she dragged Suzanne past him to the door. 'He's a good boy. And see if you can make him get a haircut.'

Seb ran his fingers through the curls, his brow puckering attractively. 'I like my hair,' he muttered to himself, sitting back down opposite Angel.

'Me too.'

He dimpled, leaning back and crossing an ankle over one knee. 'Back with us, are you?'

Her head was still spinning and she shook it feverishly, trying to focus.

'Okay, let's have it then,' Seb said.

'What?'

'Questions. I know you must have a ton,' he said. 'For as long as I've known you, you've been sticking a dictaphone in my face and asking me things. Don't tell me you haven't got anything after a bombshell like that.'

'Okay, you could start with why,' she said, trying not to fixate on his perfect lips. 'It's not the fifties, Seb.'

'Yeah. Ridiculous, isn't it?' he said with a sigh. 'The lavender marriage thing should have long been relegated to history by now.'

'Then why hasn't it?'

'I don't know. That's just the way things still are in this industry. There's a lot of homophobia. I mean, how many gay film stars can you name? I bet you can count them on the fingers of one hand. Things are changing, but coming out can still kill a career.'

It was true, thinking about it. She could barely name a handful of stars openly in same-sex relationships.

'And I suppose people like to think about their pin-ups on their arm,' Seb continued. 'Carole was a sex symbol, and men wanted to imagine being with her.'

'You haven't answered my question, though. Why? Not why generally. Why you?'

'We were worried about Carole losing out on parts, for one thing. But… well, I suppose the main reason was I wanted to protect her. Things were even worse six years ago when we married than they are now, and then there was the fact she'd been a child star. The press would've been all over it. And she's… sensitive to that kind of thing.'

283

'So it was your idea?'

'Yeah. She didn't really want to go along with it at first. Said I'd be throwing my own life away: the opportunity to meet someone. Maybe have a family. But that didn't bother me then. The kind of girls I used to go out with at the time were... well, I could take them or leave them. Career-obsessed actresses, usually. The occasional fan would go all doe-eyed at me because they loved my work, but that just seemed like taking advantage. Anyway, Carole meant a lot more to me than anyone else. And after the family life I'd grown up with, having one of my own was the last thing I wanted. So we did it, and I forgot about relationships, threw myself into work... and then you came along.' Angel coloured as he sought her eyes.

'When did she first tell you? That she liked girls, I mean?'

'When she was about eleven, I think. I was a bit older, but she was always the streetwise one. She asked if I wanted to practise kissing with her. For when we were grown up.' He reddened slightly. 'I was this shy, geeky, scrawny thing of about thirteen. Bit of an age gap, but I always did what she told me in those days. So she gave me a kiss, told me flat out I was rubbish at it and said she didn't think boys were for her. And that was that.' He laughed. 'Obviously I put her off for life.'

'Oh, I don't know, you're not so bad at it.' Unconsciously Angel brought one finger up to press her lips, still tingling from his touch.

His eyes twinkled wickedly. 'Come here and tell me that.'

She shook her head, grinning at him. 'Not yet. Or we'll never finish this conversation.'

'Okay, you'd better hurry up then. What else?'

Angel rubbed a fingernail thoughtfully. 'Why is Carole so sensitive to the press, Seb? She grew up with it, didn't she?'

She noticed his brow darken. 'Sorry. I shouldn't have asked.'

'No... it's okay. She told me I could tell you anything.' He raised a faint smile. 'Said if I trusted you, that was good enough for her. Just bad memories, that's all.'

She watched the emotions flicker across his handsome face, fascinated.

'I told you about my parents. Hugo, the years of abuse; Abigail and her problems.' A scowl tightened his features. 'Well, Carole's were worse.'

'Worse?' Her eyebrows shot up in shock. 'Jesus, Seb! Is that even possible? What did they do to her?'

He gave a bitter snort of laughter. 'The weird thing was, they loved her to bits. She was the golden girl to them, couldn't do any wrong. So much so they wanted everyone to have a share in her. They had her in that God-awful sitcom of theirs at six, styled and manicured like a thirty-year-old woman when any normal kid would've been playing dollies' tea parties.'

He frowned down at his wedding ring. 'She started wearing make-up regularly when she was about eight, with her mum's full encouragement. Sally used to throw little makeover parties for her, like she was some sort of human doll. The whole thing was ghoulish. And then as she got older they were working her harder, pushing her into more and more film roles, and the press were following her at every turn, hounding her, running those perverted "all grown up" stories they do and trying to get shots of her in a bikini. I mean, a twelve-year-old, for Christ's sake! I guess you'd be a bit young to remember.'

He looked at her, his face stern. 'And your paper was one of the worst. That scumbag Steve Clifton was editor then as well. The whole thing was sick. Really sick.'

Angel's cheeks burned with shame. She didn't need to ask herself if Steve was capable of going that low. The man would sell his own mother if he could get a front page out of it. 'God, Seb,' she said in a whisper. 'I had no idea. I'm so sorry.'

'Sorry, Angel,' he said, closing his eyes and massaging his temples with his fingertips. 'I didn't mean it to sound like I blamed you. I don't, obviously. That was a long time ago. It's just… well, it's hard not to get angry, thinking back.'

'Well? What happened to her?'

'At fourteen she had a total meltdown. It was inevitable, really. Drugs, prescription meds, self-harm, the lot. Her parents tried to cover it up, sent her off for a spell in rehab and passed it off as boarding school or something. But she was a mess.' His eyes were damp as the memories came flooding back.

'Hey. You want to take a break?' Angel asked, gentling her voice. But he shook his head, forcing himself on just as he had that day at Tigerblaze.

'When she got home, the first thing she did was get her stuff and move out,' he went on. 'Came to live with me and Moira next door. Hugo was long dead by then, thank God, and Abigail was too out of it to notice really. Carole's barely seen her parents since then. They moved to California a couple of years after and left her with us. Thank Christ. If they'd still had their claws in her, God knows what would have happened to her in the end.'

He heaved a deep sigh. 'She reminded me a bit of Abigail. What she could have been if someone had been able to get through to her like I could with Carole. But at least I could help one of them. It took years, and she still has relapses... this latest spell in rehab was a big setback. Still, we're getting there. She's been better these last couple of years, since she's had Suzanne. And getting involved with ReelKids was a lifeline too.' His voice was breaking with emotion. Angel stood up and went over to him now, sank down next to him on the sofa and took his hand.

'I do understand, you know,' she said softly, lifting the hand to her lips and printing a kiss on the backs of his fingers. 'I mean, I know it's not the same...'

'Leo?'

'Yeah. Except I couldn't help him in the end. I thought I could, but... he had to do it for himself.'

'Must've been hard for you,' he said, giving the hand he was holding a gentle squeeze. 'But he seems okay now. At least he seems to be able to be around the stuff without it affecting him. He was fine that night in the pub.'

'Yeah, now. Although to be honest I don't think it was ever the proximity of booze that was his problem,' Angel said with a shrug. 'It was just this trigger that went off in his brain, something buried inside him. He wouldn't drink for weeks, then he'd start to rub his cheek one morning and I'd know, when I got home, that it'd be the slurred speech, the glazed eyes and the half-empty bottle of vodka hidden in the toilet cistern. If he was there. Sometimes he'd disappear for the night and roll up looking like hell in the morning. I never knew where it was he went.' She gave a sad little laugh. 'He told me once he didn't even like the taste.'

'When did you end it?'

'Over two years ago now. When he disappeared for days in a row.' She winced when she thought back to that time, the most painful of her life. 'It was a weekend. I was at home, crying, trying to ring him every few minutes, worried sick, wondering whether to call the police. I knew I wasn't helping him, that we couldn't live like that any more. So when he got back and I'd nursed him past the worst of it, I packed my stuff and went to stay with Em. We spent months afterwards trying to get him into AA.' She choked back a sob. 'Jesus, I'm so glad we did! He could be dead now.'

'Hey,' he whispered, so gently it was almost a breath. 'Come here, you.'

He put an arm around her and drew her towards him. She snuggled into him, buried her face into the hollow of his shoulder for a moment. 'Oh God, Seb,' she murmured brokenly. 'Do I really get to keep you this time?'

'Always, if you want.' He planted a tender kiss on top of her head. Angel gave a small, muffled sob, breathing him in.

She took his left hand in both of hers and looked at the gold wedding ring, running her thumb over the shiny metal. 'You weren't wearing this that night,' she said quietly.

'This thing? No.' He smiled. 'Actually it's brand new. Kev made me get it. For the *Milkman* premiere. Thought it would show togetherness after that story you ran, you know? Carole never gave me a band when we married. I can't really get used to wearing it though.' He twisted it off his finger and put it down on the arm of the sofa. Angel didn't know why but she felt a sudden surge of relief and happiness. She nestled her body closer into his.

'Does he know then? Kev?'

'He knows something,' Seb said, shrugging. 'I didn't tell him, but he seems to know we're not really together. And he knew about rehab, I had to give him that. He's never said anything, though, about Carole and me. Just somehow appointed himself chief guardian of our privacy. Charmless git he might be, but he's loyal. And he's discreet.' He grinned. 'Except when he's telling everyone you're sleeping with Clifton, obviously.'

He put a finger under her chin and tilted her face up to his. 'Why did you do it, Ange?' he asked, his voice soft. He didn't say what he meant, but she knew. The honey trap. It always came back to that.

'Honestly, now I look back, I don't know. I mean, I'd always wanted to work in journalism, and Steve said… he made it sound like it could be something career-defining for me. I told you, I was only ever supposed to get your clothes off, not… well, you were there, you know what happened. I justified it by telling myself if you didn't want to cheat on Carole, you wouldn't. Used some warped redtop moral compass to convince myself you were the bad guy and not me. That I'd be doing her a favour. For a while I think I almost believed it, too.' Her cheeks burned with shame and remorse. 'When I got to the bar that night, I still wasn't sure if I'd be able to go through with it. And then you were there and I just wanted to be with you.' She stroked his fingers shyly. 'You, er, you were only my second, you know. After Leo.'

'Bloody hell! Really? How did that happen?'

She couldn't help laughing. 'Alright, no need to sound quite so amazed. I don't know, late starter I guess. Hard to do the boyfriend thing properly when you're moving from place to place all the time. And when me and Leo broke up... well, let's just say after that disaster I didn't date much.' She lifted his hand to her hot cheek, held it against her. 'God, Seb, I feel awful about that night! I don't know why you ever forgave me. I wouldn't have.'

'I almost didn't.' He ran a finger down her tear-stained face, traced the dot-to-dot freckles around her nose. 'I was angry, really angry, when I saw the story in the paper. But then there was what happened at the premiere... and afterwards when I thought about that night we spent together, I couldn't help it: all I remembered was you – how good you felt. So different from anyone else I've been with. That sweet, funny little laugh, those incredible eyes, and my God, that body...' She shivered as he ran an appreciative hand along the curve of her body, letting it come to rest at her waist. 'I haven't exactly been a monk all my life, Ange, even after I got married. But I never made a habit of picking up girls in bars. Wouldn't have been so careless. With you, though, it was like I couldn't help myself. I'd never wanted anyone that much before. And if it happened again, I'd act just the same way, I think.'

Her eyes were full when she brought them up to meet his. 'Jesus, Seb... what are you doing to me?' She guided him to her for a hot, deep kiss, feeling dazed, dizzy and so, so happy she was allowed, now, finally, to enjoy his touch without holding back.

Seb slipped the hand that had been at her waist into the small of her back and guided her up on to his lap. He held her there, pressed her tight against him, buried his face into the crook of her neck and inhaled deeply.

'You'll stay with me,' he whispered. It wasn't a question or a command. It was just a statement. She gave a tiny little nod and let her consciousness sink entirely into the consuming warmth of his lips on hers.

Chapter 27

'Come on.' Seb drew back from another long kiss, his voice husky. He manoeuvred Angel off his lap, stood up and took her hand.

'Where are we going?'

'Where do you think?' He leaned towards her for another kiss, panting slightly. 'If I can keep my hands off you long enough to get you there.'

He led her impatiently past the twinkling tree, the rows of old books on mahogany shelves, the record-player cabinet she recognised instantly from last night at the cinema, out into the passage towards the polished wood staircase leading to the second storey. Through the fog of desire she wondered which of the many windows she'd seen on the drive in had belonged to Seb's room.

'Oh God, Ange, I can't wait,' he groaned. 'I want you too much to wait.' He turned to face her, gripped her shoulders and pushed her back against the marbled wall of the passageway as he brought his mouth down hard on hers. His kisses were urgent now; greedy. She moaned, feeling the solid evidence of his arousal against her hips when he pressed his body on to hers.

'Seb… oh, God… I can feel you…' Frantic fingers reached for the buttons at the front of his shirt, fumbling them open. She untucked it from his jeans and stripped it away from his torso to the floor, planting feverish kisses along the muscles of his neck.

'Wait.' He pulled back from her with an effort, sucking in his lip to stifle the moan that would have answered hers. 'We've waited a long time for this, Angel. Let's do it right.' He ran a caressing thumb along her cheek. 'Come on. We can make it.'

'You say that to me now, when I've just got your shirt off?' she muttered, pushing him to arm's length and running trembling fingers along the taut muscles of his chest and stomach. She swallowed hard. 'Jesus, Seb, it had better not be far…'

Taking her hand, he almost dragged her up the stairs and along a long corridor. He swung her smoothly round to him and into his arms, his mouth covering hers, as he pushed her backwards through the door that led into his room.

She groped behind her in the almost-darkness, trying to get her bearings. 'Oh God, where's the bed? Where's the bed, Seb?'

'Here. Over here.' His breathing was ragged now. He guided her over to a large double bed and they fell on to it together. Taking her face in both hands, he claimed her mouth with his.

Her fingers glided up his back along the bare skin, pushed his body down on to hers. She wrapped her legs around his thighs and dragged out a low, longing moan when she felt him press into her through the denim of his black jeans.

'Oh, Angel, my Angel…'

'You've… called me that before,' she panted, running her tongue over his earlobe.

'When?'

'In a dream I had. The night before… ah!… the night before I came to Tigerblaze.' As he moved his lips to her neck, she slid her hands up into his hair, combing through the long curls. Christ, what was it about that hair that just did things to her? Asleep or awake, she couldn't keep her fingers out of it.

Angel could just see his eyes, almost glowing in the dim light, as he looked up from the line of hot, frantic kisses he was planting along her neck.

'Am I in your dreams a lot?' he breathed.

'All the time.'

'What do I do in your dreams?'

'Same as you do in real life. Drive me crazy.'

'Do I do this?' he whispered, lifting his body slightly and sliding one hand up her top, under her bra, to massage a hard, rosy nipple with his thumb.

She gasped, arching her back to press her breast into the cup of his palm. 'Yes, Seb. All the time.'

'And this?' With his other hand, he undid the fastening of her jeans and helped her wiggle them off over her hips, running soft fingers across her naked thighs.

'Yes... Seb. Oh, God...' Her head fell back, savouring his touch on her bare flesh. She let him unbutton her top too and toss it to one side.

'And do I tell you I love you, in your dreams?' he murmured into her ear. She gasped when he said those magic words, the same ones that last night had sent her seething with anger – knowing they could belong to her now and no one could take them away.

'No. You never tell me that.'

'You tell me in mine all the time,' he whispered, covering her lips with his.

As Seb's hot, tantalising mouth continued to roam over her body, Angel blinked hard, the hangover she'd been fighting all day now finally threatening to overwhelm her. Sleep was rising up to do battle with the need she had to be with him, to be as close to him as she could. And it was bloody well winning as well. *Oh God, not now! Please, please, not now! Damn you, alcohol, damn you to hell!*

'Hey,' he panted, stopping when he noticed her go quiet and her hand slide away from him. 'What's wrong, Angelface?'

She gave a sleepy laugh. 'Angelface? Do we do nicknames now?'

'Yeah, I think we do nicknames now.'

'Okay, but… might need to rethink that one.'

She guided him off her and over to her side, groaning with frustration. 'Seb, I'm so sorry. We've waited so long… but I'm exhausted. Last night, after the cinema, I was so upset… well, let's just say I'm not operating at a hundred per cent today.' She laughed sheepishly. 'Oh Christ, what an anti-climax…'

He leaned up on his elbow and looked down at her, a little half-smile curving the corner of his mouth.

'You know, some men might be offended at being told their lovemaking technique was sending a woman to sleep…'

She groaned again, a different kind of groan, as she ran her fingertips along his bare chest, into the grooves of his toned stomach. 'I want you so much right now,' she murmured. 'But the last thing I need is to pass out on you. Not after all this time. I mean, four months, Seb. I just want it to be… perfect.' She sought his eyes with hers. 'You're not too disappointed, are you? I know it's hard…' She bit her lip to stifle a giggle. 'Er, sorry.'

Seb flung an arm around her and folded her into him. He dragged the duvet over them both and buried his face in her thick hair. 'I'm lying here with a beautiful woman in my arms, who, as an added bonus, is now in just her underwear,' he said with a smile. 'What's to disappoint?' She laughed and pressed a tired kiss on to his forehead in response. 'We've got all the time in the world, Angel,' he whispered as she snuggled into him. 'I'm not going anywhere. I'll wait for you as long as I need to.'

'I love you…' she heard herself say as sleep finally overwhelmed her senses and she drifted away in his arms.

***

Angel flailed out as usual for her mobile the next morning, only to discover her bedside table had been replaced by more bed. The air was thick and delicious with the smell of frying bacon.

'Angel.' Dream voice. It was back again.

294

Wait. Not dream voice. Real voice. Seb voice.

Her eyelids flew open as she remembered what had happened the day before and where she was waking up. There he was, topless and gorgeous, sitting on a chair by the bed, wafting a bacon sandwich under her nose. She manoeuvred herself into a sitting position and reached out for it gratefully, wondering if this was what her own personal heaven would look like.

'Thank God,' he said, smiling. 'You're not veggie. I suddenly realised I'd never bothered to ask.'

'Not when there's a sexy man waving a bacon sandwich in front of me, I'm not,' she said, taking a bite. 'God, I'm starving. I hardly ate yesterday.'

Seb watched her finish the sandwich. 'Another?'

'No, I'm good, thanks.'

'Then do I get a kiss?'

She laughed, turning her face away. 'No, please! Let me brush my teeth first.'

'Nope. I insist. Right now.' He took her hand and drew her towards him, pressing soft lips to hers. 'Mmmm. Bacony.'

She giggled. 'I tried to warn you.'

'My favourite flavour of girlfriend. And coincidentally, crisp.' He kissed her again, wrapping one arm around her neck.

She flushed with happiness when he called her his girlfriend, put both arms around him and hugged him tight. His nut-brown skin smelled fresh and clean, with a hint of bergamot.

'Hey, you had a shower. That's cheating.'

'Sorry,' he said with a smile. 'I've never had anyone to tell me the rules before.'

'Seb, I'm so sorry about last night,' she murmured, looking up at him. 'I feel awful.'

'I told you, Ange. All the time in the world.'

'Time. Time! Shit! What is the time?'

'After ten. Why? Have you got plans?'

'No, but… I didn't go home last night. Em'll be worried sick.'

'Don't worry,' he said, stroking her hair. 'I rang Leo after you'd gone to sleep. Er, after I'd cooled off a bit, obviously. Thought you'd want your friends to know you were okay. He'll pass the message on.'

'Leo?' She frowned. 'Where did you get his number?'

'Texted Kev for it. It's in his little black book of press contacts. Leo does the *Investigator*'s photography at our premieres, remember?'

'Oh.' She tapped the bridge of her nose. 'Yeah. Of course. What did you tell him?'

Seb shrugged. 'Told him to let your flatmate know you were here and you were okay and I'd send you back safe and sound tomorrow.'

'Did he sound… annoyed?'

'Suspicious, definitely. Especially when he asked to speak to you and I said you were asleep. But he didn't threaten to come round with a machete or anything, so I'm guessing he doesn't think I've got you tied up in a sex dungeon somewhere.'

She stroked his face. 'Promises, promises.'

He sighed as he looked at her. 'Are you sure you want this, Angel? Me, with all my baggage? This bizarre life and everything that goes with it? It could be tough on you.'

'As long as there's a you thrown in, that's all that matters to me.'

He pushed an auburn strand out of her eye, caressing the line of her cheekbone with the back of one fingernail. 'Spend the weekend with me.'

'Here?'

'Yes. Why not? You told me you don't have any plans. Carole's staying over at Suzanne's till tomorrow, she texted me this morning. The driver's not on call at weekends but I can get a cab to take you home and pick up some clothes, and you can explain things to Emily.'

'I'd like that,' she said, smiling. 'What will we do?'

'I've got a few ideas.' He pulled her to him and nuzzled into the crook of her neck, making her gasp.

'I bet you have,' she said with a giggle, extricating herself and throwing off the duvet. 'Don't worry, I won't be long. Doesn't sound like I'll need too many clothes…'

***

'We're going to have to start charging you rent,' Angel said, discovering Leo making pancakes in the kitchen with a towel kilted around his waist, his sepia-brown skin shining and shower-fresh. Groucho was weaving about between his ankles, hoping a stray bit of batter might be coming his way in the near future.

'Did I miss a memo or something?' she asked. 'Is it Shirtless Saturday? Everywhere I go there's topless men cooking breakfast foods.' She squinted one eye thoughtfully. 'Maybe I won a competition.'

Leo turned to frown at her, tapping his wrist where a watch would be. 'And what the hell have you been up to all night? Your mother and I have been worried sick.'

'You probably don't want to know,' she said with a grin. 'God, I'm so happy, Leo. Really, really happy, for the first time in ages. Seb and me… well, it's all okay. It's sorted.'

Leo looked puzzled. 'Yeah, he rang me. I don't get it, though. Is Beaumont divorcing him or something?'

'No. Not exactly. Look, it's hard to explain. And I'm not sure I can, without betraying confidences. But trust me, it's all fine. Everybody's happy. Me most of all.'

His face spread into a smile. 'Well, if you're happy that's good enough for me, Ginge,' he said, beckoning her over. 'Hug time, I think. Then you have to go tell Em. She's even more worried than me. And she'll probably need more convincing too. She's never been a Wilchester fan.'

'Well, maybe don't hug me just yet, not till you've got some pants on,' she said. 'It's been a long time since I've seen what's under that towel, Courtenay. Probably best keep it that way now we're both spoken for, eh?'

Leo pursed his lips and shook his head in mock disappointment. 'You don't know what you're missing, Ginge.' He struck a bodybuilding pose. 'Body of a Greek god. A really fit one, mind you, not that one with the head of a dog.'

'Alright, dogface. Come here, then, I'll take my hug now. But for God's sake keep one hand on that towel.'

She grabbed his hand and drew him into a one-armed hug.

'You know, some women would worry if they walked in on their boyfriend half naked in the arms of his ex,' Emily said as she came into the kitchen.

Leo smiled, separating from Angel. 'Not my girl, though.'

'Nah. Mind you, might have to scratch your eyes out later, Ange.'

Her friend shrugged. 'Meh. I could take you.'

'Yeah, so you keep saying. I warn you, though, I may be little but I fight dirty. Straight in with the Chinese burns. Pow!'

'Alright, you two, enough,' Leo said. 'Frankly, this is verging on banter. And I stand opposed to all banter. Also, all this talk of sexy girl fights is turning me on a bit. Look, ladies, there's plenty of Leo to go round.' He put an arm around each of them.

Angel shot a worried look at the towel hanging precariously around his hips. 'Er, mate...'

He followed her eyes and dropped one arm, grabbing the top of the white cotton. 'Good point, Ginge. Let me qualify that: there'll be plenty of Leo to go round when he gets his trousers on. And now I intend to stop creepily referring to myself in the third person and dish up these pancakes. You want some?'

Angel shook her head. 'No thanks. Already ate. Seb made me a bacon sandwich.'

Emily shot her a look of concern while Leo grabbed a fish

slice and started serving up. 'Come on, then, Ange, spill. What's the story? Leo said Seb rang him last night.'

'Er, yeah. That'll be after our night of red-hot passion turned into me falling asleep on him.'

Her friend's eyebrows lifted. 'What, at his house? What were you doing there? Where was Beaumont?'

'Out with a friend. But it's fine, Em, promise. It really is. Carole's fine, Seb and me are fine, everyone who should be fine is fine. Seb and Carole… well, it turns out they're not together like that. Never have been.' She coloured slightly. 'I've just come home to pick up some clothes and grab a shower, actually. The cab's coming back for me in an hour. I said I'd spend the weekend. Can you feed Groucho for me?'

Emily still looked worried. 'It all sounds a bit… I don't know, rushed. And confusing. Are you sure this is what you want, sweetie? It's not even forty-eight hours since you were crying on my shoulder about – and this is a direct quote – "that good-looking prick and his bloody crustless cucumber sandwiches".'

'Did I say that?'

'I should probably remind you that you were very drunk. You seemed to be obsessing over the sandwiches for some reason.' She folded Angel in a hug. 'Well, if you're happy with him, Ange, and it's really okay with Carole Beaumont, then no one deserves it more, and you have my blessing. But be careful, eh? Those people live in another world. A dangerous one for ordinary schmoes like us.'

Angel smiled at her. 'Thanks, Em. I am happy, really. And I'll be fine. I promise.'

Chapter 28

Seb practically pulled her through the door when she arrived back at his ridiculous gated mansion a few hours later. He slammed it behind her and pressed her back against it as he covered her mouth in a long, passionate kiss. She brought her arms up around his neck, the overnight bag she was carrying dropping to the floor.

'Whew! Missed you too…' she gasped when he finally drew back, his moist lips parted and eyes sparkling feverishly.

He hugged her tightly until she was almost breathless, groaning while he buried his face in her hair. 'Didn't realise what it would do to me, being away from you for so long,' he muttered, his voice hoarse.

She disentangled herself from his embrace, grabbed his hand and led him towards the staircase. 'Come on.'

'What?'

'I'm taking you upstairs, Seb Wilchester, and then I'm going to rock your world. Prepare yourself.'

He pulled at the hand he was holding, swung her back round into his arms and brought his mouth down hard onto hers. She could feel his tongue caressing hers, that sensuous embrace inside her mouth, reminding her… God, she wanted to feel him inside her. Needed to. None of this would seem real until she did.

'Not if I rock yours first,' he whispered when he drew back from the kiss, smiling with triumph when he noticed her breathing had quickened into pants.

'Is that a challenge?'

'You'll have to find out, won't you? Come on, Ange. I need to be with you, right now.'

Angel drew in a sharp breath, registering the urgency in his tone, feeling the muscles stirring under her belly, her body preparing for him. She unbuttoned her coat and threw it down on top of her overnight bag. Then, taking his hand, she led him determinedly up the stairs to his room.

'Seb…' she said, pushing open the door. 'God, it's… did you do all this while I was gone?'

The curtains were closed and the bed was surrounded by rows of tiny little tealights, illuminating the room with the soft glow of dozens of baby flames. She could hear music playing in the background, Sinatra this time. Those old tunes he knew she loved.

'You said you wanted it to be perfect,' he murmured behind her.

'Right now I just want you. Come here.' She turned around to face him and moved her hands behind his head, burrowed them inside that irresistible hair of his, felt it curl around her fingers. She pressed her fingertips into the back of his scalp and kissed him deeply. 'Just make love to me already, will you?' she begged breathlessly. 'Before we both go insane.'

'Oh God, Ange, you feel amazing,' he gasped as they tumbled down on to the bed. He pulled her against him and slid his hands up inside the loose, floaty top she was wearing. 'Your skin…'

Seb's breath hitched in his throat when his hands reached her bare, braless shoulder blades. He raised a questioning eyebrow.

She treated him to a provocative smirk. 'Thought I'd make it easy for you.'

'Does that mean you're not wearing any –'

'Nope.'

His eyelids flickered as he let out a deep, harsh groan. He ran his tongue over dry lips. 'You're *killing* me here, Blackthorne.'

Rolling over on to his back, he guided her up on top of him so she was straddling his thighs. She gasped when she felt his erection press hard against her through their clothing.

'Show me,' he muttered.

Obediently, she slid her top up over her shoulders to expose her bare breasts, snowdrop curves that were canvasses for the flickering candlelight. His eyes scanned the lightshow with appreciation, his breath dragging out in short, sharp, needy pants.

'Christ, you're beautiful...'

'Pretty hot yourself.' She slid her palms along the front of the polo shirt he was wearing, trailed her fingers over the solid bulge at the front of his jeans.

He reached up and massaged one hard, pink nipple gently with his thumbtip, cupping her breast with the heel of his hand. She gave a low moan and leaned down to kiss him, but he held her back.

'Now the jeans.'

She reached with slow, teasing fingers for her fly, unbuttoned it and drew down the zip. Seb watched her impatiently. He slipped his thumbs into the waistband of her jeans and helped her slide them off, catching his breath sharply when he felt the arch of her naked buttocks under his hands.

'Okay, now stay there. I want to look at you.'

He ran trembling fingertips from the hollow of her neck over the space between her breasts, stopping just below her belly button, and sighed appreciatively, drinking her in. 'Oh yes, I remember this...'

'Tease,' she murmured, putting her hands under his shoulders and guiding his body up against hers. As she wrapped her legs around his back she could feel him stirring against her bare thighs through the coarse material of his jeans.

'How is it I'm always naked first, Seb?'

'Because you're the one worth looking at.' His voice was thick and his ragged breath burned against her ear. 'God, you're irresistible, you know that? That sweet wicked look you give me from the corner of your eye... Oh, Christ, Ange...'

He drew her to him for an intense, searching kiss, delving into her mouth with his tongue.

'Do you know how long I've been thinking about this, Angel?' he whispered, drawing back. 'Dreaming about it? Dreaming about *you*?'

'Join the club.' She reached down and unbuttoned the top of his jeans. 'Now get those things off, will you?'

'Demanding, aren't you?' He kissed along her shoulder and down the fleshy arc of her breast, his hot mouth eventually finding its way to the hard peak of her nipple. He massaged it in slow circles with the tip of his tongue.

'Yes... if I want something badly enough.' She slid her hand inside his unbuttoned jeans until she felt the solid, velveteen evidence of his arousal, sighing while she drew her fingers along its full length.

'Oh Angel...' He let out a soft moan, his head falling back and his eyes fluttering half closed while she touched him.

'Seb, please. I need you to be close to me. As close to me as you can be.' She lowered her voice to a whisper. 'Inside me.'

'Jesus, stop saying things like that, Ange. You're driving me wild here...'

'Make me, then.'

He pushed her towards him and into a hard, hungry kiss, stopping her lips with his, and she slid her fingers up into his hair. He pressed his exploring tongue deeper into the warm, inviting wetness of her mouth.

'Clothes off. Now,' she commanded breathlessly, pulling back from the kiss.

'Yes mistress...'

Angel lifted herself off him and he swung his legs over the side of the bed, feverishly sliding off his top. She dragged her lips along his neck while he wriggled out of his jeans, taking his earlobe into her mouth and massaging it with her tongue.

'Ah! Do that again,' he groaned.

'You like it?'

Seb brought a hand up to her face and pressed his index finger between her lips. She noticed it tasted a little of lemons as she touched it lightly with the tip of her tongue. 'I like everything you do with that hot beautiful little mouth,' he breathed. 'Give it to me.'

Naked and erect on the edge of the bed, he drew her up on to his lap, claimed her mouth and kissed her deeply. She felt a shiver go through her as she ran her fingertips along the bumps and grooves of his toned, shining body.

'Where?' she panted.

'There. By the bed. The drawer. Quickly, Angel.'

She reached over and fumbled inside his bedside cabinet until her grip closed on the square foil she was looking for. Tearing the condom packet open, she pinched the tip between her fingers and rolled it sensuously down over his full length.

Seb gasped and pulled her close into his body until her breasts were crushed against his smooth chest. She twined her legs around him and wrapped her ankles around his back, and he stroked her thigh appreciatively. He held one hip cupped in his hand, keeping her slightly back from him.

'I've wanted this for so long. To feel you again,' he breathed into her ear. 'Let's take it slow, okay? I'm going to enjoy every minute of you.'

His voice became suddenly soft. 'Tell me you love me.' He kept one strong hand on her hip, holding her body back from his while he waited for the words.

'Oh God… you know I do.' She gasped, feeling how ready she was, soaking wet and panting for him, as he buried his face in her neck and rained down kisses on her white skin. 'Please, Seb. I need you. Don't tease me.'

'Say it.' He sounded urgent, almost angry, demanding the words from her.

'I love you, Sebastian,' she breathed. 'God, I love you so much…'

'That's it…'

Angel groaned as finally he guided her towards him and buried himself inside her, felt her body absorb his in a snug embrace.

She gasped, bucking and pressing blindly against him, savouring him, smelling him, pushing her lips into his curls and her breasts into his chest until she felt like she was part of him. She could feel his fingers digging into her back, his hot mouth on her shoulder as every muscle, every nerve in her body awoke to that sweet pulse and swell she remembered.

'All that time… Jesus!… barely touching you because I knew if I did… I'd never want to stop…' Seb gasped out with an effort.

'Then never stop… I never want you to stop… God, Seb, that's it, that's… *ah!*' She threw her head back as she felt him harden inside her, their bodies igniting together in the blessed shattering release of orgasm. She crushed him into her, her hands filled with his hair, and it felt like ice, those unbearable, delicious shockwaves, relentless throbs of life-affirming agony…

Spent and exhausted, they slumped back panting together on to the bed and snuggled, satiated, into each other's arms.

Angel heaved a deep sigh of satisfaction, rolled over to one side and stretched herself out next to him. Seb removed the spent condom, knotted it and deposited it in a bin by the bedside cabinet, then hooked one leg over her and pulled her to him.

'What happened… to taking it slow?' she asked, breathless, once they'd had a moment to recover.

Seb gave her a soft, lingering kiss on the lips, still panting heavily. 'You happened, gorgeous. I couldn't help myself.'

Angel tilted her head to one side, noticing for the first time what song was playing.

'That what I think it is?'

'Yeah. "Strangers in the Night".'

'Inappropriate...'

'Yep.'

She giggled, hiding her face in the hollow of his shoulder and inhaling his scent, the familiar aftershave musky from the post-coital heat of his flesh. It mingled with the soft wax smell of the melting candles and the natural aroma of their two bodies, and Angel knew the same combination of scents, the sound of that song playing, would always bring back this moment, with the man she loved pressed against her.

She breathed out a happy sigh. 'Well, what now, handsome? We've still got the rest of the afternoon.'

He leaned up on one elbow. 'Sorry,' he murmured, running the tip of his index finger along the bridge of her freckled nose and across her parted lips. 'Did you think we were done here?'

She gasped when he rolled her over onto her back, brought his mouth to her breast and brushed it with lips as light as cobweb.

'Lie still,' he whispered. 'Let me do this.'

He planted baby kisses, gentle, slow, torturous kisses, around each breast, into the hollow of her stomach, along her pelvis and the tempting white flank of her hip. Each touch, each whispering breath, was as soft and teasing as his lovemaking before had been frantic and bursting with need for her. She could just barely feel the featherlight lips caressing her rosy puckering nipples, the hot air between his mouth and her skin, the light kiss of his curls against her prickling flesh. He was in control, gently holding her wrists against the mattress, stopping her from touching him, and she was... going out of her mind.

'Seb...' she panted.

'Ask me, Angel,' he breathed, his tawny eyes glinting up at her.

'Please... oh God...'

'Ask me.'

'Ah! I hate you!' she gasped as he left another bittersweet little kiss burning on her skin, spiking through her nerve endings in aching waves.

'No you don't.'

'Make me... ah...'

'Make you what, Angel?'

She shook her head. 'Don't ask me to say it. I can't.'

'Prude...'

'Oh *God*, Seb!' she panted, feeling him circle the very tip of his tongue around her belly button. 'How can you be so cruel?'

He smiled up at her wickedly. 'I won't know what you want unless you tell me.'

'Make me come, Seb. Oh Christ, please!'

'All you had to do was ask...'

She gave a heavy groan as she felt his head move between her thighs, still printing those tiny, barely tangible cobweb kisses that were driving her crazy onto her flesh. She tilted her body to bring herself closer to his taunting lips and sighed with sweet relief when finally he nuzzled into the wet scarlet heat between her legs.

Angel could feel the escaping tendrils of his gorgeous curls teasing her inner thigh. She moaned out his name while he dipped into her with his tongue, bringing her to the very edge, driving lightning-blue electricity along every nerve in her body. She pulled a hand free from his grip and grabbed the bedsheet, bunched and twisted it under her white knuckles, writhed it into creased humps beneath her.

'Don't... you dare...' she panted as Seb drew back and looked up at her to see the effect of his touch.

'God, you taste good when you're mad.' Sliding his hands under her buttocks, he pushed her up to meet his eager mouth.

Her orgasm, when it finally claimed her, was an entirely new sensation, shuddering through her in a silent, simmering fit. It slammed into every corner of her body, hard and demanding, sapping her vital energy until she couldn't even cry out. She arched her back, pushing her hips towards him, and let the boiling intensity of it fill her throbbing veins, not making a sound, nothing real to her but Seb, the feel of him, the way she felt about him, until she sank, drained and limp, back on to the rumpled sheets with a long, low groan of sheer completion.

'You… *bastard*…' she panted when he slid back up her body to join her, triumphant and flushed.

'Love you too, Ange.'

'You're evil. God, I love you,' she gasped, throwing an arm over him and guiding him to her. 'Who taught you to do that?'

He grinned at her. 'It's just a gift.'

'Come here.' She pushed against him for a deep, grateful kiss, tasting her own salt-sweet musk on his tongue.

'Hold me now,' she whispered.

He engulfed her in powerful arms and pressed his lips to her forehead. 'Sweetheart…'

'I can't believe you're really mine,' she murmured, feeling her eyes getting heavy in the warmth and safety of his enveloping arms.

'Forever…'

Chapter 29

When she awoke, a fragrant, herby scent of citrus and saffron filled her nostrils.

'Seb?' She called his name, her voice thick with sleep.

'Here, Ange,' he said, coming through from the en-suite bathroom adjoining his room in a white cotton bathrobe. He sat down next to her and ran tender fingers along her bed-ruffled hair.

'Where did you go? I missed you.'

He laughed. 'Fibber. You've been fast asleep for three hours.'

'Have I?' She rubbed her eyes and pushed herself into a sitting position. 'You should have woken me.'

'Thought you might be a bit tired,' he said. 'You know, after all the sex.'

'There was a lot of sex.' She yawned happily. 'What've you been doing, then?'

'Cooking. Lemon chicken. I fixed it earlier when you were at the flat, just needed to put it in the oven. Hope you like it, sweetheart.'

'I knew you tasted of lemons…' she muttered to herself.

'What?'

'Nothing.' She shook her head, trying to shift the sleepy feeling. 'This place is great. I'll definitely be choosing it for my holidays again next year. There's a sex-and-food dynamic I totally approve of.'

'What, nothing to say about the hunky boyfriend who delivers them?'

'I guess he's okay too.' She reached out and drew him to her for a kiss.

'So are you hungry?'

'Starved.'

'It'll be about an hour. Want to come down and wait?'

'I could really use a shower first.'

'Me too.' His face filled with mischief. 'Join me?'

She giggled. 'You're insatiable.'

'What can I say? I can't get enough of you.'

She smiled, thinking back to that night in the hotel. 'Do you ever think our sex life to date is a bit on the aquatic side, Seb?'

'There does seem to be a watery theme to it. Maybe we were mer-people in another life.' He took her hand, pulled her still-naked body towards him. 'Come on. There's just time to get you all hot and bothered again before dinner…'

***

'I don't know how you find your way around this place,' Angel said as Seb led her downstairs, wet and shining in cotton robes after their shower together. 'It's ridiculously huge. I'd say you were overcompensating for something, except, well, obviously not.'

He smirked, leaning over to kiss her ear.

'Oh no, don't start that again,' she said with a giggle. 'I think three orgasms in one day is my limit…'

'We'll see.'

'Seriously, though. How do you even keep this place? It looks like it needs a domestic staff of about fifty people just to stay on top of the hoovering.' She clapped a hand to her mouth. 'You don't have any, do you? Staff?'

'Why?'

'Just, we were a bit… loud. I sort of thought the house was empty.'

'It is. Don't worry, it's just us.'

'Ha! Sorry. I just had this image of a room full of butlers somewhere, wondering why the foundations were shaking…'

'I don't live in Downton Abbey, Ange,' he said, laughing. 'Actually, Carole and me only use about half the rooms. The rest are empty, apart from the one we use to store all Abigail's collectibles and stuff.'

'And there's the gym, of course.'

He frowned. 'How do you know that?'

'Lucky guess.' She drew her fingers along one muscular arm, smiling. 'So what about the other rooms, then?'

'All the ones on the upper floor are shut up. We don't need them, we never entertain. There's a housekeeper who comes in every other morning to tidy up and keep the place aired. Oh, and a couple of part-time gardeners, plus the driver. That's it. No butlers.'

'If you don't need the space then why live here?'

He shrugged. 'Part of the charade, I suppose. The sort of lifestyle people would expect me and Carole to have. And it's secure, isolated. Keeps us safe from a long lens.'

'Oh. Okay, makes sense, I guess…'

The kitchen adjoined the library-like sitting room she'd sat in with Seb and Carole… God, only yesterday, although already it seemed a lifetime ago. Angel was surprised to find it was a modern-style fitted affair in glass and white marble, minimalist styling at odds with the mahogany and leather of the neighbouring room.

'What?' Seb asked, noting her surprised expression.

'Nothing. Just… doesn't really match the decor next door, does it? I suppose I was expecting something more farmhouse.'

'Yeah, I got to pick the look in here, since I do the cooking. Carole picked next door. We've got very different tastes, as you can see. You like it?'

She frowned, looking around. 'I'm not sure. Looks a bit like an iceberg.'

'I guess it does.' He took her hand. 'Next time I decorate a room, you can help me.'

She blushed happily. 'Really? I'd like that.'

He flashed her an affectionate smile, brushed her fingers with his. 'Right, come on. We need veg. Do you want to take peeling or chopping?'

'Er, peeling, I think.'

He passed her a peeler and chopping board, took a bag of carrots out of the fridge and slung them to her. 'There you go, knock yourself out.'

'Damn it!' She reached down to pick up the peeler she'd dropped while catching the carrots and took it off to the sink to wash it.

'Hey,' Seb said, his voice husky. 'You could give a man fair warning before you bend over like that, Ange. If you do that again, I'm going to have to take you back upstairs, and this chicken will never get eaten…'

She giggled, starting work on a carrot. 'Control yourself, sex maniac.'

'Your fault for being so sexy in the first place.' He smiled at her over his shoulder as he opened the oven to check on the chicken. 'Half an hour. Better hurry with the veg. Well, what shall we do tonight, sweetheart?'

'Film night?'

'Didn't you recently say this was more like a bloody film club than a relationship?'

'I'm pretty sure that was before you took me upstairs and ravished me.'

'Three times…'

'Yes, well, let's not forget that.'

'Okay,' Seb said, coming up behind her while she peeled the carrots and pushing her wet hair aside to kiss the back of her neck. 'What's it to be, then? It's your choice. I picked *The General*.'

'God, yes. Seems like ages ago,' she said. 'Well, it'll have to be something good, our first film as a couple.' She gave it some careful thought. 'How about one of yours? I'd love a live director's commentary on *Unreal City*.'

He flinched, shaking his head. 'No, I hate watching my own stuff.'

'Really?' She glanced over her shoulder at him. 'You're missing out, you know. It's very good.'

'It's different when it's your own work,' he said, pinkening. 'You can't enjoy it. That's why I hate doing the commentary tracks. I mean, do you ever read your own articles after they're published?'

'Oh. I see what you mean.'

'Yeah. You never see the merits. Only how far it is from your original vision, and what could be improved... except of course it's too late.'

'Unless you're George Lucas.'

'Ha!'

'Okay,' she said, frowning while she thought through her favourite films. 'How about... wait, is this a test?'

'What?'

'Like, if I pick something awful then you'll break up with me?'

He laughed. 'It'd have to be pretty bloody awful.'

'How awful?'

'I don't know... *Porky's*?'

'Okay, then we're safe,' she said with a grin. 'Oh, I know. How about *Monkey Business*?'

He wrapped his arms around her middle and kissed the tip of her ear. 'Alright, Ange, you pass. Done. I didn't know you were a Marx Brothers fan.'

'Who isn't? I even named my cat after one of them.'

'Zeppo?'

She gave him a playful tap on the arm with her peeler. 'No, Groucho. You'll have to come and meet him one day. You ever have a cat?'

'You know I did.'

'What?' She frowned. 'Oh. The tiger.'

'Yeah.' He let out a short laugh. 'I know it must seem odd to you, that whole lifestyle. But you do adjust to it. What you know becomes the new normal.' His face darkened briefly. 'I mean, not what Hugo did. There's no way that could ever have seemed normal. But Blaze… well, it sounds weird but he was just a big pussy cat really, an oversized family pet. Food, cuddles and tummy rubs were all he ever cared about.'

'A cat after my own heart,' Angel said with a smile. 'You are not like other people, Seb.'

'Oh? In what way?'

She turned around, pulled him towards her for a kiss. 'Sexier, for a start.'

'I won't argue with that.'

'Egomaniac.'

'Well. My sex appeal's featured on the front page of the *Investigator*, you know. Hard not to get an ego when you're a star.'

She winced, smiling. 'Are you ever going to let me forget that?'

'Maybe one day I might get bored of teasing you. But I have to warn you, it's pretty unlikely. Plus, you looked really hot in those photos…'

'Naughty.' She grabbed the collar of his robe and lifted her lips up to his.

'You know, we're never getting this veg,' he said, smiling as he drew back. 'Babyleaf salad?'

'If it's a choice between carrots and snogs, then yes.' She leaned in for another kiss, folding her arms around his neck.

'You're something special, Angel Blackthorne,' he said in a low, gentle voice.

'And you're something mine…'

For a moment they were silent, locked in a tight hug.

'When can I see you again?' she asked. 'I mean, after tomorrow?'

'Me and Carole are flying out to Rome on Monday. Scouting locations for the next Tigerblaze film.'

'When are you coming back?'

'The 23rd.'

'Oh God!' She held him tighter. 'How will I cope without you for two whole weeks, Seb?'

'Hey, it's the same for me. I'll just have to get my fill of you now to keep me going.'

'Will you call me?' she asked breathlessly, tilting her head to one side while he pressed kisses under her ear and along her neck.

'If you want me to.'

'Every day?'

'If you like. Oh, that reminds me. I have to give you something.'

Extricating himself from her arms, he left the room, coming back a few seconds later with something small and black. 'Here. For you.'

'Oh!' she said, looking down at it. 'A crappy little mobile. And still two weeks to Christmas. How did you know?' She arched an eyebrow at him. 'I've got a phone, Seb.'

'This is a Pay As You Go. For me to ring you on.'

'Erm, why?'

'Just a precaution. Harder to hack. It's not registered to a named person, you see. Suze has got one too, for Carole.'

She looked at the small black Nokia, bewildered. 'I need a special Seb phone? Won't self-destruct after you call me, will it?'

'I thought your spying days were behind you.'

'So did I…'

'Sorry,' he said, reaching out and drawing her to him again.

'Probably seems ridiculous. But I think you know the dangers better than anyone. We have to be discreet about this, Angel, it's the only way.'

She slipped the little phone into the pocket of her robe. 'Yeah, I guess we do,' she said with a sigh, thinking about Steve. 'God, Seb, I wish…'

'Me too.' He hugged her to him tightly and nuzzled his face into her thick hair.

'What are you doing for Christmas?' he asked suddenly, pulling back from their embrace to look into her face.

'Er, okay, abrupt… I don't know, watching *Morecambe and Wise*, drinking mulled wine?'

'You're not going to your parents?'

'No, not this year. Australia's a long way. And expensive.'

'Then spend it with me.'

She stared at him, taken aback at the suddenness of the request. 'What, here?'

'No, at Moira's. Me, Carole and Suze are going. I'd like you to meet her and maybe get to know the girls a bit better.' He delved into her eyes to gauge her reaction. 'It would mean a lot to me, Angel.'

She coloured and dropped her gaze to the white-marble tiles of the floor. 'That's… a pretty big deal, Seb.'

'Sorry. Too soon.'

'No… no, I don't think it is. I'd love to. Thank you.' She flashed him a grateful smile. 'Are you sure Moira won't mind having me?'

'Are you kidding? She'll love you.'

'You made her sound a bit scary. I don't like to toss the word "battleaxe" around lightly, but…'

Seb laughed. 'Oh, she's not as bad as all that. I mean, when it comes to girlfriends she's always a bit suspicious. Obviously no one is good enough for me and Carole. But she loves Suzanne now. That should give you hope.'

Angel cocked a sceptical eyebrow. 'Well, we'll see. But the fact she's looking out for you makes me appreciate her.'

'Your job too now,' he whispered, pressing tender lips to her neck.

'Stop that.' She hit him with the peeler she was still holding. 'Chicken. Focus.'

'Chicken and Marx Brothers. You know, I think this might be our first proper date.'

'I think you might be right. In the four months since we first met. You are some slow mover, mister.'

'But I make up for it in quality…' he murmured, cuddling her closer to him and bringing his lips down on to hers. Abandoning her carrots entirely, she pressed her body into his and the kitchen melted away.

Chapter 30

'Well, you're certainly glowing today,' Emily said when Angel swung open the flat's sitting-room door on Sunday evening. 'How was the dirty weekend, then?' She was sitting with Leo on the sofa, twined around him as usual while they watched TV.

Angel hurled herself, exhausted, on to the other sofa. 'Un-bloody-believable.'

'Well? Come on, sweetie, details.'

'Leo, leave the room,' Angel demanded. 'This is not for your ears.'

'Oh, man!' Leo disentangled himself from Emily, looking sulky. 'You know, I'm a year older than you two,' he said, waving a warning finger at them as he pushed open the door to the kitchen. 'Why do I always get sent out of the room when there's sex talk?'

'Because it could warp your fragile little mind. And much as I love you, Leo, exes have to have some limits. Now bugger off. Girls only.'

Leo left, grumbling, to make a tea round.

'Well?' Emily said, raising a suggestive eyebrow. 'How many?'

'I lost count after five.'

'Shut up!'

'On my mother's grave.'

Emily giggled. 'Your mum's not dead, Ange.'

'She would be if she knew about this weekend. Em, that man is killing me. Jesus Christ! I'm knackered.'

'Slut.'

'S'me.'

'You know, you should really get your name changed by deed poll,' Emily said. 'It's false advertising. So, come on then, what about the other stuff?'

Angel heaved a long, happy sigh, putting her feet up on the coffee table. 'I love him, Em,' she said simply. 'I know it's all weird, with Carole and the house and the tiger –'

'Tiger?'

'Never mind. But in the end, we're just two people and I really think we're the ones for each other. Anyway, he's ruined me now for other men.'

'Ha! Soppy cow.'

'I am, aren't I?' she said. 'But happy.'

'Just don't get hurt, okay?' Emily said, with a worried look at her blissful expression. 'I picked up the pieces last time, with Leo. I'd hate to see you go through that again.'

'That's life, Em. No pleasure without risk. I mean, I've barely had a date in over two years. And I've been miserable. Obsessed with getting into a career I'm not even sure makes me happy. Well, Seb makes me happy. And I'm not letting him go, not this time.'

Emily got up from the sofa and launched herself towards Angel for a hug. 'In that case you deserve it, sweetie. And I'm so happy for you.'

'And I am for you and Leo.' Tears prickled in Angel's eyes. 'Oh God, Em. Things are finally starting to come together.' She laughed. 'Maybe we're even proper grown-ups now.'

'Well, let's not go mad…'

'Are you two still talking naked wild monkey sex or can I bring these drinks through now?' Leo called from the kitchen.

319

'Yeah, come on, then,' Angel called back. 'I think we're done with the sex portion of the conversation.'

'Just my luck.' He pushed open the door and started handing around hot drinks. 'I bet now we have to talk about grouting or something.'

'Actually I want to talk about Christmas. Are you two going home?'

'No, we thought we'd have it here,' Leo replied, throwing himself back down next to Emily. 'Be nice to spend it together, but I don't think we're quite ready to face the family Christmas yet. I'm sure you remember my dad's party piece of downing a beer and burping out "Jingle Bells". Could put Em off me for life.'

'Nice try. You can't get rid of me that easily.' Emily snuggled back against him comfortably.

Leo planted a kiss on top of her curls. 'Shame. Looks like I'll just have to keep you then.' He turned back to Angel. 'Well, Ginge? Will you be joining us for turkey and *Home Alone* in our pants?'

'Definitely not, if I'm going to be subjected to the pair of you in just your pants. Actually, I just wanted to know if you'd be here to look after the cat. I'm spending it with Seb and Carole at his old nanny's. You know, the one who brought him up.'

'Bloody hell!' Leo said, his eyes widening. 'You two don't waste any time, do you? Meeting the folks already.'

'Yeah, it's a bit scary. But… feels right, somehow. We've been dancing around each other for months. Might as well dive straight in.'

She jerked when she heard two loud beeps from her pocket.

'What's that?' Emily asked. 'Don't tell me you've broken the habit of a lifetime and actually taken your phone off vibrate?'

'Oh! I remember.' Angel reached into her jeans and pulled out the little Nokia Seb had given her. 'It's this thing. The Batphone.'

Emily regarded it with a puzzled frown. 'Why have you got a mobile from 2002, Ange? Is this some new retro phase you're going through? Miss those old games of Snake?'

'No, Seb gave it to me. Reckons I need a special phone to keep us safe from prying journalists.'

'Like you, you mean?'

'Yeah,' she said with a grin. 'Weird, isn't it?'

'Well?' Leo asked. 'What's he say?'

She opened the text and smiled. 'I can't tell you. You'll laugh.'

'If it says 'miss you already, cuddly bum' then you can just shoot me now, Ginge.'

'Good guess. That's pretty much exactly what it says. Well, minus the cuddly bum, thank Christ.'

Leo retched theatrically into his mug of tea. He turned to Emily. 'God help us. There'll be no living with her now.'

'May I remind you, Courtenay, that you don't bloody live here?' Angel said. 'You're technically squatting. Anyway, you two are just as bad.'

'Yeah, well, when we do it it's adorable,' Emily said with a grin.

'Whatever. Oh! Em. I've been meaning to ask, can you check the terms of our home insurance? Probably should've mentioned it earlier, but there's a tennis racquet under my bed worth thousands of pounds.'

***

Christmas Eve was tiptoeing into late evening when Seb's hire car pulled up at Moira's house in Somerset, headlights sparkling across two ploughed banks of week-old, frost-crusted snow rising up on either side of the road. Angel had made her own way to a small station near Bristol, where Seb had picked her up. Suzanne and Carole were travelling separately. There was an air of secrecy and subterfuge to the whole operation she was increasingly realising was now going to have to be part of her life.

'This is where Moira lives?' She frowned at the modern, slate-walled semi. 'It's not what I expected, somehow.'

Seb smiled at her as he steered the car round into the pebbled driveway. 'Why, what did you expect?'

'I don't know really. I suppose I was thinking cottage, roses around the door. Something a bit chocolate box.'

'Strange girl.'

He parked the car behind a red Corsa already in front of the house. 'Nervous?' he muttered as they piled out.

'Bloody terrified.'

He took her hand and gave it a reassuring stroke. 'Don't be. I told you, she's going to love you. Just like I do.'

'Well, not *just* like you do, I hope.' She squeezed the hand she was holding and flashed him a provocative smile.

'Oh God, don't smile like that, Ange. Not when you've been away from me for two weeks. I don't think I can bear it.' He looked around at the lighted houses along the estate. 'Come on,' he said, leading her to the front door. 'Let's get inside, before someone sees us.'

He knocked on the door, festively decorated with a holly wreath, and a grey-haired woman of about seventy answered.

Moira wasn't quite what Angel had been expecting either. She was dressed casually in jeans and a Christmas snowman jumper, with a face that must once have been very attractive. It was still striking now, although care-worn, with cut-glass cheekbones and slightly narrow grey eyes. The expression in them said here was warmth, but no nonsense.

'Here we are, Ma,' Seb said with a dimpling smile. He threw his arms around her and lifted her from the ground, the tiny old lady almost disappearing in his huge arms. 'Missed you.'

'Put me down, you big lump.' Moira's voice was muffled by his hug, but Angel could tell she was laughing. She struggled free and smoothed her dishevelled grey hair. 'Well, it's good to see you, lad. Quick, get yourselves into the warm, the pair of you.'

'Where are Carole and Suze?' Seb asked as she ushered them into the hallway. 'I saw their car outside.'

'In the sitting room, watching TV.' Moira turned her attention to Angel. 'Hello, dear. I think I'd better introduce myself, since this young man's too rude to do it. Moira.'

'God! I was just about to,' Seb protested. 'Angel, this is Moira, an old lady who is inexplicably fond of me. Ma, this is Angel, a beautiful woman who has inexplicably agreed to go out with me.'

The two women laughed at his unorthodox introduction.

'It's nice to meet you, love,' Moira said, taking Angel's hand. 'Seb tells me you're a film critic.'

'Um, yes. For the *Investigator*.'

'Oh.' Moira's eyebrows gathered. Angel could tell the *Investigator* was never going to be the publication of choice in any household Seb was connected to.

The old lady made an effort to summon a bright smile. Her foster son had obviously given her strict instructions about being nice. 'And how did the two of you meet?'

Angel flushed deeply.

'Er, it was at the premiere,' Seb said, jumping to her rescue with a massive fib. 'For *The Milkman Cometh*. Angel wrote that review I sent you. Remember?'

'Really?' Moira's smile grew a little warmer while she examined Angel more carefully. 'You said some very kind things in it, dear. I hope you weren't going easy on him just because the two of you are courting.'

'We weren't together then, Ma.' Seb turned to Angel, his eyes twinkling. 'Actually, almost the first time we met she called me a pale imitation of Billy Wilder.'

Angel landed a light slap on his arm. 'Stop it!' she hissed.

To her surprise, Moira broke into a merry laugh. 'I'm glad to hear it.' She lowered her voice and leaned over to address Angel in a conspiratorial whisper. 'It does him good to have someone keeping his ego in check.'

'You know, I can hear you,' Seb said, smiling.

'Yes, well, never you mind that. Go get your bags. I've put you in the end room, Seb, and Angel's next to me. Carrie and Suzie have got the double.'

Seb's eyebrows lifted. 'Really, Ma? Separate rooms? You do know I'm thirty-one, right?'

'My house…'

'…your rules. Yeah, I know.' He gave Angel an apologetic shrug. 'Carole gets to share with her girlfriend though,' he muttered under his breath, turning to go back to the car.

'That's different,' Moira said, overhearing him. 'Those two are practically married. Go on, get yourselves sorted and we can all settle down and have a glass of sherry. Since it's Christmas.'

'God, how will we cope?' Seb said to Angel while they unloaded the car. 'There's no way I can keep my hands off you for three days. I have to be with you tonight, Angel. I've been thinking about that body every day for weeks.'

He looked at her with feeling, and her eyes were pulled to the tempting lines of his cheekbones and stubble-flecked jaw. She reached up and drew her fingers along his face.

'And that's not helping,' he said darkly, his eyes fluttering closed while she touched him. He grabbed her wrist and held her hand against his cheek for a moment.

'Can you sneak into my room?' she asked.

'I guess I'll have to. Like a bloody teenager. And they're single beds as well…'

She couldn't help catching his eye, the corner of her mouth curling upwards. Suddenly, the pair of them burst out laughing.

'Oh, God, this is ridiculous. Sorry, Ange.'

'It's okay.' She looked up at him through lowered lashes. 'Actually I think it's kind of sexy.'

He drew her to him, into his arms. 'You think so, do you?' he said in a low voice.

'Seb, the neighbours…'

324

He sighed. 'Yeah, you're right. Come on, let's get this stuff inside then. I'll just have to control myself until tonight.'

***

'Evening, Village of the Damned,' Seb said as he and Angel entered Moira's snug sitting room, rumpling the two blonde heads on the sofa by the door.

'Rude,' Carole said, turning to look up at him. 'You took your time, didn't you?'

'Had to pick Angel up.'

'Oh yeah. Hi, Angel.' Carole beamed at her. 'Nice to see you again. Here, we've room for a little one.' She shuffled up to make space for her on the sofa, nestling comfortably into Suzanne.

'Thanks,' Angel said, tossing herself down next to the two women while Seb sank into an armchair next to a small, twinkling Christmas tree. 'And hi guys, by the way.'

'Where's Moira?' Seb asked.

'Kitchen.' Suzanne jerked a thumb in the direction of a door on the other side of the room. 'Sorting out sherry and mince pies.'

'You know she's put us in separate rooms?'

'Ha!' Carole snorted. 'Poor Seb. We'll try not to think about you when we're cuddling up in our lovely double bed later.'

'I should bloody well hope so, Car. It might kill the mood a bit.'

'Oooh! Presents presents presents!' Carole said, clapping when Seb started unloading gift-wrapped objects from the bag he'd been carrying and placing them under the tree. 'Can we open one now?'

'Nope, hands off. You have to wait till tomorrow.'

'In our house we always used to open one on Christmas Eve,' Suzanne said. 'Like a book or a selection box or something. I think it was the only way my parents could get us to go to bed.'

Moira looked at the little pile of presents with disapproval as she came in, carrying a tray loaded with mince pies and five small glasses of sherry. 'You know, when I was a lass all we got was…'

'…an apple and an orange and sixpence,' Carole and Seb chanted in unison. He turned to Moira, grinning. 'We know, Ma. You tell us every year.'

'You sound like my dad, Moira,' Angel said with a smile. 'Except he used to get a bar of soap and a gobstopper too. There's obviously a seam of money running down that side of the family.'

'I guess it was different for these two than it was for us norms,' Suzanne said, leaning forward so she could talk to Angel over Carole. 'Gift-wrapped ponies and crackers with diamonds in them, probably.'

'Caviar-stuffed turkeys by the pool…' Angel joined in.

'That's not far off, actually,' Carole admitted, taking her sherry from the tray and swirling the russet liquid around the glass. 'I mean, not the fishy turkey, that's just ick. But I did get a horse one year. I think that's why we like to keep it low-key now.' She looked over at Angel. 'We usually give something small and meaningful. And when we can't think of anything good, there's always chocolate.'

'Horses and bloody tigers.' Moira put her tray down on the coffee table and pulled up an armchair next to Seb. 'The best years of my life I gave up to chasing around after you two and your ridiculous pets.'

'We were worth it though, eh?' Seb said.

'I wonder sometimes.' She tousled his hair affectionately. 'You know, one day when you visit I'm going to wait till you're asleep and get the shears to you.'

'What is it with you people and my hair?' He ran his fingers through the curls in that way he had that instantly had Angel biting her lip. God, that irresistible hair… 'I like it as it is, okay?'

'Well, if you want to look like a mop-headed sheepdog then so be it. I'm surprised all your television friends are willing to be seen with you.'

He looked over at Carole. 'Television friends?'

'Yes, you know, Seb. All our television friends that we have.'

'Come on, don't tease her,' Suzanne said as she stood up. 'Don't worry about that washing up, Moi, I'll sort it out. I can get everyone a top-up while I'm there.'

'I'll help you.' Angel had been sipping her sherry in silence for the last portion of the conversation, fascinated by their little domestic drama and the insight it gave her into Seb and Carole's life together. Now she stood up, picked up the Delft-pattern tray from the table and followed Suzanne into the kitchen with it.

'Thanks, Angel,' Suzanne said, handing over a tea towel. 'Here you go. I'll wash, you dry.' She shook her head. 'Those two really need to buy that woman a dishwasher,' she muttered.

'Is it always like this?' Angel asked, moving the towel over the soap-sudded plate she'd been handed.

'Yeah, pretty much. Surprised?'

'A little. I'm not sure what I expected, to be honest. Something a bit more... I don't know, exotic.'

'It's Moira,' the girl said, jerking her head towards the sitting room. 'She kept them – well, like they are. I met a lot of film people when I was working as a runner, but never anyone as down to earth as Seb and Carole. I suppose that's why it was so easy to fall for her.' She smiled. 'Of course, it helped that she was gorgeous.'

Angel smiled back at her. 'Sounds familiar. So do you and Carole take turns to have Christmas with your families?'

'Er, no. Carole never comes to me. I mean, my parents don't know. About me and her.'

'They don't know you're a lesbian?'

'Oh no, they know that. They're fine with it, very supportive actually. But I can't tell them about Carole. They've never met her. Not in the two years we've been together.'

'Why?'

'Are you kidding? Carole Beaumont? *The* Carole Beaumont?

327

The first time I worked with Seb and Carole, my mum had told everyone in our village and the neighbouring ones before the end of the week. And that was just from *meeting* them. That's how most people are around them, Carole especially, because she's so instantly recognisable. They go all starstruck. Can you imagine what my mum would do if she found out her only daughter was in a relationship with someone as well known as Carole? It'd be the same as publicly outing her.'

'Yes.' Angel frowned. 'I suppose it would.'

'Hey,' Suzanne said in a gentle voice, laying a sympathetic, soapy hand on her arm. 'It's the same for you, you know, Angel. Carole and Seb are lovely people, but that's the price we paid when we fell in love with them. Whether we knew it or not. We're their little secrets. Are you going to be okay with that? I know there's your job and everything…'

'I suppose I have to be,' Angel said. 'I mean, I want to be with him, more than anything. I know there'll be sacrifices, but I love him, Suzanne.'

Suzanne stopped scrubbing her pan for a moment and smiled at Angel. 'Yeah, that's pretty obvious. I think I knew that day at Tigerblaze. I didn't know it was you who… well, you know, that front page. He only told me later. But I could tell there was something. The way he was with you.'

Angel laughed, colouring. 'I didn't love him then. We'd only met a few times.'

'I think you did. A little. Or you were starting to.'

'Maybe.' Angel changed the subject. 'So what other sacrifices have you had to make to be with Carole? If you don't mind talking about it.'

'No. It's a relief, actually, having someone else who understands. It's been pretty isolating. I mean, there're a couple of close friends we trust who know about the two of us, but no one who really gets what it's like.' She gave the pan another savage scrub with her Brillo pad. 'I suppose the biggest sacrifice was… well, I always thought I'd get to be a mum one day. That's not on the cards any more, obviously.' Suzanne looked down into the washing-up bowl, her eyes filling for a moment.

'Hey.' Angel put down the towel and slid an arm around the girl's shoulder. 'I'm sorry. I didn't mean to upset you.'

'It's okay. I just… I can't help thinking about it sometimes.'

'But isn't there any way? I mean, Seb and Carole could pretend… oh, I don't know. There must be something you could do.'

Suzanne gave her head a sad little shake. 'After their childhoods, their parents? They'd never do anything like that to kids of their own. Give them some screwed up showbizzy upbringing.'

'But things are changing, right? They won't need to live like this forever.'

'Attitudes don't change overnight, Angel. Maybe one day, Carole coming out will be no big deal and not even get a mention in the press. But it could be decades before that happens. And she's still got her own personal battles to fight: the drugs, the flashbacks, the panic attacks. No, I'm resigned to it.' Her eyes met Angel's as she handed over the pan for drying. 'And maybe it's something for you to consider too. Before you fall for him any harder.'

Angel felt her cheeks heat. 'Oh, it's too soon to think about anything like that.'

'Better to think about it now. Or you'll be so in love with him it'll be too late.'

It's already too late…

***

'Hey. Come here, you,' Seb said to Angel as she followed Suzanne, carrying the tray of refilled sherry glasses back into the sitting room. He grabbed her hand and pulled her down on to his knee, gave her a big kiss on the lips and hugged her to him.

329

'Anything wrong, sweetheart?' he asked in a low voice, noticing her moist eyes and the expression on her face.

'Nothing, just... never mind.' She tried to summon a smile. 'We'll talk about it later.'

'Okay, if you're sure...'

'We do have enough chairs, you know,' Moira said in a disapproving tone, but there was a twinkle in her eye as she made a start on her second sherry.

'Oh, come on, Ma, it's Christmas,' Seb said. Angel blushed, wriggled out of his arms and went back to join Carole and Suzanne on the sofa. 'Aren't I allowed a little kiss under the mistletoe?'

'I haven't got any mistletoe, you daft bugger. Now shut up and drink your sherry.'

'Yes, Miss.' Seb bowed his head in mock contrition, glancing up at Angel with a grin. She smiled back, trying to banish all thoughts of her conversation with Suzanne.

The TV was buzzing away in the background, and Angel recognised the *Eastenders* theme tune, just finishing after delivering its annual dose of Christmas misery to the residents of Albert Square. She listened to the continuity man announce the next programme. 'And now a classic from the nineties – the Christmas special of *Something About Sally.*'

The screen blinked off almost immediately. From the corner of her eye, Angel saw Carole with the remote and a black look on her face, her features tight and drawn.

'Excuse me.' Standing up, the little actress almost ran out of the room.

Suzanne sighed and looked over at Seb. 'You or me?'

'I'll go this time.' He stood up and followed Carole out into the hallway.

'Sorry,' Suzanne said, turning to Angel. 'This happens sometimes. It's that sitcom of her parents', you know? One of her triggers. Seb can get her through it, he understands her better than anyone. She'll be fine again in ten minutes.'

'Poor little Carrie,' Moira said, squinting sadly into her sherry. 'I wish I could have done more for her when she was still a little thing.'

'You did plenty, Moi,' Suzanne said. 'Without you and Seb, I don't know where she'd be now. Dead, probably.'

'Don't say things like that, Suzie,' Moira said, flinching. 'It's bad luck.'

Suzanne turned to Angel. 'Seb told me what you did. At the premiere. You helped her, didn't you?' To Angel's surprise, the girl suddenly threw her arms around her and hugged her. 'Thank you,' she said, her voice breaking with emotion. 'I wish I'd known that, the day you came to Tigerblaze.'

'What did you do?' Moira asked, eyeing Angel with curiosity.

'Oh, I... it was nothing much. That night at the premiere, when Carole – well, you know. I found her and got Seb. That was all there was to it, really.'

'Don't listen to her, Moi,' Suzanne said. 'It was more than that. Seb told me. She helped him look after her and sneak her out to the ambulance without anyone noticing. And she made sure it didn't get into that paper she works for.'

Standing up, Moira came over to Angel and rested a hand on her head. 'I didn't know that,' she said, her voice soft. 'Well, dear, it sounds like our funny little family has a lot to thank you for.'

Angel's cheeks were crimson as she smiled up at the old lady. 'Like I said, it was nothing much...'

Seb came back into the room now, leading Carole by the hand. Her eyes were damp and red, but she looked composed.

'Sorry, everyone,' she said in a quiet voice, sitting back down next to Suzanne. Her girlfriend put a comforting arm around her. 'I'm okay now. Let's put a DVD on or something. I've had it with TV; too full of surprises.'

Chapter 31

It was a few hours later when Seb stretched his fists into the air, giving a theatrical yawn. 'Okay, I'm shattered. I'm off to bed. I'll leave you ladies to it.' He made a motion with his eyes towards the door at Angel and she stifled a giggle.

'Actually, I think I'd better go up too. Long trip from London today.'

Carole smirked at them. 'Those two are so going on Santa's naughty list,' she muttered to Suzanne. Seb scowled at her and jerked his head towards Moira, who was nodding tipsily into another large sherry.

'Okay, night,' the old lady said, eyes heavy with sleep and Bristol Cream. 'I'll be going up myself in a minute. Get some rest, you two.'

'We're not going to get some rest, are we?' Angel whispered when she'd followed him out into the corridor.

'Bloody right.' He pulled her to him, covered her mouth with his, kissed her deeply. She pressed herself against him, relishing the comforting solid mass of his body.

'Oh God, I've missed this...' He ran his hands down the ridges of her spine, pressed against the hollow of her back to arch her body further into his. 'Come on.'

'Whose room will we use?' she asked as they hurried up the stairs.

'Mine. Yours is right next to Moira's.' He lifted the hand he was holding to his lips, pressed them against the backs of her fingers. 'Think you can be quiet?'

'With you? It won't be easy.'

He pushed open a door and led her into a small room with hideously patterned mustard wallpaper. An old, narrow bed with a metal frame was pushed back against the wall. Angel sat down on the edge and the springs gave a loud creak.

'Oh, for Christ's sake!' Seb groaned in frustration. 'I swear she's done this on purpose.'

Angel giggled. 'It doesn't matter. I'm sure we can improvise.'

'Stand up, Ange. I've got an idea.' He grabbed the corner of the duvet, twitched it off the bed and on to the laminate floor and spread it out so it was flat. 'It'll have to do.'

He walked towards her. 'Now come here, you.'

She sighed when she felt his arms go around her and hugged him back tightly around the waist. 'God, Seb, I missed you so much,' she whispered, laying her cheek against his broad chest. 'Stay like that for a minute. I want to feel you there.'

'I missed you too, sweetheart.' He kissed the top of her hair. 'I wish you could go with me sometime. Suze usually comes with Carole. It was a stroke of genius, really, giving her the PA job. Now she can go anywhere with us without questions being asked.' He laughed. 'Mind you, she's a terrible assistant.'

He held her back from him for a moment to scan her face. 'You looked upset before when you came back in from the kitchen. Did anything happen?'

'Oh, no, it was just… well, Suzanne was telling me about the sacrifices she's made to be with Carole. Not being able to tell her parents about them, and… things.'

'And you were wondering what sacrifices you'd have to make to be with me?'

'Something like that.' She hugged him tighter. 'I mean, I know there'll be some, Seb. And I do want to be with you, more than anything. There's not much I wouldn't give up. But it's hard not to wish things were different.'

'Yeah. I feel awful asking you to live this sort of life,' he said with a sigh. 'But I want you with me, Angel. I guess I'm a selfish bastard at heart.' He searched her eyes. 'Are you sure you're okay with it? If you want to back out now, I'll understand. I mean, I'll be devastated but I'll understand.'

'Oh no you don't,' she said with a smile. 'You're not getting away from me again, Seb. I love you. And I'm keeping you. That's all there is to it.'

'In that case, I'll allow you to tear all my clothes off and have your way with me. It is Christmas, after all.'

'You'll allow me, will you? How generous.'

'You don't want to? Oh, okay, then. Well, I'll see you in the morning for breakfast.'

'Tease. Stop pretending you can resist me.'

'That transparent, am I?' he said with a laugh as he drew her down with him onto the duvet.

'Kiss me, Angel.' His voice was soft now, his strong arms around her shoulders while they sat facing each other on the floor.

'Thought you'd never ask.' She took hold of his collar and pulled him to her for a deep kiss.

'And this time let's take it slow, okay?' Seb breathed, drawing back. He stroked her hair back from her face and twined a lock of it around his fingers. 'I've been away from you for a whole fortnight. Now I want to make you last.'

Angel smirked as she thought of something.

'What?'

'Nothing. Just thinking about something Leo said. He said we'd been having wild naked monkey sex.'

Seb laughed. 'Could you try not to think about your ex-boyfriend when we're in bed together, Blackthorne?'

'We're not in bed together. We're on the floor.'

'Mmmm. Pedantry. Really know how to get a man going, don't you?' He pulled her closer to him. 'Let's get these clothes off you.'

'When did you know, Seb?' she asked while she fumbled for the buttons of his shirt. 'That you loved me?'

'I don't know. It must have been building up since the *Milkman* premiere.' He divested her of the blouse she was wearing and unhooked the bra underneath. 'I suppose I knew, really knew, that night after the ReelKids fundraiser.' He grinned at her. 'I can't resist a drunk girl in black tie who tells me I'm nice.' He unfastened her jeans and shuffled them off over her hips, nuzzling her bare shoulder. 'What about you?' he asked, wriggling out of his own jeans too. 'When did you know?'

'I'm not sure, really. Suzanne says she could tell I loved you that day at Tigerblaze.'

'And did you?'

'If I did, I didn't know it. All I knew was I couldn't stop thinking about you and you were drop-dead gorgeous, and you had a way of running your fingers through your hair that… did things to me.'

'Ha! I wish I'd known that then. You'd have been on the floor.' He pushed his hands through his untidy hair sensuously. 'What, like this?'

'No, that just makes you look like you're in a shampoo advert. Like this. Here…' She reached up and combed the chestnut curls gently back from his face, letting her fingertips linger over each tempting lock.

'God, I love it when you do that…'

He guided her down so she was lying on her side next to him.

'You know you're beautiful, don't you?' he asked in a soft voice, skimming the delicious creamy curves.

'I'm thinking there's no right answer to that.'

'Well, then you can take my word for it.' He ran a soft palm along her side, over the silken contour of her hips and buttocks to her thigh, and she could feel his appreciation stirring against her.

'Christ, those legs…'

'What is it with you and legs?'

'Not just any legs. Your legs.' He trailed his fingertips over the full ivory flesh. 'Do you remember dropping your bag that night at the hotel?'

'I do. And I remember you perving at my legs then, too.'

'Couldn't help myself.'

She blushed, remembering their first meeting in the hotel bar. 'That was when I knew I couldn't resist you. Seeing you down there, with your hair brushing against me. God, I wanted you.'

'Did you?' He rolled her over on to her back, covered her body with his and nuzzled into her neck.

'So much…' she panted as he moved downward to suck at a pearly pink nipple standing out hard against the white mound of her breast.

'Tell me,' he whispered, his hot breath burning against her flesh.

'I remember I could feel your breath against my ankles, and those stupid sexy curls… God, it was torture. And I wanted you to… I had this fantasy. Kissing up my legs, your tongue… your hand…'

'Where?'

'You… know where…'

'Here?'

'Ah! Yes, Seb…' Her eyelids fluttered closed when she felt his hand slink up her legs to explore the soft, damp heat between them. 'Oh, God…' she moaned.

'Shh,' he whispered, nibbling at her earlobe. 'We have to be quiet, remember?'

'How can I be quiet when you're touching me like that?' She tried and failed to hold back a groan while his capable fingers twisted and swirled against her.

336

'You want me to stop?'

'Don't you dare… I'll be quiet, Seb. I'll try.'

'Good girl.'

She bit her lip to silence a gasp as he slid two fingers inside her, at the same time circling lightly against her with his thumb.

'Is this like your fantasy?' he said in a muffled whisper, burying his face in her hair.

'Better.'

'Why?'

'Because now you're mine.'

'Oh, Angel…'

With an effort she grabbed his wrist, stilled the hand that was still exploring her and guided him over until she was sat on top of him, wet and breathless.

'What are you doing?' he breathed.

'Taking control.'

'This isn't going to involve a ball gag and a cat o' nine tails is it, Ange?'

'It's going to involve me making you as hot for me as I am for you.'

'Is that right?'

'Yep.'

'Okay, give it your best shot, Blackthorne.' His eyes narrowed as they met hers, glittering wickedly up at her. 'Go on, I dare you. *Turn me on.*'

For a moment, she just stared down at him, her lips parted and panting. Then she leaned forward and kissed him hungrily.

'Why are you always teasing me, Seb?' she murmured, running her tongue tip over his moist lips.

'Because you look so beautiful when you're mad and horny.'

'Let's see how you like it.'

Her hands were on his firm pectorals while she lay over him. Sitting up, she ran her right hand along the bare, sleek skin to his navel. Then she lifted it to her own buttermilk curves.

Seb gasped as she ran her fingers around the swell of her breast and over the erect nipple, throwing her head back and shaking her thick auburn hair out behind her shoulders.

'Oh Jesus, Angel, don't do that…' She could feel him hardening between her thighs, his heavy breath quickening to a pant while he watched her. He reached up to follow the path of her hand along her body, but she pushed him away.

'Not yet.'

She allowed her hand to move down, down into the damp area between her legs, hearing Seb groan with longing as she touched herself in a way she'd never done in front of any man before.

'Oh *God*, Angel…'

'Tell me you love me, Seb.' She spiralled and pushed with her fingers, imitating the action of his hand moments before.

'I love you. I want you. Christ, Angel, I love you so much. Now stop tormenting me and let me touch you.'

'Ah! Not… yet.' She bit down hard on her lower lip, stifling a gasp.

Seb gave a harsh groan. 'Ange, please!'

'No. And quiet, remember?' She pressed his lips with her other hand, felt his hot breath on her fingertips, the touch of his tongue against them, and heaved a whispering groan of her own.

Tilting her hips lightly back and forth, she could feel the now rock-hard erection laid flat on his stomach sliding against her.

'Angel, please, stop, let me… I can't wait… Oh, God, it's torture…'

'Now, Seb…' Taking pity on him, she stopped the progress of her fingers. She reached for his hand, guided it up to her body.

With a shuddering sigh he pulled her towards him, kissed feverishly along her neck and shoulder, traced her ear with his whispering tongue. 'Christ almighty, Ange, what are you trying to do to me?'

He reached over to his open bag on the floor by the bed,

fumbled in the side pocket until his hand closed around the condom packet he was searching for.

'Here. Quick. You do it.'

With trembling fingers Angel peeled back the foil and reached down to roll it on to him.

'Ah… that's it… now, Ange, please…'

She slid herself over him, swallowing a gasp when she felt him enter her. 'Sit up, Seb. I want you close to me,' she whispered. She slipped her hands under his shoulder blades, guided him up so his chest was pressed against hers. Wrapping her legs around his back, she rocked her hips against him.

'When did you get to be such a bad girl, Angel Blackthorne?' he panted.

'When I met you, you sexy bastard.'

'One day you're going to stop calling me a bastard…'

'Never.'

She groaned in frustration as he grabbed her hips and guided her back and forth, slowing her rhythm to his thrusts. 'Faster, Seb, please…'

'No. I want to make this last. I want to feel your body around me for as long as I can.'

'Ah! I hate you!'

'You love me.'

'God, yes, I bloody do, don't I? Jesus Christ, Seb, faster, please! You're killing me…'

'Quiet, Angel, remember…' He dropped his hands from her hips and brought his arms up around her neck, let her set the rhythm of their lovemaking while he pressed her to him and buried his face between her breasts, moaning softly.

'That's it. My God, Seb, that feels… oh *God*…' She threw her head back when she felt the tremor of orgasm bubbling through her, stilled the thrash of her hips while it took her, sucked in her lip as she struggled not to make a sound.

'Jesus, I can feel you, Angel, I can… don't stop yet, sweetheart, please, not… quite… yet…' Seb pulled her to him, guiding her, rising and falling beneath her until he crushed out his climax against her, his fortnight's absence from her sending shockwaves bursting through his body into hers. 'Oh God, I love you so much…'

He pulled her down with him on to the duvet and for a second they lay still, tangled together and panting into each other's necks.

'Carole's right. We are going on the naughty list,' Seb said in a husky voice. He guided her over to his side so he could remove the spent condom and wrap it in a couple of tissues, then gathered her back into his arms. 'I can't believe you did that thing you just did. Naughty girl.'

'Nor can I.' She nestled into his arms and hooked one leg between his. 'It's obvious you bring out the worst in me, Wilchester.'

'Or the best, depending on which way you look at it.'

'Had you going, though, didn't I?' she said, grinning up at him.

'Bloody hell, Ange. You'll be the death of me.' He tilted her face to his for a kiss.

'At least you'll die happy.'

Seb pulled the corners of the little duvet around them, barely covering their two naked, sweat-gilded bodies.

He sighed, his eyes growing heavy with sleep. 'I guess you'd better go back to your room. I wish you could stay, Angel. I love sleeping next to you.'

'Can't we just stay here? I'm comfortable.'

Seb shook his head. 'You'll get cold.'

'Okay, but… five minutes' cuddling.'

'Ten.'

'Done. Happy Christmas, Seb.'

'Happy Christmas, sweetheart.'

Chapter 32

Angel came down next morning to find Seb and Carole on the sofa in their dressing gowns, eating toast and watching *It's A Wonderful Life* on TV.

'Clarence Odbody,' Carole said.

Seb looked thoughtful for a moment. 'Michael Gambon.'

'Stock.'

'Okay, Jim Broadbent then.'

'Meh. Better.'

'What are you two blathering on about?' Angel asked as Seb shuffled up to make room for her. She chucked herself down and snuggled into him.

'Playing Remakes,' he answered, giving her a kiss. 'Morning, gorgeous. Happy Christmas.'

She returned the kiss with added interest. 'Mmm… morning. What's Remakes?'

'Game we invented when we were kids. Cast a classic movie with modern-day actors.'

'Oh, okay. Sounds fun. And what's stock?'

'Lazy casting decision,' Carole said, smiling at her. 'I called "stock" so he had to try again. Seb makes them all the time. That's why he puts me in all his films.'

Seb cuffed her ear. 'Well. Keeps you off the streets, kid.'

'Didn't you used to play games at Christmas?' he asked, turning to Angel.

She helped herself to a slice of toast from a plate on the coffee table. 'Leo used to like to watch the *Strictly Come Dancing* special and play Shag Marry Kill. But with my parents? No, not really. Just Charades sometimes.'

'Want to play?'

'Okay. Go on, hit me.'

'Violet Bick.'

Angel laughed. 'Carole Beaumont.'

'Thanks, Ange,' Carole said. 'It'd be nice to play someone with a decent sex life for a change.' She turned an accusing gaze on Seb. 'You never write me slutty characters.'

He shrugged. 'Okay. In my next film you can be a one-legged Soho prostitute.'

'Sweet. Thanks.'

'Okay, Ange,' he said, turning to her. 'Try another. The big one. George Bailey.'

'Jimmy Stewart.'

'Er, yeah, not sure you've quite got the hang of this game, darling,' Carole said with a laugh.

'Jimmy Stewart,' Angel said firmly. 'No one can play George Bailey but him. It'd be sacrilege.'

Seb turned to his wife, lifting one eyebrow. 'She's got a point, Car.'

'Do you two always have to be talking about work?' Moira asked, coming in from the kitchen with her sleeves rolled up to the elbow and ruffling Carole's blonde bob. 'It's Christmas.'

'Ew! Get off, Moi, you've got onion hands!' Carole shrieked, jerking her head away.

'It's not work, Ma. Just a game,' Seb said.

'It'd better not be work,' Angel said, looking at him through narrowed eyes. 'I love you, Seb, but I would have to hunt down

342

and harpoon anyone who tried to remake *It's A Wonderful Life*. So be warned.'

'I wouldn't dare.' He planted an affectionate kiss on her cheek.

'I just came in to ask if one of you girls could come and help me in the kitchen,' Moira said. 'There's still lots to do before dinner.'

Carole rolled her eyes at Angel. 'Every year. It's like women's lib was something that only happened to other people.'

'Come on, Carrie. I need someone to do the stuffing.'

'Nope.' Carole tilted her little nose into the air and folded her arms. 'I'm going on strike. Make Seb do it.'

'I'll come,' Angel said, jumping up. 'I'd like to help, Moira.'

'Emily Davison threw herself in front of a horse for people like you!' Carole yelled after her as she followed Moira into the kitchen.

Suzanne was already in there, peeling potatoes.

'Okay, so Carole's version of women's lib doesn't apply to you, then?' Angel asked, coming over and taking a potato from the pile.

Suzanne snorted. 'Carole's a special kind of feminist whose principles only cover her never having to get off her backside.'

'Alright, Suzie, you've done your share,' Moira said, coming over to the girl and patting her on the shoulder. 'Go and have a sit down.'

'Thanks, Moi.' Suzanne kissed the old lady on the cheek as she walked past her to leave the room. 'Oh, and happy Christmas, everyone.'

'Best thing that ever happened to Carrie, meeting that girl,' Moira muttered. 'And you two – upstairs and get dressed, now!' she called through to Seb and Carole.

'After the film, Ma!' Seb called back. 'Nearly finished.'

Angel smiled, running the peeler over a floury potato. 'Has he always called you Ma?'

'Here. Leave the potatoes, there's plenty done already. You're on stuffing,' Moira said in businesslike mode. She handed Angel a peeled onion and a cheese grater. 'And no, not always. When he was a little mite it was always Moira. But when his mum asked him to call her Abigail, he asked if he could call me Ma. And that seemed like the right way round, in the end.'

'Do you mind talking about it?'

'Not with you, love. Seems like you're part of the family now, after what you did for Carrie.'

Angel reached over and gave the old lady's arm a squeeze.

'What was it like, Moira? When Seb was little, I mean. It must've been a pretty screwed up way for him to grow up. And Carole too. The Beaumonts sound like a nightmare.'

'Don't talk to me about those people.' Moira sniffed, pursing her lips and grating an onion savagely. 'Some folk should have to pass a test before they're allowed to have children.'

'You kept the two of them grounded, though.' Angel glanced through the door at Carole and Seb still playing Remakes on the sofa, now with Suzanne squeezed between them. 'People like Seb aren't normally… like Seb. He told me he had you to thank for that. And even Carole. Given what she's been through, she's pretty well-adjusted. Apart from… well, you know, her issues.'

'That girl would have no problems if I could've had her to myself sooner,' Moira growled, still going to work on the onion as if it had done her a personal wrong. 'Poor little lamb. Those Beaumonts… they should be in prison, if you ask me. She was in such a state when she came to live with us, needed a lot of looking after. But we pulled her through as best we could. She has her good patches and bad patches now, but we're getting there, I think.'

'My friend Emily calls that a salvation complex.'

'Anything wrong with that?'

'She'd say you can't save everyone.'

Moira looked up from her chopping and met Angel's eyes. Hers were damp with moisture that probably had nothing to do with the onion. 'You can save some. That's enough.'

Angel flung both arms around Moira and gave her a tight hug. 'What's that for?' Moira said.

'Oh, just... you know. Tea and sympathy. Minus the tea.'

The old lady gave Angel's arm a vague pat. 'Well, you're a good lass,' she said gently. 'I think you'll do well for him. He should have someone. Someone from outside that film world he lives in. It's good for him.' She held Angel away from her and looked into her face. 'And it's about time I had one good shot at being a nana.'

Angel felt her cheeks growing hot, thinking back to her conversation with Suzanne the day before. 'It's a bit soon to think about that. Let's just take it one day at a time, eh?'

She dragged over a bowl and started grating her onion into it, welcoming an excuse to lower her eyes.

'I don't know how you managed to get him through, though,' she said, picking up the threads of their conversation. 'How did you? His father sounds like he was a nasty piece of work.'

'Told you about that, did he?' Moira's brow darkened as she remembered. 'I know it's wrong to speak ill of the dead, but I hope there's a special circle of hell reserved for that bastard, pardon my French. The things he put them through...'

'I'm so sorry, Moira. It must have been tough on you.'

'Well, it was a big house. I could protect Seb from it a lot of the time. Keep him safe with me, out of the way, while his poor mother took the worst of it. Most of the time, but not always. My poor little lad...'

Angel thought about what Seb had told her the day she'd interviewed him at Tigerblaze. The little boy, sobbing in his bed with a pillow over his ears, trying not to hear his mother's screams...

'God, Moira... and what was it like after Hugo died?'

'Better. There was just his mum then, haunting the place like a ghost, and I could try to give him something that at least resembled a normal life.'

345

'Was he there when his mum died? Seb?'

'No. He was away at university. Me and Carrie were at home with her, though.'

'I remember seeing it in the papers,' Angel said gently. 'Overdose, wasn't it?'

'Yes. Poor woman. We never did seem to be able to get through to her. We tried, but she was too broken. After what that evil bastard had done to her, you know. And then fame was hard on her, she couldn't cope with it. Just like Carrie, in some ways.' She looked sadly into her bowl. 'I was the one who found her.'

'Oh my God, Moira!'

The old lady shook her head as if to dismiss the memory. 'Well, let's not talk about sad things, love. It's Christmas. And perhaps things didn't turn out so badly in the end. Here you all are, after all, and now the children have both got someone. That's reason enough to be cheerful in my old age.'

'Do you have any others? Children of your own, I mean?'

'Me? Oh, no. Just those two. I was married, but… I don't know. Somehow we never got round to it. Anyway, he's gone now. Seb and Carrie are all I've got. And they're very good to me.'

Angel put down her onion and gave Moira another hug. 'Thank you.'

'What for, dear?'

'For Seb.'

Moira laughed, looking at Angel with a glint in her eye. 'Speaking of which, I could swear I heard someone sneaking out of his room when I was getting ready for bed last night.'

Angel blushed into her onion shavings. 'Er, yeah, sorry… just went in for a cuddle. That was disrespectful. My fault.'

'Oh, never mind, dear. I know how you young people in love are. If you two want to be together, I won't put up a fight. Get that big strong lad of yours to pull the other single bed into his room and you can push them together to make a double. It might surprise you to know, I was even young once myself.'

346

Angel flashed her a grateful smile. 'Thanks, Moira.'

'And how are my girls?' Seb asked, pushing open the door and coming into the kitchen. His hair was damp from the shower and he was dressed in just a pair of tracksuit bottoms. He put an arm around them both and planted a kiss each on the top of Angel's auburn head and Moira's grey curls.

'What are you doing in here? And where's your top, you young idiot?' Moira flicked him away impatiently with a tea towel.

He shrugged. 'Just came to see if I could help.'

'He's showing off for Angel, Moi,' Carole said, following him in. 'He's like one of those randy seabirds that are always strutting about with their chests out trying to attract a mate.'

Seb grinned as he saw Carole mouth the word 'slut' at him across the kitchen, nodding his full agreement.

'Is it working?' he asked Angel under his breath, drawing her into a corner.

'Go away, Seb. I hate you,' she muttered, trying not to let her eyes wander over his glistening bronzed torso.

'You mean you want me.'

'That too.'

'Well, you're only human.' He pulled her to him for a kiss.

Carole was eyeing the raw turkey sitting on the cooker with distaste. 'Who'd have thought something as disgusting as that could be so delicious when it was cooked?'

'Alright, get out, the three of you,' Moira said, flapping her tea towel at them. 'I can't do Christmas dinner with all this fussing about and necking and insulting my turkey going on. Now go on, sod off.'

'We came to ask you to take a break, Moi,' Carole said. 'We're dressed now. That means presents. Come on.' She took the old lady by the hand and tried to drag her out of the kitchen.

'You're not dressed until Seb gets a shirt on,' Moira said firmly. 'Then we can do presents.'

'Ugh. Fine. If the sight of my body is so disgusting to you all.'

Seb rolled his eyes and removed his arms from Angel. 'I'll go get some jeans on, then. Back in a minute.' Her eyes lingered on the sleek, powerful lines of his back and shoulders, rippling enticingly while he walked out of the room.

'Where's Suzanne?' Angel asked, following Moira and Carole into the other room and taking a seat on the sofa.

'On the phone to her parents in Limerick, wishing them a happy Christmas,' Carole said, throwing herself down next to Angel. 'Her mum's probably trying to set her up on a blind date again. Happens nearly every time she rings home.' Just then, her girlfriend came back into the room and plonked herself down grumpily on Carole's lap. 'Well? Who is it this time, Suzie Q?'

'Daughter of someone in her book group who lives in Richmond. Apparently there's only a fifteen-year age gap. Divorced, two teenage kids and she still has most of her own teeth.' Suzanne grinned at Angel. 'My mum's got this idea all lesbians are automatically compatible. She's lined up someone new for me every time I speak to her.'

'She won't have all her own teeth when I finish with her. Trying to steal my woman,' Carole said with mock ferocity, wrapping her arms around Suzanne's waist. 'Bam! Right in the chops.'

Suzanne giggled, giving her a kiss. 'I love it when you go all *Fatal Attraction* on me, sweets.'

'Please, Car. You're like two foot tall. She'd take you to the cleaners,' Seb scoffed, coming back in dressed in jeans and a black Aran jumper.

'Or I'm normal sized and you're a freakish giant.'

'Alright, you two, stop pissing about,' Moira said. 'Seb, do the honours please, as the man of the house.'

'Right, who wants to go first?' he asked, seating himself on the floor by the tree.

'Just close your eyes and pick one, so-called man of the house,' Carole said, tapping her little foot. 'Stop faffing.'

'Okay, kid. Keep your bob on.' He scrunched up his eyes and reached for one of the little gift-wrapped packages.

'This one's for you, Ma,' he said, reading the label. He handed it to Moira. 'From Angel.'

'Thank you, love,' she said, beaming at Angel. 'I didn't expect anything.'

'I wanted to. I mean, it's nothing much…'

'Oh!' Moira said, opening a tin of cigars. 'Perfect. Thanks, dear. How did you know?'

'Seb said you always like one on Christmas Day. My dad used to smoke that kind.'

'I do. Only once a year, mind you. These will keep me going for a while.'

'Tsk. Filthy habit, Moi,' Carole said, pursing her lips in a superior manner. 'Give mine out now, Seb.'

Seb dug in the pile to find four flat, rectangular parcels all wrapped in silver paper with sprigs of holly on it.

'I made one for everyone,' Carole said, smiling as they each opened their gift to find a notebook in its own embroidered cover. 'When I was in – when I had a bit of time on my hands, you know?'

'It's beautiful, Carole,' Angel said, gazing in awe at the intricate beaded bird of paradise on her book's sea-green cover. 'Thank you.' She leaned over Suzanne to kiss Carole on the cheek. 'I can't believe you made these. You really are good at everything, aren't you?'

Carole flung her a suggestive smirk. 'You'll have to ask Suzie about that.'

'Ignore her,' Suzanne said, flushing. 'She already knows she is.'

'Well? Come on, come on!' Carole said after everyone had thanked her for their gifts. 'Who's next?'

'Angel can be next.' Seb smiled at her. 'Here, Ange. From me.'

'Not another tennis racquet, is it?' she asked, taking it from him. 'I could start my own club.'

349

'Did he give you a tennis racquet?' Moira asked, looking puzzled.

'Yes. For my birthday.'

The old lady stroked his curls while he sat by her feet. 'Ridiculous boy.'

'Technically it was a spaghetti strainer, but never mind that. Come on, Ange, open it. I promise it's not any item of sports equipment.'

Angel exclaimed with surprise and pleasure when she opened the heavy squarish parcel to find a set of *Rebecca the Reporter* storybooks.

'Thanks, Seb,' she said, going over to him and crouching down so she could give him a kiss. 'I didn't know you could still get these.'

'I did have to scout around a bit. They're out of print now.'

'My one was lost when we were moving barracks years ago.' She looked down at the books, smiling. 'I can't believe you remember me telling you that silly story.'

'How could I forget?' he said softly, brushing her hair away from her face just as he had that night.

'Seb...' She muttered as he pulled her over on to his knee, wrapped his arms around her middle and kissed her cheek.

'Love you, Ange.'

'Love you too, sweetheart...'

'Bleurghh. Come on, guys. Mixed company here,' Carole said, turning her face away. 'Enough soppy stuff.'

'Jealous, wifey?' Seb said.

'Ha! You wish, hubby dearest.'

'Behave, you two,' Moira said impatiently. 'Come on, Seb, do another. I need to get back to the cooking.'

'Open mine,' Angel whispered. She was still settled happily on his knee, oblivious now to embarrassment.

'Thought I got my present last night,' Seb murmured, bringing his mouth close to her ear so the others couldn't hear him. She elbowed him in the ribs, stifling a giggle.

He dug into the shrinking pile until he found her gift to him: a hard, rectangular, untidily wrapped package.

'Hmm. Not a bottle of wine, then.' He held the parcel to his ear and shook it.

'Open it and see.'

'Wrapping not one of your many talents, I see,' he said, fighting his way through the layers of tape and foil paper.

'Nope.'

'Angel…' He twisted her face around to his as he finally reached the centre of the parcel. 'It's… thank you. How did you know I was a fan? Did I tell you?'

'I sort of assumed,' she said, a shy blush creeping up into her cheeks while he examined the handsome leather-bound volume of TS Eliot poetry she'd given him. 'I mean, your first two films. The titles are from *The Waste Land*, aren't they? And then you mentioned him in that interview.'

'Oh God, don't mention that interview. Arrogant bastard, wasn't I?'

'Oi. Language,' Moira said, cuffing him.

'Come on, Ma, you swear all the time.'

'Yes, well. I'm allowed.'

'So? Do you like it?' Angel asked. 'I mean, it's not a first edition or anything fancy. Just a book. It's hard to know what to get you when you can probably afford to buy whatever you want and I'm only a poor journalist.' She wriggled round to face him.

'It's perfect,' he said softly. 'Perfect because it came from you. Thanks, sweetheart.' He kissed her again, Angel doing her best to ignore Carole gagging theatrically in the background.

***

'Come upstairs a minute, Ange,' Seb said once all the presents had been given out and Moira and Suzanne had gone into the kitchen to deal with the delicate operation of stuffing the turkey. 'I've got something else for you.'

Carole snorted from the sofa. 'I bet you have.'

'Shut up, you. Not that,' he said, giving her a look. 'Come on, Angel. Five minutes.'

'What is it, Seb?' she asked, following him up to his room.

As soon as the door had closed behind her, he wrapped his arms around her neck, drew her to him and claimed her for a long, passionate kiss that left them both out of breath.

'Huh... So Carole was right, then.'

'No,' he said, smiling. 'I just thought since I had you here... God, Ange, I've wanted to do that all day. Anyway, wait a sec...'

Seb let her go and turned to rummage in his holdall. He pulled out a small gift-wrapped box.

'Here. For you.'

'What is it?'

'Open it and see.'

She peeled off the paper and opened the little box to find a Yale key on a leather keyring.

'Er, thanks. What does it open?'

'It's for the Hippodrome.'

'Your cinema?'

'Ours, Angel.'

'Seb... really?' She looked down at the little silver key in her hand, moved. 'That's so sweet.'

'It is, isn't it? Now kiss me again, Ange.'

'Come here, then.' She grabbed his jumper and brought her lips up to his.

'You know, we don't have to go straight back down,' he whispered, moving his lips to her ear.

She giggled. 'You've got stamina for an old man, I'll give you that.'

'Cheeky,' he breathed against her neck. 'I'm only four years older than you.' He took her earlobe into his mouth and massaged it with his tongue.

'Yep. Ancient.' She tilted her head to one side and closed her eyes. 'And by the way, don't think I've forgotten you teasing me with your shirt off this morning. I'll get my own back later.' She sighed. 'But not now, Seb. We should go and help Moira with the dinner. It's not fair to leave it all to her and Suzanne.'

Seb gave a dismissive shrug, moving his lips along her neck. 'I don't need to help. I'm the man of the house, remember?'

'Don't let Carole hear you say that,' Angel said with a smile. 'She'll give you her Last of the Suffragettes speech again.'

'Ha! She wouldn't dare. That woman hasn't cooked a thing in the six years we've been married.' He drew back from her neck, lifted her chin so he could look into her face. 'How are you finding it, Ange? Not too weird?'

She laughed. 'Well, maybe on paper the family Christmas with your boyfriend, his wife the film star and his wife's secret girlfriend sounds like a reality TV show waiting to happen, but –'

'Don't forget Moira.'

'Yes, chuck an ex-nanny in there too, why not? But it's like you said before. What you know becomes the new normal, doesn't it?' She hugged him to her. 'It's an unusual little family group you've grown up with, but they're lovely people, Seb. Really. I've enjoyed getting to know them better.'

'It means a lot to me that you like them,' he said gently. 'I knew you would. And they love you already, I can tell.'

'And so do you, right?'

'You know I do, Angel. More than anything.'

'Well, maybe we don't need to go straight back down,' she mumbled, pulling his lips on to hers.

'That's my girl…'

Chapter 33

'I hate having to leave you here,' Seb said as he dropped her off at the station the day after Boxing Day. 'It seems ridiculous, when we're both going to London. Safer from any lurking paparazzi, though. Present company excepted, of course.'

'Hey. Film critic, thanks very much. Leo's the pap.' She grabbed the hand resting on the gearstick and pulled him over to her side for a kiss. 'Do you really see a lot of them?'

Seb couldn't help a smirk. 'I've seen a lot of one of them. Sorry, sorry, film critic, I know…' He reached up to stroke her hair, brushed a few escaping strands away from her face. 'But no, not really. Not me, anyway, apart from for a couple of weeks after that *Investigator* front page when I was followed around a bit by a bunch trying to catch me getting my leg over with any flame-haired temptresses.' He grinned at her. 'Unfortunately for them they were a few months early.'

She winced at the reference to the honey trap and rapped him lightly on the arm. 'Oi. None of that flame-haired temptress stuff, you.'

'Anyway, generally it's Carole who gets the attention. That's what I'm worried about. Me, you, her… them working out that connection. It puts us all at risk. I mean, that's kind of why we met in the first place, Ange. Sorry to bring it up. Clifton was only ever interested in me because of Carole really.'

'God, I hate this. Seb, I wish…'

'What, Angel?'

'Oh, I don't know. That we could be together properly. You could come and meet the folks, all that stuff. Things couples do. Other couples.'

'You think I don't want that?'

'I know you do,' she said. 'You're right, though, it's not safe. I love my parents, but… well, my mum thinks you're God's gift to filmmaking as it is. I told you before. She might try to be discreet, but I don't think she could help herself. One glass of wine too many at a dinner party…'

'I'm sorry, Ange. I wish things were different.' Pulling her into a tight hug, he buried his face into her hair and kissed the top of her head. 'I just hope in the end you think I'm worth it,' he whispered, his voice muffled.

'And more.' She kissed him again, let herself run her fingers through those tumbling curls she loved.

'Go on,' he said with a sigh. 'You'll miss your train. I'll see you soon, won't I?'

'Whenever you like. I can meet you at the cinema, now I've got my shiny key.'

'Still a film club?'

'Film club with benefits.'

'Sounds like heaven. I love films. And as for benefits…' He pressed another kiss on to her lips with an air of finality. 'Now go on, go. There's only a few minutes to get to your platform.'

'Okay, okay, I'm going,' she said, smiling. 'Since you're so keen to get rid of me.'

'Is this one of those "you hang up" things? Are we that couple now?'

Angel laughed. 'We're just lucky Carole's not here, rolling her eyes and making vomit sounds. Really knows how to kill the mood, that woman.'

'Well, wife's prerogative, I suppose. Go on, Angel. I'll see you soon. Call me when you get home, won't you? Love you, sweetheart.'

'Love you too.' She gave him one last kiss, then grabbed her bag from the back seat and headed to her platform to find the train.

***

It was over three hours later when she pushed open the door to the flat.

'Hello? Have you guys got your clothes on? I'm back,' she called out.

'Ange… thank God…'

The door to the sitting room opened to reveal Emily, looking pale and drawn. Angel could see Leo standing behind her, looking just as anxious and haggard as his girlfriend.

'Oh my God, are you okay?' Emily hurled herself forward to give her friend a hug. 'We've been worried sick, sweetie. We couldn't get you on your phone.'

'Er, yeah, sorry, I forgot to take my charger,' Angel said. 'Are you guys alright?' A pang of worry arrowed through her. 'Did something happen while I was gone? Where's the cat?'

'He's fine, Ange, he's here…' Emily nodded down at Groucho, weaving around her feet as usual.

'Christ, haven't you seen, Angel?' Leo said at the same time.

Angel shook her head in confusion. 'Okay, guys, one at a time. And seen what, Leo? I don't know what you're talking about.'

'Today's *Investigator*. You really haven't seen it?'

'No… what?' She felt a sudden chilling sensation in the pit of her stomach. 'Oh my God, Leo, what is it? Show me. Quick.'

'Here.' He ushered her into the sitting room and pointed to a newspaper on the coffee table. 'Sit down first.'

The front page showed a grainy long-lens shot of Carole and Suzanne kissing, taken through the window of a London flat. Overlaid on the photo, one of Steve's typically sensationalist headlines was screaming out to her:

Bonking Beaumont's lesbo shame! Hubby's PA is former child star's secret lover!

Oh God… was she going to be sick? It felt like she was going to be sick…

She buried her face in her hands, tried to fight the sudden surge of nausea, get her head around what had happened. 'How, Leo?' she asked, turning helpless eyes up to him.

He sank down on the sofa next to her, looking bewildered. 'I don't know, Angel. Honestly. Steve never said a word about any story he was planning to run on Carole Beaumont. You know I would've told you.'

'I know…' She stared blankly ahead, in shock. Then her eyes narrowed in anger. 'And so did he. That's why he didn't tell you. That *bastard!*'

'I need to ring Seb,' she said suddenly. 'Oh Christ. He must be going out of his mind.'

'Wait a sec, Ange,' Emily said, sitting down on the other side of her. 'Have you seen the rest?'

'What do you mean, the rest?'

'It's all in there.' Emily's voice dripped sympathy. 'I'm sorry, I know you don't want to hear this. But it's not just that. It's everything. The suicide attempt that night at the premiere, rehab, everything…'

'Oh Jesus, Em!' Angel gave an anguished sob. 'This could kill her!'

'I know, sweetie, God, I know. Go on, ring him. He'll want to hear your voice right now. Make sure she's okay.'

Angel fished in her pocket, her hands shaking as she took out the little black Nokia Seb had given her. She pulled up his number, the only one on there, and hit the call button.

'Angel.' She felt a surge of relief when she heard him say her name at the other end of the line.

'Oh God, Seb, sweetheart, I just heard. Are you okay? Is Carole?'

'She's bearing up. We're back at the house. Had to fight through an army of press to get in.'

'Just you two?'

'No, Suze is with us. Her flat's crawling with the bastards as well, and Carole needs her right now. She might as well be here. She might as well, now.' His voice sounded hollow, emotionless.

'God, Seb... is there anything I can do?'

'Angel. Tell me honestly.' He hesitated. 'Did you do this?'

If Angel had been standing, she'd actually have staggered. It felt as if she'd taken a fist to the gut.

'*What?*'

'Did you leak it? Just answer me.'

'You can't think...you... you... bastard!' She stared at the phone in disbelief, feeling her brain start to fog and her ears ring as she absorbed what he was accusing her of. It felt as if she was sinking slowly underwater, gaping, struggling to breathe. 'Do you really... how could you even think that? You think I'd sell Carole out just for a step up the ladder at the bloody *Investigator*, even now? You still don't trust me, seriously? For Christ's *sake*, Seb!'

'I'm not talking about your career, Angel. God, I hope we're past that now.' His voice broke when he spoke again. 'I meant for me.'

'For...'

'What you said this morning. About being together. A proper couple. Suzanne told me what you talked about before...'

'You... you arrogant *prick*, Seb! Arghh! I can't believe you! You think I'd do that to Carole? You think I'm that kind of *monster*? After everything!' She let out a choked sob. 'And I really believed you loved me. Oh, God!'

'Angel, wait…'

The phone hurtled against the wall of the sitting room and smashed into pieces.

'Arghhhhhh!'

'Hey,' Emily said, eyeing Angel with deep concern. 'Come here, crazy phone-smashing lady. Don't bite my hand off, will you?' She stretched her arms around Angel's neck. 'Are you okay?'

'Christ, no, I'm not okay. Do I look bloody okay? How could I be okay? Oh God, Em… he said… he told me…'

'Yeah, I think we got the gist, sweetie.'

Angel let herself collapse into broken sobs in her friend's arms, limp and spent. Emily stroked her hair and made soothing sounds over her.

'Hey, Ginge,' Leo said gently, hugging her from the other side. 'You've still got us, eh? We'll get through it all together, like always.'

'Anything we can do, sweetie,' Emily said, nodding.

'I don't know if I can get through. Not this time…' Giving in to the heaving, grief-filled sobs, Angel slid into an oblivion of misery in her friends' soothing embrace.

***

Later that afternoon, Angel marched through the *Investigator* offices, ignoring the surprised stares of the skeleton staff manning the place over the Christmas break. She flung open the door to Steve's office, chucked that day's paper down in front of him and slammed both fists on to his desk.

'You son of a *bitch*, Clifton.'

'I thought you might say that.' The editor looked up to meet her blazing eyes, and for once he wasn't grinning. 'Look, calm down a minute, can you, Blackthorne? Sit down. Try and remember I'm an old man before you go ahead and thump me.'

She glared at him for a full minute before she lifted her fists from his desk and threw herself into the seat facing him.

'Okay, pet, let's have it,' he said with a resigned sigh, pushing the paper with Carole's story on the front page away from him. 'Get it all out, eh?'

'You absolute, total, complete – how did you get that story?'

'Got some spies around. And I had a few clues coming in to point me the right way.'

'Clues… oh my God! I should've known!' she exploded with a sudden realisation. 'You hacked Seb's phone, didn't you? Is that how you always knew – everything? About where I'd been and when I'd seen him? Is it? Tell me, you bastard.'

'Alright, keep your voice down. That glass isn't completely soundproof, you know,' he said, looking nervously out at his staff. Several of them had turned to peer, with great curiosity, through the glass front of his office. 'Some of these people are temps. I don't fancy a prison sentence at my time of life, that could just about finish me off. And no. Not his, love.' He narrowed bleared eyes at her. 'Yours.'

'My… *what*! You couldn't! You… prick, Steve! For *Christ's* sake!' she said in a choked voice. 'You played me, seriously? How did you even… when?'

'I knew there was something going on between you and Wilchester. That night you went to the premiere. People saw you leave with him and Beaumont, or someone answering to your description, anyway. I've been dipping into your texts and voice-mail for months. You should change your default PIN, Princess.'

'Oh my… God!' Angel shook her head in shock and disbelief. 'Christ, you are one evil bastard, Steve. Don't even look at me. I can't stand the sight of you.' She turned away from him, scowling over the office with narrowed, salt-stinging eyes. 'I mean, what gave you the *right*? That's a violation of my privacy and, I don't know, of *me* somehow! God! I thought…'

'Thought what, love?'

'I don't know. I guess I got this mad idea from somewhere that you respected me.' She looked down, tried to squeeze back the tears that were threatening to seep out. 'I mean, Jesus Christ! I knew you were an amoral prick but I thought you had some professional ethics. Hacking your own staff! That's a new low, even by your standards.'

To her surprise, she heard him sigh. 'You're right, Blackthorne,' he said. 'I crossed a line. And I'm sorry for dragging you into it. Look, if it makes you feel any better, the story about you and Wilchester would've been explosive enough on its own, and I had more than enough to run that a month ago. I wanted to keep your name out of it.'

'How the hell is that supposed to make me feel better?'

'Well, maybe it isn't, I don't know. Listen… maybe I should've told you this before. Things aren't going well for us, not for any of the print media. It's all online these days. The bloggers, click-bait, all that free viral content on the web. Makes us obsolete. Who wants to read a story that broke on Twitter an hour ago tomorrow morning? Old news. It's a brave new world out there, and it's trying to edge us out.' He cast a glance down at his front page, his eyes darting over the photo of Carole and Suzanne embracing. 'A good, dirty exclusive is just about all we've got to offer these days. I needed something big to put us back on top.'

'What, and you thought you'd sell out Carole Beaumont to do it? After everything you've done to her already? That's sick, Steve! You're sick.' Angel glared at him, her expression radiating shock and disgust. 'Jesus, how can you do these things to people? Screw with their lives like that? Carole's one step away from a nervous breakdown thanks to people like you. No, scrap that. People who *are* you. *You*, Steve. You homophobic, exploitative little… *shit*. You did this to her. You've been on her case since she was bloody knee high. Haven't you?'

He shrugged. 'Beaumont knew the risks. She was born to this.'

'*No*, Steve! No one's born to anything! She's just a woman. Like anyone: your wife, your granddaughter. Don't you see that? Christ, she's a human being, not some performing animal born into captivity to be gawped at. And you nearly destroyed her. Or is that just what you need to tell yourself so you can sleep at night, you mad bastard?'

'What makes you think I sleep at night?'

'God, don't you feel guilty at all? Don't you feel anything? A woman could be dead because of you! I mean, she came this close. I was bloody there, I saw it. And it wasn't the first time, either.'

He shrugged again. 'That's the game we play, Blackthorne. That's the business. You knew it going in, so don't come over all moral-high-groundy about it now. You were a part of this, whether you like it or not.'

'What? I never asked you to hack my phone!'

'Not what I meant, love. I mean you're part of this industry, the old set-'em-up-and-knock-'em-down.' He shot her a significant look. 'You played your part, didn't you? Don't remember having to force you at gunpoint, either.'

She winced at the reference to the honey trap, but she refused to drop his gaze.

'You're right, I did play my part, and I can't take it back now. But that's it, no more. I'm done, Steve, with all of this, for good. I'm not hanging around this moral vacuum trying to convince myself people aren't people until the day I wake up and I've turned into someone like you. Consider this my notice. I quit.'

'Blackthorne, wait…'

But she'd already marched out of his office, letting the door slam shut behind her.

Chapter 34

Angel glared at the buzzing phone on the coffee table, willing it to stop ringing through the sheer power of her scowl.

'God, Ange, let me answer it if you don't want to,' Emily said, coming in from the kitchen with a cup of tea for her. 'It's driving me insane.'

'Leave it.'

'How many is that today then?'

'Five so far. He usually gets up to eight or nine before bed.'

'You can't keep doing this, sweetie. Talk to him. You know you want to.'

Angel didn't answer. She just carried on stroking Groucho, who purred away obliviously on her lap, and scowling at the phone.

'Oh God, you're not going catatonic on me again, are you?' Emily asked, waving a hand in front of her vacant eyes. 'Not going to start wittering on about cucumber sandwiches?'

'No. We're out of wine, for one thing.'

'Right.' Emily leaned over, picked up the now-silent phone and shoved it into Angel's hand. 'Ring him back. Now. Come on, Ange. You can't sit here being the jobless, boyfriendless Mad Cat Lady all your life. Hear what the man has to say, at least, before you decide what you want to do. You're stuck in an infinite misery loop and it's doing my attractively curly head in.'

Angel scoffed. 'What happened to "you can never be part of that world, Ange, you big fat ordinary person loser"?'

'Pretty sure I never called you a big fat ordinary person loser. Anyway, it's different now, isn't it? He doesn't need to live that lie any more. You can make your own life, your own future. I mean, I guess there'll still be… challenges. With his unusual job and his screwed up parents and everything. But nothing you couldn't work through. Take it from the woman who's going out with the recovering alcoholic.'

She sank down next to Angel and curled a comforting arm around her shoulders. 'I mean, think about it. I've never seen you chippier than in those few weeks you and Seb were officially an item. He's like the perfect man for you, isn't he? Mr Tall, Dark and Gagging-for-it. He makes you a romantic picnic, gives you a thoughtful – not to mention priceless – gift from your favourite film, dances with you to your daft old music, takes you to meet his family… what else?'

'Well, there was some bloody incredible sex. Quite a lot of it, actually.' Angel sniffed. 'And topless bacon sandwiches as well.'

'Yeah, okay, let's stay off the sandwich theme, shall we?' Emily twisted her friend's face around to look at her. 'Look, Ange, how many guys do that kind of thing? I know what he said. And he was wrong to say it. But he does love you. It's obvious to anyone with eyes. And you love him, don't try to pretend you don't. Talk to him, go on.'

'I don't know, Em. I do miss him… God, so much. And he did make me happy. Very happy. And yes, alright, I still love him. Obviously.' She gave a muffled sob, hiding her face on Emily's shoulder for a moment. 'But I don't know if I can forgive him. I just can't believe he could ever think I'd do that to Carole.'

'Well, sweetie, you do have some previous there, you know. Something as big as that, you don't just forget it.'

'That's what makes it worse,' Angel said. 'I really thought we'd got past it, Em. Could laugh about it, even. How can I forgive him if I feel like he can never really trust me, that he'll always be thinking about it?'

'Well, you won't know if you can forgive him until you try. Ring him. Go on.'

'I'll… think about it.'

'Think about it fast. Your miserable face is giving me a head-ache. It's that or move on, Ange. You've wallowed long enough. It's been nearly two weeks.'

'Bloody hell, don't go easy on me just because I'm upset, will you? Look, I said I'd think about it.' She grabbed her mug of milky tea off the table and without thinking took a long swallow, wincing as it burnt her mouth. 'Ow! Bugger. Where's Leo to play Good Cop anyway?'

'At AA. And then he's got that exhibition, so I'm afraid it's Bad Cop only for you. Now come on. Finish your tea and man up. You're not getting babied today.' Emily stood up, folded her arms and stood over Angel with pursed lips.

'God, you're scary when you're strict.'

Emily's face broke into a grin. 'Leo says it turns him on when I do that.'

'Ha! Yeah, he would. He'll have you in jodhpurs with a riding crop next.'

'Well? Are you going to ring Seb?'

'No. Not yet. Give me some time, okay? I need to think a bit more.'

The phone buzzed again.

'That's him, isn't it, Ange? Go on, answer it. I dare you.'

'It's not a call, it's a text,' she said, picking it up and scanning the screen. 'Wants me to meet him at the cinema to talk.' She looked up at Emily. 'Did I tell you he gave me a key to the place for Christmas? Said it was ours.'

'Really? That was sweet.'

'Yeah. It was, wasn't it? Bastard…'

'So will you go?'

'Okay, if it'll shut you up. If I'm going to talk to him, I'd rather do it in person.'

'What will you do, sweetie? Think you'll get back together?'

'I don't know, Em. I honestly don't know.'

***

There was no sign of Seb when Angel pulled up to the tiled white façade of the Hippodrome in a cab later that evening. Reaching into her pocket, she took out the little silver Yale key he'd given her and unlocked the door, wondering idly why he didn't get some better security on the place. It felt like there should be an alarm or something, with all his priceless film reels in the projection room. Maybe there was CCTV around she hadn't noticed.

She made her way along the exposed brick passage, pushed open the door leading to the teal auditorium – and burst into tears.

God, she remembered… getting to know each other, the picnic he'd made her, the way he'd picked out records he knew she'd like and held her while they danced. The way he'd told her for the first time that he loved her, his handsome face buried in her hair, his hot breath close against her scalp and his tears on her cheeks. The way he smelled, the way he looked, the way he dimpled when he smiled, the way he kissed her, the way he touched his curly mop of stupid hair, the way he teased, the way he tasted. The way she loved him. Christ, so much!

And she knew then the answer to the question he'd asked her that night at Moira's. She knew when it was she'd first realised she loved him. It was the moment he'd brought her here.

'Angel.'

She jumped when she heard that deep, crushed-velvet voice behind her. 'Seb…' She turned to face him, stood motionless as he walked towards her, his face grey and haggard but gorgeous, as always, to her. And then she threw herself forward into his arms.

'Oh God, Seb, I missed you so much,' she sobbed, burying her face in his chest, inhaling his woodsmoke-chocolate scent greedily. 'So, so much…'

'Angel, my Angel… God, I'm so sorry.' She could feel his tears falling on the top of her head while he pushed his face into her hair.

'No,' she said with an effort, pushing him from her and backing away. 'Don't touch me. I can't, Seb.'

'You know, that's what I like about you, Ange. You're unpredictable.'

'Don't joke with me, you…'

'Bastard?'

'Bloody right. I mean it, Seb. Stay the hell away from me.'

'Angel, please…' He tried to wrap his arms around her again, but she pushed him back savagely.

'Okay, Ange,' he said, sounding drained and sad. 'I won't hold you if you don't want me to. But please, just talk to me.'

'How could you, Seb?' She was heaving out silent sobs now, her body shaking as she sank down into one of the leather chairs in front of the big cinema screen. 'How could you, after everything?'

'I'm sorry,' he said hoarsely, throwing himself down next to her. 'Carole and Suze won't let me hear the end of it. Moira too. She's been on the phone nearly every day, just to give me my daily dose of bollocking for buggering everything up as usual.'

'Good. I hope she gives you hell.'

'The thing is, I wasn't even angry. Even when I thought briefly you might have… I just thought what a selfish bastard I'd been to ask you to make so many sacrifices.' He turned damp, feeling eyes on her. 'You were right, Angel. Everything you said. You do deserve better. Someone who can be fully in your life, not sneaking you around like something secret and shameful. I was an idiot not to realise that. Selfish, stupid… I just wanted to be with you, that's all. That was all I could really think about.'

'No…' She reached out and took his hand, gave it a gentle squeeze. 'I knew what the price of being with you was when I signed up. It wasn't right to make you feel guilty. You couldn't help the way things were. It was only because you cared about Carole so much… and that's one of the things I love about you.'

'Angel… then you still love me?'

'Love doesn't just disappear, Seb. Still,' she said, dropping his hand and turning blazing eyes towards him. 'How could you ever think I'd do that to Carole? Did you really believe I'd sell her out like that?'

'Oh God! I knew you wouldn't. As soon as I said it I knew, but I was upset about the story, and angry at the paper, at the press generally for everything they've done to her over the years. Everything they did to us both… to Abigail too. And I took it out on you. That was wrong. I'm sorry, Angel, I'm so sorry.' His voice cracked. 'Give me another chance?'

'I don't know if I can, Seb. Not now I know you still don't trust me. I'll always be thinking about it, worrying…'

'Oh Christ!' He let out an anguished cry and covered his face with his hands. 'I've ruined everything, haven't I? Oh God…'

He looked up suddenly, his expression wild and impetuous. 'Marry me, Angel.'

'*What?*'

'You heard. Marry me.'

She snorted through her tears. 'Don't be so bloody ridiculous. Jesus! Do you really think you can propose your way out of this?'

'Come on, Angel. I love you, you know I do. I want to spend my life with you, if you're up for it – Carole and me are getting an annulment. Will you?'

'What, after six weeks together? No I bloody won't!' She shook her head. 'Seriously, Seb, what did you think you were going to achieve by that?'

'I guess I was kind of banking on you finding it either ador-able or funny.'

'Try absurd.' Suddenly, she burst out laughing. 'You nonsensical bastard. Is that your solution to every problem, marry your way around it?'

'If I can't think of anything better.'

'So what was your back-up plan then, for when I said no?'

He shrugged. 'Take my shirt off again?'

'You should've tried that first. Come here.' She grabbed his collar with both hands, drew him towards her and delivered a soft kiss on his lips, feeling his hot tears against her face and swapping them for a few of her own.

'Really, Ange?'

'Yes, Seb. Really.' She sighed. 'Come on, you always knew I'd let you talk me round eventually.'

He hooked a stray tendril of hair from her face and twisted it around his finger. 'Call me a bastard again,' he said softly.

'You're a bastard. A sexy, gorgeous, ridiculous bastard. And I love you.'

'I love it when you sweet-talk me, Ange.'

He kissed her again and she let herself melt into his strong arms, felt his body warmth surging through her.

'And that was a definite no to marriage, was it?'

'Yes it was. You can't go all your life collecting wives, Wilchester. You showbiz types…'

'Oh God, Angel, I was so scared I'd lost you,' he breathed brokenly, nuzzling his nose into her hair.

'You nearly had.'

'That bloody paper. Always there between us.'

She looked up at him. 'You do know I quit, right? The day that story broke. Angel Blackthorne is no longer employed by *The Daily Investigator*.'

'What?' He held her back from him. 'You did that? Why? Not – for me?'

'Ha! Get over yourself,' she said in a teasing tone, tracing the outline of his ear with her finger. 'I couldn't work there. Not after that. Not after what they did to Carole.'

'Oh, Angel, sweetheart… come here to me.'

He guided her out of the cinema seat, over on to his lap, and wrapped his arms tightly around her middle.

'Such a waste, though,' he said, his mouth close to her ear. 'You were a great critic.'

'You would say that. I gave *Milkman* five stars.'

'Well, there is that. So what will you do now, Ange?'

She shrugged. 'I can always freelance. I've got a good enough portfolio now. And there are other papers. Better papers.'

'Or you can come and work for me.'

'What?' She laughed and twisted around to look at him. 'Seriously, that's as bad as the proposal. You can't employ your way into my good books either, Seb. And I've already been accused of sleeping with one boss, thanks.'

'I'm serious,' he said, smiling. 'You'd be great in PR. Even if we'd never met, I would've snapped you up just on the strength of your writing.'

She curled her lip in distaste. 'So you want me to go and churn out press releases for Kev, do you?'

'Ha. No, I wouldn't inflict Kevin on you. I wasn't talking about Tigerblaze actually. It's ReelKids I need someone for. It'd be perfect for someone with your skills and background. Rewarding too. I mean, you'd have to apply properly, do an interview with the board, but…' He kissed the top of her ear. 'Think about it?'

'Well, maybe. I'm still working out my notice anyway.' She scanned his face, noticing the red rim of each eye, the dark circles. 'So how's it all been for you, sweetheart? How's Carole holding up?'

'She's engaged.'

'*What?*'

'Yep. She popped the question to Suze as soon as we'd shipped off our annulment papers to the lawyer. They're probably at home looking through hat catalogues, or whatever it is these brides do.' He looked down at his fingernails in mock offence. 'Some people's proposals aren't met with howling derision, thanks very much.'

'Idiot.' She pressed a kiss on to his lips. 'Wow, though! That's massive news. I bet Suzanne's chuffed to bits. Everything she always wanted.'

'Yeah. And she's been great too. The press pack started to break up after a couple of days, but she's still protecting Carole's privacy like a tigress. Never knew she had it in her. She's like a female Kev.'

Angel shuddered. 'Well, let's not go that far. I like Suzanne. So she's going to be okay? Carole?'

'We're taking it one day at a time, but… yes, I think so. Or I hope so. It was nowhere near as bad as either me or Suze expected, to be honest. I mean, we didn't want to leave her alone, not for the first few days. But I think she was actually a little relieved the whole thing was out there, especially once the press had started to move off to look for fresher meat. And now she can be with Suze, which is what will really do her good. Publicity for the next film will be a challenge, the interviews, but… like I said, one day at a time.'

'What about parts?'

'Too early to say. She's got plenty on at the moment, though. We've got another Tigerblaze production filming from next month. Obviously she'll still be working with me, whatever happens with other roles.'

Angel tilted her head and let out a deep, happy sigh as he started kissing along her neck, brushing her hair back behind her shoulder with his feather-soft fingertips in that way she loved.

'Seb…' she said breathlessly. 'Oh God, I'm so happy you're mine again.'

'Sweetheart…'

'God, I love you.'

'I love you too, Ange.' He nestled her closer to him. 'More than anything.'

'Stay with me.'

'Forever, if you like.'

For a moment there was silence as they locked in a tight embrace.

'So, Angel, what shall we do tonight? Anything you want,' Seb whispered, stroking a tender thumb along her waist in the gap between her top and her jeans.

She smiled fondly at him, running her fingers through those untidy curls she could never get enough of.

'Film night?'

Acknowledgements

This bit's like my Oscars speech, right? And by the end I'll be drunk as a lord and sobbing like Paltrow. Sounds good, especially as I'm writing this at work.

So in order of unimportance, I'd like to thank all these lovely people and animals:

Harpo the cat for never leaving me alone while I was writing and for inspiring his fictional brother, and Minky, Pinky and Sage for leaving me alone to get on with it (and consequently not making it into the book); oh, and Hutchy the rabbit, she should probably get a thanks as well, for, er, garden-based frolicking and services to dandelion demolition. To my friends, especially Bob, Amy, Nige and Lynette, for the support, the ideas and the booze-ups; my American critique partners Lyndsey and Donna for their great feedback; the good folk at NaNoWriMo, without which event I never would have written this book; Charlotte Ledger and Sam Gale at HarperImpulse for taking a chance on me and being brilliant throughout the publishing process; anyone at work in Skipton who got sick of me talking about my book but were too polite to say so (which was everyone); and most importantly, my partner Mark for his love and understanding as I retreated from the world into "novelist mode", his

373

excellent beta reading skills and for letting me buy that top hat.

And finally, to my loving and supportive family for encouraging me to read and write pretty much from the womb, and who for reasons that should become obvious around chapter three are never allowed to read this book...

Oh, and my characters, can I thank them? Thanks, characters, for bringing yourselves to life. Love you all. Especially you, Leo: mwah mwah.

Printed by RR Donnelley at Glasgow, UK